The Fallout

Also by Yrsa Sigurdardóttir

The Thóra
Gudmundsdóttir
novels
Last Rituals
My Soul to Take
Ashes to Dust
The Day is Dark
*Someone to Watch
Over Me*
*The Silence of
the Sea*

Standalones
I Remember You
The Undesired
Why Did You Lie?

The Freyja and
Huldar Series
The Legacy
The Reckoning
The Absolution
Gallows Rock
The Doll
The Fallout

About the Author

Yrsa Sigurdardóttir works as a civil engineer in Reykjavík. She made her crime fiction debut in 2005 with *Last Rituals*, the first instalment in the Thóra Gudmundsdóttir series, and has been translated into more than thirty languages. *The Silence of the Sea* won the Petrona Award in 2015. *The Fallout* is her fifteenth adult novel and the sixth in the Freyja and Huldar Series.

About the Translator

Victoria Cribb studied and worked in Iceland for many years. She has translated some forty books by Icelandic authors including Arnaldur Indridason, Ragnar Jónasson and Sjón. In 2017 she received the Ordstír honorary translation award for her services to Icelandic literature.

The Fallout

Yrsa Sigurdardóttir

Translated from the Icelandic by Victoria Cribb

HODDER &
STOUGHTON

First published in Great Britain in 2022 by Hodder & Stoughton
An Hachette UK company

First published with the title *Þögn* in 2019 by Veröld Publishing, Reykjavík

1

A CIP catalogue record for this title is available from the British Library

Hardback ISBN 978 1 473 69353 1
Trade Paperback ISBN 978 1 473 69354 8
eBook ISBN 978 1 473 69355 5

Typeset in Sabon MT Std by Manipal Technologies Limited

Printed and bound in Great Britain by Clays Ltd, Elcograf S.p.A.

Hodder & Stoughton policy is to use papers that are natural, renewable
and recyclable products and made from wood grown in sustainable forests.
The logging and manufacturing processes are expected to conform
to the environmental regulations of the country of origin.

Hodder & Stoughton Ltd
Carmelite House
50 Victoria Embankment
London EC4Y 0DZ

www.hodder.co.uk

Pronunciation guide
for character names

Agnar Grétarsson (Aggi) – AK-nar GRYET-ars-son
  (AGG-ghee)
Aldís Ellertsdóttir – AL-dees ELL-erts-DOE-teer
Andrea Logadóttir – AND-ray-a LOR-ga-DOE-teer
Baldur – BAL-door
Bríet Hannesdóttir – BREE-ett HAN-nes-DOE-teer
Dröfn – Drerbn
Droplaug Thórdardóttir – DROP-lohg THOHR-thar-DOE-
  teer
Einar Brjánsson – AY-narr BRYAUNS-son
Ellý Thórdardóttir – EL-lee THOHR-thar-DOE-teer
Erla – ED-la
Freyja – FRAY-a
Gudbjörg (Gudda) – GVOOTH-byerg (GOOD-da)
Gudlaugur – GVOOTH-lohg-oor
Hanna Lúdvíksdóttir – HAN-na LOOTH-veeks-DOE-teer
Huldar – HOOL-dar
Íris – EE-ris
Jói (Jóhannes) – YOE-ee (YOE-han-nes)
Kristbjörg – KRIST-byerg
Lína – LEE-na
Lúdvík Jónsson – LOOTH-veek YOHNS-son

Mía Stefánsdóttir – MEE-ya STEFF-auns-DOE-teer
Númi – NOO-mee
Ólína Traustadóttir – OH-lee-na TROES-ta-DOE-teer
Rögnvaldur Tryggvason – RERK-val-door TRIGG-va-son
Rósa – ROH-ssa
Sædís – SEYE-dees
Stefán (Stebbi) – STEFF-own (STEBB-bee)
Valgeir – VAHL-gyayr

Eleven years earlier

Prologue

The shower was far hotter than Númi was used to. He was someone who preferred to avoid extremes: he didn't like overly spicy food, swimming in the sea, loud music, CrossFit, neon colours, tequila slammers or anything else outside his comfort zone. Including scenes. He hated scenes.

But the heat of the shower wasn't a mistake; he had pushed the temperature controller as far into the red as he dared. While the water was heating up, he pulled off his clothes, dropping them in a pile on the floor as if he were fifteen again. As he stepped naked onto the cold tiles, he almost expected to hear his mother's voice calling out of the past, yelling at him to pick his things up off the floor.

The clouds of steam in the shower cubicle gave a hint of what was in store. Númi braced himself, then ducked under the scalding jet. Some things were better got over with fast, and anyway he didn't have much time. At first the heat was unbearable. His skin turned instantly scarlet and stung all over, but he stuck it out and the discomfort soon passed. Once the pain had receded, the boiling sensation felt good. He needed it.

Númi placed the flats of his hands on the tiled wall, leant forwards and let the water pummel his aching shoulders. His muscles weren't sore from exercise as would once have been the case: running and sessions at the gym had taken a back seat in

3

recent months, like so many other things that had been part of his life pre-Mía. The arrival of his daughter had opened a gulf between his old and his new existence, and so much had been left behind on the other side: sport, freedom from worry, overtime, eight hours' sleep, dry-clean-only clothes, marathon TV sessions and a number of other things that Númi regularly reminded himself he could do without. Because life on this side, with Mía, was so much better than what he had been forced to give up.

He had to hold on to that thought. In spite of all the crap that was going down at the moment, he couldn't complain. Apart from this recent temporary blip, life was good for him and Stebbi: new house, new baby, a new maturity in their marriage. All three required an effort, but then you couldn't expect to have anything for nothing. The hassle over Mía would be worth it in the long run, and, if Stebbi was right, the ordeal would soon be over. The work on the outside of the house was finished too and the builders were finally packing up their tools – months behind schedule but, still, it was something to be celebrated. According to Stebbi, they were close to settling with the contractor over the bill too, though Númi had his doubts – doubts that he tried to push away. Sometimes it was good to allow oneself a few unrealistic expectations. He had enough other crap to put up with, like his boss grumbling about his paternity leave, which had unfortunately coincided with a collapse in the markets. And now all these scenes.

Stebbi didn't think the drama would last much longer. Númi disagreed, but self-deception was a more comfortable option. Like when he compared weather forecasts and always chose to believe the most favourable one. These days Stebbi's confidence suited him so much better than his own pessimism.

In his heart of hearts, he didn't believe it would ever end. No doubt they would eventually reach a settlement with the building contractor, but a conclusion to the Mía saga could take many years.

That mustn't be allowed to happen. He and Stebbi had to be given a chance to look after her themselves, without interference. They were more than capable of it.

Thanks to the internet, with its bottomless well of information, there had been few big surprises. No one could say they hadn't been prepared for Mía's arrival. In the months leading up to her birth they had immersed themselves in reading everything they could lay their hands on, especially accounts and advice from couples in a similar position to their own: two men bringing up a child, and couples who had used surrogate mothers, whether legally or not – these had proved the most helpful.

Then, not content with that, they'd read everything from academic articles to badly organised and largely uninformative blog posts by parents, ranging from the ridiculously positive, through the over-the-top humorous, to the downright fear-mongering.

They had memorised every last thing, however unhelpful. Their knowledge ended up being so encyclopaedic that nothing about their child could take them by surprise: milk intolerance, being born with teeth, every kind of chromosomal or birth defect, ear problems, sleeping problems, jaundice, premature birth, chronic hiccups, super-sensitive skin, reflux . . . They knew all the basic advice in these cases, as well as in countless others.

But it's one thing to be well informed, another to be confronted by the issues in real life, as they had been for just over four months now. They no longer lived in constant fear of losing or accidentally injuring her, but they were still learning. Mía changed by the week and you could say they were always absolutely confident about what to do – or, at least, they had been yesterday. Who knew what new things tomorrow would bring? She grew, put on weight, stayed awake longer, smiled and laughed as she discovered herself, the two of them and the world about her. She became conscious. It would still be a long time before she realised that her situation was different from that of most children, but for now everything was equally strange and new to her. Hopefully she would be allowed to go on feeling this way for a long time – preferably forever.

Númi stretched and wiped the water from his eyes, then reached for the soap and lathered himself all over. The shower immediately rinsed off the foam, so he went over himself a second and a third time to be sure. He could do with a good clean, stinking as he did of baby vomit and diarrhoea. Mía had an upset stomach and he had been caught in the firing line. The internet gurus had skipped the bit about how best to deal with projectile bodily fluids.

Luckily, Mía's stomach seemed to have settled down and she was sleeping peacefully outside in her pram. Númi had grabbed the chance to jump in the shower, something he had been meaning to do the moment she dropped off. Instead, he'd been forced to stand arguing at the front door yet again, with vomit and worse on his face. As always, he had tried to be sympathetic and polite but had quickly lost his temper. There could be no compromise in a dispute in which one side – he and Stebbi – would not give an inch. But the fact was they were in the right.

His hair hadn't been spared either. Númi put down the soap and fumbled for the shampoo. He didn't have much time. Long showers were yet another thing that belonged to his old life.

The back of his hand brushed against the waterproof radio beside the shampoo. These days he no longer hummed along to music while having a leisurely wash. Instead, he kept an ear tuned to the silence from the baby monitor on the vanity unit, and stressed himself out by hurrying.

The transmitter was in Mía's pram. As long as he didn't hear anything, he could feel relatively relaxed. But the instant she made a noise, it meant she was waking up. Then he'd have under two minutes to dry himself, dress, run downstairs and out onto the terrace. If he didn't pick Mía up within that time, she would start crying and it was astonishing the volume those tiny lungs could produce. None of the neighbours could fail to hear her. The girl would have a bright future as an opera singer – or an air-raid siren.

Númi squeezed the last drops of shampoo out of the bottle and started washing his hair. As he massaged his scalp, foam trickled into his ears, blocking his hearing. Or not quite, because just then he caught a faint sound from the baby monitor. He paused, wiped a hand across his face to get the soap out of his eyes, rubbed his ears and listened.

Then he froze.

The noise emerging in a burst of crackling from the monitor wasn't Mía crying. It was a voice warily hushing her. Was it possible that she'd woken up and one of the neighbours had jumped over the low hedge to tend to her? Could the builders have returned? Or the postman have come round the back of the house? Númi deliberately ignored the most likely explanation.

There was a mumble of protest from his daughter. Then nothing. No shushing, crying or crackling. Either the battery had run out or the person standing by the pram had switched off the transmitter.

His hair still covered in shampoo, Númi leapt out of the shower, almost slipping and falling flat on the wet tiles in his panic. Flinging his dressing gown over his soaking body, he tore downstairs, taking them two at a time, sprinted to the French windows and peered out onto the terrace.

In his haste, he had left his glasses behind on the vanity unit, but he could see that the cover had been loosened and was hanging down beside the pram, still fastened by a popper. Númi peered at the white quilt inside and breathed easier as he made out the shape of Mía lying underneath it and a glimpse of her little hat.

His shock gave way to relief, then to fury. It must have been some stupid kids. What on earth had they been thinking? He opened the door to the terrace, feeling the cold stealing up his wet legs. Pausing to wrap his dressing gown more tightly around himself, he scanned the garden but there was no sign of any children.

Fuck, fuck, fuck. Perhaps it wasn't safe to let Mía sleep outdoors any more. If so, he would have even less time to get anything else done during the day, because she slept so much better outside in the fresh air, Icelandic fashion, than she did in her nursery.

Then Númi noticed that someone had been tampering with the monitor. It wasn't where he had left it. Instead, the aerial was sticking up between the side of the pram and the quilt. He picked up the monitor. It had been switched off.

Númi shivered. He didn't know whether it was from the cold or the fact that some kids had been messing around with his baby. Both, no doubt. He decided to take Mía inside, though she was bound to stir if he moved her.

He drew the quilt gently back, hoping he could carry her indoors without waking her.

It took him a moment or two to work out what he was seeing. The baby's face was grey, its small lips were cracked, its wide-open eyes dry and unseeing. It was dead.

But the dead child was not Mía.

Five months earlier

Chapter 1

The little white coffin could hardly be seen for all the flowers. The wreaths and bouquets came in a wealth of different colours: pink, red, white, yellow, and one made up mainly of green. It wasn't as if people could have chosen their floral tributes according to his daughter's favourite colour or flower, as Íris's life had been too short for her to form a definite opinion on these things. And, anyway, she had spent a large part of it in a hospital ward. She'd had a favourite food: pizza, a favourite dessert: ice-cream, and a favourite animal: a panda. She'd had six favourite songs too, which formed the playlist he'd made for her and never had a chance to add to. Not that it had seemed to matter. She'd been perfectly content to listen to them on repeat, using the pink headphones with the pussy-cat ears that her grandparents had given her for Christmas.

Apart from that, Íris had had few treasured possessions, with the exception of a cuddly toy that she'd rarely let out of her grasp. This was the little penguin that was now lying on her chest under her crossed arms in the coffin.

At Rögnvaldur's side, his wife, Aldís, was silently weeping, the tears running down her pale cheeks to drip onto her chest. Ever-expanding wet patches decorated the colourful top that she was wearing while everyone else, including him, was in black. When he'd found her sitting on their bed before they set off for church, he'd asked if she was going to put on the black dress that was laid out beside her. But she'd just sat there, staring into space, and shaken her head. So he'd nodded and let her come as she was, in the clothes she'd been wearing the night their daughter died. She had taken off the shirt when they got home, put it in a bag and shoved it in the wardrobe. He hadn't asked any questions, just assumed she'd wanted to preserve the smell of Íris, who had been lying in her arms when she drew her last breath. By then she'd been in hospital for two weeks and to him barely any trace had remained of her own sweet, innocent scent. It had been replaced by the smell of hospital: a reek of drugs, disinfectant and dressings. A taint of impending death.

The vicar announced that they would now sing a hymn, then turned to the altar and started fiddling with something.

Rögnvaldur felt a sudden impulse to stand up and scream. To silence the choir and throw out the mourners. Although most of the congregation were genuinely upset by Íris's death, their grief was nothing compared to what her parents were going through. He and Aldís were like zombies. They moved, breathed and ate without any need of oxygen or appetite for meals. Friends and family members regularly brought them offerings of food, but apart from those they went without. Once the supply of meals dried up, he supposed they would shrivel up and die. It was inevitable that people would withdraw their support. He and Aldís weren't exactly easy company at the moment, answering if spoken to but contributing nothing to the conversation beyond that. They had nothing to say. Not yesterday, not today or tomorrow. Probably never again.

The hymn came to an end and the vicar turned to face the congregation. There was silence in the church apart from the odd polite sniff. He and Aldís were past trying to hide their weeping. Actually, he had no tears left, but she was crying openly, heedless of their surroundings.

The vicar began to talk about Íris's life. He had come round to their flat to discuss the details of the funeral and elicit information for his eulogy, but they hadn't been able to give him many pointers as their daughter had only been ten years old. They couldn't list her sporting achievements, the clubs she'd belonged to, the different places she'd lived or her exam results. She hadn't been a member of any club, had never played any sport or taken any major exams in her life; she'd never even got old enough to take her driving test. The only thing they could stammer out was that at seven she had been diagnosed with leukaemia and from then on had spent much of her time in hospital. Things had been looking up until her suppressed immune system had come into contact with the measles virus. Due to a recent bone-marrow transplant, she had lost the preventive immunity provided by her childhood vaccinations and it had taken the virus only two weeks to overwhelm her poor little body.

Of course, there were plenty of other things to be said about her that had meaning for her parents. Their daughter wasn't defined by her time in hospital. But neither of them had wanted to share their memories with anyone else. Her first steps, her first words and first smile were nobody else's business. Nor were the poignant stories they clung to at first and took it in turns to recall for each other between their sobs.

The vicar had got to hear none of this. After listing the basic facts of Íris's life, they had sat there without speaking. It was fortunate that Rögnvaldur's mother-in-law had been there to fill out their brief, dry contribution.

Rögnvaldur noticed out of the corner of his eye that Aldís's head was drooping. Turning to her, he looked down at her greasy parting. He was in the same state. Although he had put on the black suit his parents had bought him for the occasion, he hadn't had the energy to get in the shower, shave or wash his hair. His own appearance, and other people's opinions, no longer mattered to him. Only one thing mattered. And it wasn't pretty. He would probably be kicked out of the church if he were to share it with the vicar. Not that he'd care if that happened.

The vicar finished and the choir resumed. Yet another standard funeral hymn that the singers could no doubt have intoned backwards if required. He and Aldís had been invited to choose the music themselves – tunes Íris liked, for example – but he had hastily declined the offer and shut up his mother-in-law when she mentioned the playlist. Those six songs hadn't been written for funerals; they had been written to make people smile and sing along. And he wasn't sure he could bear to hear her favourite songs being played in the presence of her coffin. He had also vetoed the suggestion that his daughter's prize-winning poem should be read out in church. Íris had been one of four winners in the children's poetry competition held by the Reykjavík City Library, as his mother-in-law had informed the vicar. The poem had been written after her bone-marrow transplant, when every-thing had appeared to be looking up. It listed all the things she was planning to do once she'd got her strength back.

A more inappropriate text for the occasion would be hard to imagine. Aldís had agreed with him, though not in words. She had simply broken down and wept. She had still been in floods of tears when the vicar finally decided he had got enough material and said his goodbyes.

Aldís's shoulders were shaking now as they had been then. Her sobbing grew more violent, shaking her unwashed hair. It pierced his heart and he clenched his teeth to bite back the scream that was desperately seeking an outlet. It wasn't that he wanted to spare the congregation; he was just afraid that if he started screaming, he wouldn't be able to stop.

Rögnvaldur closed his eyes and two heavy tears ran down his cheeks. Instead of allowing himself to cry as his heart desired, however, he sniffed hard and squared his shoulders. He couldn't let himself break down. He needed to be there for Aldís. He wanted to give her his arm as they followed the flower-decked coffin out of the church, but he wouldn't be able to do that if he himself needed support. He had to be strong today. He had to be strong tomorrow. And the day after. Life hurtled on like a relentless juggernaut; a juggernaut that couldn't care less about those that got in its way and were dragged along, more dead than alive. Like him and his wife.

Ever since Íris died he had been trying to deflect his grief by obsessing over who could have infected their daughter. No other thoughts worked as well. Rögnvaldur turned in his pew to survey the packed church. As he peered at people's faces, most dropped their eyes. There were family members, both close and distant, friends and acquaintances, a few colleagues from work, the odd member of staff from the hospital, neighbours, and faces here and there that he recognised but couldn't place. He assumed that the group at the back, whose faces he couldn't see, were made up of a similar cross-section. There was every chance that the guilty party was lurking among those sitting here today. It wasn't as if his daughter had had contact with that many people.

Aldís sniffed and Rögnvaldur turned to face the front again. As he did so, he was fairly sure that the people behind him all let out a sigh of relief. No one wanted to meet the eye of a father who had just lost his child. The infection carrier must have been most relieved of all – if the person in question was present.

There was no information to be had from the hospital. Rögnvaldur had asked various members of staff the same question after his daughter had been admitted with measles. The answers were always the same. At present they were not aware of any other case of measles in Iceland. Only one report had reached the Directorate of Health but that had come from abroad and wasn't considered reliable. It had been an application for sick pay by a foreign labourer who had left the country. He claimed to have fallen ill with measles while he was in Iceland. The doctor who shared this information with Rögnvaldur had added that the case had been dismissed as attempted benefit fraud.

At the Directorate of Health, he had hit a brick wall. They told him that the infection would be investigated but that even if they discovered its origin, the results would not be shared with him. No investigative body was going to hand over to him and his wife the name of the person who had infected and killed their daughter. This became clear when a representative of the directorate came round to take a statement from him and Aldís. The conversation was one-way: the representative asked the questions and their job was to answer.

After Íris died, Rögnvaldur had sat down at his computer. It hadn't taken him long to find out the relevant information. Measles was caused by a highly contagious virus that was transmitted by droplets in the air and collected in the nasal cavity and throat of the victim. If an infected person sneezed or coughed, the virus could survive without a host for two hours on surfaces or in the air of an enclosed room. One to two weeks after infection, a person would fall ill if they did not have immunity. Three to five days later a rash would appear. Four days before its appearance, the host could infect others and would remain infectious for eight days in total.

The information fitted with the period the man from the Directorate of Health had asked most of his questions about. Where had they taken Íris and who had she met during the two weeks before she fell ill? They had thought back and reported everything they could remember, though it wasn't as if they had been out and about much, as Íris had been shielding. She had visited her cousin of the same age but no one had been ill there. They had gone for a short walk by the sea but hadn't encountered anyone who was sneezing or looked otherwise suspicious. They had gone to the local playground but there hadn't been any other children there since they were all at school or in day-care. They had twice taken her to hospital for check-ups but had been kept separate from the other patients. Apart from that, they had gone for a few drives, bought ice-creams and enjoyed the view of the sea or mountains. They couldn't remember anything else, since Íris's life post-treatment had consisted of taking it easy and being careful. Their daughter hadn't gone to the shops with them or to the cinema, theatre, the swimming pool or to any sports matches. Because her immune system had been compromised, she had been supposed to shield as far as possible.

Nothing they could think of explained how she had been infected. Not yet, anyway. Perhaps it never would. Perhaps the carrier had been a tourist who had left the country before falling visibly ill. Except they hadn't encountered any tourists. Or any foreign labourers. There hadn't been any building work going on in their block of flats or anywhere else Íris had been.

The vicar recited the Lord's Prayer but Rögnvaldur didn't hear it. He was remembering Íris's birth and the moment she was laid in the arms of her exhausted mother. All sticky and bloody, wrapped in something white, with clenched fists, a gaping mouth and tightly closed eyes. He and Aldís had both cried, but those had been very different tears from the ones they were shedding now.

He remembered the overpowering sense of responsibility and the promise he had made himself: that nothing bad would ever happen to mother and daughter while he still drew breath. The longed-for child had arrived at last, after the terrible ordeal of the previous few years. He'd meant to do everything he could to ensure that his daughter's life would be easy. But look what had happened – he had failed her when it really mattered.

Yet another hymn. Then the vicar took over again. He recited a standard text designed to mark an end and a new beginning. Dismal words if you weren't religious and didn't believe the third line.

Dust thou art,
and unto dust shalt thou return,
and from dust shalt thou rise again.

Rögnvaldur didn't weep. Instead, he felt an uncontrollable rage close around his heart like a fist. He couldn't leave it like this. He wanted revenge. It was the only thing that mattered now. Once he had accomplished that, he couldn't care less what happened to him.

Now

Chapter 2

Monday

Erla's distended oval belly bumped into the edge of Huldar's desk, rippling the cold coffee in his mug and sending a pencil rolling away to finish up against his keyboard. It wasn't the first time she had collided with the office furniture, but then she didn't seem to have adapted to the temporary change in her body shape. Nothing at navel height was safe: the edges of desks, doorposts, printers, shelves, chair backs – they had all got in the way of her bump. But Huldar and his colleagues in CID all tactfully turned a blind eye, though they couldn't help noticing the protruding belly that appeared in advance of Erla whenever she rounded a corner. Apart from this, she had nothing in common with the other pregnant women Huldar had known. His five sisters' baby bumps had formed a wide bulge all the way round, as if they were stuck through the middle of an exercise ball. Whereas Erla looked as if she shoved a ball down the front of her jumper every morning that was gradually expanding, first to the size of a handball, then a football and now an inflated beach ball. Seen from behind, she was exactly the same as before. In fact, if you ignored her bump, she still had the physique of a lean marathon runner – or would do if you put a bag over her head.

Because her face gave her away. It was adorned with puffy dark shadows, which made her eyes look as if they were resting in twin hammocks. Her skin was blotchy too and her short hair clung, dry and lifeless, to her head. Some women bloomed during pregnancy. Others didn't.

Huldar hadn't a clue how far along Erla was but assumed she must be about to drop any day now. On the few occasions he had tried asking her, the answers had been vague. He had stopped altogether after she bit his head off, accusing him of being impatient to warm her seat. The truth was, he had absolutely zero interest in the position of departmental manager that he had once held himself. And she, of all people, should know that.

He had no idea who the father was either. He had asked twice and got the same answer both times: *No one you know.* Her manner had discouraged any further discussion. For all he knew, Erla could be living with someone. But if he had to bet, it would be that she was about to become a single mother. She never received phone calls when they were working late, unlike the members of CID who had partners. And recently she had turned up to work with toilet paper sticking out of her trouser leg. There's no way a live-in boyfriend wouldn't have noticed and stopped her on her way out of the door.

'Are you free?' Her voice was strained, evocative of tiredness and sleepless nights. Huldar's sisters had complained a lot about that sort of thing: lack of sleep, fatigue, water retention and endless trips to the loo. Bringing a child into the world certainly started with a bang but what followed didn't seem to be much fun. He reckoned birds had worked out a far better system. If only Erla could have laid an egg and shoved it in the microwave on a low temperature for nine months, she would be standing in front of him now as perky as she had been on the day the child was conceived.

Huldar shoved himself away from the desk in his eagerness to escape his computer, so hard that his chair rolled backwards into the shelves behind him. 'I'm free. Free as a bird.' He hoped this was going to involve a trip outside in the fresh air. His eyes ached from staring at the screen, not helped by the useless office lighting. As part of the police's new environmental policy, they had recently installed a smart lighting system. It was supposed to be self-adjusting, but by some miracle the designer had managed to ensure that the level of illumination was always inappropriate. The older members of CID had mostly resorted to bringing in desk lamps from home in order to be able to see to work. As a result, the energy saving was lower than envisaged and global warming continued apace.

Erla shot a glance at the empty workstation next to Huldar's. 'Where's Gudlaugur?'

'He got an invite to attend a course. Cultural sensitivity training or something like that.' Huldar braced himself for a stream of invective.

But Erla merely nodded, then got to the point. 'I've just had a phone call that should have gone to the switchboard but came to me by mistake. It's no big deal but I need to get some fucking air, so I decided to grab the excuse. Any chance you could come with me and see if there's anything to it or it's just a load of time-wasting bullshit?'

Pregnancy had done nothing to temper Erla's tongue, even though she hadn't used the opportunity to spew expletives all over the course Gudlaugur was attending. It wouldn't surprise Huldar if the baby emerged from the womb swearing like a trooper. 'I'm up for it,' he said. 'What's it about?'

'An abandoned car. A woman rang to say it's blocking her drive. It hasn't been moved since it appeared there on Saturday night and she wants it towed away.'

'Then why didn't she ring a tow company?'

'She spouted some crap about the car possibly being involved in organised crime and insisted it was a police matter.'

'Eh? How did she work that out?'

'She says she looked through the window and it's full of rubbish. She even claims she saw a syringe. That's where she got the idea it could be linked to a criminal gang. But of course that's just a fucking pretext: she's afraid of being charged to have it towed away.'

'Did you get the number plate?'

'Yes. It's registered to a lab technician called Bríet Hannesdóttir. She doesn't exactly sound like the head of an international crime ring.' Erla hovered, looking impatient. 'I tried her mobile but it's switched off. Are you coming or not?'

'Yep, I'm coming. Absolutely.'

Erla left Huldar and went to fetch her car keys and coat. She hadn't bothered to buy any new, roomier, work clothes, just made do with her old official police jacket. As a result, she couldn't zip it up, which made her bump even more conspicuous, if that were possible.

Huldar pulled on his own coat and they met by the exit. From there they descended the stairs to the car park, though Huldar would have considered the lift a more sensible option for Erla. But she'd been walking up and down the stairs ever since she joined the police and, typically bloody-minded, had no intention of breaking the habit, even temporarily. Then again, perhaps it was sensible of her, because changing one's habits could be a bad idea. Even changing tiny details. If Erla ever took it easy, she would find out how nice it was, and then she might never rediscover her old spark – the one that kept her permanently stressed and in overdrive.

'Would you like me to?' Huldar held out a hand for the car key, since he seriously doubted Erla would be able to reach the steering wheel in her present condition. He received a filthy look in return.

'I'm perfectly capable of driving, Huldar. I'm pregnant, not ill or handicapped.' She glared at him over the roof of the unmarked police car. 'How do you think I get to work in the mornings? On a scooter?'

Huldar got in and closed the door. When you didn't have a clever riposte on the tip of your tongue, it was better to keep your mouth shut. Anything else was a recipe for trouble with Erla. And there was still a chance that this trip might prove tolerably pleasant.

Erla had to move the seat back before she could squeeze behind the wheel. While she was struggling with the mechanism, Huldar diplomatically gazed out of the passenger window. As a result, she kept her cool and the atmosphere grew less tense. Their chat didn't touch on anything Huldar wanted to know, like when she was expecting, who the father was, or who would replace her while she was on maternity leave. Instead, they discussed the weather and politics. Only then did Erla really let rip.

It didn't take them long to reach their destination. Apart from a teenager who dawdled over a pedestrian crossing, absorbed in his phone, and a narrowing of the lanes due to roadworks, there was nothing to delay them. The traffic was still comparatively light and the address they wanted was in a post-war housing estate that wasn't too far away. The drivers they met didn't seem to be in any hurry beyond catching the next green light. It would be different on their return journey, when they would hit the rush hour. Just as well they'd be heading back to the centre while most people were streaming out towards the suburbs. Huldar reflected that the traffic in Reykjavík behaved like the tides, flowing into town in the morning and out again eight hours later.

'There's the car.' Erla pointed to a white Skoda that was noticeably badly parked. Apart from this aberration, you'd have thought the street was inhabited solely by driving instructors. Every other car was perfectly parallel and suitably close to the kerb. No one had parked too close to any fire hydrants and a decent amount of space had been left between each vehicle. Only the little white Skoda was parked right up against the car in front, leaving hardly a finger's breadth between the bumpers. Ignoring the marked spaces, the driver had left it half blocking a drive and jutting out into the road. Huldar contemplated this evidence of careless driving. 'Bet you anything the bloke who parked that was drunk.'

'Woman, not bloke. The car's registered to a woman, remember?' Erla squeezed skilfully into a free space on the other side of the blocked drive. 'But I agree. That could also explain why she hasn't come to fetch the car. Maybe she can't remember where she left it.'

Huldar got out and sucked in a lungful of fresh wintry air, only to be hit by a craving for a cigarette. He decided to ignore it out of consideration for his pregnant colleague. However hard he tried to direct the smoke away, it invariably sought out the nearest non-smoker. Even upwind. So instead of lighting up, he used the time Erla took to work her way out from behind the wheel to survey his surroundings.

He examined the house of the woman who had reported the car. It was small, with a corrugated-iron roof and an attic, identical to the other houses on the estate. It stood closely flanked by two others, separated by compact gardens. Behind them, he could glimpse the houses in the next street through the naked branches of the birch trees that lined the edges of the plots.

Huldar had always liked this estate, which was known as the small-residence district. In the post-war period when it was built, the housing shortage had been as dire as it was now, so an area of small plots had been designed for people to build their own houses. The government had provided the plans, built roads and laid pipes, then more or less handed a spade to the lucky owners of the plots and given them the go-ahead. To Huldar, the idea of all those families toiling away in their free time to build a roof over their heads was a brilliant one. He just wished they could come up with something similar to solve the current housing crisis. If they did, he would be the first on the scene with his tools. Not necessarily to build a place for himself, but to muck in and help out. To hammer nails into planks, dig ditches, cart building materials. Hard physical labour with a purpose – there was nothing to beat it.

Erla didn't waste any time looking around or reflecting on the history of the estate. Instead, she marched straight over to the car and bent down to peer through the driver's window. 'It's full of crap. The woman wasn't making that up, at least. Though I can't see any syringes.'

Huldar joined her and looked in the windows, front and back. He refrained from voicing the thought that immediately popped into his head concerning women and mess. In his opinion, most women were slobs by nature, and the clearest evidence of this was the state of their cars and their bathrooms. The Skoda wasn't much worse than the cars that had belonged to the women in his life – although, on second thoughts, there was something different about this. It wasn't just the usual chaos of packaging, plastic bags, torn magazines, hair ties and empty Coke bottles.

'That's not a handbag, is it?' Huldar moved round to the other side to get a better look. 'On the floor there, on the passenger side.'

Erla came to peer in beside him. 'That black thing?'

'Yes.'

Erla straightened up, pressing her hands to the small of her back and grimacing. 'It's definitely a handbag. Weird to dump it on all that rubbish on the floor. Perhaps she didn't want passers-by to see it. Or she was too drunk to aim for the passenger seat when she put it down.'

Huldar was still peering through the window. He noticed that the rear-view mirror was askew. Perhaps the woman had twisted it round to check her face before she left the car. He'd done that himself a few times when he didn't have a mirror in the sun visor. But he'd always, without exception, returned it to its original position. Then again, the mirror seemed very cloudy. Anyone who tried looking in it wouldn't notice if they had two black eyes and both their front teeth missing. It was as if a dirty cloth had been smeared across it. On closer inspection, the surfaces of some of the other objects in the car looked as if they had been wiped with the same cloth. The dashboard was similarly smeary and covered in dark streaks. The woman who owned the car must be half blind if she thought this had had the effect of improving it. Unless she'd used the wrong cleaning fluid and only managed to make matters worse.

Huldar spotted another anomaly. 'The car must be unlocked, Erla. The keys are in the ignition.' He took a step backwards. Like the other cars in the city, the Skoda was filthy from the slush and grit that were an inevitable downside to winter driving. But the door handle and the area immediately around it were free from dirt. Huldar did a circuit of the car and observed that the same was true of the driver's door and the boot, whereas the handles of both rear doors hadn't been touched.

Erla worked out what he was looking at. 'Isn't that just proof that it's a case of drink driving? She forgets the keys in the ignition and her bag on the floor. Drunks don't necessarily think logically. Maybe she thought her fingerprints might give her away and so she wiped the door handles clean. Possibly the steering wheel too. She must have been pissed out of her skull to do something that pointless, seeing as her fingerprints would be all over the car anyway.'

'You mean it isn't linked to an international crime ring after all?' Huldar grinned. 'Too bad.'

Erla ignored him. She took out her phone, saying she was going to have another go at reaching the owner. At that moment, a woman appeared at the front door of the house. She didn't smile but nor did she frown as she greeted them. She was small and appeared to be around retirement age, in spite of her youthful face. The knobbly veins on her hands gave her away, along with the badly thinning, dyed hair. Like so many others, she had tried to disguise its sparseness by blow-drying it into a bouffant style that wasn't fooling any-one. She folded her arms against the icy winter air. 'What's happening? Aren't you going to remove it?' This was followed by a litany of complaints about the fact that the contractor responsible for digging up the water mains in the street kept blocking the parking spaces on weekdays, the city council wasn't doing a good enough job of clearing snow from the road, and the free newspapers she had long ago cancelled just kept coming. The woman obviously had great faith in the powers of the police to sort out all these woes.

Huldar asked her politely to go inside again while they were finishing up, promising that they'd knock on her door before leaving. She seemed unconvinced, since she reappeared almost immediately in the window overlooking the drive. They wouldn't be able to sneak away. Not that this was their intention. Or not his, anyway. He couldn't answer for Erla.

While she was making phone calls, Huldar decided to step aside for a smoke, taking care to stand a good distance away from her and out of sight of the vigilant woman in the window. He guessed she would be disgusted by his behaviour.

As he savoured his cigarette, he tried to visualise the sequence of events that had led to the car being abandoned. He found it hard to reconcile the wiped-clean door handles with the idea of a drunk driver. He could easily imagine the bag and keys being left behind and the mirror being knocked askew, but not why the pissed woman would have taken the trouble to clean the door handles, particularly the one on the boot. Even if she'd had some confused idea about hiding the evidence of her drink driving, it was hard to see where the boot would fit in.

He still hadn't come to any conclusions by the time he stubbed out his cigarette.

Erla was returning her phone to her pocket when he rejoined her. The owner of the Skoda wasn't answering her landline and her mobile was still switched off. According to the Police

Information System, she had never received a traffic fine or been picked up for public drunkenness. But even respectable citizens could do foolish things under the influence.

'I suggest we take some pictures of the car in case we need them later,' Huldar said. 'Then I'll move it, we'll take the keys with us and everybody'll be happy. Except the owner, who'll have to pick them up from the station.' He gestured to the empty space in front of the car that the white Skoda was nestled up against. 'Of course, we won't be able to prove it was a case of drink driving, but it'll be enough of a punishment for the woman to have to explain herself to us.'

Erla made a face. 'Yes. That's probably the best idea. If we have it towed away, we'll have to hang around here, waiting for the tow truck, then fill out a load of forms. And you can bet the owner will make a complaint and protest about the cost. I've got enough on my plate without that kind of bullshit. Not to mention the fact I'd have a tough job explaining why I decided to deal with this in person. There's nothing in my job description about being responsible for badly parked cars.'

Huldar didn't waste any more time. He had no wish to be dragged through the complaints system either. He opened the door of the Skoda and got in, then had to move the seat backwards. This didn't surprise him. He was tall and the car belonged to a woman who had presumably been the last person to drive it.

He closed the door, took hold of the key and prepared to start the engine.

But the instant the fresh air had been shut out, he became aware of a familiar odour – the metallic stench of blood, much stronger than if it had come from a nosebleed or a minor graze. Immediately letting go of the steering wheel and key, he pulled his sleeve over his left hand, opened the door and got out. Before shutting it again, he fished a pair of latex gloves from his coat pocket, put them on, then pushed the button under the dashboard to open the boot. Under the watchful eyes of the woman in the window, he bent down to whisper in Erla's ear.

Her expression hardened and she nodded to show that she had understood. They walked round the back of the car and Huldar lifted the door of the boot, releasing a pungent stench of blood. But rather than a dead body or severely injured person as he had feared, the boot contained a number of black bin bags. There couldn't be a body inside them as the contents were too small. Both he and Erla emitted sighs of relief.

The door mechanism was broken and wouldn't stay open, so Huldar had to hold it up while he was studying the bags. 'I'm guessing that's game – ptarmigan or reindeer.'

'Or something from a freezer that's broken down. Christ, can you smell vomit too?' Erla took a step backwards, exhaling in disgust. 'Imagine what the stench would be like if it was summer.' She donned a pair of latex gloves as well, then bent down to the bags, finding one that was open and peering inside. It turned out to contain neither game nor food from a broken freezer.

The instant Erla had withdrawn her arm and moved back, Huldar dropped the door of the boot.

Erla sighed. 'I'd better call it in.'

They stood side by side, leaning against the woman's fence while they waited for back-up. 'What are you going to say when we're asked about this callout?' Huldar knew Erla would be the one facing the music, not him. She was his boss, after all.

'I'm just hoping I won't be asked. There's enough other stuff to think about. But if I am, I'll just say I needed some fresh air. It's true and I doubt anyone will comment on it, in the circumstances.' Erla fell silent. The sun, which had been low in the sky when they arrived, had now vanished behind the nearby houses, and the twilight made the circles under her eyes less obvious. She wore the expression of someone who is resigned to what's to come.

They were both silent for a while, contemplating the car. A very ordinary white Skoda with a far from ordinary cargo in the boot. Knowing what was in there made it hard to look at and Huldar averted his eyes, gazing down the street instead, at the rows of houses. There was an unusual number of them, due to their small size, and it was clear that CID would have their work cut out knocking on all those doors. And judging by all the cars parked here during the day, many of the residents were likely to be senior citizens, who were unlikely to have been out late on a Saturday night. So the car might well have arrived unseen at its unorthodox parking space.

Erla broke the companionable silence. 'What about you, Huldar? Do you sometimes think about chucking all this in and finding something else to do?'

Huldar stared at the fenced-off trench at the end of the street where they'd been digging up the water mains; at the shabby Portakabin and yellow earth-moving machinery that had been parked on the verge beside it. He couldn't deny that he felt an urge to roll up his sleeves and get stuck in. But the longing was like the wave of nostalgia that had hit him when he thought about the history of the estate. It was one thing to dream, another to commit yourself. If he started work as a carpenter again, he would soon miss CID. 'I sometimes want to get back into carpentry,' he said, 'but not as a full-time job. As a sideline, maybe.' He looked at Erla and smiled. 'What about you?'

Erla folded her arms on top of her bump. 'Me? What else would I be capable of? Cake decorating?'

Huldar couldn't quite picture it. At least, not cakes for conventional occasions. For stag or hen parties, maybe, but clearly not for christenings, confirmations or weddings.

'Being a cop is all I know. And I don't want to do anything else.'

'Great, then you can be content that you're in the right job.' But when Huldar looked back at Erla, he saw that she wasn't. He checked the impulse to give her a good-humoured nudge. Erla was afraid her job in the police wouldn't be compatible with single motherhood. The shifts, the long hours and heavy stress load. She wasn't from Reykjavík, either, so she didn't have the usual family support network nearby.

Before he could think of anything encouraging to say, their back-up arrived.

Chapter 3

Monday evening

It was such a typical single guy's bedroom, it might have been cut out of a furniture brochure. All dark shades and low lighting. A big bed with a firm mattress. A small, shiny, bright-red fridge, probably intended for beer. A clothes rack and a massive chest of drawers. A bulky dark-brown leather chair that had been distressed in the factory to make it look as if it had come from a hunting lodge in the Scottish Highlands. Walls hung with framed photos from the world of international sport, together with the skull of an impressively horned beast on a wooden plaque. It had probably come in a job lot with the chair. And as if that wasn't pretentious enough, two wooden oars had been set up in one corner, as if the flat were in Venice and the owner travelled everywhere by gondola.

Which couldn't have been further from the truth. Right now the owner wasn't going anywhere since he was locked up in a prison cell. While he was out of circulation, Freyja was renting his flat complete with all its contents, which included his pet: a fat python whose brown markings toned with the bedroom furnishings. It was quite possible that the person responsible for the interior design had chosen the pet to match.

The heavy headboard of the enormous bed was banging rhythmically against the wall. It was made of repurposed wooden planks and had no doubt cost a fortune, but it wasn't actually that solidly built – at least the screws weren't very secure – and the headboard was coming loose. Huldar would have to bring his toolbox with him next time he visited. The bed belonged to the jailed owner and it wouldn't do to destroy it. Huldar couldn't quite picture Freyja explaining the damage to her landlord. She was a prude by nature, though fortunately she managed to leave this character trait behind at the bedroom door.

The train of thought caused him to lose focus and slow his frantic rhythm. Since this was by no means his first time, he knew what was going to happen and did his best to hold back, but when Freyja started moaning, he was lost. His mind emptied and for a few brief seconds he felt a lot better than he deserved to. Judging by Freyja's blissed-out expression, she felt the same.

Huldar remained perfectly still on top of her while he caught his breath. Then he rolled off onto his back, although it was the last thing he felt like doing. He had no choice. His body was ready to slump, powerless, and he was afraid of crushing her – not that she looked as if she'd suffered any discomfort from his weight up to now.

He and Freyja had been seeing a lot of each other, though usually on a more brother–sister basis than was the case at this moment. They had come to the joint conclusion that they worked better as friends than as a couple, and were keeping it like that. Mostly. It was better that way. He was into football and camping; she was into concert halls and hotels. She had even encouraged him to try Tinder, then laughed at his attempts to find a match there. His method, which had provoked her amusement, consisted of swiping right on every single woman in his age group who fulfilled one basic condition: her profile did not contain any mention of global warming, religion or poetry. Apart from that, he saw no reason why he and the woman in question shouldn't get along. That is, if he ignored the fact that he would prefer to have Freyja beside him. This latest failure in her resolve would do nothing to diminish his longing.

He had dropped round after work, once his colleagues had taken over at the housing estate. Although he didn't say a word about the investigation to Freyja, she'd seemed to sense that something was wrong, but she hadn't asked any questions and he was grateful for that. The purpose of his visit was to distract himself from what he had seen in the boot of the car, not to bring it all back by telling her about it. He hadn't been expecting her to be up for it all of a sudden, but certainly hadn't complained when this turned out to be the case.

Freyja flicked her eyes open as she lay back on the pillow, her hair a wild halo, as if she'd just had an electric shock. 'Oh, Christ.' She propped herself up on one elbow, staring at him in horror. 'Not a word about this to anyone. Not at work. Or anywhere else. Don't even mutter it into your coffee.'

Since he wasn't in the habit of discussing his private life with his colleagues, she needn't have bothered asking. He had got used to not mentioning their friendship to anyone. Nevertheless, he reassured her: 'No problem.'

The concealment had its reasons. Huldar wasn't convinced they were sound or even good, but that didn't change the fact that they were important to Freyja.

She had accepted the position of consultant psychologist with the police. It was a new role, designed to improve the force's relations with the Child Protection Agency. Over the years, communication between the two had been less than satisfactory, at times downright chaotic. By appointing a child psychologist, senior management wanted to avoid potential blunders in the investigation of future cases involving children. As the new liaison officer, Freyja was supposed to see to this.

She had said goodbye to her old workplace, the Children's House, cleared out her office and turned up at the police station with all her stuff in two overflowing cardboard boxes. These she had dumped in a rather poky office – an office that was not unlike the one she had been relegated to at the Children's House following her fall from grace.

At first, Huldar had welcomed this change in her situation. He had looked forward to working closely with her and seeing her more often than during his weekly visits. To eating lunch with her, dropping by for a chat and bringing her coffee. But nothing had come of this. It turned out that Freyja didn't want them to talk to each other at work, unless it was strictly business. So their paths didn't cross much at the office. They said hello as they passed in the corridors and nodded to each other at staff meetings. But she wanted to be judged on her own merits in her new workplace, rather than having her achievements overshadowed by her association with him. Huldar hadn't put up much of an objection. She was right. If their friendship became common knowledge, she would be suspected of having got the job through him, however unlikely that was. In truth, a reference from him or an attempt on his part to influence the decision would have had exactly the opposite effect. But gossips rarely let a little thing like the truth get in the way of a good story.

Since it was Huldar's fault that Freyja had lost her dream job as head of the Children's House, he had to accept her decision. If she lost another job because of him, there would be zero chance of their ever getting together. Fortunately, although Reykjavík was a small world, no other police officers lived in the upmarket block of flats on Seltjarnarnes where she was renting, which meant he was safe to visit her there. And his offer to take over feeding the snake that came with the apartment had made him a welcome guest.

Perhaps it was the python, but he often felt as if he were playing a game of Snakes and Ladders with Freyja. He would land on a square with a ladder and shoot up it, but this would invariably be followed by a square with a snake, which would send him hurtling down again. Right now, he was at the top of the longest ladder.

Huldar closed his eyes. He'd always been someone to whom sleep came easily and sex tended to knock him out like an anaesthetic. If he started counting, he wouldn't make it to ten even if he kept his eyes open and pinched his arm.

'Hey!' Freyja gripped his shoulder hard and gave him a shake. 'Don't fall asleep. Baldur's coming over with Saga and you've got to go.'

Huldar had landed on a square with a snake. He raised his head. It wasn't only work that got in the way of his relation-ship with Freyja. Her brother, Baldur, had a criminal record as long as your arm and according to her he couldn't stand cops or judges. In fact, he held judges in even lower esteem than cops. Yet somehow Baldur didn't seem bothered by the fact his sister had started working for the arch-enemy. Presumably, like so many people, Baldur inserted exemption clauses into his life rules when it came to his own family.

His little daughter, Saga, on the other hand, was a great fan of Huldar's. Since she was extremely picky, her liking for

Huldar had probably played a part in advancing his friendship with Freyja. After all, if Saga liked him, he couldn't be all bad.

'Have I got time for a shower?'

Freyja reached for her phone. 'Do you use conditioner?'

'No.'

'Then it should be OK. But you'll have to hurry.'

The bathroom was an en suite. Since it had no door, Huldar half hoped Freyja would come and slip into the huge shower cubicle with him. But no such luck, so he concentrated on washing. By the time he returned to the bedroom she had her dressing gown on and was sitting on the edge of the bed, constantly checking the time on her phone. Seeing this, he hastily started dragging on his clothes, still damp from the shower.

It was strange to think that not so long ago this arrangement would have suited him perfectly – no-strings sex. But now that he found himself in this position, it wasn't quite the unmitigated pleasure he'd imagined. He wanted to be wrapped up in a dressing gown himself, making them both coffee, and perhaps stepping out onto the balcony for a smoke. He wanted to fall asleep with Freyja, wake up with Freyja and hang around with Freyja, doing nothing in particular. He still hoped that day would come.

But it wouldn't be any time soon.

Before leaving, Huldar checked on the snake. As usual, it was lying coiled up in the huge glass tank, but even so he could see how plump and well fed it was looking. That was his fault. He had overfed the creature on his too-frequent visits. It felt like a very basic arrangement: snake feeding in return for payment in kind.

The flat head lifted when it became aware of Huldar and the black forked tongue appeared. He knew that pythons sensed smells by sticking out their tongues and flickering them back and forth. He had been forced to read up on the species when he took over the care of the animal, not out of curiosity but from a desire to know the risks involved, which turned out to be considerable.

As Huldar was closing the door, he saw the python blink and lick its lips.

Before saying goodbye to Freyja, he hesitated a moment, wondering if he should say something clever about continuing with this more intimate relationship. But the moment passed. It was better not to say anything.

He had no sooner stepped out of the building than work began to intrude on his consciousness again, presenting him with the images he had left behind by the post-boxes in the lobby on his way in.

He had a vivid flashback to the boot of the car, as if he were still standing in the housing estate with Erla. The black bin bag she'd opened had turned out to contain a lower leg attached to a foot with red-painted toenails. There had also been a glimpse of the sawn-off, bloodied end of another limb that was probably an arm. Huldar's nose filled again with the sickening metallic stench that had put him on the trail in the first place. It was a smell that never boded well in his job, so his sudden realisation had not been the result of any particular brilliance on his part. Come to think of it, he couldn't think of a single job where the smell of blood would be good news, except perhaps in an abattoir.

Huldar got in the car and tried to distract himself with thoughts about the supper he was belatedly about to eat. There were three choices: one of the city's fast-food joints, which had long ago lost their appeal for him; a hot dog from the petrol station, or pot noodles and toast at home. None of these were tempting enough to drag his mind out of that boot. But he had to eat something, so the petrol station it was.

He was assailed by boredom as he stood at the plastic table with the paper-napkin dispenser, surrounded by shelves containing bottles of engine oil and windscreen cleaner. He finished the last bite of his first hot dog, then pulled the phone out of his pocket and rang Erla. Since he couldn't stop thinking about the body parts, he might as well hear the latest update. A lot could have happened since he'd finished his shift. At that point, the only thing that had changed since they'd first opened the boot was that the car had been taken to a hangar at the domestic airport for forensic examination, the collection of specimens and to be photographed. When the car was towed away, the black plastic bags full of human remains had still been in the boot, but by now they must have taken them out and perhaps discovered who the victim was.

Erla picked up instantly. 'What?'

'I just wanted to hear the latest. Do you know who was in the boot?'

'Nothing's been confirmed yet but by far the most likely answer is that it's Bríet Hannesdóttir, the owner of the car. We can't get hold of her and we know that the body parts belong to a woman. The post-mortem's scheduled for tomorrow morning and after that we'll have more information. It should be interesting. Presumably the examination will take longer than usual because of . . . well, you know.'

Huldar shuddered, his eyes on the second hot dog, which was resting in a red plastic holder on the table in front of him. It didn't look very appetising all of a sudden. He coughed. 'Yes, right.' Then he tried to change the subject to something less grisly. He was still hungry and was hoping to get the next sausage down without gagging. 'Does this woman Bríet live alone?'

'She's a single mother. She has a ten-year-old daughter who's staying with her father at the moment on some kind of extended daddy weekend. He last saw Bríet on Thursday when he picked up the girl but hasn't heard from her since. I spoke to him briefly on the phone.'

'And that didn't strike him as odd? How does it normally work when parents share custody?'

'Why are you asking me? Like I've got a fucking clue.' Erla's burst of anger suggested she'd read more into Huldar's question than he'd intended.

'It was just a general observation. I only meant would it seem normal or not that he hadn't heard from her? That's all.'

Erla was silent for a moment, and when she answered her tone was friendlier, so apparently she believed him. But she didn't apologise. 'He said he hadn't been expecting to hear from her. Of course, he was very curious to know why I was calling but I just said it was in connection with her car. I'm not sure he bought it, though. Especially after I asked if she had any tattoos, scars or breast implants.'

'And did she?'

'No. No tattoos, no scars, no implants. Not when they divorced, anyway. I also called her parents, using the car as a pretext there as well. They hadn't heard from her either, not since Friday. But they didn't find that unusual. They said she was studying and working part time, and that she was probably up at the university, which was why her phone was off. According to them, she was planning to use the weekend and her child-free weekdays to study. Unlike her ex, they didn't see through the car story.'

'What about work?'

'She works at the National Hospital and the woman I talked to there spoke well of her. She said Bríet's a reliable and helpful lab technician who's liked by everyone. She hasn't made any mistakes on the job or received any reprimands during the time she's been working there. The woman also mentioned that Bríet was supposed to do the night shift on Sunday evening but didn't turn up. So I'm fairly sure it's her. But, according to management, fairly sure isn't good enough for us to start contacting her closest relatives with bad news. They want us to hold off. At least until tomorrow.'

'That's probably smart. I mean, maybe it isn't Bríet. Maybe it's someone who got on the wrong side of her. She could be on the run after . . . you know, those bags . . .' Huldar moved aside for a customer who needed to get to the shelves behind him. He turned his back to the man, as if this would give him more privacy, and just hoped the guy knew what he wanted and wouldn't start perusing the labels on all the spray bottles.

'Is there someone there with you?'

'Yes. I'm at a petrol station.'

'Why are you calling me from a petrol station?'

'I was bored.'

Erla sighed. 'I'm still at work. It's not my problem if you're bored. Go home and watch Netflix like any normal person. Jesus.'

Huldar merely replied that he would drop by her office when he got to work in the morning. But he felt compelled to ask one more question before she could hang up on him. He couldn't spend the rest of the evening wondering about it. 'How many body parts were there?'

'Seven.'

While Huldar was trying to visualise this, Erla added: 'But there's one bit missing.'

'Oh?'

'The top. The head wasn't in the boot.'

Erla hung up without saying goodbye. But then a cheery 'See you!' wouldn't have seemed appropriate after the information she had just shared with him.

Huldar shoved the phone back in his pocket. He picked up the hot dog and tossed it in the bin on his way out.

Chapter 4

Tuesday

Freyja had dressed up for work, in a skirt that she felt was office-rather than party-wear, a smart shirt, modest heels and, after a little thought, large gold hoops in her ears. She'd received a summons from her boss the previous evening and wanted to make a good impression. The email, which had arrived after Baldur left, had simply said *Meeting* in the subject line, and stated the time and place but nothing about the purpose or who else would be there. As a result, she had taken it to mean that the meeting was about her performance at work. Had she known that it related to a murder inquiry and that Erla and her entire team would be there, Freyja would never have glammed up. As it was, she stuck out like a sore thumb, since the proportion of people sporting fleeces wouldn't have been out of place at an engineering firm.

So far no one had paid much attention to her. When they entered the meeting room, no one had commented on her clothing, except for one man who helpfully informed her that her earrings were a health hazard; they could get caught in something and tear her earlobes. She thanked him for his warning and said she would be careful. Apart from that, no one had appeared to notice her until now, when all heads turned in her direction. Erla had asked a question that was clearly aimed at her, although she hadn't mentioned her by name. Up to that point, Freyja hadn't contributed to the meeting at all, just sat and listened.

Erla had shared only very general information about the new case, stressing that the investigation was just getting off the ground. Since nothing that had been said so far was remotely relevant to Freyja's role, she had begun to wonder why she had been ordered to attend. But now it was clear. She was required, as a psychologist, to enlighten them about what possible motivation someone could have for dismembering a body.

It was uncomfortable feeling all eyes on her as she was forced to express an opinion on a subject she had no experience of, either professionally or academically. It felt like one of those oral exams she was always taking in her dreams, exams that she had invariably forgotten to revise for. But she had to say something; she couldn't just stare blankly at them. Especially since she knew that most of the people in there regarded her presence in the police as mere window dressing. What mattered to them was good solid detective work, based on collecting evidence and interviewing witnesses. It was up to her to earn their respect by providing an intelligent, professional answer to Erla's question. Freyja sat up straighter and smiled weakly. 'I won't claim to be an expert in this area, but—'

Erla immediately jumped down her throat. This was worse than any oral exam, whether in her dreams or in reality: teachers and examiners at least let their students ramble on without interruption, in the hope that they'd eventually come out with something that made sense. But Erla wasn't about to cut her any slack. She was just looking for a chance to catch Freyja out. 'No *buts*. I was hoping for a professional opinion. If you don't know anything about it, we've got better things to do with our time than—'

Freyja saw red. '*If* you'd let me finish . . .'

Clearly unaccustomed to being interrupted like this, Erla shut up.

Freyja's momentary rage evaporated and her mind cleared. She could do this; she knew all about humanity and its more warped outliers. 'I think we can all agree that we're dealing with an abnormally horrific act.' With the notable exception of Erla, most of those present nodded faintly, and Freyja went on: 'Human beings are programmed to show empathy and compassion. We come equipped with a certain moral threshold, which makes most of us abhor extreme violence or torture, for example. We also have an innate or built-in system that means that from the age of two we are revolted by and recoil from anything that could be dangerous: rotten food, raw meat, vomit, boils, waste products, and so on. The act of sawing a human body into bits would fall into that category, which means that not everyone would be capable of it. Most people would experience such powerful feelings of revulsion that they wouldn't be able to start the job, let alone see it through.'

'So? What kind of individuals would be capable of finishing the job? I'm not interested in the ones who couldn't do it.' Erla had got over her momentary surprise at being called out.

'The first thing that comes to mind is someone experienced in dissecting or cutting through flesh, like a surgeon, a reindeer hunter or someone employed in the meat industry. It's possible they'd be capable of going through with it.'

'So our killer's a surgeon, a hunter or a butcher?' Erla didn't look particularly happy at the prospect.

'Not necessarily. I mentioned those professions because they would find it easier than someone who works in an office from nine to five. The killer, or rather the person who dismembered the body, could also have been in a state of acute psychosis and therefore free from the restraints that would make such an act impossible for the rest of us. Certain drugs would have the same effect, though I doubt that an individual on drugs would have the stamina or concentration to finish the job and pack the body parts into bags. But a psychopath could have done it because they wanted to. In that case, the murder might have been incidental and the real purpose have been to experience what it felt like to cut up a dead body.'

'You're assuming the victim was dead. That's not a given and we won't know for sure until after the post-mortem.' Erla's expression suggested she wasn't making this point simply to disconcert her.

The possibility hadn't even occurred to Freyja. She felt sick to her stomach and the flesh prickled on her arms. She made no attempt to disguise her shock. If fitting in here at CID meant turning into an unemotional automaton, she wasn't interested. However, glancing around, she saw that most of the others had had the same gut reaction. Some shifted in their seats, others grimaced or shuddered. Huldar had done all three.

Freyja was careful not to let her gaze linger on Huldar. She must concentrate and not let herself be distracted by wondering what had got into her yesterday.

He must have known about the discovery of the body parts when he visited her, yet he hadn't said a word. At first, she had been offended by this, but Erla hadn't been talking long before Freyja understood. She could never have faked the appropriate level of amazement and horror if she'd heard about it beforehand.

She cleared her throat and replied to Erla. 'I hadn't considered that possibility. But if that's the case, you're definitely looking for a psychopath.'

'A butcher, a hunter, a surgeon, a psychotic or a psychopath. And possibly, though it's unlikely, a drug addict.' Erla let her sarcasm shine through. Pregnancy had done nothing to mellow her.

But Freyja didn't rise to her tone. 'No, actually. He or she may not belong to any of these categories. If the body was only cut up in order to move it, the frame would be much wider. People are capable of unbelievable things when they feel cornered. The survival instinct is powerful enough to enable them to overcome various obstacles that would normally be beyond them. Maybe the perpetrator thought there were only two choices, either to cut up the body into manageable parts or to be caught. If so, we could be talking about anybody. But in that case I believe the person in question probably knew the victim. And it would have made the job easier if he or she had been in a frenzy of rage or filled with hatred for her.'

Erla was listening attentively now.

Freyja continued: 'Or the perpetrator could have done something terrible before and therefore already crossed the boundary that would limit most people's behaviour. If so, it's safe to assume that they've taken a step that would have changed them. You can't just carry on with your life as if nothing's happened after committing an act like that. Even if other people haven't noticed the change, it will be there.'

Freyja lapsed into silence. She reckoned she had done all right, judging by the expressions of those present, who were all looking noticeably friendlier. Of course, Huldar had been looking positive ever since she opened her mouth, but that didn't mean anything. Nor did it help much, since he was careful never to look in her direction. That in itself was suspicious. Just as well no one seemed to have noticed.

Erla took over again. 'Right, well. For now, we're not concerned with what the perpetrator might get up to in future. We just need to track him down and provide the prosecution service with enough evidence to make sure he gets the severest sentence possible. As long as he's inside, he can't do much harm.'

Huldar shifted in his chair. Then he addressed a question to Freyja, while studiously avoiding looking at her. This was so peculiar that she thought everyone was bound to notice. 'Who would be more likely to do this, a man or a woman? From a psychological point of view.'

Freyja tried and failed to meet Huldar's eye. 'A man. They're more likely to use violence than women are. The body was cut up into eight parts, according to what we've just heard. If this was done to facilitate its removal, it would suggest that the perpetrator isn't particularly strong. In other words, it could have been a woman. But it may also have been done to transport the body as inconspicuously as possible, and therefore have nothing to do with physical strength.'

'So we're none the wiser about the sex of the killer. Either a woman or a man.' Erla slammed shut the folder lying on the table in front of her. 'Can psychology provide us with any answers about why the head was removed and is still missing?'

Freyja was silent. There might have been a psychological explanation but she was in no position to speculate. It wasn't as if she had anything to go on, since the identities of the victim and the murderer were as yet unknown.

One of the detectives present took advantage of the silence to ask a question. It was addressed directly to Freyja. 'Seeing as the body was beheaded, isn't it possible that an asylum seeker did it? It's not like Icelanders are known for that kind of thing.'

The other people round the table watched Freyja closely. She got the feeling that the question was an attempt to sound out her position on the issue. She didn't know about the others but she suspected that the detective who'd asked was hoping to hear that it was bound to be an asylum seeker. She would never dream of giving such an irresponsible reply. 'Well, it's not as if the asylum seekers in Iceland are known for beheadings either. But the description I gave earlier doesn't rule out any particular group or nationality. It could be an asylum seeker. It could be an Icelander. Or a tourist, for that matter. It's your job to find out who it was.'

She reckoned that would do. Nobody spoke but she read in most of the faces around the table that her answer had just about passed muster. No one looked pissed off but they didn't exactly look enthused either.

Erla broke the silence. 'Quite. Anyway, I've reported it to the Identification Commission, but in the circumstances they didn't see any reason to involve the entire committee. It seems probable that the body is that of Bríet Hannesdóttir, the owner of the car, so only one representative of the committee will take part in the investigation. He'll stay in the background and only get involved with the aspects that are relevant to making an identification. Like attending the post-mortem. Please be polite to the guy.' Erla glanced at the clock on the wall. 'Right, well. I'm late, so we'll wrap up for now. When I get back I'll have more information, as the post-mortem should shed some light on the matter. And the search of Bríet's house, too.' She surveyed the faces present, her gaze pausing on Gudlaugur. 'You do the house search. Take one of the team with you and two guys from Forensics. The warrant's on my desk.'

Gudlaugur nodded, looking satisfied, until Erla added: 'There's a chance you'll come across the head there, so don't lose your breakfast if you do. We don't want the scene to be contaminated.'

She turned back to the others. 'You lot divide up the other tasks I mentioned earlier. The most important is to carry out a thorough examination of the car and to work out which CCTV cameras cover the housing estate and surrounding area. We'll need to pull all the footage. According to the woman whose drive the car was blocking, it wasn't there at suppertime on Saturday evening but had appeared by nine on Sunday morning, when she happened to look outside. You'll need to act fast. Use that as your rough time frame. We'll have a progress report when I get back. We need to knock on doors in the neighbourhood and find out if anyone saw the car arriving. Remember that it's probably Bríet, the owner of the car. The body was naked but the bags also contained items of female clothing that need to be identified. To start off with, check her social media accounts to see if we can find a photo of her wearing them. That way we won't have to involve her parents until we're sure of the victim's identity.' She scanned their faces. 'Any special requests for jobs?'

Huldar jumped in. 'I'll knock on doors in the estate.'

'No. You're coming to the post-mortem with me and the guy from the Identity Commission.'

There were sighs of relief from everyone except Huldar. No one wanted to go anywhere near this particular post-mortem.

Once the meeting was over, everyone dispersed to get on with their appointed tasks. Everyone except Freyja, who hadn't been given a job. This was hardly surprising, since none of the assignments related to child protection. During her job interview, it had been made clear that her colleagues could also consult her about other matters requiring psychological expertise, but up to now these had been thin on the ground. She had been asked a few times to judge whether a prisoner in custody was merely drunk or also suffering from mental health issues. But it wasn't often that she recommended someone be admitted to the psychiatric ward. And once she had been asked to speak to two members of staff who had fallen out over whether the window by their workstations should be open or closed. In that case she had recommended that they be separated. None of these exactly counted as demanding jobs. As for her contribution to the meeting, she had managed not to disgrace herself but didn't feel she'd helped to progress the inquiry at all.

She got the feeling that Erla hadn't requested her presence at the meeting and guessed that it had been forced on her. No doubt the manager who'd appointed Freyja had been responsible, since he was keen to use her as much as possible. She suspected, however, that the need for her expertise had been overestimated. She had recently been appointed to three committees that dealt with objectives, image problems and equality issues in the police. She had also been appointed to the anti-bullying team and a group that was supposed to deal with sexual harassment, should any cases arise. Since all three committees and the two teams were already fully staffed, it was fairly obvious that this was a rather desperate attempt to keep her busy. It had been a mortifying realisation.

Almost as mortifying as her situation now, all dressed up with nothing to do, surrounded by detectives who were run off their feet. The most obvious solution was to go back down to her poky little office, but she didn't want to. It was uncomfortably reminiscent of the one she had left behind at the Children's House and whenever she sat there, staring at the wall, she was overwhelmed by doubts about whether she had done the right thing in taking this new job. There was nothing else for it, though. If she stood by the coffee machine any longer, people would realise she was just killing time.

Freyja tilted back her head and emptied the last drop from the paper cup down her throat. When she straightened up again, Lína, the diminutive intern, was standing there, her porcelain-white face framed by a thick mane of wavy red hair. She was wearing the inevitable fleece, zipped up to the neck like a tourist.

'What did you learn at the meeting?' Typically, Lína didn't bother with small talk. Freyja hadn't noticed her absence that morning, but then she hadn't been aware that Lína was back doing another spell of work experience with the police.

'Probably nothing you haven't already heard.' Freyja wasn't sure if she was allowed to discuss the meeting with someone who hadn't attended it. 'I gather there's going to be another progress meeting tomorrow morning, when there should be more information.'

Lína folded her arms, her expression thoughtful. 'Do you know if I'm supposed to be there?'

Freyja shrugged. 'I haven't a clue. I seriously doubt I'll be invited, though, as it's not that sort of case. But I'd be surprised if you weren't given a job.'

This was what Lína wanted to hear. 'Yes. Me too.'

'Why weren't you at the meeting earlier, by the way?' Freyja asked quickly, to keep Lína chatting. As long as they were talking, she wouldn't have to crawl back to her office and sit there twiddling her thumbs.

'I've been in a different department for this latest part of my internship. But they sent me up here to help out. Maybe Erla forgot I was coming today. Otherwise I'm sure she'd have invited me.' She didn't sound quite so confident as she said this last bit.

'Oh, yes. Absolutely.' Sometimes it was best to give people what they wanted to hear.

Lína didn't look either pleased or displeased. Instead, she returned to the point. 'Did you learn who the murder victim was?'

'No. They don't know yet.' Since this information could hardly be regarded as a military secret, Freyja felt she could answer. The news had already broken about a murder in Reykjavík, although so far the reporters had been given so little to go on that it was barely more than a headline.

'Why not? Is it a foreigner?'

It was a natural enough question; it wasn't usually difficult to identify the recently deceased in Iceland. But since Lína didn't know the answer, it was obvious that no one had told her the details. And as Freyja was unlikely to be the first person Lína had asked, it was better to avoid telling her the reason: that it was hard to identify a body without a head.

'They simply don't know. Hopefully the post-mortem will provide an answer.' Freyja felt it was time to extract herself from Lína's interrogation before she was forced to say bluntly that she wasn't at liberty to share any details with her. Lína had been one of the few members of Erla's department to be at all friendly to her – though the fact that she could be considered part of this group was a sign of how limited it was. After all, Lína hadn't been exactly friendly, she just hadn't been actively unfriendly. That was all it took for Freyja. 'Hopefully you'll hear the latest at tomorrow's progress meeting. Then maybe you can fill me in.'

Lína frowned. 'No, sorry. What's discussed at the meeting is confidential.' She didn't bat an eyelid as she said this.

'Yes, of course.' Freyja smiled blandly at her.

She noticed that Lína's gaze was fixed on her earrings. But instead of complimenting them, the younger woman frowned again. 'Are you aware that earrings like that can get caught in things and tear through your ear? I'd take them out if I were you. Especially if you're going to be entering a building site.'

'I hadn't actually planned on doing that any time soon, but if I do, I'll take them off.' Freyja tossed her paper cup in the bin and said goodbye to Lína. On the way downstairs to her office she wondered what, if any, assignment would fall to the intern. Perhaps Lína was too young to be part of a case involving dismemberment and beheading. She herself wouldn't recommend it if the subject came up in one of her committees.

Freyja went into her cramped office, sat down at the computer and stared at her reflection in the dark screen. Her attention was drawn to her earrings, which had now lost all their charm. She would never be able to put them on again without picturing a torn earlobe. But she was damned if she was taking them off today. She smiled as the computer started up and the wallpaper appeared. It was a photo of her little niece, Saga. The girl was sitting on the floor, her plump arm resting on the back of the dog, Molly, who was sound asleep beside her. It was an adorable, feel-good picture, apart from Saga's expression. She was glowering darkly at the camera, her mouth turned down in its characteristic perma-scowl.

Freyja fiddled with the keyboard as she met Saga's gaze, trying in vain to think of something useful to do. She could read up on the police's equal opportunities policy yet again, or go into the appraisals and objectives area and see if anything new had been added.

She was saved by the phone. They wanted her to come down and talk to a man who was refusing to leave his cell. This wasn't some repeat offender, just an ordinary middle-aged bloke with a drink problem. They wouldn't agree to extending his custody as it was high time he took himself home and made up with his wife. A spot of old-fashioned bother, in other words; nothing to do with corpses or dismemberment. Grateful for this small mercy, Freyja jumped up and hurried downstairs.

Chapter 5

Tuesday

Sædís had parked on the pavement. There were no free spaces near the police station and she needed to keep an eye on the entrance, which was difficult with the snow coming down so heavily, reducing visibility to a few metres.

The pedestrians gave her dirty looks as they squeezed by but she turned away, pretending not to see them. Not for the first time, she wished they had a smaller car. It was a big four-by-four, jacked up on huge tyres, totally inappropriate for city driving but her father obviously derived some pleasure from it that she didn't even try to understand. She was happy with her own little banger, though it was reaching the end of the road, so to speak. She automatically crossed her fingers, hoping that it would prove possible to repair. Preferably today. Her dad needed his four-by-four and she couldn't manage without a car.

Her father finally emerged from the police station. He looked terrible, his hair dirty and matted, his jacket crooked on his shoulders, and his trousers stained and creased. She assumed he'd lost his glasses as he wasn't wearing them. Instead of starting down the steps, he patted the pockets of his jacket. Sædís was familiar with the gesture. He was looking for cigarettes. No doubt the packet had been lost along with his glasses. He raised a hand to his eyes and squinted around through the thickly falling snow.

He spotted the car, despite his bad eyesight and the poor visibility. It was unavoidable, really. Their eyes met and even through the snow Sædís thought she could see the sadness in his expression. Neither wanted to share this moment.

Best get it over with. He needed to go home. If he didn't, he was perfectly capable of heading straight to the nearest bar and carrying on drinking.

For a moment or two it looked as if he was going to make a run for it along Hverfisgata but instead he came towards the car, his shoulders hunched. Sædís felt a pang. He might not be perfect, but he was her dad. And she loved him, in spite of his flaws.

She reached for the handle on the passenger side and opened the door. Large snowflakes blew inside and collected on the seat, only to melt almost instantly as it was heated. There was no point trying to wipe it dry, as her dad was unlikely to be bothered by a little wetness right now. He would be too preoccupied with his headache and his shame.

The police had called her to say that her father was in the cells after being arrested twice in short succession for being drunk and disorderly. The first time had been early on Saturday evening, the second on Monday evening, after he had been released late on Sunday. According to the police officer who rang, he had begged them to let him stay and sleep it off on Sunday, following his first arrest, and he had tried the same ploy again today. Sædís had been asked to come and fetch him to make sure there wouldn't be a third time. The officer she spoke to had pointed out that the police cells were not a drying-out clinic and recommended that her father seek help from the rehab centre.

Long experience had taught Sædís that her father didn't need treatment. He had fallen off the wagon before but managed to clean up his act again. She didn't know much about alcoholism but suspected he wasn't a typical drunk. He had given up without any help before, when he'd had enough, replacing the bottle with hard work. Instead of spending every evening sitting half pissed in front of the TV, he had kept himself busy.

Now that Sædís was an adult herself, she had a better insight into what caused his lapses. It wasn't her fault, as she'd believed as a child. The drinking and the long hours at work were simply crutches he used to avoid coming to terms with her mother's illness. He just couldn't handle the mood swings, the sadness and depression that accompanied her mental health problems. If he'd only displayed more initiative and resolve, her mother might have been persuaded to take medication for her condition. But he hadn't. He'd just switched off and seemed to be waiting for everything to get better on its own.

But when one support gives way, the next has to bear more weight to keep the structure from collapsing. And this was Sædís's fate. While he buried himself in work, she took care of what needed to be done at home.

Her father got into the car, carefully avoiding Sædís's eye, and stared straight ahead through the windscreen instead. As he did up his seat-belt, she saw that his hands were shaking.

'God. I'm so sorry. I'm so bloody sorry.' His voice shook as badly as his hands.

'We need to talk.' Her words conveyed her meaning quite precisely. Neither wanted to talk but they needed to, nevertheless.

'Not now, please. Later. I just can't.' Her father's voice cracked.

It was no use trying to force the issue. 'Home?' she asked instead, though anywhere else was out of the question. He needed to recover there: take a shower, have something to eat, talk to her bed-bound mother, then sleep off his hangover. Work would have to wait, although he must be itching to get back to it. Work was his way of hiding from problems. Work and alcohol. The conversation they were both dreading so much would have to wait as well. 'I'll fry you some eggs,' she said. 'We've got fresh bread too. You must be starving.'

He nodded and she moved off. As she turned the wheel to make a right onto Snorrabraut, she twisted her body, which made her belly more conspicuous. Luckily, though, her father was still staring rigidly ahead and didn't notice anything.

Sædís turned up the windscreen wipers, which were fighting a losing battle with the snow. This was definitely not a good time to tell him her news.

Chapter 6

Tuesday

The children entered the classroom, their cheeks ruddy, their hair ruffled from hats and hoods. Their eagerness had diminished since the beginning of break time, when they'd been jostling each other out of the way in their desire to get outside. It was hardly surprising. Not many of them were really interested in the lesson that was about to start, dealing as it did with the settlement of Iceland. Their interest in the ninth century was limited as it was so far from the world they knew. The original settlers of Iceland couldn't go online or watch Netflix or play computer games; they knew nothing about football and never took selfies. To Kristbjörg's disappointment, even their weapons held no attraction for pupils used to computer games. The children were unimpressed by swords and axes. Such primitive weapons wouldn't stand a chance against the automatic ones they were familiar with from their games. The boys' drawings, in particular, often featured such guns. She had even started recognising the names of the main ones: Minigun, Uzi, Desert Eagle, Arctic Warfare, Kalashnikov. When the names were written on the drawings they were never spelt wrong. Even boys incapable of spelling the word 'egg' could write 'bazooka' without any problem.

'Hurry up and sit down. The sooner we start, the sooner we'll be finished.' This wasn't actually true. The lesson was supposed to last for forty minutes and the pupils couldn't speed it up by sitting down any faster. 'Then turn to page six in your textbooks.'

One by one the pupils took their seats and the majority also obeyed her instruction about the textbooks. She repeated the page number when three pupils stuck up their hands simultaneously to ask about it. Before long they were all sitting with their books open in front of them. The entire class was facing Kristbjörg and waiting in silence for further instructions.

They were all good kids but in combination they were a difficult group. There were twenty-five pupils in the class. A handful of them managed to span almost the entire gamut of diagnoses. In addition to that, there was an immigrant whose Icelandic was limited, another kid who was struggling with gender dysphoria, and a third who was gifted and more demanding than all the rest put together – with the exception of the pupil who was the offspring of a law professor and a doctor of physics. Not a week went by when the couple didn't kick up some sort of fuss. Sooner or later Kristbjörg would be goaded into responding to an email or phone call from them by saying that they would simply have to accept that their child was very ordinary and didn't excel in any way. The blame for that did not lie with the school, and no amount of complaining would change it.

There was a squeaking of chair legs on lino, a sure sign that the class was growing restless. As usual, the disturbance started at the rear of the room and spread towards the front. At the round table at the back, a girl leant over to the boy next to her and whispered something in his ear. The boy didn't seem particularly pleased by what she had said. He made a face, leant away and gave the whisperer a shove.

'What's going on?' Kristbjörg raised her voice. She knew from long experience that it paid to nip this sort of thing in the bud.

Both pupils answered in unison: 'Nothing.' Kristbjörg also knew from long experience that children always answered like that when put on the spot, no matter what the circumstances.

'You know it's forbidden to whisper. It's rude to the people around you.' Kristbjörg glared in the hope of hammering her message into their heads. 'And you should pay attention in lessons. You can talk during break. Understood?'

'Don't blame me. I wasn't whispering. It was her.' The owner of the ear was indignant, perhaps not unreasonably. He moved his chair away from the whisperer. 'I didn't do anything.'

As the aggrieved child was the son of the two academics, it would be as well to resolve this straight away. 'I'm not blaming you in particular. I was talking to the whole class. It's rude to whisper and that applies to all of you.' Kristbjörg hoped this would be enough to smooth things over.

But her argument cut no ice with the son of the doctor and the professor, who folded his arms, scowling. 'You *did* mean me. Anyway, I think it was unfair of you to tell everyone off when she was the only one whispering.'

The chances of the evening news being interrupted by a phone call from his parents had just shot up. Kristbjörg felt like groaning aloud but she fought back the urge. 'I'm not telling everyone off, I'm teaching you all some manners.' This came across a bit harshly, so she corrected herself. 'I mean I'm

instructing you. It does us all good, me included, to be regularly reminded of our manners.'

The academics' son did not look mollified. He was after
something more, perhaps an apology.

He wasn't getting one. 'Right, kids. That's enough of that.
Let's turn to the settlement of Iceland. Last time we were
talking about Ingólfur Arnarson's high-seat pillars. Who
remembers what role they played in the settlement?'

The gifted child's hand shot up and waved eagerly. As no
one else made any move to answer, Kristbjörg was forced to
choose her.

While she was showing off, Kristbjörg noticed that the
whispering had started up again. She waited for the gifted
child to finish, then asked sternly: 'What was I just saying
about whispering?'

The academics' son pushed his neighbour away. 'I can't
help it. She keeps whispering in my ear.'

The boy had a point. Kristbjörg addressed the girl: 'What
is it that the rest of us aren't allowed to hear? Are you answering the question about the seat pillars, by any chance?'

'No.' The girl looked sheepish. She blushed and dropped
her eyes to her lap.

'Right. Then I suggest you stop that and concentrate
instead on what's happening in the lesson.' Kristbjörg didn't
want to come down on her too heavily. The girl had a difficult
time of it and was generally no trouble. She had two friends
and as long as she wasn't sitting with them, she behaved perfectly well but, if left together, the three of them did nothing
but giggle. Since Kristbjörg had taken to splitting them up,
the girl had been trying to make friends with her neighbour,
the academics' son, who wanted nothing to do with her. No

amount of effort on her part had changed his mind about that, as demonstrated by this latest incident. 'How about I split you two up for now?'

While Kristbjörg was scanning the room in search of children to change seats with them, the boy protested: 'I shouldn't have to move. She was saying sick things to me. She should be sent to the head teacher's office.'

The girl looked hurt. There was no knowing what she'd said to the boy but she obviously hadn't expected him to find it sick. She had presumably been hoping he'd think it was cool.

Kristbjörg now found herself confronted by the backs of the children's heads. Even the gifted child had turned round.

One of the pupils asked: 'What did she say?' Others chimed in with the same question. It wasn't every day they got to hear something sick in a lesson.

'She said—' The boy was forced to shut up when the girl jumped on him and put her hand over his mouth. He tore it away and carried on speaking, holding her off as well as he could. 'She said she'd seen a head.'

'A head?' The rest of the class looked disappointed. 'What's so sick about that?'

Kristbjörg clapped her hands. 'Turn round!' She pointed to the table at the back. 'You two! Stop fighting at once!' They subsided instantly, the girl returned to her seat and Kristbjörg continued: 'I don't know what on earth is going on, but both of you stop it—'

She wasn't allowed to finish. The academics' son interrupted. 'It *was* sick! It wasn't just a head. She said she'd seen a *chopped-off* head. A woman's head. Like in a horror film.'

The other children's eyes grew round and several shuddered, including the girl's two friends.

71

Kristbjörg gave in and moved the girl.

At the end of the lesson, she asked her to stay behind for a chat. The child walked up to the desk looking sheepish and stood there chewing her lower lip, her hands behind her back. 'Are you going to tell me off?'

Kristbjörg gestured at the two friends to step away from the door where they were lurking, clearly trying to eavesdrop. Once they had gone, she turned back to the shamefaced child. 'Yes, but not much.' Kristbjörg gave her a friendly smile. It was impossible to be angry with the poor kid. She was so vulnerable somehow, so small, thin and sickly. She had problems concentrating and her eyes were forever flickering to and fro behind her glasses, which always seemed to sit crookedly on her nose. She had as many problems socially as she did academically. Apart from her two friends, who both had problems of their own, she seemed incapable of fitting in. But the girl's situation could change. She had one very important advantage – the support of a loving family. Kristbjörg knew she was adopted and, as is often the case with adoptive parents, they lavished love on her. Her packed lunch was always prepared with great care, although it usually returned home untouched. Her clothes were smart and clean, but they always looked dishevelled by the end of the day. In the mornings, her hair was neatly tied back in a pony-tail and secured with clips. But, like her clothes, her hair soon became a mess; the elastic band slid down her thin pony-tail and the clips became dislodged.

Her friends weren't nearly as well cared for. One was unusually tall, the other of perfectly average height. The smaller of the two was a noticeably better student, but otherwise they had much in common. They often came to school without a packed lunch, pencil or eraser, were inadequately dressed for the weather and were frequently absent – the taller girl in particular. Kristbjörg's attempts to get the girls' parents to keep a closer eye on their attendance hadn't had an effect. It was as if they didn't feel any responsibility towards their kids, and she couldn't detect much interest in how they got on either. It was no wonder that the threesome mostly went round to the third girl's home after school, as hers was by far the least chaotic.

Kristbjörg put on a serious face. 'You know I don't like it when children in my class don't listen.'

The girl nodded, her head drooping. 'Sorry.'

'I'll forgive you if you promise to listen in future and stop whispering and interrupting during the lesson.'

'I promise.'

It was so easy to make promises. Harder to keep them. But Kristbjörg left it at that. 'Good.' She would have to mention the head, though, before the girl ran out to join her friends and started spouting the same nonsense to them or anyone else. 'Just one thing before I let you go: don't make up stories about chopped-off heads. It's not a nice thing to do. If you go on like that, I'll have to talk to your parents and tell them they need to be more careful about what you're allowed to watch on TV. You shouldn't watch things that are banned for children.'

'I don't.'

Of course, the girl resorted to denial. What a surprise. 'What were you thinking, to say you'd seen a chopped-off head?'

The girl looked shifty and avoided Kristbjörg's eye. 'I never said that. He was lying. I never said anything about a head.'

Kristbjörg stared at the girl in silence. This wasn't the right moment to give her a lecture about the difference between truth and lies. Perhaps she should leave it at that. Where would their conversation lead if she continued it? To an impasse, that's where. The more the girl denied having said it, the harder it would be for her to back down. And, of course, that bloody boy could have been lying. Or have misheard.

Perhaps that was it. 'All right. But remember what I said about whispering. It's not allowed.'

The girl nodded and Kristbjörg watched as she scampered off to join her friends. Shortly afterwards, Kristbjörg left the classroom herself, went up to the staff room and sat down for a coffee with her colleagues.

The story of the head gave way to other, more enjoyable topics. After all, it was absurd.

Chapter 7

The smart clothes had come in useful in the end. The hung-over man in the cells had mistaken her for a lawyer, accepted the police's offer to ring his family, and agreed to go home. Freyja had then returned to her office and started searching online for material that could help her understand what was going on in the killer's head. Before she'd got far, her manager rang and asked her to drop by his office. He wanted to talk to her about the murder and her role in the investigation. Afterwards, she wasn't sure if this had been yet another attempt to find a job to fill up her day or whether her skills were genuinely needed. She was inclined to believe they were, though no doubt there was an element of time-filling involved.

He was specifically concerned about the police's interaction with the dead woman's family. The horrific mutilation of her body would make talking to her relatives an extremely delicate matter but they needed to hear the ugly truth, and he felt it would be only right if Freyja was present when the news was broken. Ideally, she should also be present when the police interviewed Bríet's daughter – assuming the remains were those of her mother. In addition, Freyja was to assist the investigation team in their attempts to assess the perpetrator's mental state, if required. Finally, the investigators themselves might need trauma counselling. Few members of CID had seen anything like this before.

Freyja had responded enthusiastically to everything her manager said, mainly by vigorous, repeated nodding. Although he didn't seem to expect any input from her, she did manage to slip in one question at the end: was Erla OK with all this? The answer was vague but gave rise to a question about whether Erla had been causing difficulties. Without a moment's hesitation, Freyja assured him she hadn't. She was no telltale.

As she was leaving, her manager had coughed and added that looking people up on the Police Information System without good reason was frowned on. It was irrelevant whether the individuals in question were family, friends or strangers. He went on, awkwardly, to say that maybe this hadn't been made clear to her, but he was rectifying that now. Baffled, Freyja said she didn't know how to access the system. At this, her manager looked even more embarrassed and merely repeated his words, then thanked her for dropping by. Since this didn't exactly invite further discussion, she left it at that.

After the meeting, she sat down at her computer again and resumed reading where she had left off. The material she had found so far related to excessive violence, both from a psychological point of view and from other perspectives. Although her research left her with a bad taste in her mouth, she felt herself growing more desensitised to the horror with every article she read.

There was a knock at the door and she hastily closed the window she was looking at. This was silly really, since her colleagues in CID were used to grim realities, in spite of her manager's concern for their mental wellbeing. Much more used to them than she herself was, ironically enough. She called out 'Come in,' and turned to the door.

Huldar appeared in the gap. It was obvious from his coat and the cold he was radiating that he had just come in from outside. He didn't often drop by; during the few months she had been working for the police, he had only twice looked in. On both occasions he had been there on other people's business and had only put his head briefly round the door. But this time he came in and closed it behind him. He looked ill; pale and glassy eyed, much more subdued than he had been at the meeting earlier, not to mention yesterday evening.

'Is this a bad moment?'

'No.' Freyja refrained from reminding him of their agreement about avoiding all unnecessary contact at work. Perhaps he really was here on business, though she doubted it. On the previous occasions he had seemed very conscious that he was contravening the terms of their agreement. But this time any such worries appeared to be far from his mind. Perhaps he had misunderstood what happened yesterday evening and was under the impression that they were in a relationship and had nothing to hide. But then she realised that there was something wrong; Huldar wasn't himself.

'Has something happened?' Her tone was solicitous and so was the sentiment behind it. She had come to care for him. As a friend. Nothing more, despite yesterday's slip-up. As much as she had enjoyed it in the heat of the moment, she vowed it would be the last time she crossed her self-appointed boundary. If their relationship moved to another level, sooner or later it was bound to end in disaster. And, strange as it might seem, she didn't like the thought of losing him as a friend.

In some mysterious way he had succeeded in overcoming her doubts about his character. Instead of concentrating on his faults, she had started noticing his good points. It had taken her by surprise to discover that there were so many. He was laid-back, but this suited her surprisingly well since she herself was so stressed and anxious by nature. And her niece Saga had taken to him, which she certainly hadn't with any of Freyja's other friends. The dog Molly too. There wasn't an ounce of snobbery or affectation in his nature, and although he wasn't exactly a new man, he was capable of showing great sympathy. On top of that, he had earned himself a big bonus point for taking on responsibility for the snake.

She avoided thinking about his prowess between the sheets. It would only trigger flashbacks to yesterday evening, and there was no knowing where that might end. Possibly with a repetition here on the desk. He was guaranteed to be up for it, however pale and quiet he seemed. 'Are you ill?' she asked.

'No. Nothing's happened. Or not really. And I'm not ill, just feeling a bit dazed.' Huldar sat down. It was the first time the visitor's chair in her office had seen any use. As a rule, no one lingered in her room, whether for work purposes or to chat: they simply dispatched their business in the doorway, then left again. 'I've just come back from the post-mortem on the body parts.' He puffed out his cheeks, then exhaled with a shudder. 'Jesus Christ, what a nightmare.'

It looked as if Freyja had just got her first candidate for trauma counselling. There was nothing surprising about this, as the post-mortem was without doubt the worst part of the whole inquiry. Huldar put his elbows on his knees and buried his face in his hands. Looking at his tousled head, Freyja decided to do her professional duty. 'Do you want to tell me about it, Huldar? I can imagine it must have been a horrible experience. At times like this, it can help to talk about what you've been through.'

Huldar sat up and regarded her in astonishment. 'What do you mean? Are you trying to do some kind of shrink stuff on me?'

Freyja shrugged. 'Not exactly. I just thought you might want to talk about what's distressing you. I promise you'll feel better if you do. You don't want to carry around images of it forever, do you?'

'To be honest, I'd prefer that. But thanks anyway.' Huldar drew himself up and tried but failed to look cheerful. His familiar laid-back smile made a brief reappearance before his features resumed their half-stunned expression.

'No problem. But would you mind telling me what came out of it? Just to satisfy my curiosity.'

'Ye-e-e . . . yes.' He sounded reluctant, as if suspecting her of trying to lead him into a trap.

She wasn't. If he didn't want help now, he might accept it later, but there was no point trying to force it on him. So she asked the most straightforward question she could think of. 'Did you find out who it is?'

Huldar shook his head, messing up his hair even more. Realising, he ran his hands through it, but to little effect. 'No. Not with any certainty. But it's a woman of around the same age as Bríet, the owner of the car, with the same sort of physical attributes. No tattoos or operation scars, which matches her ex-husband's description. I'd be surprised if it wasn't her. But they've taken fingerprints which will be compared to those found in her home, and biological samples for DNA testing. The results will be compared to samples from her closest relatives, once we've got them. With luck, those two should be enough to confirm our guess. You don't need the head for that. Though of course we're hoping it'll turn up. It has to.'

Freyja couldn't agree more but felt it was better to leave the missing head out of the conversation for now. It was bound to conjure up an image of the neck stump and she would rather not have that in her mind. Although Erla hadn't shown any photos during the meeting, Freyja had come across some pretty grisly images relating to incidents abroad during her online search, including one of a headless torso. The picture had been bad enough; seeing it in real life must have been horrific. 'What about the cause of death? Has that been established?'

'Yes, more or less. All the indications are that the woman was strangled. There are signs of bruising on the stump of the neck that's still attached to the torso, though most of the area where the pressure would have been applied is missing. So are the hyoid bone and larynx, which tend to be damaged during strangulation.' Huldar closed his eyes and breathed through his nose for a moment before continuing. 'In other words, a large part of the neck is missing, which means the findings can't be a hundred per cent certain. But it's the most likely cause of death. There were injuries to the right ankle too, sustained just before she died, and also bruising down the right-hand side of her torso, as the result of a struggle. Neither injury was fatal, though.'

Freyja nodded, unsure what exactly the implications were for the investigation. Was it a major problem that they couldn't be sure how exactly the woman had died, or was that irrelevant in terms of solving the case? She assumed it might be a serious issue during the trial. 'The head wasn't found when her house was searched, then?'

'No. Gudlaugur rang Erla during the post-mortem and told her there were signs of a struggle. Small blood-stains, a kitchen chair on its side and stuff on the floor. But no head. And no sign that the woman was dismembered in the flat either. Apparently the amount of blood was nothing like what you'd expect in that case. But it does suggest Bríet was hit, possibly on the head, as none of the injuries on the body had bled. Of course, she could have landed a blow on her attacker, in which case the blood might be his. We'll find out once we get the DNA results. The blood group is the same as Bríet's, so we can't rely on blood type to settle the question.'

'Couldn't the killer have cleaned up the blood after dismembering her? Used the bathtub, for example, then rinsed it out?'

'Very unlikely. We use special chemicals to show up traces of blood, and Gudlaugur says it's out of the question that the butchering was done in the flat.' Huldar paused to rub his eyes. 'According to him, there was a plate with an unfinished slice of pizza and a glass of water on the kitchen table. There was a takeaway box too, containing several leftover slices, and the delivery note showed it had been ordered on Friday at around six. The post-mortem turned up some barely digested pizza in her stomach.' Huldar rested his elbows on his knees again and bent over, burying his face in his hands. When he went on, his voice was muffled as he was directing his words to the floor. 'I'll never be able to eat pizza again.'

Freyja thought it would probably be a while before she did too. Since they were on the subject of gruesome matters, she asked the question that had been gnawing away at her ever since this morning's meeting. It wouldn't help him feel better, but she had to know. 'What about the dismemberment? Was it done after the woman died?' Freyja clasped her hands tightly under her desk.

'Yes. That news was the best thing to come out of the whole horrible business. I'm not sure I could have survived in there if it had been the other way round. Another positive bit of news is that there were no signs of rape. But who knows? The body had been undressed and washed before the pieces were put in the bags, so some kind of sexual assault could have happened without causing any detectable damage to the cervix. The washing was almost certainly intended to destroy any biological traces. The clothes that had been stuffed into the bags with the body parts had also been hosed down.'

Freyja loosened her fingers. Another question in the same macabre vein was troubling her. It was odd enough that it might just kick Huldar into gear again, so she went ahead and asked. 'Do all the body parts fit together?'

The question did the trick: Huldar dropped his hands and raised his head in surprise. 'What?'

Freyja reddened a little under his incredulous gaze. 'I mean, do the remains all belong to the same person?'

Huldar's face returned to normal. 'Yes. One person, minus the head.'

Neither of them spoke for a while. Freyja guessed they were both thinking the same thing: what had happened to the head? But she didn't ask what theories he or the other members of the investigation team had come up with. Their speculation was unlikely to be any better informed than her own. She had learnt a thing or two about decapitation from her online research, including examples of what the killers tended to do with the heads afterwards. No one severs a head from a body for any good reason. But she got the impression that it would be better to spare Huldar the details she'd found, in his current state. So she changed the subject.

'What about the time of death? Has that been established?'

'Yes. The woman died on Friday evening. But unfortunately the time frame is very vague. We found her body on Monday, nearly three days after her death. As a result, rigor mortis had passed and the temperature of the body parts had adapted to that of the boot of the car. Those two factors make it impossible to calculate a more precise time of death.' Huldar shivered, his mind perhaps still on the pizza. 'But her stomach contents give us a better idea. We're waiting to hear from the pizza place about what time her takeaway was delivered, since there could be as much as half an hour's difference from the time on the receipt. We also need to talk to the delivery guy in case he noticed anything. But we're working on the basis that the pizza was delivered at six thirty and eaten within half an hour. If that's correct, Bríet must have died between seven and eight o'clock, according to the pathologist. Give or take. It's not very precise.'

'That should help, shouldn't it?' Freyja tried to inject a note of optimism into her voice.

'Sure. Assuming the pizza wasn't eaten cold later that evening.'

Freyja was struck by a thought. 'But didn't the car appear in the housing estate on Saturday evening or early on Sunday morning?'

'Yes. According to the woman who reported it. We won't get an exact time until we've located the car on the CCTV recordings of the area. If it appears there. The network of cameras is gappy and most are privately owned by people who don't put them up to record the traffic, though the street view sometimes ends up in the frame.' Huldar stretched. 'We still need to find out what happened between her death and the appearance of the car in the estate. It must have taken time to saw up the body and put it in bags. Though no more than twenty-four hours, of course. Still, things will become clearer in due course.'

Freyja sat there puzzling for a while. 'I can't quite work it out. The woman's killed on Friday evening, very probably at home, then her body's taken somewhere else to be chopped up. Then the body parts, minus the head, are loaded into the boot of her car, which is abandoned in a neighbourhood where Bríet didn't live. Isn't the whole thing peculiarly complicated? Why all the toing and froing? Why didn't the killer just leave the body in Bríet's flat?'

'Well, that's one of the things we need to find out.'

But Freyja hadn't given up trying to understand. If she were to provide the team with insights into the way the murderer's mind worked, she would have to figure out what had motivated his behaviour. 'I don't understand why the body was cut up into bits. If it wasn't done at her flat, the murderer would have had to get the body out of the building in one piece. Which means it can't have been chopped up in order to make it easier to transport or to sneak it out to the car. Where *did* Bríet live, by the way?'

Huldar ran his hands through his hair again. 'Salahverfi in Kópavogur. In a ground-floor flat with a small, fenced-in back garden. I've examined the aerial view in the online telephone directory and it wouldn't have been too difficult to carry her body outside after it got dark. From her garden, it's only a short way to an access path that leads to the block's dustbins. If her car had been moved round there, it could have been achieved without much problem. But it's possible she was killed some-where else and cut up at the scene. Maybe the circumstances there made it necessary. Or the perpetrator wanted to make it easier to dispose of the body. It's much simpler if it's in bits.' Huldar sighed.

'In that case I find it pretty strange that he just shoved them in the boot of her car. Why didn't he throw them in the sea, for example, or down a volcanic fissure?'

Huldar agreed. 'Yes, it is strange. And from the way the car was parked, you'd think the person who left it there was hoping it would be found as quickly as possible. I can't get my head round any of it. And only two of the five bags were closed. If they'd all been tightly tied at the neck, we might not have worked out what was going on until much later. It was the smell of blood that alerted us.' Suddenly Huldar bright-ened. 'But the good news is that we've found biological traces in the boot that almost certainly belong to the perpetrator.'

'Blood?' Freyja couldn't see how it would be possible to work out whether some of the blood in the boot came from another person – not without performing a series of tests, anyway. And that would take time. Unless blood groups could be identified using simple paper strips, like a litmus test, and these had revealed the presence of more than one blood type. But her next question proved unnecessary.

'Not blood, vomit. There was vomit on one of the bags in the boot. Bile. Not a huge amount but enough. The person had probably thrown up several times already. At least, that's the theory. And it doesn't take a genius to work out when that would have happened.'

Freyja nodded and wondered what it meant. If the killer had vomited repeatedly while dismembering the body, he or she was unlikely to be a psychopath. Surgeons and butchers also slipped several places down Freyja's list of possible culprits. They would be too inured to such things to throw up in the middle. 'Isn't it a bit odd to go to the trouble of washing the body to get rid of any DNA, then vomit on the bags and not clean up after yourself?'

Huldar shrugged. 'Yes and no. Perhaps the car wasn't supposed to be found with the bags in it. Perhaps the killer was tired and confused by then. Perhaps an opportunist thief thought they'd steal something since the car was unlocked, and threw up when they saw what was in the boot. Or stole the car, drove it away, then noticed the same smell as I did, stopped, had a look in the boot, chucked up on the bags, and legged it. I expect there are other possible scenarios too. Anyway, the bile sample's been sent abroad and we're trying to fast-track the DNA analysis. But it's not guaranteed that they'll accept our request. Not many labs deal with vomit, which means we're not in a good position to apply much pressure. Most limit themselves to blood, hair, saliva or sperm. They're less keen on excrement and vomit, for obvious reasons. Let's just hope they manage to push it through, because the DNA could lead us to the killer. You never know, the perpetrator might be in our database of DNA samples.'

Freyja lifted her right hand and crossed her fingers. 'Please let that be the case.'

Huldar didn't sound optimistic. 'Yes, but don't count on it. I have a feeling this murder isn't going to be that easy to solve, because we're dealing with one sick fuck. The post-mortem also revealed that the dismembering was carried out with some kind of coarse-toothed power saw, very probably a circular saw. That wouldn't require any particular physical strength, so theoretically anyone could have done it. All it would have needed was a massive dose of insanity.'

Their eyes met and there was no need for words to express their agreement on this last point. Freyja guessed that, like her, Huldar was picturing the scene. At least, his expression was regaining the stunned look it had worn when he'd first appeared at her door. Freyja broke eye contact. She reached for her mug and handed it over the desk to Huldar. 'Have some coffee. It's cold and nasty but it'll do you good.'

Huldar took a sip. 'Thanks.' He put the mug down on her desk and smiled. 'Possibly the worst coffee I've ever tasted.' Then he slapped his knee and rose to his feet. 'Anyway, I should get moving. Erla will be wondering where I am. I pretended I was going for a smoke when she went upstairs.' He smiled. 'The truth is, I couldn't have coped with a cigarette just then.'

'You should take the opportunity to quit.' Freyja thought this was an excellent idea but clearly Huldar didn't agree. He opened his mouth, evidently couldn't think of anything clever to say, and closed it again. It crossed her mind to ask what he thought of her manager's odd comment about the Police Information System but she decided to leave it. Huldar had enough to contend with at the moment. Instead, she pointed out that help wasn't far away, should he change his mind. 'I'm here if you ever want to talk about things. You know what I mean.'

Huldar merely smiled awkwardly and said goodbye. She thought it unlikely he would be knocking on her door any time soon in search of counselling. But he paused in the doorway and turned back. 'Don't get me wrong, they're very pretty earrings, but you know that—'

He didn't get any further: Freyja cut him short. 'Relax. I know all about the terrible risks and I'll be careful. Honestly, what is it with you people and my earrings?'

'They're prohibited under the police clothing regulations. This may not apply directly to you, but that's the reason. Mind you, there are new regulations in the pipeline, so the rule might change. But until then . . .'

Freyja nodded, embarrassed. 'I see.' If there was a plan to change the regulations, there was bound to be a committee convening on the issue of clothing. She was privately grateful that this morning's meeting hadn't been to discuss that. If she'd turned up wearing rule-breaking, potentially hazardous earrings, it would have been like walking into the meeting and giving them all the finger. 'Clearly, I should read them.'

After he had gone, Freyja sat there alone in her poky office. Unable to face opening her browser and resuming her research, she stared thoughtfully into Saga's eyes on her screen. Then she looked up the regulations and skimmed through them. Huldar was right: for safety reasons it was forbidden to wear hoops in one's ears. Only plain pearls or studs were allowed, and then only for women. No wonder a new set of regulations was in preparation.

Freyja removed the offending earrings. Then she checked her emails in the hope that she'd received a message from someone who needed her assistance. But there was nothing new in her inbox.

Her fingers tapped an impatient tattoo on her paperless desk while she tried to come up with something to do. Something that might help the case along. The only thing she could think of was to call her brother Baldur. Although he claimed to have left crime behind in accordance with his new-found status as a model citizen, she only had his word for that. And she had heard it before. Surely it wouldn't hurt to try asking, she thought.

Except that it did. Baldur was offended. She saw his shocked face clearly on their WhatsApp call.

'So you think . . . what? That someone in my social circle beheaded a dead woman?'

'No, that's not what I meant at all.' It was, but Freyja hastily backtracked. 'I just thought you might have heard something on the grapevine. From one of your old pals. Or someone you did time with.'

'No, Freyja, I haven't.' Baldur still seemed affronted. His handsome face looked stern, and he was running his hands in an agitated way through his blond hair. 'I socialise with a different crowd now. And anyway, nobody I know from before would kill a woman, much less chop her head off.'

The conversation wasn't going the way she had hoped, so Freyja refrained from pointing out that this was exactly what the murderer's family and friends would say about the culprit before he was caught. If killers walked around looking and acting like murderers all day, policing would be a piece of cake. She changed the subject. 'So, what's new?'

Baldur quickly relaxed and almost reverted to his usual easy-going self. They exchanged a few words about Saga and he told her that some tourist companies had put his name down as a back-up guide in case any of their regulars had to cancel. How he'd managed to achieve this was beyond Freyja. Guides were usually expected to have some kind of qualification, but this was typical Baldur. When he turned on the charm, people seemed to put their normal reservations aside. Women in particular. Freyja would bet her meagre life savings on the fact that the obliging tour operators who had put him on their back-up lists were women.

The funny thing was that his good looks and charisma were also his biggest flaw. They had enabled him to sail through life without much thought for the consequences of his actions. Too often he had been able to charm his way out of a corner. But not always, and when this happened, it invariably took him by surprise. Freyja pushed away visions of tourists falling into glacial crevasses that he had ignored. Maybe he was serious about turning his life around this time. To be fair, he had been acting a bit more like a proper grown-up recently. Maybe he had met someone who expected more of him than just looking good and being entertaining. She wanted to ask but decided against it in case he retaliated by interrogating her about her own love life. She didn't want to have to lie to him.

After the conversation ended, Freyja checked her inbox again. Nothing. She groaned. She wasn't used to kicking her heels, waiting for someone to rescue her. It was up to her to create a demand for her new position and her skills. It wasn't her manager's job to do this.

Freyja hurried over to the lift before she could get cold feet. She couldn't remember having walked this purposefully since she started with the police. Normally she moved as slowly as possible, setting off early to meetings, so early that she had to dawdle on the way so she wouldn't get there an embarrassingly long time before everyone else.

But this time it was different. She hammered the lift button repeatedly, then folded her arms and waited, tapping her foot, for the doors to open at the right floor, stepping out the moment the gap was wide enough. Then she charged into Erla's department, making a beeline for her office. After knocking once, she opened the door without waiting for an answer. If Erla wasn't going to get in touch with her, Freyja would have to take the initiative.

Erla was sitting at her computer with headphones in her ears. She looked astonished when she saw who had burst in. Moving the headphones down to her neck, she adjusted the microphone so it wouldn't bump into her chin. 'What?'

'I just wanted to remind you that I'm supposed to be assisting with the inquiry. So it's only right that I should be kept in the picture – attend meetings and take part when appropriate. That way I can provide a better insight into the killer's thought processes and psychology – if required.' Freyja stopped talking and braced herself for the storm. She had rehearsed her speech in the lift but, as is so often the case, it had sounded better in her head than when she said it out loud. She had also been planning to offer Erla trauma counselling following the post-mortem, but changed her mind. Erla was even less likely than Huldar to be receptive to that sort of offer.

Erla tilted her head back a little, raising her eyebrows. Through her tight uniform shirt, her bump visibly twitched as the baby kicked. Perhaps that was why she didn't imme-diately throw Freyja out or give her the bollocking she had been expecting. Instead, she said perfectly calmly: 'Yes, OK, no problem. There's a meeting tomorrow morning. Make sure you're there.'

Freyja was momentarily lost for words but she recovered fast. She thanked Erla, said she'd attend and exited the office. As she turned away, she saw Erla putting the headphones back on, then heard her start talking and realised that she had barged in right in the middle of a phone call. Erla said her manager's name and added that he could relax – Freyja would be given a role, as he had no doubt heard.

Freyja was glad she had her back to Erla when she realised it was her manager on the line and that he had overheard their entire conversation. From what Erla said, it seemed the phone call had been about her and a possible role for her in the investigation. Freyja didn't know the man well enough to be able to guess what he would make of the scene. He might think she was being pushy by pre-empting him like that. Or perhaps he would be relieved: if she was going around the building demanding jobs, it would save him the bother.

Either way, she would have to prove herself; have to do something to move the investigation forward. Then all would be forgiven.

Freyja left the department, taking care not to look in Huldar's direction. Out of the corner of her eye, she noticed that he didn't show the same self-discipline. His gaze followed her all the way to the door.

Chapter 8

Tuesday

Rögnvaldur took two steps backwards to get a better view of the sitting-room wall. He was holding a packet of Blu Tack in one hand and a marker pen in the other, and wearing nothing but pyjama trousers and a white vest. Aldís had gone to bed hours ago and the silence in the flat was broken by the occasional rattling snore from the bedroom. These days she took sleeping pills to knock her out and stimulants to wake her up. The drugs did their job, but no more than that. She woke and she slept. She described her sleep as dreamless, as if a stop button had been pressed and she had been temporarily shut down. The drugs she took in the morning and during the day started her up again, but she wasn't herself. Neither was he, for that matter. They were both silent and stooping; they kept the curtains closed and as few lights on as possible. Both had switched off their phones so they wouldn't have to deal with people who still saw a purpose in life; people who were determined to draw them out of their shell.

The entire wall was covered and he could have done with more space, but it couldn't be helped. He would have to make do with what he had. The painting that used to hang there was now lying face down on the floor. This probably wouldn't do it any good but Rögnvaldur couldn't care less. Nor could

Aldís. She had noticed the painting when he'd started on his project two days ago but hadn't said a word. Nor had she commented on the new position of the sofa, which had previously been pushed up against the wall but now stood aslant in the middle of the room, crammed against the coffee table that had also been moved out of place. In the process, a vase had fallen off the table, rolled over against the radiator and broken. The pieces were still lying on the floor.

Rögnvaldur folded his arms as he surveyed his masterpiece. It had no artistic value but then that wasn't the point. The point was to plot his family's movements during the period when Íris had become infected. He was hoping that this graphic representation would help him trace the transmission.

And if he traced the transmission, he would find the culprit.

The period in question consisted of two weeks – the weeks immediately before she fell ill, during which she must have been infected. On the giant wall chart, every day had its column, every hour its row. As Íris had never woken up before 7 a.m. and had always gone to sleep by 10 p.m., he left out the nights. In total, allowing for the time it took her to get up in the mornings and get ready for bed in the evenings, he reckoned he needed to fill in their movements for thirteen hours a day over fourteen days. One hundred and eighty-two boxes, each the size of half a sheet of A4. There was still plenty of free wall space either side of the chart but hardly any above or below.

He had already filled in a great many boxes but there were still a number of empty ones, noticeably more the further back he went in time. Nevertheless, he had managed to remember a surprising amount. Perhaps it wasn't so surprising, though, since he was relying on information from his mobile phone's tracking system. His lack of interest in such gadgets meant that he had spent a minimum of time setting up his phone. If he had gone through the process more thoroughly, he would probably have ticked the box that prevented the phone from saving this kind of information.

But it wasn't enough on its own. The phone told him nothing about his daughter's movements when he wasn't there. After her bone-marrow transplant, he had started working half-days in the office, which had been easy to arrange. His colleagues were used to his frequent absences in connection with his daughter's struggle against leukaemia. While he was at work, Íris had been with her mother, but unfortunately Aldís's phone had mostly been offline when she was outside the house. She was too careful with her data allowance to switch on 4G.

Nor could the phone tell him who had visited them during this period or who had entered their building, leaving their infection lingering in the corridors or lift. That information wasn't available anywhere. The same applied to various other factors over which he had no control, but that didn't stop him trying.

Before coming up with the idea of the wall chart, Rögnvaldur had tried various other methods of identifying the source of the infection. He had knocked on the doors of every flat in their block and asked if any of the occupants had been ill during the period when Íris could have been infected. He had been careful not to ask directly about measles but most of his neighbours had seen through him. Though they obviously thought he had lost his mind, they had taken pity on him, since his daughter's death was no secret. But none of the neighbours knew of any serious illness. One recalled having a stomach bug. Another had broken his wrist, but that didn't count. Rögnvaldur hadn't yet managed to get hold of one of the residents, an old woman whose neighbours didn't know what had become of her, though they thought she had probably got a place in a home. As no one had seen her during the critical period, he didn't bother to track her down.

Rögnvaldur had also visited his office and knocked on the door of the human resources manager to ask for information about staff sick leave during the two-week period, thinking that it was possible he had brought the infection home with him. The woman had refused his request, citing data protection. This had led to an unpleasant scene, which would no doubt have a detrimental influence on his next pay review. Not that he cared. The upshot was that he had been forced to question each of his colleagues individually. They had reacted like his neighbours. First they had been puzzled, then full of pity, but no one admitted to having been ill. Two younger colleagues, a woman and a man, said they could see from their time sheets that they had been off work then because their children were ill. But only for two days each and, according to them, their children hadn't had measles. Both made a point of mentioning that they'd had their children vaccinated, which implied that they had guessed why he was asking, like his neighbours and his other colleagues, no doubt.

He had wasted time on other efforts that had proved similarly futile. For example, he had tried in vain to prise information out of the Directorate of Health about whether they were making any progress in tracing the transmission route. In the end he had given up, when suddenly all the people he wanted to talk to were permanently in a meeting when he called – even when he rang two days in a row, at fifteen-minute intervals, asking to speak to every employee named on the directorate's website. They were all in a meeting until the switchboard closed and voicemail took over. Only a crisis of the magnitude of a zombie apocalypse could have explained such a marathon round of meetings.

He had also spent a lot of time on chat forums in which anti-vaxxers spewed out their 'wisdom'. What he'd read had made him feel sick but he had forced himself to persevere. Ironically, fate seemed to have missed an obvious opportunity to teach these idiots a lesson: none of their children had been infected or fallen ill. He had come across one post asking about the risks associated with measles, dating from the week in which Íris had most probably been infected. He had found this suspicious at first but the comments had convinced him that it wasn't associated with an actual infection. Everyone had jumped in and belittled the risks. *Huh, measles are just the usual: fever, runny nose and cough. Really, it's just flu with a rash. That's all.* The person whose post had triggered the discussion had cast doubt on this, pointing out that there were warnings online about serious complications, including the risk of children going blind. Were they saying that was wrong? The group had piled in, saying that there might be something in it but not necessarily. The odds were maybe one in a million. Another member had improved on this, saying it was more like one in a gazillion. The discussion had continued in the same vein but he had ploughed through it anyway. By the end, he was convinced that none of these people had any personal experience of the disease.

After a bit more online detective work, he had found an article about a study at the University of Iceland into the immunisation of primary-school children. The students responsible were investigating the circumstances of children who had not received their immunisations, with a special focus on their general health, medical history and the reasons why the vaccination or vaccinations in question had not been taken up. The children were listed in the central vaccination register, a database Rögnvaldur couldn't access and which the Directorate of Health refused to let him see. His pestering about the register was one of the reasons why they were no longer answering his calls.

This was intolerable. The register itself wasn't exhaustive, though, as permission to keep it had only been obtained in 2002. Since information about vaccinations prior to that date was held piecemeal by individual doctors' surgeries, health centres and hospitals around Iceland, he could forget about trying to get hold of those records.

But that didn't mean he wasn't interested in the data that had been centralised. He had got in touch with the two women who were working on the university study. To begin with, they had been very friendly and welcomed his interest, especially when he explained the reason for it. He had even had a meeting with one of them during which she had regaled him with tales of their problems with the Data Protection Authority. According to her, the authority had delayed their study for months while deciding whether it would violate any laws. In the end, they had been granted permission with certain conditions attached: the findings should be anonymised, permission was to be obtained from the parents by means of a formal letter, and all personally identifiable data was to be destroyed once the study was complete.

After enduring this speech, Rögnvaldur felt he had earned some answers and cooperation. He was hoping that the authors of the dissertation would be in possession of information about recent infections and prepared to share the names of the children who had not been vaccinated. But in this he was mistaken. It turned out that the woman had misunderstood the purpose of the meeting. She'd thought he wanted to share his experience as a parent, so they could use his daughter's medical history in their study. She'd actually believed he had come to meet her in the colourful little hippy café to share his daughter's story with the academic community. That he'd sat on an uncomfortable wooden chair, sipping watery coffee with almond milk from a flowery cup belonging to someone's long-dead grandmother's coffee set, just in order to chat to her about the gaping wound in his heart. Well, he wasn't interested. Their study would do nothing to prevent future infections and certainly nothing to save his daughter. It was far too late for that.

But he had failed to make a good enough case. It hadn't helped that he had taken one of his wife's pills before coming out. It was supposed to perk him up, straighten out his hunched shoulders and put a bit of a sparkle in his bloodshot eyes. Well, it had certainly straightened him up and opened his eyes wide, but unfortunately they had darted continually from side to side and he'd been unable to keep his hands still. In that cosily decorated milieu he had come across as downright weird and untrustworthy.

Rögnvaldur hadn't given up, though. Nor had he stopped taking the drug. His next step had been to approach the other woman who was working on the study, but that had gone no better. In fact, it had gone worse. Infinitely worse. As badly as it was possible to go. He didn't want to think about what had happened. He reminded himself that sometimes bad things had to happen if you were to achieve your goal. At least it had brought him much closer to his. And the police hadn't knocked on his door yet. Perhaps they never would. Perhaps he'd got away with it. In which case he could prob-ably risk seeking assistance to break the password. Things were looking up.

The marker pen emitted a sucking sound as Rögnvaldur pulled off the lid. He walked over to the huge wall chart and carried on entering the information he had collected so far.

Chapter 9

Few sights are as unsettling as the signs that Forensics have been at work. Although there were no chalked outlines of bodies in Bríet's flat, there were several demarcated spots in the kitchen and entrance hall where blood-stains had been found, accompanied by small numbered photo-evidence markers. Similar markers had been placed by a chair lying on its side in the middle of the kitchen, by a broken salt mill and a thick English medical textbook that was lying open on the floor, its pages crumpled from its rough landing. There was no doubt that this had been the scene of a struggle.

Huldar's hands were itching from the blue plastic gloves. He was also becoming uncomfortably conscious of the almost airtight white boiler suit he was encased in. To increase his discomfort still further, the air in the flat was polluted by the fine powder used for fingerprinting. Worst of all, though, was the oppressive feeling of being in the home of a person who would never come back. He couldn't wait to get outside.

'Who do you think it was?' Huldar asked Erla, who had brought him along to Bríet's place after the Forensics team had returned to the police station. Their work wasn't finished and would continue tomorrow, but she wanted to grab the chance to examine the scene while no one was there. The flat was small and having detectives blundering around tended to get on the forensic technicians' nerves.

Erla glanced around the compact kitchen. 'To be honest, I haven't a clue. Her mother said she'd been intending to study at the weekend. But the dress we found in one of the bags with the body parts was quite smart. And tights? Who gets all dolled up in a dress and tights to spend the weekend studying alone at home?'

'Don't forget that she was wearing indoor shoes.' The smart dress and tights had been totally at odds with her foot-wear. One of the plastic bags had contained the kind of comfy orthopaedic sandals that Huldar associated with health work-ers, certainly not with going out on the town.

'What do I know? Maybe she was trying on the dress because it was new. It hasn't turned up in any of the pictures of her on Facebook. But the sandals were in one of them. Per-haps she always dressed up. Some people do. Who knows?' Erla gave a barely visible shrug. The forensic boiler suits weren't designed for pregnant women and she'd had to put on the largest size in order to accommodate her bump. As a result, it was hopelessly baggy except where it stretched over her stomach; the sleeves and legs were far too long and the crotch drooped to her knees.

Huldar thought about Bríet's bedroom wardrobe. It hadn't exactly been bursting with smart clothes. On the con-trary, the wardrobe suggested a woman who generally dressed casually and didn't go out much, which would be consistent with the fact that she was a single mother who worked along-side her studies. In circumstances like that she'd hardly have been propping up a bar every weekend. 'No, I'm fairly sure she was intending to go out. Perhaps with the man who killed her.' Huldar tugged at the elastic that held the hood of the boiler suit around his face, admitting a little air, much to his relief. 'But definitely not out to dinner, given the pizza. Her footwear suggests she wasn't going out straight away. Maybe she still had to put on her make-up or do her hair. We'll find out if her head ever turns up.'

Erla corrected him: '*When* her head turns up.'

'Yes, of course. When it turns up.'

Erla continued: 'Whether Bríet had plastered her face with make-up or not won't necessarily tell us anything. Not all women put on war paint and blow-dry their hair every time they go out on the town. Though I agree with you that she must have been planning to go out somewhere – and not to a library.'

Erla lapsed into silence and carried on surveying their surroundings. She was behaving like someone who doesn't know what to do with themselves, aimlessly opening drawers, reading envelopes and peering into cupboards. Never spending long on anything.

Muttering something inaudible, she turned from the cutlery drawer she had just opened and looked at Huldar. 'There's no computer here. No laptop or desktop. Can the killer have taken it?'

'I wouldn't have thought she'd have a desktop computer. There's no desk with an empty space where it could have been. But she must have owned a laptop. I don't suppose it's possible to study without one.'

'No, of course not.' Erla continued poking at things with her blue gloved fingers. 'There's no sign that anything else has been taken. Not that there's much here to steal.'

Huldar looked round the kitchen. There was nothing that would be worth much, especially not as stolen goods. The same applied to the sitting room with its cheap TV and furniture that no one would bother lugging out and trying to put on the market. Nothing appeared to be missing in there or in either of the bedrooms. Of course, that didn't rule out the possibility that money or other valuables like jewellery or silver were missing, but the discovery in the wardrobe of a small box containing a few necklaces, two rings and a bracelet suggested otherwise.

'I don't buy the idea that it was a burglary.' Huldar picked up a clear plastic jar half full of ground coffee, only to put it straight down again. He was just fidgeting now, like Erla. 'For one thing, not many thieves would break in that early in the evening. And for another, I can't see why a burglary should escalate into murder. If Bríet took a burglar by surprise, the odds are he would have legged it.'

'Anything's possible.' Erla bent down with difficulty to peer under the kitchen table. 'I can't see any laptop charger.'

'Perhaps it was taken along with the computer. The laptop could have been in a bag with its lead.'

Erla extracted her head from under the table and straightened up with an effort. 'No. Forensics found a backpack in the hall that Bríet seems to have used for uni and took it away for examination. It had a compartment for a laptop, but there was no computer or charger inside.'

Huldar went over to the fridge. Pinned to it was a book recording school marks, with 'Hanna Lúdvíksdóttir' written on the front, which showed that Bríet's daughter was a model pupil. There was also a class photo, marked '5B'. Huldar searched for Hanna's face, going by the framed photo of the girl he had seen on Bríet's bedside table, and was quick to find her, as she was the tallest in the class, standing a head above the others. It was weird to think that the girl was out there somewhere with her father, blithely unaware that her mother was dead. He looked away. 'When are the family going to be informed?'

Erla rubbed her hands in an attempt to alleviate the itching caused by the gloves. It wouldn't work; Huldar had already tried. If anything, it made it worse. But Erla kept doing it. 'First we need to be sure it's her. But we can't wait long. One of the neighbours in the building clocked Forensics and now that we've started knocking on doors, the victim's name's bound to leak out. I'm going to talk to the guy from the Identification Commission later and agree a time.'

Huldar looked back at the photo. 'Any chance it's not Bríet?' For the girl's sake, he hoped so. But the relief would be short-lived. The fact was that the body belonged to a young woman and, even if she wasn't Bríet, there was every chance that she had one or more children of her own.

'No. It's her all right.'

Huldar nodded gloomily. He hoped Bríet's young daughter was enjoying her day because it would be a long time before she had anything to be happy about again. 'One thing, Erla. About that laptop. Is it possible it was taken because of the information it contained?'

'Like what?' Erla had finally given up trying to scratch her hands.

'I don't know. Sensitive data. Communications with the killer, for instance; messages they exchanged in the lead-up to the murder. Could it have been some bloke she'd got involved with, then dumped?'

'Yeah, sure. Could be. Though I can't really see a couple declaring their love for each other by email these days. But maybe there's something incriminating in her messages. It's a bloody nuisance the laptop's missing. And her phone. They didn't find it in the car or in her bag, which is obviously going to hold us up. Forensics have established that her mobile was last connected to the network here in her flat on Friday, at around the time she's believed to have died. Presumably the killer switched off the phone, then got rid of it. Which is a bugger. If we had her electronics we could access her browsing history, photos, all her recent movements, etcetera. Now we've got the hassle of having to apply to big international companies to get most of the information we need.'

There was no point getting riled about this, Huldar thought. Life had a tendency to throw obstacles in the way of their inquiries. But occasionally it was on their side. He would a thousand times rather have the help of modern technology than not.

Erla had run out of things to examine in the kitchen. 'I'm going to take another look in the hall.'

Huldar followed her, though they'd already checked the narrow entrance hall, then wished he'd stayed in the kitchen. In his efforts to avoid treading on something belonging to Forensics, he kept colliding with Erla's bump. Although the collisions weren't violent, he was afraid of hurting the unborn baby. Not only that, he was terrified he might accidentally trigger the onset of labour. His stomach tightened with horror at the thought of having to deliver a child, encumbered by his plastic boiler suit, among the coats and shoes belonging to Bríet and her daughter. So he hung back, letting Erla turn in circles in the cramped space.

He watched as she tried the handle of the front door, opened it and checked the lock, then closed it again and examined the inside of the door at head height. A blood-stain had been marked there and also on the floor below. 'There's no way the killer broke in,' Erla observed. 'The door and the lock are intact. She must have opened it, then he slammed the door into her head and forced his way inside. A blow like that could also explain the injuries to her left-hand side and her leg. Or perhaps she started to shut the door when she saw who was outside and he threw himself at it before it could close. One or the other.'

Huldar nodded. 'He wouldn't have had to be buzzed in from the lobby, so that's quite possible.'

The house search had taken place during working hours, when few people were at home. But in a large block of flats like this there was always someone coming or going. Gudlaugur had accompanied the forensic team to the scene and encountered a very surprised resident. He had deftly sidestepped the man's questions about what the police were doing in the building, and at the same time discovered why the front door had been – and still was – unlocked: apparently the stairwell was due to be redecorated. The job was supposed to have begun on the Friday and the front door had been left unlocked so the decorators could bring in their materials and tools, but they still hadn't turned up.

Huldar gripped a coat hook with his blue-gloved fingers. 'I wonder if things would have turned out differently if the decorators had bothered to tell someone they weren't coming. Then the front door would have been locked.'

Erla shook her head. 'Judging by the way he treated the victim's body, the killer wouldn't have let a mere door stand in his way. He'd probably have broken in through the back.'

'Yes, I suppose so.' Huldar let go of the hook. 'The more I think about it and the more I see, the more convinced I am that it was a man.'

Erla shrugged and looked at him wearily. 'Shall we call it a day? I've seen enough.'

They quickly pulled off their plastic boiler suits in the corridor outside – but not quickly enough. An older woman in a down jacket, who was on her way out of the building, spotted them trying to get free of their trouser legs. Letting go of the front door, she came over, her face puzzled. Huldar and Erla hastily turned their backs on her, but it was no good.

Huldar felt a finger tapping his shoulder.

'Excuse me, are you the decorators?'

Out of the corner of his eye, he saw Erla grimace. The woman repeated her question, then asked if they spoke Icelandic.

They both turned and the woman's eyes grew round when she spotted Erla's bump. 'Are you allowed to paint if you're pregnant?'

'We're not decorators,' Erla snapped.

The woman's eyes narrowed. 'Oh? Then what are you doing here?' She turned to Huldar, who was too slow to hide the logo on his fleece. 'The police? What's happened? Is someone hurt? Is it the woman in that flat?' She pointed at Bríet's door.

Huldar waved the woman away. 'We can't discuss our business with you, I'm afraid. We'll have to ask you to move along.'

The woman opened her mouth to object. Then she looked back at the door and noted the number of the flat before asking a final question. 'Is this connected to the murder that was on the news?'

'I'm afraid we can't discuss our business with you. Please move along.' Huldar repeated the only thing he could or wanted to say to this woman.

'Then it is the murder. Or you'd have said no.' The woman turned on her heel, went back to the front door and hurried out.

Erla rubbed her forehead. 'Shit, shit, shit. Now at least two people in the building know about the operation. Tomorrow it'll be fifty and by the next day a thousand.' She lowered her hand. 'We'll have to talk to the next of kin before the rumour reaches them.' Furiously, she kicked off the remaining trouser leg. 'ASAP.'

Chapter 10

Tuesday evening

Freyja's feet were killing her after the unusually long day in heels. They weren't by any means spike heels but the few centimetres they added to her height had taken their toll all the same. Her shirt was crumpled too and her smart office skirt was beginning to look more like a party skirt – after the party. It was becoming increasingly likely that she'd be going to work tomorrow in a fleece. She tucked her shirt into her waistband and ran a hand down her skirt, trying to smooth out the creases, then drew herself up, focusing on the door in front of her and blowing out a breath.

'Ready?' Gudlaugur was standing beside her, eyeing the door as well. Neither of them wanted to knock.

Erla and the representative from the Identification Commission had come to a joint decision that Bríet's parents needed to be informed at once. Waiting for the DNA results was out of the question since they wouldn't be available until the end of the week at the earliest. A comparison of the fingerprints taken from the body with those lifted from Bríet's flat would have to do, though Forensics had objected on the grounds that there had been a lot of prints and they hadn't all been processed and catalogued yet. They asked for the deadline to be extended to the end of the following day, but their request was refused.

Before leaving the office, Freyja and Gudlaugur had been reminded yet again that they were not to tell Bríet's parents she was dead, only that there were a number of indications that the body that had been found was hers. A formal identification and death certificate would not be issued until the DNA analysis was complete. But, in the meantime, the investigation team needed to be able to talk to the victim's family and friends without having to hide what had happened. The first step in this direction was to inform Bríet's next of kin about the discovery of the body.

The media were breathing down the police's neck too. They knew that human remains had been discovered, that it was a woman and that her death was a criminal matter, but they hadn't yet learnt that the body had been dismembered or that the head was missing. The moment that leaked out, all hell would break loose. And the clock was ticking. It was vital the police talk to Bríet's parents before that particular bombshell dropped.

Gudlaugur had drawn the short straw and Freyja had been sent along with him to provide psychological support, if necessary. As if anyone imagined the parents would take this calmly. Before they left, Erla mentioned that if they got the chance, they should ask the parents whether their daughter had been expecting any visitors the evening she vanished off the radar. And also whether she had been planning to go out on the town. Any background on Bríet's ex-husband, Lúdvík Jónsson, would also be useful. Freyja felt it was a bit premature to be grilling the parents, but she understood that the police were in a hurry to find the killer, and for that, they needed information.

So far, there were no suspects, but partners or ex-partners were among the most likely culprits in murder cases. Erla told them that CID had conducted a quick inquiry into the circumstances of Bríet's divorce. According to the local magistrate, it hadn't been any more or less acrimonious than usual, and the issue of custody had been settled. But it was possible that Bríet's parents might take a different view of the couple's break-up.

Erla mentioned a whole list of other things that Gudlaugur was to do during the visit, including taking DNA swabs from both parents, enquiring about Bríet's computer, any connection she might have had to the housing estate where her car had turned up, and any boyfriends, as well as showing the couple photos of the dress and sandals that had been found with the body parts. It was hard to see how he was supposed to achieve all this during a first visit. Presumably he would have to pick and choose his questions carefully.

Freyja glanced at Gudlaugur and nodded. 'Let's get it over with.'

He knocked and they both unconsciously clasped their hands behind their backs, as if forming a guard of honour. Neither moved a muscle while they were waiting for the door to open, which took longer than normal.

The couple were expecting the police and knew the visit was about their daughter, as they had been notified in advance. Although no more details had been given, the gravity of the situation had been obvious. It wasn't hard to put oneself in their shoes and understand their reluctance to open the door. They wanted news but not bad news. Until they opened the door, they could cling to the hope that it was all a misunderstanding; that their daughter, like Schrödinger's cat, could be simultaneously alive and dead, as long as no one opened the door – or box.

Finally, the couple appeared together. They were both around sixty; he was a delivery driver, she was a nursery school teacher. Clearly, they were beside themselves with anxiety but trying to put a brave face on it. The father avoided eye contact; the mother asked if she could offer them tea and kept wringing her hands. An awkward speech followed about whether it was a bad idea to drink coffee in the evenings. Once they could get a word in, Gudlaugur and Freyja politely declined her offer.

They went into the sitting room and all four perched on the edges of the three-piece suite, as if poised to get this over with as quickly as possible, then leap to their feet. Gudlaugur was the first to speak. He told the couple that the body referred to in the news was connected to their daughter. It had been found in the boot of her car and all the indications were that it was hers. He finished by saying how sorry he was to have to bring them this news. Then he fell silent, waiting for it to sink in.

'Wait, what are you saying?' Bríet's father asked, suddenly angry. He leant forwards, the blood risen to his cheeks, glaring at them. 'How long have you known this? Did you know she was dead when you rang yesterday, claiming it was about her car? Did it not occur to you to tell us then?'

Gudlaugur replied steadily: 'The body was discovered yesterday. Late in the afternoon. But we couldn't be at all sure who it was until now. We came as soon as the information was available.'

The father's rage receded before a wave of incapacitating grief. The mother sat there, rigidly staring at the wall in front of her, tears sliding down her cheeks.

Gudlaugur coughed and carried on. This was the part they had been dreading the most. 'I'm very sorry to have to tell you that the body, which the evidence suggests is Bríet, was badly treated after death.'

The couple both turned their heads to him. The mother clutched at her heart, squeezing her jumper, her knuckles white with the effort. She was staring at him, open-mouthed. 'What do you mean?'

'We would rather have spared you the details but they will have to be made public sooner or later.' Gudlaugur drew a deep breath before continuing. 'The body has been dismembered. I repeat that this was done after her death.'

'How did she die?' The father's voice was devoid of emotion, which Freyja knew meant nothing: he was as shattered as his wife. Some people cried, others froze when grief came knocking at the door.

'The woman in question was very probably strangled.'

'Very probably?' The mother's voice was close to breaking. She was still clutching her jumper for dear life. 'What does *very probably* mean? Is she in such a state that you can't tell how she died?'

Gudlaugur looked ready to bolt for the door. Freyja silently pleaded with him not to do it. She didn't want to be left alone here and have to break the news about the head. But it didn't come to that; after a moment, Gudlaugur started speaking again, as steadily as before. 'I shouldn't have put it like that. All the evidence suggests that the woman was strangled. But it wasn't as clear as we would usually expect. You see, I'm afraid her head is missing. It wasn't in the car.'

The couple sat there, frozen. The father was blinking uncontrollably, as if he had a twitch in both eyes. The mother opened and closed her mouth, unable to find any words.

Freyja judged that the moment had come for her to take over. She offered the couple trauma counselling to help them deal with the terrible news and, when they refused it, gave them some sound advice anyway. They also turned down her assistance with breaking the news to Bríet's daughter, though not quite so emphatically. They accepted her card, at least. In closing, Freyja stressed that, if they changed their minds, they could turn to her any time – it didn't have to be during working hours. She thought privately that she wouldn't find it an imposition to have a TV programme interrupted or be woken in the middle of the night if she could be of service to these people.

The moment she'd finished, the mother said: 'I want to see her. Where is Bríet?'

Gudlaugur threw Freyja a look of panic, but she couldn't help. She hadn't a clue how these matters were organised or whether family members had the right to see the bodies of their loved ones in circumstances like this. Judging by Gudlaugur's answer, he was equally in the dark. 'The body is being kept at the National Hospital. But I advise you not to insist on this. If it does turn out to be Bríet and you want to see her, it would be better to do so after she's been laid out by the funeral parlour. By then, you'll have had more time to recover from the initial shock.'

'I want to see her,' the mother said stubbornly.

Freyja thought it unlikely they would be able to sort it out there and then, so she came to Gudlaugur's rescue with a compromise, in the hope that they would then be able to turn to the other questions they needed to ask. 'We'll discuss it with the detective in charge of the inquiry when we get back to the station. We don't have the authority to grant permission ourselves. In the meantime, please think carefully about whether you really want to do this. It would be better to focus on Bríet's life rather than her death and the circumstances surrounding it. It's not easy, I know – but it is possible. And do bear in mind that it hasn't yet been conclusively established that it is Bríet.'

The mother didn't seem remotely placated by this answer. She merely repeated her wish and the father seconded it. 'We want to see her and no one's going to stop us.'

'See the fucking body? Are you out of your tiny minds? Why didn't you just say no?' Erla was so outraged that she exploded out of her chair and loomed forwards over her desk, her bump resting between her hands. 'You can't seriously have thought there would be the faintest chance of that happening? Do you want to fucking kill them? Maybe you'd like Bríet's daughter to join them on their little sightseeing jaunt?'

Freyja and Gudlaugur reacted very differently to this outburst. He was better prepared as it clearly wasn't the first time he'd received a bollocking like this. But when Erla ran out of steam, Freyja was the first to reply. Her feet were killing her, she was feeling mentally and physically drained after the visit, and as a result she had zero patience with being treated like a naughty school kid who's been caught vaping behind the bike sheds. 'If we'd answered like you wanted, that would have been the end of the conversation. We'd have been out on our ear. But feel free to tell them yourself, because we promised them you'd be in touch. Besides, we can't be sure that it would be psychologically damaging for them to see her. They'll already have horrific images in their heads, which may be far worse than what they'll actually see at the mortuary. The main thing is to prepare them properly. Which I could do – if it comes to that.'

Erla gnawed at the inside of her cheek, then dropped back into her chair, suddenly deflated. She picked up one of the labelled specimen jars that Gudlaugur had handed her when they'd first come in, and held it up to the light. There was no telling what she was hoping to see, since the jars contained swabs with saliva samples from Bríet's parents that would mean nothing to the naked eye. No doubt she was just buying time while she tried to come up with a retort. She tilted the jar this way and that before putting it back on the desk. 'OK, what else did they say?'

Before Gudlaugur or Freyja could reply, Huldar's voice spoke behind them. 'Everything all right?' He must have heard Erla shouting and charged to their rescue like the cavalry. This contravened the terms of his agreement with Freyja, but sometimes you had to make exceptions. Not in this case, though, since the storm had already safely blown over without doing any damage.

Erla raised her eyebrows, then beckoned him in. 'Feel free, why don't you? Is there anyone else out there who'd like to join us?'

Ignoring her sarcasm, Huldar closed the door behind him. 'What did you learn from your visit?'

'I was just getting to that when you barged in.' A twinge of pain distorted Erla's face and she pressed her hands to her back. To Freyja's astonishment, neither Huldar nor Gudlaugur asked if she was OK. But before Freyja had a chance to remedy this omission, Erla gritted her teeth and started speaking again. 'Go on, Gudlaugur. What did the parents say?'

'They confirmed most of what we already know about Bríet. She was divorced with a ten-year-old daughter. According to them, the break-up was difficult but not uncivilised. No temper tantrums and no violence on his side. The marriage had just run its course and the decision to end it was mutual. Which is consistent with what we learnt from the local magistrate.'

'Any boyfriends?' Another twinge of pain crossed Erla's face as she spoke. Again, Huldar and Gudlaugur behaved as if this were completely normal.

Now that Freyja thought about it, everyone in CID seemed to be in denial about the fact that their boss was on the point of giving birth. Well, she had no intention of playing this game. 'Sorry, but are you OK?'

'Yes,' Erla snapped, so irritably that Freyja could understand why people turned a blind eye to her bump. Absurd as it seemed, Erla's pregnancy was clearly a sensitive topic.

'Go on, Gudlaugur.'

He obeyed. 'According to the parents, there was no new man in her life. She'd been so busy that she'd had no time for that sort of thing. Though I suppose it's possible she was seeing someone but hadn't told her parents. They say she didn't have any enemies and she was well liked at work. They don't believe the murder can have anything to do with her private life, her work or her studies. She didn't have any alcohol or drug problems, and she wasn't involved in any disputes. There's nothing to explain what's happened.'

Erla flapped a hand at Gudlaugur. 'Keep going. What about Friday evening? Could they give you any information about whether she was expecting a visitor? When I rang them on the pretext that I needed to get hold of Bríet about her car, her mother said she'd last talked to her on Friday. Did Bríet say anything about what she was planning to do that evening?'

'No. According to the mother, she didn't mention any visitors. She'd been planning to work on her Master's dissertation on Friday and to use the weekend for studying. Her dissertation partner was going abroad on holiday, so they wanted to get as much done as possible that day. They'd been studying together a lot because they're around the same age, both older than most of the other students. The mother also mentioned that Bríet was supposed to be taking a night shift at the hospital on Sunday evening. That was pretty much it. Though they did mention some friends Bríet was in touch with. I took down their names. Maybe they'll know more about her plans for Friday evening.' Gudlaugur laid a page from his notebook on Erla's desk. 'They also gave me the name of Bríet's dissertation partner, in case she knows anything. She's called Andrea. They don't know her patronymic but they say she works as a yoga teacher, so it shouldn't be too hard to track her down. None of Bríet's friends live in the housing estate where she was found, or not as far as they know. Mind you, they don't actually know where this Andrea lives.'

Erla scanned the list of names, then put it down again. 'What about brothers or sisters? Did Bríet have any siblings who could have dropped in? Family quarrels can get out of hand.'

Gudlaugur answered flatly: 'No.' Then added: 'Unfortunately.'

He didn't need to explain. It was terrible to lose a child, even when that child was an adult. But when it was an only child . . . They were all silent as they digested this tragic fact.

Erla seemed even more tired now than when Freyja and Gudlaugur had first come in, though at least she had stopped grimacing with pain. 'No link at all to the housing estate?'

'None that they knew of.'

'What about computers? How many did she have?'

'They said she had a laptop. But they didn't know what make it was or where it could be, only that it was black. Apparently it was usually on the kitchen table when they went round.'

'What about clothes? Did you show them the pictures?'

Gudlaugur dropped his gaze. 'No, I'm afraid not. They couldn't take any more.'

No one said anything for a long moment.

Erla rubbed a hand over her face. 'OK. Anything else?'

'No. Except that they said Bríet had been doing incredibly well in her studies. They wanted us to know that.'

Huldar chipped in with a question. 'What was she studying?'

'Public health. Apparently she was very interested in the subject.'

Freyja took over from Gudlaugur. 'They're going to talk to Bríet's daughter this evening. They didn't want any help with that, but if you think it's necessary to interview the girl, I would expect to be present. Ideally, I'd like a chance to talk to her privately after that, just to check how she's coping. Independent of the inquiry.'

'Yes.' Erla left it at that. She sat there thinking, massaging the back of her neck. 'What am I going to say to them about their request to see the body?'

'Fob the problem off on the guy from the Identification Commission.' Huldar's suggestion wasn't such a bad one.

'Call him and let him make the decision. After all, it comes under identification, doesn't it? If they confirm that it's their daughter, the commission can tick the box marked "direct identification". That should please them.'

Erla brightened up a little, but she didn't thank Huldar for his suggestion. 'Yes. Maybe.' Although she sounded doubtful, none of them were fooled. It was blindingly obvious that she was going to seize on this as a way out. 'Right, if there's nothing else, I need to get on. I've got to finish going through everything that's come in today and prepare tomorrow morning's progress meeting. But you're free to go.'

No sooner had they stepped out of the office than they heard her voice from behind the closed door. There wasn't a shadow of doubt in Freyja's mind that she was on the phone to the man from the Identification Commission.

Chapter 11

Photos connected to the case had been pinned to the wall of the meeting room in a grim montage, their subjects revealed in unsparing detail by the smart lighting system, which seemed to have concluded that flood lighting was required. It was ironic, Huldar thought, because if ever there had been an occasion for low lighting at work, this was it: the wall display did absolutely nothing to raise morale.

The visuals included a picture of Bríet from her Facebook page and photos taken during the examination of her flat, of the bags in the boot and the other contents of her car. Huldar's gaze kept returning to the image of her when she was alive, which had nothing to do with the murder. However comfortable it was to think of her as a name and identity number, it was salutary to be reminded that the victim had once been a living, breathing human being.

Nothing about the picture gave any hint of what was to come. It was a selfie, apparently taken on a mountain hike, and Bríet was doing her best to look good. She was wearing a windproof jacket and woolly hat, holding walking poles and gazing proudly into her phone with a view of distant lowlands behind her. Huldar couldn't place the mountain but it obviously wasn't one of the higher or more strenuous climbs. Yet the pleasure radiating from Bríet's face couldn't have been greater if she'd just scaled Everest. There was nothing particularly striking about her appearance: light-brown, shoulder-length hair sticking out from under her hat; grey eyes; an unremarkable nose; red cheeks and a medium-sized mouth. A very ordinary thirty-five-year-old woman who seemed perfectly content with her lot and unlikely to cause any ripples.

Huldar felt a burning desire to see her murderer brought into the police station in irons.

A large map of the capital area had also been fastened to the wall, with red circles drawn around Bríet's home in the Salahverfi area of Kópavogur, and the housing estate where her car had turned up. The most likely routes between these two points had also been marked in, with notes on how long each took to drive, and the location of any CCTV cameras along them. The problem was that the body hadn't been dismembered at Bríet's flat or where the car was parked, so logically it must have been driven to a third location between these two points. They still hadn't found anything to connect Bríet to the housing estate, but it was possible that the killer had some link to it. Perhaps he lived there or had access to premises in the area where he had chopped up the body. At this stage, though, it was pure speculation, like so many other aspects of the case.

The photos of Bríet's body parts, exposed in all their horror by the cruel lighting, made for extremely disturbing viewing. It didn't help that Huldar had been present at the post-mortem. In fact, it probably made things worse. There was a sign on the meeting-room door saying: *No Entry*, presumably to deter the cleaners from coming in. Apart from them, it was unlikely that anyone without a link to the investigation would wander in here. The only meetings held in the department in the near future would be those relating to the inquiry. Even the senior management's work-flow committee, whose meetings usually took priority, would have to take a back seat for a while. Missing these was no hardship for Huldar, though he would have liked to have seen the committee's faces if they'd walked in there without warning. It would do them good to see such stark evidence of what the job really entailed, before they had whittled it down to brief statements, crammed into boxes on their charts and connected by arrows.

In addition to the photos and map, there was a list of outstanding jobs, another with the names of people who needed to be interviewed, and a timeline of the events, which was pitifully sketchy as yet. But that was to be expected. It was only thirty-six hours since Bríet had been found. In fact, CID had achieved a reasonable amount in that time, since the entire department had been co-opted to work on the investigation and everyone had been pulling their weight.

Erla had borne the brunt, though. Huldar didn't know when she'd left the office last night, but she had still been there when he went home just before eleven. He'd been intending to stay as long as her but had given up. Judging by how exhausted she'd looked at this morning's progress meeting, she must have been at it until the early hours.

Huldar sat on the edge of the conference table, nursing a mug of coffee. He was tired from yesterday's efforts but knew that today would be no less gruelling. He let his gaze wander back and forth over the wall display, hoping for some kind of revelation, but nothing leapt out at him. So far, they hadn't come across a single possible reason why Bríet should have been butchered and shoved in the boot of her own car. On the surface, she appeared to have been your ordinary law-abiding citizen, who had no gripe with God or her fellow men.

They had skimmed through her posts on social media without finding anything of interest. She wasn't particularly active, didn't post political declarations or use strong language or put the boot into minorities. She had expressed no opinions on the third energy package, the need for a new constitution, the recently proposed Reykjavík busway, or the annual New Year's Eve satire on TV. Her contributions were all perfectly anodyne and so were her photos: plates of food, her daughter, and selfies like the one she'd chosen for her profile picture. She hadn't posted anything since Friday afternoon when she had put up a photo of a coffee mug beside the textbook that had later been found lying on the kitchen floor, adding various hashtags to do with university, studying, etcetera.

Since the post-mortem had revealed no evidence of a sexual attack, they could probably rule that out as a motive. Her ex-husband wasn't a suspect, though that might change after his interview later today. The missing laptop left open the possibility of a burglary, but there was no other evidence in the flat to support the idea: nothing had been torn from the cupboards and no drawers had been pulled out.

If Bríet had been involved with a new man, she had kept it very quiet, which made it unlikely that the perpetrator was a psycho boyfriend. A drugs link was also looking implausible. Bríet's parents were adamant that she hadn't been a user or addict of any kind, and the blood tests had confirmed this: there had been no traces of alcohol or narcotics in her system. Early this morning, the police had contacted her workplace and the university, but nothing of significance had emerged.

The National Hospital ruled out the possibility that Bríet had made any mistakes in her job that could have affected anyone: she had a spotless record. The university tutor they spoke to had also given her a good report. As a student she had been conscientious, keen and caused no problems, though the tutor did point out that the supervisor of her Master's dissertation would be in a better position to provide a character reference.

That appeared to eliminate a disappointed lover, an angry ex-husband, a fellow student, a hospital patient or a vengeful relative, or a drug dealer. Nevertheless, somebody had seen fit to throttle the woman, cut her into eight pieces and walk off with her head. All the police were left with by way of suspects was a burglar or a crazed attacker with no personal connection to Bríet. Both scenarios would suggest a random event, which, if true, would be a nightmare to investigate. Fortunately, however, there were some indications that Bríet might in fact have known her attacker.

Yesterday evening, Erla had got hold of the pizza delivery guy, who turned out to be a kid at sixth-form college, working alongside school. He remembered delivering to Salahverfi and recalled Bríet because she had behaved so oddly. He'd rung the bell, but instead of opening the door, Bríet had called out: 'Who is it?' When he said he was delivering a pizza, Bríet had asked what chain he was from. Only after he had answered this did she open the door, and then only a crack. Apparently, she had jammed her foot against it as if she was expecting him to try and force his way in. He hadn't been aware of anyone else in the flat; hadn't heard any voices behind her or seen anyone else when she took the pizza from him. The plan was to get the boy into the station to give an official statement, as what he said suggested that she had been expecting someone she didn't want to let in. The delivery boy had also been able to confirm that Bríet had been wearing orthopaedic sandals with a leather strap over the instep. But he hadn't been able to get a good view of what else she was wearing, apart from her sleeve, which might have been either blue or grey.

The police had spoken to several of Bríet's neighbours yesterday evening, once her parents had been informed, but almost nothing useful had emerged. For example, no one remembered seeing Bríet's car, or indeed any other car, parked round the back of the block, next to her small, fenced-in garden. This was unfortunate, since Forensics reckoned they could detect signs that Bríet's body had been dragged out through the garden. The neighbours hadn't noticed any unfamiliar vehicles in the car park either. This was a pity too since, if the killer had driven there, the police might now at least have a colour and perhaps a make of car. Huldar was inclined to believe he had arrived by some alternative means, as otherwise it was hard to understand why he had put Bríet's body in the boot of her car rather than his own. Unless he was being clever and trying to avoid getting any biological traces in his. In which case, he could have come back later to retrieve his own vehicle.

The cars currently parked in the spaces belonging to the block of flats had all been checked and accounted for. If the killer's car had ever been there, it was now gone.

The police had also spoken to the city's taxi companies, but there had been no trips to the building on Friday or Saturday, and although there had been other jobs in the area, none of the customers had seemed remotely dubious. They had all paid by card, too, which didn't suggest they were trying to cover their tracks. Nevertheless, the names of the card owners would be collected and checked out.

None of the other residents in the building had noticed a possible perpetrator. The only potentially useful information the police had obtained from these conversations was the statement of the man who lived in the flat above Bríet's. He said he'd heard a noise and thought it had come from downstairs. There had been a loud quarrel and screams and he had thought the voices were those of a man and a woman. He hadn't been able to make out any words, though, and said the disturbance hadn't lasted long. No one else had heard a thing. The neighbours who lived either side of Bríet had been out at the time, and the others' flats were too far away for the noise to have carried. Besides, most of the residents had had their radio or TV on.

The only problem was the timing. According to the upstairs neighbour, the row had taken place before the pizza delivery boy arrived, or just after 6 p.m. But he wasn't entirely sure about this, so it was possible he'd misremembered. Alternatively, the killer could have come round twice; once before the pizza was delivered, when he'd had a row with Bríet, and then again shortly after the delivery, in an even more murderous rage. Today, the police were going to talk to the neighbours they hadn't got hold of yesterday evening, in the hope that they might be able to shed light on the sequence of events or even have caught a glimpse of the killer.

In other words, there was a hell of a lot to do for the understaffed team.

As it was now officially a murder inquiry, they were waiting for permission to examine Bríet's bank and card statements. So far, all they'd received was a general statement from her bank to the effect that there was no evidence of anything untoward and her cards hadn't been used since she had paid for the pizza on Friday evening.

There had been no wallet or cards in the handbag found in her car. If the killer had taken them, he hadn't given in to the temptation of using them.

Huldar took a mouthful of coffee, then carried on contemplating the wall display. Had it really been a random attack? Could the murderer have got the wrong person? Could Bríet have unwittingly seen something she shouldn't have? Unlikely. What could be so bad that it would necessitate killing a witness? Huldar's mind was blank.

But if it wasn't a random killing, the explanation had to be out there somewhere. The question was, where?

'What do you think?' Lína's youthful voice piped up behind Huldar. She had entered the meeting room without his noticing. 'I put some of it up for Erla this morning.'

Huldar turned to her with a smile. 'It's great. Though I doubt I'll be asking you to decorate the walls of my flat any time soon.' He turned back to the pictures and carried on studying them. 'What do you think happened, Lína?'

Lína sat down at the conference table beside him. She was so short that her feet couldn't touch the floor. 'I don't know. But I am sure that the person who did it was out of his mind with rage.'

'You don't say.' Huldar immediately regretted his comment. Lína might think he was sneering at her, which wasn't the intention. 'What kind of thing would drive someone insane with rage like that?'

Lína thought for a while. She had done such an outstandingly good job during her previous spells of work experience in the department that she was probably reluctant to spoil her record by coming out with something ill-considered now. 'I'm assuming it's a man. And I'm guessing it could tip some men over the edge if they felt they'd been humiliated, two-timed or cheated in some way. Then there's revenge, of course. And no doubt other reasons too.'

'We can forget about two-timing. Bríet wasn't in a relationship. And unless the last person to drive her car was a very short man, it must have been a woman. But all the same, I think it's unlikely the perpetrator was female.'

'I agree. A woman has never killed another adult woman in Iceland, except maybe in the distant past. But, having said that, there's nothing in the academic literature that gives me reason to believe we can rule out a woman.'

Huldar smiled. 'And the academic literature doesn't lie. Surely you haven't been grappling with anything like this on your course?'

'No. Not exactly like this. But plenty of nasty stuff – most of it from abroad.' A thoughtful furrow appeared between Lína's eyes. 'Could it have been a case of mistaken identity? Could she have been mistaken for someone who led a very different sort of life – one which might explain what happened? A woman who had recently divorced a violent psychopath, for example.'

'Maybe. But it's strange that she let the murderer in if she didn't know him. There's no indication that it was a break-in. She opened the door to him, though of course there were signs of a struggle in the hall, as you can see from the pictures. So he probably forced his way in as soon as she opened the door a crack. Or maybe it was unlocked and he just walked straight in. But after hearing what the delivery boy said, I don't buy it.'

They were both silent. Huldar took another sip of coffee while Lína studied the wall gravely.

She pointed to the photos of the body parts. 'Then there's the missing head. That can hardly be considered normal.'

'Nothing on that wall is normal.'

Lína started swinging her legs, as if bored of the subject. 'Do you know what job I'll be assigned?'

Huldar shook his head. 'No idea. I didn't even know you were joining us.'

Lína drew herself up, her face smug. 'I was in another department this time. But I was asked to stay on and help out CID. Apparently there's so much to do that you're going to need every hand you can get.' She turned to Huldar and he was transfixed by the band of freckles that started on her nose and spread out over her porcelain-white cheeks. She pushed her wavy, bright-red hair behind her ears and he found himself picturing some distant female Irish ancestor, carried off as a slave by one of Iceland's Viking-age settlers. If she had been as tough and determined as Lína, no doubt the roles of master and slave would soon have been reversed. 'Did you know I came top in my Christmas exams?' she said.

Huldar smiled at her. 'Congratulations. Maybe you can fill in for Erla when she goes on maternity leave.'

Lína misinterpreted this as mockery and her freckles were hidden by a blush. 'Ha ha.'

'I wasn't joking. I'd be happy to work for you.'

The blush faded and Lína grinned. Then she leant over and asked in a conspiratorial whisper, with a sweet puff of the minty lip salve that she had repeatedly refreshed during the meeting: 'When's Erla actually expecting? She threw me out of her office for asking.'

It was Huldar's turn to grin. 'Don't ask me. She won't tell me either, so don't take it personally. It must be any day now, though.' He stretched and got to his feet. Lína's closeness and the scent of her lip salve were disturbingly pleasant. He couldn't afford any trouble of that sort. 'What's the betting she'll give birth here in the office? You don't by any chance know how to deliver a baby?'

Lína's expression turned serious again. 'No, but maybe I should google it.'

It occurred to Huldar that this might not be a bad idea. If his prediction came true, it would be good to have Lína on hand. He would be worse than useless himself. 'Just make sure Erla doesn't catch you watching childbirth videos.'

As they left the meeting room, Huldar turned off the lights and shadow fell across the wall, softening the gruesome images.

Chapter 12

Wednesday

The snow was turning to slush. It had already melted on the roads and been dirtied by the cars and soon the pavements would go the same way. The pristine white world that had delighted Sædís's eye first thing this morning was turning into its antithesis: a filthy, grey quagmire. She cursed her stupidity in wearing her new shoes instead of her boots, but she had wanted to look smart. Now they would be ruined, with a white line of salt on the suede that would never come out. Silly as it was, she wanted to weep over the fate of her shoes. But she mustn't give in to the urge: she needed to come across as hard as nails, with both feet firmly on the ground.

Sadly, though, this wasn't the case. She was hopelessly tender-hearted and over-sensitive. She couldn't bear to see suffering, and was always imagining it even when it wasn't actually there. Her heart went out to anyone who was downtrodden, having a hard time or ill, and to all animals, large or small. She even felt pity for inanimate objects, attributing feelings to them, which meant she could never throw anything away. If she got rid of an object she no longer had any use for, she would be distressed for days afterwards over its fate, picturing it being crushed in landfill or gathering dust in the Good Shepherd charity shop, where no one would appreciate it.

It was this kind of sadness she was struggling with now. She was filled with remorse over the fate of her shoes, which had been so smart and had deserved to remain so for much longer.

Sædís was driving her old banger again. The repairs hadn't cost as much as she'd feared, though the mechanic had commented that he couldn't keep it on the road much longer. She would have to buy a new one sooner rather than later. This news had done nothing to cheer her up since she was as sentimentally fond of the old wreck as she was of all her other possessions.

She reached out to switch on the radio. It didn't work properly – you couldn't change stations – and like everything else in the car, it was about to expire. But, she reminded herself, it wasn't as if she needed to be able to listen to more than one station at a time.

The light turned green at last and the traffic crawled off again. Sædís wiped the mist from the windscreen, but this didn't do much to improve the view. She carefully avoided looking at the clock on the dashboard. It too was wrong but she knew how many minutes it was out by. There was no point getting stressed. She had set off in good time but the traffic had been heavier than expected.

When she finally drove into the National Hospital car park, she saw that he was already there, punctual as ever. She tried in vain to feel grateful for the fact, but his correctness always made her feel inferior. It wasn't deliberate – he was always very considerate to her – but she couldn't help the feeling. Neither of them could help what they were like.

Even her new shoes probably didn't look smart to him. She had tried to dress up for the occasion before, buying herself an outfit from H&M that she'd thought looked classy. But when they'd met she had read in his eyes that he saw through the cheap material and shoddy tailoring. He didn't say anything, but that in itself was telling, because he usually began by commenting on how well she was looking. This would be followed by questions about her diet and general health, to which she always gave the same answer: her health was excellent and so was her diet. Sometimes she was tempted to blurt out that she'd lost her appetite because she'd recently starting smoking crack, but she'd never do it. For one thing, she wasn't the sarcastic type and, for another, she didn't want to hurt him with a joke in poor taste.

Sædís finally found a parking space. It was at the other end from the hospital, as the grounds were in chaos due to building works. Only a few spaces close to the entrance had escaped the disruption and only visitors who turned up early – like him – had a chance of nabbing them. Whereas she would have to wade through the slush. There were some plastic bags on the back seat and she toyed with the idea of using them as shoe covers, but he was unlikely to be impressed. He'd probably offer to buy her some proper snow boots. She didn't want that, though. He'd already paid for more than enough.

She undid the seat-belt, accidentally brushing against her bump. Looking down, she was forced to face up to the fact that it wouldn't be possible to conceal it much longer. Thick jumpers would only work for another week. After that, anyone who cared to would be able to see through her attempts to disguise her condition.

Her parents still hadn't noticed. Her mother was experiencing one of her frequent lows and had hardly got out of bed lately. Her father had taken himself more or less straight to bed after she'd driven him home from the police station. He had eaten the eggs and toast she had made for him without saying a word. She had said, 'Here you go,' when she put the food on the table and he had said, 'Thanks,' when he got up again. These were the only words they had exchanged. She judged it wiser to wait until he was in a better frame of mind before making another attempt to talk to him about what had happened.

By the time she got up, he had gone to work. They would probably never have the conversation, but then that was typical in their house. If their family was a business, their motto would be: *We sweep problems under the carpet.*

Her pregnancy, on the other hand, would be impossible to ignore. Sooner or later they would have to discuss it – a prospect she dreaded.

The slush reached halfway up her shoes when she stepped out of the car. Instead of setting off, she stood still for a moment and took a deep breath. She needed to compose herself. She searched her mind for positive thoughts but they were thin on the ground. The only thing that occurred to her was that her unborn child would be fortunate in life. It would have opportunities that she herself had been denied. It wouldn't have to spend its childhood fretting over its mother's depression and its father's absences.

Not like her. Or her sister Selma.

Sædís was assailed by a terrible feeling of guilt. Soon her life would be transformed and she would be able to leave home, but her little sister would be left behind in the silence that reigned in their house; their mum in bed, their dad at work. No one to talk to her or encourage her. If Sædís was to be honest with herself, this just wasn't an option. Somehow she would have to take her sister with her. Perhaps a lawyer could help her prove that Selma would be better off with her. She wouldn't have to go far to find that kind of support. Not any more. On the other hand, she would never actually dare to ask for it.

Everything seemed so hopeless, almost everywhere she looked. Sædís was aware of a familiar sense of dread, only this time it felt more ominous, like the threatening black banks of cloud that sometimes loomed on the horizon, biding their time before creeping inexorably closer and developing into a storm. Was she turning into a depressive like her mother? If she did, what would become of Selma? The thought made her feel even worse until she reminded herself that her dread was normal. Really, in the circumstances, it would have been far more worrying if she hadn't felt this terrible sense of despair.

She instinctively stroked her belly through her jumper. She had to get a grip on herself and push these worries away. A small person was growing inside her. A small person who might sense her misery and anxiety. She couldn't bear the thought. This child must have the best possible start in life.

She clenched her toes as the icy slush started seeping through the seams of her shoes. She would have to start moving before her feet got soaked. Taking another deep breath, she closed her eyes and counted to ten.

Then she zipped up her coat to hide her bump and started walking. She felt better immediately. She always felt better when her bump was out of sight. She had recently taken to dressing and undressing in the dark to avoid having to see it. When the bump was invisible, it was so much easier not to think about the child. She was determined to see this through and the only way she could do that was by not forming a bond with her unborn baby. So it was unfortunate that nature pro-grammed both body and mind to demand just that. The scan she was about to have wouldn't help either. The last thing she needed was to see an image of the foetus. After that it would be even harder to pretend it wasn't happening. So far, this was the approach that had worked best for her. She obviously took after her family in her ability to live in denial. But this wasn't the time to try to throw off the familial yoke. For her own sake she needed to behave as if she wasn't pregnant. Or not exactly pregnant. She was just hosting a child for someone else. It was almost like babysitting. Because it wouldn't be her child.

Appealing to her sense of generosity had also helped. Not everyone was capable of having a child but she could. For that reason, it went without saying that she would make the sacri-fice – surely?

One ought to be generous with what one had. She had never had much to share with others but had always tried to live according to that maxim. If she followed this thought through to its logical conclusion, though, she would be forced to admit that this wasn't a case of sharing: she was *giving* the child away.

For a very respectable sum, of course. A sum of money that would enable her to leave home and start a new life on her own terms – with her sister. Otherwise it would never hap-pen. She could never be happy if her sister didn't benefit from her good luck, so Selma would have to come too.

If Sædís had wanted to, she could have raised the money by other means. In recent years her father's business had been thriving. He'd bought himself a monster jeep and they had exchanged their modest flat for a decent-sized house, though they'd stayed in the west end as her mother handled change badly. Apart from that, things went on the same. She didn't ask her father for anything beyond what she needed to buy for the household, and it hadn't occurred to him to offer her any money above and beyond that. This didn't matter much to her as she could look after herself. Her wages were quite enough for her. She wasn't high maintenance and had no intention of scrounging money from her dad or anyone else. Yet Sædís knew he wouldn't hesitate to give her what she needed without saying a word. He was kind, despite his air of detached indifference and apparent ability to switch off all normal feelings. But Sædís wanted to make her own way. In any case, she doubted he would be keen to finance her move out of their dreary household, since she was the one who actually kept it going.

There was no denying that the lump sum would come in useful. Sædís's dream was to rent a pretty flat in a traditional wooden house, where she and Selma could make a cosy little home for themselves, far removed from depression and chronic indifference. She would leave all the bad memories behind, refusing to let them into their new home. In her mind's eye, their flat was decorated entirely in pastel shades, almost like the pink and white of a fluffy cartoon bunny. There the two sisters would be able to cuddle up on the sofa in their pyjamas with cups of tea, and read or watch films together.

The thought raised Sædís's spirits. She started walking more briskly and waved to the waiting man who was beginning to shift impatiently from foot to foot. There was no need to get stressed. They were a tiny bit late but on all her previous appointments she had been kept waiting. They would have to sit and flick through the dog-eared, out-of-date magazines until their turn finally came. After all, they couldn't chat while they were waiting because he felt it would be best if no one knew they were together. Of course, when her name was called and she was summoned for the scan, it wouldn't be possible to keep up the pretence any longer, but that couldn't be helped. He had declined her offer to pretend to be his sister and say something loud and clear in the waiting room to back up this impression. She was rather relieved. It was more comfortable sitting in silence, without having to make conversation. She was used to that.

They shook hands as formally as if he were about to give her a graduation certificate, but then he pecked her on the cheek. He did it so lightly that it felt almost as if she'd been brushed by a butterfly's wing.

As they went inside, Sædís made up her mind. She wasn't going to look at the screen during the scan. Instead, she was going to close her eyes and picture her flat; picture her and Selma enjoying their new life. She just hoped a caption wouldn't pop up saying: *This cosy existence has been paid for by your unborn child.*

Chapter 13

Wednesday

Freyja wasn't the only person waiting to see Erla. Gudlaugur was leaning against the wall beside her, next in the queue. Erla's office door was open a crack and they could hear the murmur of a conversation that went on and on, as if it would never end.

Gudlaugur closed his eyes as if on the point of nodding off, but then he wasn't alone. As Freyja had crossed the open-plan area to Erla's office, everyone she'd passed had looked worn out, slumped in their chairs, red-eyed from staring at their screens, where usually they seemed like poster children for exemplary posture. Every desk was decorated with a coffee mug, in some cases a whole collection.

Freyja was feeling pretty shattered herself after the long day yesterday, though nothing like as bad as the rest of the team. When she left, they had still been hard at work. So the fact she was looking brighter than most had nothing to do with good genes, an expensive mattress or a healthy diet. But it had had the unfortunate effect of making her stick out like a sore thumb again at this morning's meeting. It had actually occurred to her to yawn and slouch in the hope of blending in. The one compensation was that Lína had been in the same boat: the intern had been so bright-eyed and alert that she'd put Freyja in the shade.

Huldar was somewhere in between. He didn't look as unnaturally healthy as an actor in an Icelandic *skyr* advert like Lína, but nor did he resemble a ferry passenger the day after the notorious Westman Islands Festival like the rest. At present, he was sitting at his desk, directly in Freyja's eye-line, busily working his way through a list of people who needed to be interviewed. He was speaking on the phone, his eyes on the screen in front of him, oblivious to her presence. Becoming aware of unfamiliar feelings stirring inside her, Freyja looked away. She nudged Gudlaugur. 'Tell me, do you know anything about accessing the Police Information System?'

Gudlaugur's drooping eyelids flicked open and he pulled his sagging body upright. 'The Police Information System? What do you mean? Do you need to access it?'

'No, I don't. Not at all. I was just wondering if it was normal for people to look up friends and relations on it.'

Gudlaugur seemed surprised. 'Why do you ask?'

'Because my manager suddenly blurted out that I wasn't to do it. I don't understand what prompted him to bring it up, so I wondered if it was a common problem.'

'And you're sure you've never accessed it for personal reasons? You've never given in to the temptation?'

Freyja tried not to let his questions rile her. 'Yes, I'm quite sure. I don't even have a log-in. I'm not interested in getting one either.'

Gudlaugur appeared relieved. 'Good. I expect he was just warning you, then. Because it's no joke if you get caught. The IT department monitors all searches on the system. They can see who's logged in and what they've looked at. If it turns out someone's used the system to satisfy their curiosity, the person in question will find themselves in deep shit.'

'How deep?'

'Depends whether the news gets out or whether the matter can be dealt with in-house, without the press getting wind of it. We could be talking anything from disciplinary measures to criminal prosecution. It depends what the purpose was. If you looked someone up, then used the information to blackmail or intimidate them, that would constitute a criminal offence. Just as an example.'

Freyja nodded. 'I see. It still seems odd that he brought it up out of the blue like that.'

Gudlaugur shrugged. 'Yes and no. Maybe they're planning to grant you access. If they do, bear that in mind.' Suddenly embarrassed, he added: 'Not that I believe for a minute that you'd abuse the privilege. But the stuff on the system is just so tempting. It contains almost all the details of everyone who's ever been on our radar.'

In the ensuing silence they could hear Erla still rabbiting away on the phone. Freyja folded her arms, checking her watch as she did so. In her opinion, the phone call had been going on for an unnecessarily long time. Personally, she tried to keep her calls as short as possible, otherwise they had a tendency to drag on with neither side able to bring them to a conclusion. She was too impatient for that. 'What are you looking at, by the way?'

'CCTV recordings. I've watched so much passing traffic I think I'll walk home via the coastal path this evening just so I don't have to set eyes on another car.'

If today turned out to be as long as yesterday, Freyja doubted he would do it. He would be so eager to get home to bed that he'd opt to drive. 'Found anything useful?'

'Yes. That's why I need to talk to Erla. I've finally found footage of Bríet's car being driven out of the area on Friday night. There are no proper cameras in the residential streets but it was caught on a security camera belonging to a private property on the outskirts of Kópavogur. So at least that gives us a time for when it was on the move.'

Freyja smiled at him. 'Congratulations. What time was it?'

'A quarter past twelve. Midnight.'

'What? Weren't they saying Bríet died between 7 and 8 p.m.?' Freyja did some quick mental arithmetic. Four or five hours would have passed between Bríet's murder and her body being driven away. She had seen photos of the flat and it wasn't particularly large. If the perpetrator had been lurking in there all that time with the body, he must be very disturbed indeed. Most people would have got out of there as fast as they could – fled so they didn't have to face up to the atrocity they had committed. 'That's weird.'

'What's even weirder is that the car didn't appear in the vicinity of the housing estate where it was found until Saturday night. Almost exactly twenty-four hours later.' Gudlaugur started to yawn but managed to suppress it. 'It would have been better if the car had been on the move an hour or two later in both cases. There's so much less traffic in the early hours of the morning that it would have been much easier to track. Whereas there are quite a few cars still on the road around midnight at the weekend. And just to make life even harder for us, the Kópavogur choir held a concert on Friday evening, which finished at around the same time. So there were a whole load of cars heading in the same direction. We'll find it, though. It's just a matter of time.'

'Is the driver visible?'

'No. Unfortunately. A driver can be seen as the car's leaving Bríet's flat, but he's wearing a hood – the big kind, like on a parka – and we only get a side view, so the hood hides his profile. The image is very grainy too, as the camera's set back from the street. But we might be able to estimate his height – it looks to me like a man. In the other footage, where the car appears to be on its way to the housing estate, the driver's not visible at all. The camera's pointing at the empty passenger seat. And the picture quality's terrible too.'

After this, neither of them added anything. In the sudden silence, they realised that Erla had finally finished her conversation. Freyja pushed off from the wall and invited Gudlaugur to come in with her, as what she had to say wouldn't take long. She refrained from adding that she felt more comfortable about confronting Erla in her lair if she had someone with her for moral support.

'What?' Erla glanced up, her headphones round her neck, as Freyja tapped at the door, then pushed it open.

'Er, Bríet's mother was just on the phone, repeating their demand to see the body. I told her the same as you did: that they would just have to wait.' Erla and the representative from the Identification Commission had agreed that the parents shouldn't be allowed to see Bríet's body as matters stood. Badly though the couple had taken the news, there was little they could do about it.

Erla leant back in her chair. 'Good. I don't know why she was wasting her time calling you, though. It's not like you can do anything to change the decision.'

Freyja was careful not to get angry. 'They've got my card. And she was calling about another matter too. She said Bríet's ex-husband, Lúdvík, was interested in getting me to talk to their daughter. Apparently he's unsure how much he can safely tell her. The girl's asking awkward questions.'

'Good. Do it. Absolutely. You go with her, Gudlaugur. Get some information out of him while you're there. We can use the answers to prepare for his official interview.'

Erla was just putting her headphones back on when Gudlaugur coughed and said he had some news. Freyja seized the chance to slip out. She could fetch Gudlaugur once she'd arranged the visit.

The girl's sobs echoed around the sparsely furnished room. She was sitting on the sofa beside her father, in a pair of colourful pyjamas that she'd almost outgrown. It was very late in the day not to be dressed, but when you're ten years old and your mother has just been murdered, the rules about that sort of thing go out of the window. On the coffee table in front of the girl lay a school textbook and an exercise book, a green propelling pencil and a furry pink pencil case. She had clearly been doing some homework to distract herself. It would probably be a while before she finished the questions she appeared to be halfway through. Then again, she might start doing her sums again tomorrow. As Freyja knew, children react very differently from adults when they lose a loved one. They can only cope with powerful emotions for short periods at a time, so, when dealing with grief, they have a tendency to intersperse their periods of weeping and misery with apparently carefree play, as if nothing had happened. Observers can easily misinterpret these intervals of high spirits as lack of feeling, but in this they would be quite wrong. Few if any traumas can equal the devastating impact of such a loss in childhood.

Hanna was ten but tall for her age. She looked nothing like the picture Freyja had seen of her mother, though this meant little as the girl's face was swollen and blotchy from crying. Freyja studied her as she leant against her father. She was still weeping, with a child's noisy lack of inhibition, not caring how the sobs contorted her face, so different from the restraint adults often feel they have to exercise. Mercifully, she was too young to understand how dramatically things were about to change as a result of being motherless. The changes would affect every aspect of her life, from the everyday to the special occasions. Her confirmation would be different, as would Christmas and birthdays and other celebrations that have a tendency to stir up old grief. Her packed lunches would no longer be the same, and it would be a while before her long hair received the attention it needed. Hopefully she would be able to take care of that herself.

Several years ago, Freyja had assisted a weekend father on behalf of children's services. He had been left alone with his daughter after her mother's sudden death. When Freyja had first met them, the little girl had long, curly hair, and as the meetings with father and daughter went on, the girl's hair had become ever more unruly. By their fifth meeting, it had all been cut off. The therapy sessions finished before her hair had grown back to its former length, though Freyja assumed it would eventually. The girl's outfits had also become more eccentric with every session; nothing ever matched, and once she had even turned up in fancy dress. Of course, this didn't matter in the great scheme of things. What mattered most was the father's genuine willingness to adapt to his new role.

She hoped the same would be true of the man now sitting in front of her and Gudlaugur. He was in too great a state of shock for her to be able to assess the likelihood, but his deep love for his daughter shone through. He held her in his arms, indifferent to the tears and snot smearing his shirt. His own eyes were dry, but then his feelings for his ex-wife were probably no more than a distant memory. They had divorced three years earlier and presumably their love had been cooling for a good while before that.

'So you didn't hear from Bríet after you picked up your daughter for the weekend?' Gudlaugur was at great pains not to sound like a police officer demanding answers. Instead, he was doing a good job of conveying gentle concern. 'No phone calls or messages?'

'No. But there was nothing odd about that. The whole thing had been arranged. Hanna was due to stay with me for the week and there was no reason for Bríet and me to talk on the phone while she was here. I collected her on Thursday and was going to drop her off at suppertime this coming Friday. So there was nothing else to be said.'

'Did you have custody on alternate weeks?' Freyja was hoping he would say yes. If Hanna was used to spending every other week with her father, the change in their situation would be easier. For both of them.

'No. Hanna usually spends every other weekend with me, but I have so much unused summer holiday that I was asked to take my days off while things are quiet. I work for a hotel and they'd rather I didn't disappear when things are hectic at the height of summer. So I had a week off and wanted Hanna to spend it with me. We're supposed to have equal or joint custody but in practice it doesn't work out like that. Bríet didn't have any objections, though – she agreed to it immediately.'

'What about you, Hanna? Did you hear from your mum at all after you came to stay with your dad?' Freyja tried to make eye contact but the girl buried her swollen face in her father's shirt. 'Did she ring you, or did you call her, maybe? Just to say good night the day you arrived, or good morning when you woke up next day?'

The girl shook her head, keeping her face hidden.

'What does it matter?' Lúdvík tightened his arms round his daughter's thin shoulders.

'It doesn't really, at this point. We'll talk to you both again in more depth later on.' Gudlaugur shot a quick glance at Freyja. 'I'm just here to see how you're doing and to introduce you to Freyja. She can help Hanna work through her grief. We gathered from your ex-mother-in-law that you thought it was necessary and would be grateful for a bit of help.'

Lúdvík's face was blank. 'I may well have said something like that. I don't really remember much about the conversation. Or about the phone call when she first rang to tell me the news. It's all a bit hazy.'

'That's understandable.' Gudlaugur left it at that. 'Anyway, Freyja will be your contact with the police if anything arises in connection with the investigation or with Hanna. She'll also be present at all our conversations with Hanna, should we need to talk to her at a later date.'

Freyja smiled faintly at Lúdvík. She had introduced herself when they arrived, explaining that she was a child psychologist. She didn't think there was any need to repeat this and assumed that Lúdvík had taken it in, though he had looked tired when he came to the door. 'Hanna. I don't know if you were listening, but my name's Freyja and I work with helping children who are hurting inside.'

The girl obviously took this in, though she didn't answer. She became still in her father's arms and her sobs petered out.

Freyja continued. 'I know you feel terrible. I lost my mother too when I was young. I felt so bad I thought I'd never be happy again.'

Hanna twisted in her father's arms to see Freyja's face. 'Did you ever feel happy again?'

'Yes. It took time but slowly I did feel better.'

The girl sniffed. 'Did you live with your dad?'

Freyja smiled at her. 'No, sadly. I wasn't as lucky as you. I lived with my grandparents instead.'

'Was your mother killed? Did the murderer go to prison?'

'No, she died because she was ill. No one went to prison.'

'My mummy worked at a hospital. Maybe she could have made your mother better.' The girl bit her lip. Her hair was a mess and her eyes were red. 'My mummy wasn't ill. She was killed. Daddy won't tell me why.' Rather than breaking down again as Freyja had feared, Hanna started asking her own questions. 'Did the strange man kill Mummy? When will he go to prison? He'll never be allowed out again, will he?' The tears started trickling down her cheeks once more and she turned away from Freyja to bury her face in her father's chest.

Freyja tried not to let her excitement show: Hanna's words suggested she had a specific man in mind. Freyja would have to tread extremely carefully and avoid putting the girl under any pressure that might make her clam up. This wasn't the moment to explain the sentencing laws for murder. Assuming her mother's killer wasn't insane, he would be released from prison one day. But first they had to catch him and put him away. 'We don't know yet, but the police will take care of it. Gudlaugur's a policeman.' She turned to him. 'Aren't you?'

He nodded. 'Yes.'

It didn't have the desired effect: the girl kept her back to them. Freyja tried another tack. 'Have you met the strange man, Hanna?'

150

The girl's arms tightened around her father. He shifted warily, putting a hand under her chin and gently raising her head until he could look into her eyes. 'Hanna, love. This is very important. We must help the police. Will you do that?'

The girl didn't look at Gudlaugur or Freyja but kept her gaze fixed on her father's face as she nodded. The movement was so slight as to be almost imperceptible.

'Have you met the strange man?' Lúdvík's voice was calm and steady.

No pressure must be put on the girl at this stage. If she refused to answer, Freyja would suggest that they left and came back later.

When Hanna remained stubbornly mute, her father repeated the question in slightly different words. This time they heard a muffled 'No' from the girl. She sniffed, then added, almost in a whisper: 'No.'

'What about your mummy?'

'I don't know.'

Freyja was silent for a moment or two while considering her next question, then asked: 'Who told you about the strange man?'

'Mummy. She said he was strange. A bad man. And angry. She said I must be careful of him.'

Freyja needed to find out where her mother knew this strange, angry, bad man from. 'Did she tell you where she'd met him?'

'No.' Hanna sat up a little. 'Is he outside?' Her eyes were suddenly wide with fear. 'Mummy said he had a red car. Is there a red car outside?'

'He's not outside. There's no red car, no man. He's nowhere near you. You needn't worry about him. The police will deal with him.' This was stretching the truth a bit, which was unfortunate, as Freyja didn't want to lie to the girl. It could have an impact on any future interaction with her. No one expected them to extract a perfect witness statement from her on this visit. Hopefully they would be able to talk to her again in a well-prepared interview conducted at the Children's House. Freyja would stress the importance of this in her report. 'Hanna, did your mummy tell you what he looks like? It would help Gudlaugur arrest him if we knew.'

Hanna shook her ruffled head, then collapsed in a terrible fit of weeping. They couldn't get any more out of her, but what they had was better than nothing. Someone Bríet knew, or knew of, had been making her nervous. And it was a man.

Freyja and Gudlaugur didn't wait to be shown out or politely asked to leave. They both rose as one and thanked Lúdvík, who freed himself from his daughter's arms, leaving her lying prone on the sofa. After dropping a kiss on her head, he escorted them out.

He closed the sitting-room door once they were in the hall, then went to the front door with them and waited while they put on their shoes. 'What exactly happened? Who killed her? You must have some idea.'

'The investigation is still ongoing, so I'm afraid we can't answer that. Not at this stage.' Gudlaugur finished tying the laces of one shoe, straightened up and asked in return: 'Did Bríet or Hanna ever mention this strange man before?'

'No. Not to me. But Bríet and I only ever discussed Hanna. Bríet's quite a private person and after we separated, we didn't have much contact.' Lúdvík was still referring to his ex-wife as if she were alive, but then it always took people a while to get used to talking about the dead in the past tense. 'What happens now? Will I be kept updated? For Hanna's sake? I'll have to explain it to her one day. I can't fob her off forever by just telling her that her mother was murdered.'

Freyja shared with him all the advice she felt would help. 'You'd better start by calling the school and letting them know that Hanna's mother's dead. There's no reason why she should go in at the moment, though if she wants to, by all means let her. But bear in mind that as soon as the news breaks about what was done to Bríet's body, it will slowly filter down to the younger age group. It's vital that she hears the story from you, not from one of her classmates. But keep it from her for now; she doesn't need to know anything else at this stage. She's got more than enough to cope with as it is. And be careful that she doesn't get sucked into a downward spiral of grief. If she wants to play or go to the cinema or see people, it's important to let her. Just be incredibly kind to her, but then it looks to me as if you're already doing that.'

Lúdvík's shoulders straightened a little. 'Don't worry, I will. I'm going to ask for more time off work. As long as it takes. But if there's anything else I can do . . .'

Gudlaugur bent down and tied the laces of his other shoe, answering as he was doing so: 'We'll be in touch. You'll need to come in and give an official statement shortly, and I'm assuming we'll need to talk to Hanna too. Rest assured that her interview will be very carefully prepared, to avoid causing her any unnecessary distress.'

Freyja was wearing boots that were easy to pull on, so she didn't need to bend down and fiddle with them. She handed Lúdvík her card with her contact details. She still hadn't got used to seeing her name beside the police logo and official address. 'Call me. Any time.'

They said goodbye but Lúdvík wouldn't let them go. He kept bombarding them with questions. 'When will I get Hanna's things? I'm running out of clothes for her and they can hardly count as evidence, can they? Unless the flat's in a terrible state? Was anything stolen? Was it a burglary?'

Gudlaugur fielded the questions as well as he could but decided to call it a day when they showed no sign of letting up. Saying a very firm goodbye, he started walking towards the unmarked police car parked outside. Freyja followed, then turned and told the man to get in touch if he had any questions about Hanna's interview. Lúdvík, who was still holding her card, glanced down at it. She got into the car at that point and so couldn't guess if he was likely to take her at her word or simply chuck the card in the bin.

'Christ, I'm glad that's over.' Gudlaugur sighed heavily. 'I keep asking not to be sent to talk to the next of kin.' He started the car and pulled away. 'God.'

'You did well.' Freyja looked in the mirror and saw Lúdvík still standing in the doorway, watching their departing car. He must be dreading going back inside.

'Huh. Don't tell anyone that. It would be better if you said I was hopeless.'

Freyja just smiled.

Gudlaugur stopped the car at a red light and leant forwards to be ready to set off again the instant the lights changed. 'I reckon the strange man's our killer. I was always pretty sure it would be a man. I just can't picture a woman committing an act as brutal as that. But perhaps that's naive of me.'

The lights changed to green and Freyja left it too long while thinking of something to say, which made it hard to pick up the thread again. She focused instead on looking out of the window. There would be more than enough discussion of the case back at the police station. The whole thing would become clear in time – it had to. But that wasn't why she was annoyed with herself for failing to continue the conversation. It would have been a welcome distraction, preventing her from thinking about everything she needed to face up to in her own life.

Top of the list was her problematic relationship with Huldar, followed by worries about her brother Baldur and his daughter Saga. Her concern about those two was a constant theme in her thoughts, but she was becoming inured to her brother's nonsense. He never listened to her advice, never had done and never would, so there was little she could do about that. She had to admit, however, that he had been improving lately, behaving more responsibly and talking about getting his act together. So maybe her words had had an effect after all. But she doubted it. More likely, it had something to do with his coming to terms with being a father. Or possibly with a new girlfriend who had talked some sense into him. Whatever the reason, Freyja could only hope the change was here to stay.

Huldar was another matter, though. She was the one in charge of that situation. And the nature of the problem was different. She hadn't a clue what to do. Should she carry on as things were, as friends with benefits? Or cut all ties with him? Or keep on meeting him purely as a friend, without any kind of sexual element? Or allow the relationship to develop into something more serious, as it probably would if she let it?

She transferred her attention back to what was happening outside, watching the people waiting at the bus stop or sitting in the approaching cars or the very few who were on foot. They all had problems like her. Different ones, of course – maybe less serious, maybe more so. Freyja sighed. Like the murder case, everything would resolve itself in time. And given the present crisis, any further thoughts about the situation would have to wait.

For now, work had to take priority.

Chapter 14

The card reader bleeped. That was good news. He hadn't been sacked, then. But Rögnvaldur didn't smile. He'd opted to use the staff entrance at the back of the building to avoid having to walk past reception. Last time, when he'd come in to interrogate his colleagues, the receptionist had given him an odd look as he was leaving. It was quite different from the look she'd greeted him with when he arrived; that familiar mixture of pity, sympathy and more than a hint of relief and gratitude at not being in his situation. Which he could well understand. If their roles were reversed he would react in exactly the same way. But her changed manner when he left the building suggested that she'd heard about what had happened, very probably from the HR manager who'd had to intervene and order him to go on immediate leave. He suspected she'd asked the receptionist to warn her if he showed up again, presumably so that he could be escorted straight off the premises. He didn't like the thought of that.

Rögnvaldur tightened his grip on the cloth bag he'd brought with him and headed upstairs to the floor he wanted, then strode purposefully towards the IT department. The door was locked but his staff card let him in.

He was met by a sign announcing that the IT department was the beating heart of the company. It wasn't new and he had often paused by it, thinking how much he disagreed with the claim. To him, the IT department was more like the company's kidneys, but of course that wouldn't look as good on a sign, however accurate it was. The IT department purified the waste from the email system just as the kidneys purified the blood. They also controlled the flow of information, in the same way as the kidneys controlled the flow of blood through the veins. Occasionally, there would be a blockage in the server that had the same effect as a kidney stone, at least judging by the suffering the staff had to endure while the system was down.

In his pocket was the marker pen he'd used to create the chart on his wall at home. Taking it out, he crossed out the word 'heart' and wrote 'kidneys' above it. It didn't give him the buzz of satisfaction he'd expected.

A member of staff walked past Rögnvaldur as he stood there contemplating the new, improved version of the sign. The man gave him a brief nod, speeding up as he did so. Clearly, he had no intention of getting trapped in a conversation with Rögnvaldur. But that didn't matter because Rögnvaldur wasn't here to chat. His business was with another man in IT.

The man in question turned out to be sitting at his desk. He had three screens in front of him and was peering hard at one as he entered something on the keyboard. He was so absorbed that he didn't notice as Rögnvaldur came to stand beside him.

Rögnvaldur put his bag down on the desk. 'Hello, Jói. I need a favour.'

Jói looked up and didn't even try to hide his dismay. 'Aren't you on leave?'

'Yes. That doesn't alter the fact that I need a favour.'

'Put it in the request box. You know how it works. Use the app.' Jói withdrew his hands, leant back in his chair and clasped them behind his head. He was wearing a black T-shirt emblazoned with a picture of the supreme leader of North Korea. Kim Jong-un grinned at Rögnvaldur from beneath his Lego-figure haircut. 'I can't promise anything, though. There's a mega-upgrade in progress and I'm rushed off my feet.'

'No. That won't work.' Rögnvaldur patted the bag. 'I need you to do me a favour now. You owe me. Remember?'

The IT guy sat up again, with a shifty glance around him. And no wonder. The favour Rögnvaldur was calling in was the kind that no one would want to get around.

'What is it?'

'A laptop. My sister's laptop. She's forgotten the password and needs to get into it.'

'OK. Leave it with me and I'll take a look at it this evening. Or before the weekend, anyway.'

'No. I want to pick it up later today. My sister needs to hand in a university assignment tomorrow and the unfinished version's stuck in here.'

Jói muttered for a moment before giving in. 'I'll try. Come by again just before we close.'

Two years earlier, Rögnvaldur had hauled Jói from the cloakroom of a restaurant that had been hired for the company's Christmas party, shoved him in a taxi and sent him home. His prompt action had saved the man from being caught half-conscious, having just puked up all over the boss's overcoat. As a result, the mystery had never been solved and suspicion had fallen on gatecrashers. Jói had whispered to

Rögnvaldur on the following Monday that he could never thank him enough. Now, though, they would be quits.

'I'll be here at a quarter to. The laptop needs to be ready by then.'

Jói took it out of the bag. 'Any particular password she wants me to replace it with? Preferably something she can remember this time.'

Rögnvaldur gave him a mirthless smile. 'Yes. Scorched earth.' He felt this was suitably fitting for the situation. But his pleasure was short-lived.

'A password can't be two words. Just one word, containing at least one symbol and one number. You'll have to choose something else.'

Chapter 15

Wednesday

The woman Huldar and Lína were due to meet at the University of Iceland was running late. There was no point ringing and chasing her as she was teaching and knew they were there. Lína kept speculating about what could be keeping her: perhaps she'd been surrounded by dissatisfied students protesting about their marks; or there were exams coming up and her class wouldn't let her go; or she was trying to boost the ego of a demoralised student.

Huldar nodded every time Lína came up with a new explanation. He had nothing to contribute. He watched the students streaming past, mostly in small groups, as if the flow had curdled into lumps. The majority looked young, in their early twenties, but there were a few mature students, distinguishable from the lecturers by their backpacks. Huldar identified the members of staff by the fact they were only carrying books or papers and weren't wearing coats; obviously on their way to the staff room or office rather than about to plunge into the howling blizzard outside.

Lína was still chattering away when Huldar spotted a middle-aged woman, minus coat and backpack, heading towards them. She walked quickly and purposefully against the tide of people leaving the building, a pile of papers clutched to her chest as if they contained state secrets. She had to be the person they were waiting for.

He was right. She stopped at the office door and held out her hand. 'Hello! Sorry about the wait. I'm Ellen.'

Huldar shook her warm hand and introduced himself and Lína.

'Come in.' Ellen put down her lecture notes and performed a quick tidy-up. The visitors' chairs were hardly visible under piles of books and papers, and her desk and shelves were similarly overflowing. In the end, she gave up trying to find a free surface and dumped her things in two piles on the floor, then sat down behind her desk and twisted her shoulder-length hair into a bun, fixing it with an elastic band. 'Take a seat.'

The smell of dusty books reminded Huldar of libraries when he was a boy. If he'd made more of an effort to read something other than Donald Duck and Tintin comics, he might have ended up here. But the thought didn't spark any regrets: he'd found his niche and he was content with it.

He and Lína sat down. The office was on the small side and once he was seated, his knees pressed against the desk, whereas the short-legged Lína had plenty of room. He began by getting the social niceties out of the way, so they could get down to business. 'Thanks for agreeing to see us at such short notice.'

'No problem. It's not every day I have a visit from the police.' Ellen adjusted her monitor to be able to see them properly. 'The woman who called wouldn't tell me what it was about, so I have to admit I'm curious.' She looked at Lína. 'Was it you I talked to?'

Lína's gaze had been wandering along the bookshelves, but now she snapped her attention back to the woman. 'No, that was my manager, Erla.'

'I'm afraid our visit is connected to some very sad news that we must ask you to keep to yourself for the moment.' Huldar laid a photo of Bríet on the desk. 'I assume you recognise this woman?'

Ellen drew the picture over and raised it to her face. 'Yes, that's a student of mine – Bríet Hannesdóttir. I'm supervising the Master's dissertation she's working on with Andrea Logadóttir. It's worth sixty credits, so we have more contact than usual.'

'How do you mean?'

'A big project like that involves independent research rather than simply a review of the available literature, as is the case with a thirty-credit dissertation. And, as it's a joint effort, a proper methodology is essential.' She put down the photo. 'I find it hard to believe that Bríet would do anything to break the law. And the same applies to Andrea. They're both very nice, very conscientious women.'

'Bríet isn't suspected of any wrongdoing.' Huldar took a quick breath before giving her the news. 'I'm afraid she was found dead on Monday, believed murdered.'

Her supervisor didn't move for a moment, then said, in a stunned voice: 'Murdered? You mean Bríet's the woman in the news?'

Huldar nodded. 'Her body was discovered on Monday but she's believed to have died on Friday.'

'Wait, what? Why?'

Even if Huldar had known the answer to that, he wouldn't have been at liberty to tell her. 'I'm sorry, we can't divulge any information about the investigation.'

'But what are you doing here? You don't think I or the university have anything to do with this?'

Nothing of the sort had crossed Huldar's mind. 'No, we're simply talking to all the people Bríet was in contact with. When did you last see or speak to her?'

'Me?' Ellen seemed flustered, but this didn't necessarily mean she had something to hide. The news must have come as a shock and it would take her a moment to recover enough to think back and give the correct answer.

'We're in no hurry. Take all the time you need to remember.' Lína's voice was calm and sounded deceptively mature for her age.

Ellen was silent while she gathered her thoughts. When she spoke again she'd recovered some of her composure. 'I last saw them both a week ago. We have regular supervisions on Wednesdays to discuss their progress. They behaved no differently from usual.'

'What time's the supervision?' Huldar checked his watch. 'Is it supposed to be later this afternoon?'

'No. It's at eleven in the morning. But they both asked to be excused today.' Noticing their interest, Ellen immediately put a damper on it. 'Andrea was going abroad on holiday and planning to be away all week, so they asked if they could postpone this week's meeting.'

'Do you have Andrea's phone number and email address? We need to talk to her but so far we haven't had any luck getting hold of her.' Her name had been on Huldar's list of people to call but she was one of the few he hadn't succeeded in reaching yet.

The woman turned to her computer. After a brief search, she read out the details the university had for Andrea.

Huldar noted them down, then looked up the details he'd been given earlier. 'I think that's the number we already have.

Do you have any idea where she was going? Outside Europe, maybe?'

'No. If she told me, it must have gone in one ear and out the other. She's into yoga and the trip had something to do with that. I'm pretty sure she said she'd be away for a week and that her flight was last weekend. But I don't think she mentioned whether it was on Saturday or Sunday. It could have been on the Friday, for all I know.'

Huldar nodded. He guessed Andrea had gone somewhere outside Europe and didn't want to run up huge roaming fees by using her phone. She should be able to check her emails, though, assuming there was wi-fi at her hotel. 'What's their dissertation about? Anything controversial?'

'Controversial?' Ellen shook her head. 'I wouldn't say that. Important, though. Do you know what public health involves?'

Lína nodded gravely and Huldar said he had a pretty good idea.

Ellen launched into teaching mode. 'It's a field concerned with everything that affects people's health, including prevention and other measures to promote good health in the population. Bríet and Andrea were studying the immunisation of primary-school children, using a database provided by the Directorate of Health, to find out for example whether Iceland's herd immunity could be jeopardised by parents refusing to have their children vaccinated. And also to analyse the reasons informing people's decision not to vaccinate, and the general wellbeing of the children involved.'

'Idiots.'

Huldar thought Lína must have blurted this out inadvertently, but to his surprise she didn't turn red or show any other sign of regretting her reaction.

Ellen didn't seem at all disconcerted. 'Yes, in the case of some parents. But not all of them. Occasionally children can't be vaccinated for valid reasons, such as when they have a weakened immune system. But people who believe they're saving their kids from mercury poisoning or autism are doing them no favours – especially not the children who have pre-existing conditions which mean they can't be vaccinated. The anti-vaxxers seem to be mainly worried about the combined eighteen-month MMR vaccination against measles, mumps and rubella. Bríet and Andrea are—she corrected herself – '*were* analysing the trend over a ten-year period in connection with that specific vaccination. In other words, is the proportion of eighteen-month-olds who are not receiving the vaccination increasing or is the misconception about the effects of childhood immunisation on the wane?' Ellen shook her head dispiritedly. 'I don't know what will happen to the study now that Andrea's on her own. It's far too much for one person to cover.'

Huldar had no doubt that this would make life difficult for Ellen and Andrea, but he had rather more serious matters on his mind. 'Did they talk to any of the parents? To any of the anti-vaxxers, I mean?'

'Yes, they did, via email or occasionally over the phone. They didn't meet any of the participants, or only in exceptional circumstances. But you mustn't get the idea that they were on some sort of crusade to change the parents' minds. They were simply recording the reasons for their decision – when the individuals in question were willing to participate in the study. They also sent out questionnaires about the children's general health and medical histories. They never spoke to or met any of the children involved. And their questions

were entirely factual and in no way controversial. The participants were under no obligation to answer them, either.'

'So she didn't have run-ins with any of them? Or with
anyone else at the university – like other students or even
teachers?' It was becoming clear to Huldar that they weren't
going to gain much from this visit apart from Andrea's email
address. Still, at least they could tick the interview off their list
and turn to the next task awaiting them.

'I can assure you she didn't have run-ins with any of her
teachers. And I'm not aware of any friction with the other
students. She mostly just worked with Andrea – they were a
bit older than the others on their course. I wouldn't have said
they had any difficulties with the parents they talked to either,
although they did mention that things got a little heated on
occasion, usually because the parents who didn't want their
children vaccinated were very keen to convert them to their
way of thinking. And obviously that wasn't going to happen. Apparently some of them took it badly when Bríet and
Andrea weren't interested in hearing about the imaginary science behind their anti-vax theories.'

'Who were they? Do you have their names?'

Ellen was silent for a moment. 'I didn't mean in a way that
could possibly have led to murder. Far from it.'

Huldar ignored this, merely repeating: 'Do you have their
names?'

Ellen folded her arms across her chest. 'I'm afraid I can't
release any information from this database. We were only
granted access to it under very strict conditions. It's impossible
for me to reveal the names of any of the children or parents.
And there's no way any of these people could be connected
to the murder. It's just not that kind of study. I mean, there

are no interests at stake. No one's going to tear these children away from their parents and drag them off to be vaccinated—' She broke off, seeming to change her mind. 'Actually, now I come to think of it, there was one incident. Andrea had a very uncomfortable meeting with the father of a child who'd died of measles. He approached her, so his name's not on the database. He didn't attack her or anything like that, but I could see how shaken she was when she described their encounter. I can try to track down his name without contravening any privacy laws.'

'Yes please,' Lína and Huldar said simultaneously. Anything was better than nothing.

Ellen rooted around in the papers on her desk. 'I know it's here somewhere.'

While she was searching, Huldar turned to the next question. 'Bríet's laptop is missing. Does she have a locker or office here at the university where she could have left it?'

Ellen looked up from the mess of papers. 'No. Only a workspace shared with lots of other students. She wouldn't have left it there except by mistake.' She carried on turning over papers.

Judging by the chaos in her office, the search could take ages and might not turn up any results, so Huldar ploughed on with his questions to make use of the time. 'Could there have been any material on the computer that someone else might have wanted to get hold of?'

Ellen straightened up triumphantly. 'Here it is!' She was holding a handwritten page of notes. 'Funny you should ask about her laptop. Both Andrea and Bríet have copies of the database on their computers and this man was demanding access to it.'

'To the database of vaccinations?' Huldar tried to imagine what possible use it could be but nothing sprang to mind.

'Yes. He wanted to find the person who'd infected his daughter. As I said, she died of measles.' Ellen handed Huldar the page of notes. 'His name's there, at the bottom: Rögn-valdur. Rögnvaldur Tryggvason.'

Huldar tossed Lína the keys and asked her to drive. As soon as they were in the car and he'd done up his belt, he rang Erla. Far from welcoming his call, she demanded to know what was so urgent that it couldn't wait until he was back at the station.

'I'm up to my ears, Huldar. The call log has come in and the CCTV footage is piling up. If I don't keep an eagle eye on this lot, they'll get it all out of order. No one'll have a clue which footage comes from which camera.'

This was grossly unfair, but Huldar didn't comment. When Erla was stressed, she tended to take an unduly pessimistic view of things. Not that it was any different when she was in a good mood. 'We've got the name of some weirdo who was hassling Bríet's supervision partner. He could well have been hassling Bríet too.'

'What's his name?'

'Rögnvaldur.' Huldar glanced down at the yellow Post-it note the supervisor had given him. 'Tryggvason.'

There was a pause, then Erla barked: 'Get your arses back here *now*.'

Chapter 16

Wednesday

Molly sniffed eagerly at the lamppost she herself had weed on at the beginning of their walk. Before becoming a surrogate parent to Molly, Freyja had been under the impression that dogs urinated to scent-mark their territory. But if Molly was anything to go by, they hadn't the faintest clue about who had urinated where.

Her brother Baldur had received an unexpected request to take over a tour group in the north of Iceland, after they'd fallen out with their guide. Apparently fed up with their endless demands, the man had stormed off the bus in the middle of nowhere and walked almost two hours to get to Akureyri Airport. There he had handed in his notice by text message and boarded the next flight to Reykjavík. As a result, Baldur had been given the job at extremely short notice, but luckily Freyja was at a loose end when he'd rung her in a panic. Judging by the way people were leaping into action around her, there had been a major development in the investigation, but so far no one had bothered to tell her what it was.

Baldur had asked if she could look after Saga and Molly, and, as usual, she'd unhesitatingly said yes. Though how she was supposed to babysit Saga in the middle of a murder inquiry was something she'd just have to play by ear. In the worst-case scenario, she would only be able to work during nursery-school hours. She'd just have to roll up her sleeves, forget about coffee breaks and go into overdrive. Anyway, some jobs could be done perfectly well from home. To be on the safe side, she would ring round her friends this evening to see if she could fall back on them in an emergency. Since she'd helped them out from time to time, there should be no difficulty about asking them to return the favour.

Molly had evidently sniffed to her satisfaction. She peed a few drops beside the lamppost, then carried on walking. After all that hanging about, she was now in a tearing hurry and immediately began pulling hard on the lead. The dog reminded Freyja of one of her friends who always took forever to get ready but, the moment she had her coat on, would start chivvying everyone else around her as if the place were on fire.

Saga was the polar opposite: she would not be hurried. Since she refused to sit in her buggy these days and insisted on walking, Freyja had to lead her by the hand as she dawdled along the badly ploughed pavement in her little snow boots. Like Molly, she was forever stopping, but never in the same place as the dog. As a result, they proceeded by fits and starts, and Freyja's arms were almost pulled out of their sockets as she was repeatedly dragged in different directions.

She was standing like this, torn between the two, when her phone started ringing in the pocket of her coat. In order to answer, she had to trap Saga between her legs, clamp the phone between ear and shoulder, then reach down again for the little hand in its woolly mitten, before she could continue walking.

It was Erla. Freyja stopped dead in astonishment and almost went flying when Molly jerked her lead.

'Where are you?' Erla wasted no time on small talk. But then, if she had picked up the phone to call Freyja, it must be serious. Freyja hoped she wasn't going to get a tongue-lashing for skipping off work early, or, even worse, be kicked off the investigation.

There was nothing for it but to tell the truth. 'I'm at home. Out walking the dog.'

'Turn round.'

Freyja smiled. 'I'm looking at my building. Do you want me to turn back and do another lap?'

Erla ignored this. 'You need to get straight back to work.'

'That could be tricky.' Freyja had assumed she would at least have this evening to activate her emergency plan of asking her friends for help. 'I'm looking after Saga—'

Erla cut her short. 'Leave her at home. Dog-sitting is no excuse. I need you here now.'

'Saga's not a dog, she's a child. My niece.'

Erla groaned so loudly that Molly turned her head to see what was going on. 'How old is she?'

'She's nearly three.' Freyja smiled at Saga, who had heard this and was looking up. The little girl held out one small hand, wiggling her fingers in her mitten, hopefully to show three fingers rather than one or two. She was always being reminded about her birthday in the hope that this would teach her to say her age, at least with her fingers. Freyja and her other family members had long since abandoned any false hopes about the child's ability to express herself.

There was silence at the other end while Erla was thinking. 'Bring her along. She's too young to understand. Lína or someone can look after her.'

Freyja began to suspect the worst. 'Have you found the head?' She shuddered. 'You do realise it's totally inappropriate to subject a three-year-old child to something like that? Even if it's only to talk about it?'

'It's not about the head. You'll be told everything you need to know when you get here.'

This was the first time Erla had personally requested Freyja's presence. It didn't sound as if she'd been bullied into calling by a senior manager either, which meant it must be serious and therefore impossible to refuse. 'I'll be there in fifteen minutes.'

No 'Thanks' or 'See you in a bit'. Just silence. Erla had hung up.

Saga surveyed the office, immediately spotted Huldar and tore herself loose from Freyja. She ran over as fast as her clumsy little boots would allow, calling out his name in her own unique manner, dropping the H and R, as if she were French: '*Ulda!*' Freyja was privately grateful that Saga couldn't talk properly. Baldur would not be best pleased to hear that his daughter had not only visited the enemy camp but been delighted with the experience.

Erla was watching Saga from her office doorway. 'Huldar seems to have worked his charm on the kid. She's obviously no judge of character.'

Freyja ignored this. Her gaze had been fixed on Huldar as he bent down to pick up her little niece. She could see his thigh muscles tense against his trouser legs and her mind immediately jumped in a direction that had nothing to do with murder or missing heads. Feeling her cheeks begin to flush, she turned smartly back to Erla, as the sight of her was bound to cool her down. 'Right, I'm here. What do you want me to do?'

Erla was still watching Saga as she filled Freyja in. She looked distinctly unimpressed with the little girl. 'We're going to arrest a man who's almost certainly our killer and bring him in for questioning. We're pretty sure he's the strange, bad man Bríet warned her daughter about. At least, he has a red Toyota registered to his name and he's one of the people who rang Bríet the day she died, according to the call log from her phone that we got hold of today. Gudlaugur spotted the car on CCTV driving into Salahverfi at around 6 p.m. and leaving again around 7.30 p.m., which is the likely time frame for Bríet's death. The man threatened her dissertation partner, Andrea, as well, so it sounds as if he's the guy we're after. But he's not answering his phone and hasn't responded to messages ordering him to come in for interview. We need you there since the guy's almost certainly nuts. The arrest and the aftermath need to be a hundred per cent by the book.'

Freyja merely nodded. 'Where is he?'

Erla finally dragged her gaze away from Saga and back to Freyja. 'That's the question. We called him at work and were told he was on leave. His wife says he's not at home but his mobile is in their flat, according to Forensics, so we're going to try there. She's probably shielding him. When I spoke to her on the phone, she sounded very odd. I got the impression she was . . . I don't know . . . out of it.'

'Out of it?' Freyja queried. 'Do you mean she was on drugs or that she's got psychiatric problems?'

'Both, either, doesn't matter. We've scraped together some background on the couple and it seems they recently lost their only child. That's bound to affect people badly, but, even so, murder would be an excessive reaction. The guy must already have been unbalanced.' Erla turned away to watch Huldar scoop Saga up and sit her on his lap at his desk. When she looked back at Freyja, her weary face was inscrutable. 'Their daughter died of measles and Bríet's dissertation was about vaccinations. That has to be the link, because they didn't know each other before, as far as we can tell. What motive the guy had for murdering Bríet is a mystery, though. We'll have to prise it out of him.'

'What's the plan? Should I stay outside in the car or come to the door with you? I'm just thinking about Saga. What am I supposed to do with her in the meantime? I can hardly take her with me.'

'Oh, shit.' Erla pressed both hands to the small of her back. 'I was going to ask Lína to look after the kid, but . . .'

They were both looking in Huldar's direction. Lína had gone over, no doubt to ask disapprovingly who the child was. Saga's reaction was to scowl and stick out her tongue, then grab an eraser from the desk and try to hurl it at Lína. But since she still had her mittens on, it dropped harmlessly to the floor.

Freyja shook her head. As Saga was unlikely to change her mind about Lína, it would be a disaster to have them both in the back seat of the car. 'Huldar's the better option.'

Erla glanced at the clock. 'He'll have to take her some-where. She can't stay here.'

'The bus. He can take her for a ride on the bus. It's her favourite treat.' Freyja could tell from Erla's expression that she didn't think much of Saga's taste in entertainment. There was no point trying to explain that for Saga the chief attraction lay in sitting there, passing judgement on the other passengers.

At least, this was the conclusion Freyja had come to after taking her niece on countless bus trips to keep her amused.

'Huldar!' Erla bellowed across the open-plan office. 'Get your coat on. You're going for a bus ride and you're taking that brat with you!'

Freyja saw Saga close her eyes with pleasure when she heard the word 'bus'. With her, this counted as a smile. Then she opened them again and directed a glare at Erla, conveying the message that, like the unfortunate bus passengers who crossed her path, Erla had been judged and found wanting.

The SWAT team went ahead in two cars and Freyja followed in her own. If she'd had any idea it was going to be used for a police operation, she would have cleaned it. Both inside and out. Well, she'd have considered it, at least.

The police cars drew up in front of a block of flats in Háaleiti. Fortunately, there were enough free spaces for them all to park, though not together. Freyja chose a space as far from the building as possible, in the shelter of a van. Although Erla had assured her they had no reason to believe there were any firearms in the flat, so there shouldn't be any danger outside, Freyja thought it better to be safe than sorry. She didn't like the idea of getting bullet holes in her little car. Only a rapper would think that was a cool look.

As the police officers emerged, the slamming of car doors drowned out the low drone of traffic from Miklabraut.

They gathered by the entrance. Apart from Erla, most had their faces hidden. The SWAT team wore grey helmets and balaclavas, which left only their eyes visible. When Freyja joined the silent group, she felt as if she were walking into a computer game. No one greeted her and she kept quiet, not wanting to disturb the concentration they must need for their job. She felt a wave of fear wash over her as she stood there among a group of people preparing for combat with a possible armed suspect – a man who had nothing to lose. She would be worse than useless in that situation. Psychology was best practised in peace and quiet. Any attempt by her to reason with the suspect in the middle of a struggle would be futile.

They entered the lobby and Erla raised her finger to the bell labelled with the names of Rögnvaldur and his wife Aldís. Glancing over her shoulder, she warned the SWAT team to be alert and ready for anything, then told Freyja to keep back at a safe distance and not to interfere unless asked. Freyja nodded. This was one order she would have no trouble obeying. Although she and Erla weren't exactly friends, Freyja hoped she would take her own advice. A woman on the point of giving birth had no more place in an armed encounter than a psychologist did. But she didn't say anything. Erla was no fool and must have given thought to her own and her unborn child's safety.

Erla pressed the bell and they waited in a huddled mass for an answer. Nothing happened. She pressed it again and this time, after a brief pause, they heard a woman's husky voice over the tinny little loudspeaker.

'Hello.'

'Hello, Aldís. This is the police. We need to speak to Rögnvaldur. I rang earlier. Could you let us in?'

'He's not home.'

'Could you let us in anyway?'

'No.' The woman hung up.

Erla tried again and got the same response. A flat refusal, then the entryphone went dead. She pressed the bell twice more but got no answer at all. In the event, though, there was no need to break down the door, because just then a young woman came out of the building and they seized the opportunity to pile inside. The woman was left standing there, gaping in astonishment, but then a lobby full of special-squad officers wasn't an everyday occurrence.

Once they had climbed to the right floor, Freyja hung back at a safe distance, while the others took up position by the door, the SWAT team on one side, Erla on the other. She held her finger on the bell for a long time. No one answered. She repeated the action, shouting to Aldís to open up. When nothing happened, Erla called that they were from the police and had a search warrant; they were coming in whether Aldís opened up or not. She made one more attempt to get the woman to see sense, then signalled to the SWAT team to break down the door. At that moment they heard the lock click.

The door still didn't open. Erla reached out and tried the handle. At that, the door opened a crack and the police officer who was nearest pushed it wider. They waited without moving for a moment or two, backs pressed to the wall. Freyja assumed this was in case Aldís or Rögnvaldur came storming out, brandishing a knife or worse. But nothing of the sort happened.

Erla announced that they were coming in and ordered the couple to kneel down and put their hands behind their heads. It seemed unlikely the woman would adopt this position, though, judging by the trouble they'd had in getting her to obey orders so far.

One by one the SWAT team passed noiselessly inside until Erla and Freyja were the only ones left in the corridor. They heard doors being flung open and repeated orders to kneel down, this time issued in a deafening shout – so deafening that Freyja only just stopped herself from instinctively dropping to her knees. While all this was going on, she watched Erla, marvelling at her stony expression. She might as well have been queuing for the till at the supermarket.

One of the officers appeared at the door. 'You're safe. We've cuffed her. The man's not here but his phone is.'

Erla couldn't hide her frustration. The whole purpose of the operation had been to arrest Rögnvaldur. With a jerk of the chin, she signalled to Freyja to follow her and they stepped inside, into the home of the man who was suspected of having murdered a woman and chopped up her corpse. From the little Freyja knew about Rögnvaldur, he didn't appear to fit into any of the categories she had thought the perpetrator might belong to. According to Erla, he wasn't a hunter and, given that he worked for an insurance company, he presumably wasn't used to cutting up large animals or people as part of his job. They still had to examine his life in more detail, though, so it might emerge that he had worked at an abattoir in his youth. If not, Freyja was pretty sure he must be either a psychopath or suffering from acute psychosis.

As she entered the flat behind Erla, everything she saw led her to believe the latter. All the curtains were tightly drawn, and the flat was dark and airless. Freyja carefully observed every detail of the interior to form a picture of the people who lived there. It reminded her inescapably of the photos she'd seen of abandoned homes in Chernobyl. All that was missing was the vegetation that had forced its way through the walls. Everyday life in ruins.

Every surface was covered in dust. Unopened post and rubbish lay strewn all over the floor. Through the door to the kitchen she spotted plates of half-finished food and glasses of curdled milk. But it wasn't hard to imagine how the flat had looked when it was still being regularly cleaned, the lights were on and the curtains pulled back. Before disaster had struck.

Most bizarre of all was the sitting room. It had been turned upside down, the furniture shoved aside, paintings and pictures on the floor, along with the fragments of a smashed vase or bowl. Pens and papers were scattered everywhere, as if they had been thrown up in the air and left lying where they fell. There was an empty pill blister pack on the sofa, labelled with the brand name of a common stimulant, suggesting that either the husband, or the wife, or both were on it. If they were taking more than the doctor recommended, it didn't bode well.

The longest wall in the sitting room had been commandeered to make a homemade mural or collage of paper, with information scrawled all over it. Freyja managed to snap it quickly with her phone before Erla called her into the bedroom.

There was the wife, Aldís, on her knees. She didn't have her hands on her head as they had been cuffed behind her back. She was wearing a white T-shirt and pyjama trousers that clearly hadn't been near a washing machine in a long time. Her hair hung in a greasy tangle to her shoulders.

As there was a special squad officer standing either side of Aldís and a third just behind, Freyja assumed it was safe to crouch down beside her. She would have no chance of making contact with the broken woman if she was towering over her as if in judgement.

'Aldís.' Freyja tilted her head in an attempt to meet the woman's eye, but Aldís turned away. 'They're going to take you to the police station. It would be best if you didn't resist. Do you understand?'

Aldís stared straight ahead at the bedroom wardrobe. She gave no sign that Freyja's words had filtered through.

'If you resist, there's a risk you'll get hurt. We don't want that.'

Aldís just kept staring at the fitted wardrobe that occupied the wall behind Freyja. All the compartments had been opened, presumably in search of her husband, and perhaps of Bríet's missing head too. The woman seemed dazed. For all Freyja knew, this could be a normal reaction to the police bursting into one's home; equally, it could be the effect of medication or severe depression.

Erla had come to stand beside the officer who was behind the cuffed woman. She pointed at Aldís's head and started mouthing at Freyja. It took Freyja a while to grasp that Erla was telling her to ask about Rögnvaldur, but then she was no lip-reader.

'This is very important, Aldís. Where is Rögnvaldur?'

Aldís's eyes moved from the wardrobe to meet Freyja's. 'I don't know. So could you all just go away?'

'Is he somewhere in the building?'

'I don't know.'

'Have you got a garage?'

Aldís shook her head.

'It would be better for him and everyone else if we could find him as soon as possible. If you know where he is, please tell us now.'

'I don't know where he is. So you can let me go. I don't know anything. He was here this morning but now he's gone.'

All the questions Erla mouthed to Freyja received the same answer. *What time did he leave? Did he take your car? Did he take something with him? Where does he usually go? Does he have another phone? Does he have money or a card on him?*

'I don't know.'

The only question that received a definite answer was when, at Erla's urging, Freyja asked about firearms.

'Does your husband have access to a gun?'

'No.' Aldís didn't seem remotely surprised by the question. If she was on sedatives, that might explain it. That might also explain why she hadn't asked what was going on. Freyja tried asking a question of her own.

'Do you understand why we're looking for Rögnvaldur?'

Aldís didn't drop her gaze. Her voice was toneless, her face blank and devoid of emotion when she answered flatly: 'Yes. Murder. Rögnvaldur's killed someone.'

After that she said no more. Freyja was left with the feeling that she should have tried harder or used a different approach. She had a hunch that the woman knew something, something she needed to get off her chest but couldn't. What this might be was anyone's guess, but intuition told Freyja that Aldís was withholding some devastating secret.

Chapter 17

Thursday

Outside it was as fine a winter's day as you could ask for: perfectly still, the sky cloudless and everything covered in a pristine layer of snow. As soon as the sun crawled a little higher it would be the ideal day to go skiing. It was sod's law that the good weather had fallen on a weekday. The forecast for the weekend was a cocktail of strong winds, blizzards and general misery. Not that this would make the slightest difference to Huldar since he would be stuck at work. The investigation was still in full swing, even though they believed they had tracked down the killer. In theory. In practice, the man was still out there.

Huldar leant against the wall in the yard behind the police station and pulled a cigarette from his pocket. He lit it, took a drag, then blew out a thick stream of smoke that formed great billowing clouds in the frosty air. He might as well savour the moment since another busy day lay ahead. A day that would be spent in interview rooms, meeting rooms, on the phone or in front of the computer. Not exactly an enticing prospect in glorious weather like this. He felt a flicker of envy for the ordinary uniformed officers on the beat.

The door to the yard opened. Huldar quickly checked to see who it was, praying it wasn't one of the anti-smoking evangelists, of whom there were far too many in the building. It wasn't: it was Erla. She didn't like smoke either but she had long ago given up nagging Huldar about it, realising that she might as well have a go at the sea for making waves.

She didn't notice him at first, just stood there with her eyes closed and her face raised to the sun. Then she put her hands to the small of her back and arched it, causing her bump to jut out so far that Huldar had a sudden horrible fear the skin might split and the baby pop out. Then she relaxed again and the bump returned to its normal dimensions.

'Get a good lungful. You're going to be breathing nothing but stale office air for the rest of the day.' Huldar slapped the wall beside him. 'This spot's free.'

Erla came over and propped herself beside him, gasping down the fresh winter air as if she had just surfaced from a dive. 'Where the hell is Rögnvaldur?'

Huldar could have done without talking shop, even if only for the five remaining minutes of his break. But the investigation was weighing heavily on everyone, Erla most of all. 'He'll turn up. It's only a matter of time. Can't you get any sense out of his wife?'

'No. Fuck all. I can't work out if she's pretending or telling the truth. The only thing we've got out of her is that she thinks Rögnvaldur's killed someone. But she doesn't know who, where or when. All she wants is to go home.' Erla tutted. 'Don't we all?'

Huldar ground out his cigarette on the tarmac to avoid getting smoke in Erla's face. 'She could be telling the truth. Maybe she doesn't know anything. I gather she hasn't left the house for weeks, if not months. She's just been lying there, doped up on prescription drugs.'

'Yes. So it appears. Apparently she had a difficult night – puking her guts up and so on from withdrawal symptoms.' Erla inflated her lungs again and held the air down as long as she could. 'The good news is that there was blood on the pair of shoes we found while searching their flat. The same blood type as Bríet's. The fingerprints we lifted from his flat also match several found at Bríet's place, including on her garden door. His car shows up on CCTV in her neighbourhood on Friday and the time fits with when she died. Plus there's the fact he kept ringing Bríet and sending her messages in the days leading up to her murder, which shows he was after her. He's our man, all right.'

Huldar agreed. 'Any news of the DNA results?'

Erla was still doing her breathing exercises and it was a moment or two before she answered. 'Apparently we can expect something tomorrow. It's a bugger that there'll be another delay after we've caught Rögnvaldur and taken swabs from him for comparison. Not that I think the DNA test will be key. He's guilty. The analysis of the vomit will be just one of many pieces of evidence in our case against him. It's a pity his motive is so obscure. But who knows? Maybe he'll be able to explain the whole thing when we catch him.'

Huldar tore the plastic off his cigarette packet and wrapped the butt in it. 'No. He'll never be able to explain or make us understand why he did it. Nothing could explain something that sick.' He shoved the butt and packet in his pocket. 'If the wall art in his sitting room is anything to go by, he's obsessed with finding out who infected his daughter. Which is pretty fucked up but at least it's understandable. Whereas killing Bríet, who had absolutely nothing to do with it, makes no sense at all. You can't seriously blame a university student, who's doing a study of vaccinations, for the fact that someone didn't choose to give their kid the measles jab. I mean, what was she supposed to do about it? I just hope he gets a bloody long sentence.'

'Then you'd better start by finding the guy for me. He can't be locked up until we've arrested him.' Erla filled her lungs again, then slowly released the air. She put her hands on her hips and made a face. Huldar guessed she was experiencing a pregnancy-related twinge but decided it was wiser not to comment. One of his sisters had come to Reykjavík to give birth and had stayed with him for the last two weeks of her pregnancy. Once, when she was pacing round the room, beside herself with pain, with a bag of ice cubes pressed to her back, he had suggested she lie down and try to empty her head, since pain was largely in the mind. His reward had been a stream of curses and he'd only just managed to duck when the bag of ice cubes came flying in his direction. So he thought it was better to keep his mouth shut and just hope that the pains weren't the onset of Erla's contractions.

'We'll find him. He's just an ordinary guy. No one's going to hide him from the police. A wanted notice has been circulated to the media and people will be on the lookout. Trust me, he'll turn up before the end of the day.'

'Yeah, right,' Erla said sceptically. 'The public's already ringing in with tip-offs, most of them complete fucking bullshit, not to mention the reporters who won't get off my fucking back for a minute. I don't know how we're expected to man the phones. Do you know how many calls I get a day?'

As if on cue, her phone started ringing and she muttered that it was bloody typical. But she'd only exchanged a few words with the person at the other end before her manner was transformed. By the time she hung up, the weary pessimism had vanished, to be replaced by triumphant excitement, though she still managed to swear. 'Come on. The fucking head's turned up.'

Huldar was behind the wheel. He'd grabbed the keys before Erla got a chance, afraid she might drive recklessly in her excitement and do herself an injury. If the seat-belt locked, her bump was bound to get in the way.

He slowed down as they entered the small road leading out to Grótta, the nature reserve on the tip of the peninsula at the west end of the city. The area was popular with the public for walks along the beach and out to the tidal island with its lighthouse. At the end of the short road was a car park and, as it was empty, Huldar had a choice of any spot he wanted. There was a spectacular view north over Faxaflói Bay to the mountains and headlands of the west coast, revealed in all their glory by the brilliantly sunny weather.

He had hardly come to a stop before Erla jumped out. While Huldar was parking, she gestured at him impatiently to hurry up. The instant he got out and joined her, she was off, moving so fast that she slipped in the snow and only his quick action saved her from falling. 'Be careful, Erla. There are some big rocks up ahead.'

Reluctantly, she slowed her pace and together they crossed the expanse of snow between the car park and the path that ran along the top of the beach. The couple who had found the head were sitting on a bench. Even if there had been other people around, it would have been easy to pick them out as they looked exactly how you would expect someone to look if they had just found a severed head in a plastic bag. The young woman was bent forward over her knees as if to stop herself from fainting. The young man beside her on the bench was sitting upright with his head craned back. Only the mongrel at their feet seemed oblivious to the fuss. It was the first to notice Huldar and Erla and its whole body began squirming in eager anticipation. The lead jerked, causing the young woman to look up. When she saw them, she nudged her companion and they both rose to their feet.

'Oh my God, I thought you'd never get here.' The young woman introduced herself as Dröfn. 'It's no joke waiting with that *thing* just over there.' She glanced at her phone. 'And Aggi's going to be late for work. Can we go now? We don't want to hang around here a minute longer.' She sounded close to tears.

'Thanks for waiting for us.' Erla didn't waste any time shaking their hands or offering them trauma counselling. Neither she nor Huldar were particularly adept in that department. 'You're not going anywhere, I'm afraid.'

'But I have to.' The young man buried his bare hands in his coat pockets. 'I've got to go to work. I can't be late.'

'Where do you work?' Erla had taken out her phone.

The young man named a restaurant in the centre of town. 'I usually work after my classes but I've got the day off uni today so I promised to take a shift. And I just can't afford to lose this job.'

Huldar's gaze fell on the expensive designer bag Aggi was carrying over his shoulder. He wouldn't be surprised if the young man had taken out a loan to buy it and was now grafting alongside his studies to pay it back. Young guys with bags like that were becoming an ever more common sight. It was a mystery to Huldar how anyone could walk into a consumer trap like that with their eyes open. It used to be mainly women who fell for that kind of nonsense. The owners of the big fashion houses must be rubbing their hands with glee over the influence exerted by all those spoilt, consumer-mad rappers abroad.

He had to remind himself that he and Erla weren't here to teach these kids any life lessons. Unfortunately, they were here about a severed head – something that was unlikely to become a fashion accessory any time soon.

Erla had found the number of the restaurant. She called it. 'Aggi . . .' She turned to the young man. 'What's your full name?'

'Agnar, Agnar Grétarsson.'

Erla turned back to the phone. 'Yes, Aggi – Agnar Grétarsson – won't be able to come in on time today. He'll be late. Very late. In fact he may not make it at all.' She was silent and they could hear the faint echo of a voice at the other end. 'Yes. Well, anyway, Agnar can't come in, so you'll just have to make other arrangements. And no, I can't provide him with a note. I'm from the police and that's not our job.'

Agnar opened his mouth indignantly, and Huldar noticed Dröfn squeeze his upper arm, as if she feared he might go for Erla. But he could be mistaken. Maybe she just wanted to commiserate with him because now he'd lose his job and might have to sell his bag. They both visibly relaxed when Erla added that he wasn't suspected of any wrongdoing; he was just a witness.

'Right, so you've got the day off.' Erla turned back to the young man. 'Which school do you go to?'

'I'm at the University of Iceland. In my third year of business studies.'

'What about you? Have you got the day off as well?'

The young woman nodded. 'Yes. I'm at uni too. Doing law.'

'Should you be at work as well?'

'No. I was going to study today. Though there's no way I'll be able to now.'

Erla nodded. She got out her notebook and jotted down the information, then took the young woman's full name and both their phone numbers. While she was doing this, Huldar contemplated the bare bars of the old wooden fish-drying racks that stood beside the path, relics of the past, only there for decoration these days.

Erla looked up. 'Where's the bag?'

The young couple pointed towards the beach. It was separated from the coastal path by a strip of grass, which sloped down gently from the car park but grew gradually steeper to the south, where a retaining wall of rocks and small boulders had been raised along the shoreline to prevent erosion. It was to this area that the couple pointed. While Agnar was zipping his coat up to the neck and shivering, Dröfn described the spot. 'It's, like, a black bin bag. It was caught between the rocks in the sea wall. You can't miss it. We pulled it out because Tína refused to move away from it. She kept scratching at this one spot, so we went over to see what it was. I wish we hadn't bothered. I wish someone else had found it.' It was her turn to shiver. 'We'd never have gone for such a long walk if the weather hadn't been so nice.'

Erla caught Huldar's eye. 'Check it out.'

He set off at once, overcoming his reluctance. Although he couldn't think of anything he wanted to do less, protesting was out of the question. Best treat it like a plaster: rip it off without stopping to think. However gruesome it was, at least he wouldn't have to hang around long. They were expecting back-up to guard the crime scene and Forensics would follow just as soon as they'd got their gear together. After that, there would be no further need for him.

Once he had located the bag, he clambered along the line of rocks that made up the sea defences, taking care to stay well above the black plastic. If a person had jammed the bag between the rocks, they must have done so from below, from the beach, which meant Huldar wouldn't be destroying any evidence as long as he stayed above it. Though if the head had been there since Friday or Saturday, he reflected that it was unlikely there would be any incriminating evidence left, unless the killer had dropped something from his pockets. He doubted they would be that lucky, but Forensics would search the area anyway. If they could prove that Rögnvaldur had put the head there, they would have such a watertight case that the trial would be over before lunchtime.

The tide was out. On the beach below, weed-covered rocks that would be submerged at other times poked out of the sand. There was no snow to be seen except a sprinkling here and there on the old piles of seaweed that had collected against the line of boulders. Two pairs of footprints ran along the sand between the rocks and the water's edge. Presumably they belonged to the young couple, who had apparently walked along the beach from the direction of the golf course. The tracks left by their dog could also be seen, zigzagging wildly from one side of the beach to the other. Clearly it hadn't been on a lead – as it should have been, since this was a protected nesting site. The dog's trail led up to where the bag was sticking out of the rocks, and you could see where the young couple had turned back and come over to take a closer took. All perfectly consistent with their account.

Huldar inched his way closer until he could hook the black plastic bag with his retractable pointer. At his first attempt, he managed to tug it up a little – far enough to see that this was no mistake or hoax. Inside the bag there was a glimpse of dirty, wet, brown hair.

Huldar let the bag drop back into place. Then he perched on an icy boulder, turned his face to the sea and concentrated on some ducks that were swimming peacefully near the water's edge. After a minute or two, he shook his head, got to his feet and climbed back up to the path.

Chapter 18

Thursday

The change in Erla was extraordinary. She had gone from being the personification of gloom to more optimistic than an Icelandic concert organiser. She stood tall, her face no longer looked like a thundercloud and she finished on a positive note whenever she spoke or issued orders. The shadows under her eyes had faded and her cheeks had regained their colour. Freyja thought she looked almost amiable.

It wasn't hard to guess what had brought about this transformation. Bríet's head had turned up, which meant there was no longer any need to worry about where it was, whether it would ever turn up and who might find it. Freyja gathered that it hadn't occurred to the young couple who had stumbled on it to take any pictures, so there was no danger of the head finding its way onto social media. It was now safe in the hands of the pathologist. The post-mortem had been postponed, however, as there was a possibility that Bríet's parents would be allowed to identify the body, in which case it would be better if the head hadn't been cut open. The situation was macabre enough without that.

But this wasn't the only reason for Erla's good mood. The first part of the DNA analysis had come in. An update was expected from Forensics any minute, and although they would still have to wait to hear if there was a potential match with Rögnvaldur's DNA profile, based on a hair taken from his brush, nevertheless it represented a turning point in the investigation.

The only bad news was that one of the CCTV cameras on Seltjarnarnes, the suburb where the head had turned up, had been out of order the weekend of Bríet's murder. There were two cameras covering the routes into the city centre, and, since Rögnvaldur didn't show up on the footage from the southern shore, it appeared he must have driven out to Grótta along the northern side of the peninsula, where the camera had been down. As a result, the police didn't know whether he had been driving Bríet's car or his own when he'd disposed of the head. But they believed he must have done it at the weekend, since the camera had been repaired on Monday and there was no sign of either car on the CCTV footage after that.

The movements of the two cars were still obscure, then, apart from the fact that Rögnvaldur's red Toyota had been driven into Salahverfi on the Friday at around 6 p.m. and had left again at around 7.30 p.m. Someone had then left the area in Bríet's white Skoda shortly after midnight, and twenty-four hours later, the car had reappeared on its way into the housing estate where it had later been found abandoned. The assumption was that Rögnvaldur must have returned to Bríet's flat on foot in order to take the body away in her car. It took roughly one and a half hours to walk from his home to hers, which would be consistent with the time frame established from the CCTV recordings. Where he'd driven after that had yet to be discovered, but the police were still collecting security-camera footage from various points around the city.

Irrespective of Rögnvaldur's movements, the inquiry had finally received the boost it needed to get it out of the rut and onto the home straight. They would soon have their hands on some solid evidence; after all, no one can deny their own DNA. Of course, a number of details still remained to be filled in, including the location of the place where Rögnvaldur had dismembered the body, but the absolute priority now was to find the man himself.

They had put out a wanted notice but the phone calls from the public hadn't provided any leads, only wasted precious time as the undermanned team were sent all over the place to follow up tip-offs. It was inevitable that Rögnvaldur would be tracked down in the end. The staff at Keflavík Airport had been alerted, so the police were fairly confident that he wouldn't slip through the net there. And no one could stay hidden for long in Iceland. Not as long as they were alive. If he had killed himself, that would be different. In that case there were ways of ensuring that one's body would never be found.

Freyja had been asked to read through the background information they had collected so far on Rögnvaldur, to see if there were any hints to be gleaned there about his possible next steps. Was there a risk he might attack again or was he more likely to be suicidal? She was also supposed to gauge whether anyone who had denied knowing his whereabouts might be lying. The police had talked to an astonishing number of people since Rögnvaldur had come onto their radar the day before; some on the phone, others in formal interviews. But this mammoth effort had got them nowhere.

A work colleague thought he had seen him on the premises the day before, but when the insurance company's IT department was asked to look into the matter, there was no record of Rögnvaldur's having accessed the building. They insisted it was out of the question that he could have destroyed the evidence of his presence, as only the IT team would be capable of that. And as this seemed highly unlikely, it appeared Rögnvaldur's colleague must have been mistaken.

No close relative or friend would admit to sheltering him or helping to conceal him from the police, and Freyja had no way of telling from their statements whether this was true or not. Words on a page were seldom sufficient on their own to catch people out in a lie. For that, it would be necessary for them to contradict themselves or come out with something that was patently nonsense. Freyja needed to be able to read their body language and listen to their tone of voice. She had soon given up on the statements and turned instead to analysing Rögnvaldur's mental state, as described by those close to him. Later, she might have time to watch recordings of the interviews that had been conducted at the police station.

The results of her efforts were pretty underwhelming, but then the police's questions hadn't been designed to elicit information about the man's state of mind. From what she had to work with, it seemed there had been nothing to suggest Rögnvaldur was on the point of crashing so far through the barriers of civilised behaviour that he would commit murder. It was obvious he had been in a bad place psychologically, but there had been nothing to suggest that his grief would explode into the kind of savagery he was suspected of. According to his parents and brother, he had never been the violent type, as a child or an adult. On the contrary, Rögnvaldur had always been quiet, gentle and slow to anger. Aldís's parents had backed this up.

Still, traumatic events could transform even the gentlest soul. The statements of those closest to the couple suggested that grief had developed into full-blown psychological problems in both their cases. Freyja assumed earlier traumas had played a part in that. Rögnvaldur's mother seemed to have been the most talkative and had virtually laid her son's entire life story on the table. She seemed to be one of those people for whom the floodgates open under pressure. As a result, Freyja found her statement the most informative, though the police officers who interviewed her must have been shifting restlessly in their seats by the time she was done.

One significant piece of information to come out of the mother's account was that before giving birth to Íris, Aldís had suffered two miscarriages and one stillbirth. It went without saying that it must have been devastating for the couple to lose their longed-for daughter on top of these earlier bereavements. It was unfortunate for everyone concerned that they had rejected all offers of help in coping with their grief. Had they accepted, it would have reduced the likelihood of things going as badly off the rails as they had. If Rögnvaldur's mother's description of the couple's state in recent months was to be believed, they were both showing signs of PTSD and complicated grief disorder, though manifesting them in different ways.

Aldís had withdrawn into her shell so completely that it was as if she were trying to vanish off the face of the earth. She had shut herself in her bedroom, indifferent to the attempts by family and friends to draw her out again. At present, she was almost catatonic. It was nearly twenty-four hours since her arrest but the police still hadn't got any sense out of her. Two attempts had been made to question her and Freyja had been present on both occasions. The interviews had been quickly suspended because Aldís had simply sat there mute, her head hanging. Freyja had also paid her a visit in her spartan cell and felt a pang when she saw the pathetic figure. The woman was lying on the mattress, her face turned to the wall, her vertebrae and hip-bone jutting through her thin T-shirt. Almost all Freyja's attempts to get through to her were in vain, although she knew Aldís was conscious. At one point the woman had turned to face Freyja, opened her mouth as if to say something, then apparently changed her mind and turned back to the wall. Her expression had been profoundly sad, as if what she was about to say was devastating. This did nothing to quell Freyja's suspicion that Aldís knew something important, but none of her efforts to coax it out of her had any effect.

The accounts of friends and family suggested that Rögn-valdur had also cut himself off from the outside world after his daughter's death. Unlike his wife, though, he hadn't taken to his bed with his duvet pulled over his head. Rather, he had gone back to work, half-days at first, then more sporadically, until in the end he had stopped going in altogether after an unfortunate incident at the office. This had been related to his growing obsession with the accident of fate that had brought them to this tragic state of affairs. The chart on his sitting-room wall couldn't be interpreted any other way, nor could the tales of how he had tried to interrogate everyone he had been in contact with about their health. How this fixation had spiralled until it drove him to commit an appalling atrocity was impossible to explain, except by talking to the man himself over a number of sessions – a concept Erla was having trouble grasping.

'So you haven't a clue why Rögnvaldur lost the plot?'

Freyja took care over her answer, despite the crudeness of the question. '"Lost the plot" isn't the term I'd use, but the death of his daughter was clearly the trigger for these horrific events. I won't know exactly how it happened, though, unless I get a chance to talk to him. But right now I don't suppose his motive is the most important consideration?'

Erla shrugged. 'No. Maybe not. What I'm mainly trying to find out is whether this . . .' she waved her arms dismissively, this character profiling of yours can tell me whether or not Rögnvaldur is likely to attack someone else.'

Freyja didn't take offence. At least Erla hadn't put air quotes around the word as she often did when referring to Freyja's expertise. It seemed their relationship was improving. So it was a pity that Freyja's answer was unlikely to oil the wheels any further. 'I wouldn't like to try and predict that.'

But Erla was in too good a mood to let this get on her nerves. 'Fifty-fifty, then.'

'Yes.' Freyja reached for a sachet of ketchup that Erla had her eye on and passed it over. To her surprise, Erla actually thanked her before tearing it open.

They were sitting in the police-station canteen with a handful of others, stuffing their faces with chips that Huldar had picked up to celebrate the turning point in the investigation. If they'd been Formula One racing drivers, they would be showering themselves with champagne. Although Freyja didn't especially like chips, she reflected that they were preferable to being drenched in booze. Especially as she was due to collect Saga from nursery school shortly, where the smell of ketchup was unlikely to raise any eyebrows but the smell of alcohol certainly would.

For the first time since starting her new job, Freyja felt at home here. Felt she was part of a team, rather than just a bit of window dressing. It was extraordinarily pleasant to get the sense that her contribution mattered for a change. She felt almost weepy as her fears about the wisdom of her move vanished in the blink of an eye. But she got a grip on herself. If she started crying now she was sure to fall out of favour again. The others were not the type to let their emotions get the better of them.

The door opened and Gudlaugur appeared in the gap. He sniffed appreciatively, his eyes on the feast spread out on the table. 'Anyone know where Erla is?'

'Are you joking?' Erla leant forwards into view, squashing her bump against the table. She raised her hands and jabbed both forefingers towards her own head. 'Hello! Do I have to put a plate on my head for you to notice me?'

Gudlaugur flushed bright red, but as Erla was in a good mood, she didn't string it out, just beckoned him over to join them.

He didn't wait to be told twice but sat down and tucked in, the flush fading from his cheeks as the first chip disappeared down his throat.

Erla waited for him to swallow before saying: 'So, out with it, then.'

Gudlaugur swallowed again to be sure. 'We've found his car. It's parked at the Laugar fitness complex, in the busy area outside the gym. Judging by the amount of snow on the roof, it's been there all night, at least.'

'Did you get recordings from the gym's CCTV?'

Gudlaugur nodded. 'The car's parked in a space that looks as if it's covered by one of the cameras, so we should be able to see when he parks it and whether he gets into someone else's car afterwards. We'll need to check what clothes he's wearing too, as it could be useful, assuming he hasn't had a chance to change.'

'Have we got the car under surveillance? In case he comes back? He might get fed up with walking and be tempted to risk using it again. So far, no one's admitted to lending him theirs.'

'Lína stayed behind and there are officers on their way to relieve her. Just as well – it's bloody freezing out there.' The red spots on his cheeks when he'd arrived had borne witness to that.

Erla nodded and helped herself to more chips. 'Good. I need to talk to the legal department about Aldís. It would be crazy to let her go but I'm not convinced custody is the right answer. There's clearly something very wrong with her, though I don't believe she was involved in the murder. She seems incapable of combing her hair, let alone of doing anything more drastic. Do you agree?' Erla poked a chip in Freyja's direction.

'Yes. Based on what I saw in the interviews earlier, she's not up to much. I don't think she belongs in a prison cell but she shouldn't be left alone at home either. My recommendation would be to get her admitted to the psychiatric ward. I don't know if you want to have her sectioned or if you'd be satisfied with a regular admission. Personally, I think the latter would do, because I agree that it's unlikely she took part in arranging a murder. She may have suspected what was up but hardly more than that. The blood test yesterday showed that she'd been taking way more than the prescribed dose of sedatives. She must have been almost completely out of it.'

'Does the blood test show how long she'd been on such a high dose?' Huldar asked. 'I mean, could she have knocked back a handful of pills just before her arrest but been straight before that?' He took a sip of coffee. He hadn't touched the chips, although they had been his suggestion and he'd gone to pick them up.

'No. We know nothing about that—' Erla's phone rang, interrupting her. After exchanging a few words with the caller, she got to her feet. From her half of the conversation, the others had gathered that it concerned the results of the DNA analysis.

Erla left the canteen without a word. Huldar and Gudlaugur immediately got up and followed her, and Freyja decided to do the same. There was still half an hour before she had to collect Saga and with any luck she might get to hear the latest development in the case before she left. She hadn't been able to read anything from Erla's face during the phone call, which meant the news could be either good or bad.

The only people left sitting at the table were two members of CID she didn't know by name. They had been hanging back up to now, but as soon as they were left alone with the chips, they began eagerly tucking in.

The instant Freyja had taken up position between Huldar and Gudlaugur against the wall in Erla's office she regretted it. She really ought to have found a better place to put herself. For one thing, she was pressed up against Huldar and could feel the warmth of his hard body, something she found incredibly distracting. For another, what if the forensic technician was still talking when she needed to slip out? It would mean having to interrupt Erla's conversation with him. The office was too small to fit five people without a crush, but maybe she could squeeze past Huldar and behind the technician without being too conspicuous. He was taking such a long time to get to the point that she would soon have to put this to the test.

Freyja wasn't alone in feeling impatient with the man's longwindedness. Erla's eyes had narrowed and she was showing all the warning signs of an imminent eruption. Her mood had soured the moment Huldar, Gudlaugur and Freyja had crowded into her office, eager to get in on the act. But she hadn't thrown them out as they would normally have expected.

'Could you cut to the chase? I don't give a shit about longitudinal variability or whatever it is you're on about. I just want to know what emerged from the DNA comparison of the blood and the vomit. When you rang just now, you said you had some extraordinary news. So far all you've given me is a string of extraordinarily boring gibberish.'

The technician looked as if he'd like to retort in kind. Although he didn't give in to the urge, his deeply offended tone betrayed him. 'Since you're not interested in how the results are obtained, I'll proceed straight to the findings.'

'Great.' Erla drew her lips back in a smile of the kind that a waiter puts on when a customer says they're allergic to water or some such nonsense. 'Get on with it, then.'

'The blood samples from Bríet's flat originate from two different individuals. Both female. The comparison with the samples from the body show that one of them was Bríet. The other is unknown.'

Erla eyebrows drew together in a frown. 'Two women? So neither could be from Rögnvaldur? I mean, he could have been injured in the struggle.'

'No.' The technician didn't seem to mind having to break this bad news to Erla. 'Not unless Rögnvaldur is a woman.'

'Don't try to be funny. It's such a bad look for Forensics. Rögnvaldur hasn't undergone a sex change – he was born male in a man's body.' Erla turned to her computer screen and moved her mouse. 'This morning I got an email from Forensics saying that you'd found fingerprints in Bríet's flat that matched a set at Rögnvaldur's place.' She located the message and threw an angry look at the technician. 'That was several hours ago. But now you're telling me the perpetrator was a woman?'

'I'm not telling you anything of the sort. The information about the fingerprints is correct. I'm telling you that the blood in the flat came from two women. We compared the DNA profiles to the profile obtained from the body. The comparison confirmed that one of them was Bríet. It's not our job to find out who the other woman was. That's your headache. But I can confirm that there's no DNA profile in our database that matches the unidentified blood, either in the Identity Database or the Trace Database.'

While Freyja was wondering what the difference was between them, Huldar weighed in. 'Just let me get my head round this. We're now faced with the possibility that the perpetrator was a woman, possibly working with Rögnvaldur. Or that there were two victims – both women. One possibly injured but still alive, whereas Bríet is obviously dead.' He held up a hand to stop the technician who'd put on a long-suffering expression and opened his mouth to speak. 'I'm not asking your opinion or expecting you to solve the case for us. We'll take care of that. I'm just thinking aloud.'

'Carry on,' Erla told the technician, ignoring Huldar's interruption. 'What about the DNA from the vomit? Are you telling me that's from a woman too?'

'Yes.' The more displeasure Erla showed, the smugger the technician looked. 'A third female. The DNA profile doesn't match either of the other two.'

The last vestiges of Erla's good mood evaporated. 'What are you telling me?'

The technician held out the top page of the papers he'd brought along. 'This is a short summary I made of that particular sample.'

Erla made no move to take the report. 'I don't need to read a hard copy. We're meant to be saving paper. Wasn't it enough to upload it to the case folder?'

'No, actually. I think you'll want a copy of this.' The technician was obviously relishing Erla's baffled expression as he placed the paper on her desk. 'Now we come to the part I told you was extraordinary.'

He paused, obviously itching to be asked. But since Huldar, Gudlaugur and Erla all remained silent, the job fell to Freyja. She was in a hurry, after all. 'And? What's so extraordinary?'

Although the technician would clearly have preferred it if Erla had been forced to beg, he replied to Freyja's question. 'I ran the DNA profile through the Identity Database. Nothing.' Another dramatic pause, then: 'After that, I tried the Trace Database. And hit the jackpot.'

'In the Trace Database?' Huldar moved towards Erla's desk and reached out for the report but Erla snatched it first.

This had clearly got them interested. To her frustration, Freyja didn't know why. Although the clock was ticking, she had to ask. 'What's the Trace Database?'

The technician turned back to her, pleased by her interest. He bestowed a friendly look on her while addressing her in a didactic tone. She was sure his kids would turn out to be geniuses and his wife would go nuts if he spoke to his family like this, but despite her irritation, she was hooked. 'The two databases contain DNA profiles related to investigations. The Identity Database holds the genetic profiles of individuals convicted of serious crimes, while the Trace Database holds DNA profiles from the scenes of unsolved crimes. In this case, I found a match with an old case.'

Erla slammed her hand on the desk and the technician and Freyja both snapped their attention back to her. She was holding the report. 'Is what this says correct?'

The technician nodded. 'Yes, it's correct. The probability is ninety-nine point nine per cent.'

Erla buried her face in her hands. 'How the fuck is that possible?'

The technician pouted. 'That's your job to find out. I was asked to analyse the genetic profiles and that's what I've done.' His manner softened slightly as he went on. 'There's no doubt. The profile belongs to Mía Stefánsdóttir, an infant who vanished from her pram eleven years ago and was believed dead – which I can now confirm categorically not to be the case.' The man released a breath. 'Nothing else can explain the presence of her DNA in the vomit. It didn't come from an infant and had never been deep frozen. In other words, the girl is alive.'

Chapter 19

Thursday evening

The dining table was covered with exercise books. Most were closed, indicating that the homework for those subjects was finished. The only book still open was the one in front of Selma. She was poring over it, poking at the text with a pencil stub and emitting frequent sighs. If it had been her favourite subject, Icelandic, she'd have been working away enthusiastically, without a word of complaint.

Sædís smiled at her sister and ruffled her hair. 'Had enough for now?'

Selma flopped forwards over the table in a melodramatic gesture of surrender. 'Yes. I can't take any more.'

Of course she could. The truth was that everyone could take more than they did. They just differed in how easy they went on themselves. Sædís knew she hadn't pushed herself hard enough, but then her education had ended prematurely. She hadn't even finished her school-leaver's exams before she'd started working in reception, where she had stayed until she'd accepted her father's invitation to join him in the office just over a year ago. It wasn't her dream job. Although the company was reasonably large, the office itself was small, with only her, her father and the payroll clerk working in there. In fact, her father was rarely there since he was always out and about, so mostly it was just her and the payroll clerk, an old bloke who had lost his left arm in a work-related accident. Her father had taken pity on him and found him a new role within the company. Now he picked away at the computer keyboard with one hand, stopping regularly to exclaim: 'What the heck?' Working on a computer didn't suit him at all and sometimes Sædís felt that most of her time was wasted on helping him navigate his way around the screen, searching for files that had 'just disappeared'.

Her salary was respectable enough, but you couldn't call the job stimulating. She answered the phone, took messages, made coffee and ordered food, which she then rushed around delivering to the workforce. At Christmas, she wrote cards to all their clients and stuck ribbons on the accompanying bottles of wine. That was about it. Out of sheer boredom, she had suggested adding the cleaning to her list of tasks, first in the office during working hours, then later in the warehouse and workshop as overtime. After taking over this role, she had persuaded her father to buy more environmentally friendly cleaning products, which gave her the feeling that she had finally achieved something at work that genuinely mattered. In addition, the overtime put a little more money in her pocket every month. This didn't change her lifestyle much: she spent nothing on luxuries or eating out, just put the bulk in a savings account. At first, she had done this because she had so few outgoings and wanted to look after what was left. But before long it had turned into something of a personal challenge: a challenge to save up as much as possible and watch her balance slowly but steadily growing.

Soon she would have to give up the cleaning. The sooner the better. Just thinking about having to mop and wipe the workshop again made her feel sick to the stomach. Maybe she should stop now. Although the chemicals were supposed to be environmentally friendly, they were unlikely to be good for the baby and she had to make sure it was healthy when she handed it over. She didn't look forward to telling her father, though, as there were few things he disliked more than dealing with hiring staff, and the current arrangement suited him perfectly. But he wouldn't say anything. All things considered, what could he say? And anyway, the news she had to break to him would be a far greater blow than this.

Selma swept up her exercise books and stuffed them into her backpack. 'Can Rósa come round? I promise we won't make a noise. And maybe Gudda too?'

It was almost suppertime and although Rósa was allowed out at any time of the day or night, there was no question of Gudda getting permission. 'No. It's too late. You'll just have to chat to them online. Anyway, it's nearly the weekend. If you like, I can take you all to the cinema tomorrow night.'

It was a deal. Selma skipped off to her room. Sædís remained sitting at the dining table for a while, reflecting with pleasure on how well Selma seemed to be getting on with her schoolwork. She was good at the subjects she enjoyed and muddled through in the rest. It would be enough to allow her to continue into higher education. Not all kids could take that for granted. She herself had suffered from being isolated during her studies because neither her mother nor her father had been engaged enough to push or encourage her. Sædís felt it was her responsibility to make sure history didn't repeat itself in Selma's case, because no one else would bother.

She heard a clatter of dishes from the kitchen. Her mother was back on her feet, feeling better than she had in a while.

Sædís stood up, carefully wrapping her long cardigan around herself. She leant in the kitchen doorway and offered to help. Her mother turned, smiling warily, and declined. After a moment, she added that it was high time she did it herself, now that she was well again. Turning back to the kitchen table, she started putting out the plates. She was looking pretty good – clean hair, bright eyes – but she was painfully thin and her hands were shaking, although she tried to disguise the fact.

'Is Dad coming?' Sædís assumed he must be, since her mother was cooking. The question was designed to provide an opening for a conversation about his bender at the weekend. Perhaps her mother would feel better if the family brought things out into the open, once in a while.

But her mother let the chance slip through her grasp. 'Yes. He rang to say he's on his way. I'm cooking your favourite – spaghetti bolognese.'

Sædís nodded. She had never particularly liked the dish and neither had her father. But this wasn't the time to mention it. There was something about this family that meant the right time never came, though they always seemed to be hovering on the verge of it. They were like cartoon donkeys with a carrot dangling from a branch in front of their noses.

'I'm going to have a quick nap.'

Her mother nodded and put on another feeble smile. 'You do that, love. Go on.'

Once Sædís was lying flat on her back on her bed, her bump stuck up like a tussock on a poor piece of grazing land – a simile prompted by her bad conscience, because the fact was, she hadn't let on to the prospective parents about her mother's depression. They hadn't asked about her family history and she hadn't volunteered it. This was something she had wanted to do and she was afraid of spoiling her chance. After all, she wasn't depressive herself, though she could be described as a bit over-sensitive.

Sædís closed her eyes. She hoped the child would inherit the best qualities from both its parents. A scene from the intra-uterine insemination procedure flashed into her mind and she flicked her eyes open and stared up at the white ceiling. It was better to contemplate the paint than relive that.

A tear that Sædís hadn't ordered ran down one cheek and into her ear. Was she doing something stupid? Had she let the parents' tragic story influence her into making a big mistake? If so, it was the fault of her sentimental streak. Because she was the one who had suggested it, taking every-one by surprise, not least herself. They hadn't immediately accepted her offer, so she couldn't claim she'd been led into a trap. No, she had voluntarily stepped into a trap of her own making.

Through the wall she heard Selma's friend Rósa giggling and squealing. They were obviously chatting on FaceTime. Sædís was grateful for the interruption. Now she could dis-tract herself by thinking about Rósa and how odd the girl was. Sædís had often been on the point of reporting her parents to social services but had never actually done so. It wasn't as if she had any solid proof of bad treatment or neglect, only her suspicions. The girl had far too many days off school 'sick', missing a lot more than either Selma and Gudda, neither of whom were particularly robust. Rósa was much bigger and more mature than them as well and would probably start messing around with boys earlier than they did. It had better not spread to the other two. There was no rush.

The Fallout

Sædís heard the front door open. It must be her father. He didn't call out 'Hello!' like her friends' dads, just closed the door and came inside. She sat up and drew a deep breath. Had the big moment arrived? Would there be any better time than now to admit to her parents what she had done? Maybe even take her father aside after the revelation and have the dreaded conversation about his latest bender that they had both been avoiding?

But by the time she had swung her legs off the bed and was sitting on the edge, the impulse had died. No. Not yet. Her dad was still recovering. And her mother had only just got back on her feet.

Later. There would be a right time later.

Chapter 20

Thursday evening

Sídumúli was deserted. Not because the street had just been evacuated or because of the bad weather or because Eurovision was on TV. It was like this every evening. Nobody lived there and the businesses weren't the kind where people worked in the evenings or at night. Rögnvaldur knew the area well as the insurance company where he had been employed for nearly seven years was based there. On Fridays, the car doors would start slamming at four in the afternoon and there would be another wave of slamming at five. By six, all would be quiet. He used to be one of the few people there to witness the last trickle of office workers heading home. Whenever Íris had been admitted to hospital, he had been allowed to start work at lunchtime and stay on until late. It had meant he could be at the hospital in the mornings when there was the best chance of getting to talk to the doctors.

A gust of wind whirled loose snow into his face, the ice crystals stinging his already freezing cheeks. The same gust swept a collection of litter into the corner where he was standing and a grubby credit-card receipt landed on one of his shoes. He shook it off and stamped it into the snow to prevent it from going any further. Then he looked up and scanned the street again. Nothing. No one. Not even a cat. Even animals avoided this apocalyptic wasteland.

God, it was a dreary place. They hadn't even tried to make the office buildings attractive. They had just thrown them up with a minimum of effort. Walls to keep out the elements, windows to let in light and air, and a roof so it wouldn't rain on the office drones and their paperwork.

It wasn't somewhere Rögnvaldur would have chosen to spend his evening. He was here because he couldn't go home. He had seen the police outside his building the day before, just in time to do a U-turn before they spotted him. He had driven into a nearby street and parked at the bottom of a cul-de-sac, behind a dirty wreck of a caravan with two flat tyres. From there he had run back towards his building, then walked unhurriedly past on the other side of the road. By then, the police had vanished from sight but their cars were still there.

Rögnvaldur had walked to the neighbouring block and slipped into the lobby. There he had rung the bells of the flats on the top floor and been let in. Instead of going up, he had hurried down to the basement where he had lurked until he calculated it was safe to go upstairs again. He hadn't wanted to risk encountering the person who had buzzed him in, just in case they had come down to check who was at the door.

On the staircase between the floors there was a window offering a good view of the entrance to his own building.

It wasn't long before the police officers had begun to pour out again. He'd watched quite calmly until Aldís was led out between two masked members of the SWAT team. What on earth did they think she'd do? Run away? Attack them? They didn't need a special squad to arrest Aldís. The puppies of

PAW Patrol, the kids' programme Íris had loved so much, would have been more than up to the job.

Rögnvaldur's knees had buckled and his eyes had stung as he watched his wife being led across the car park. Aldís's head was drooping. She was wearing nothing but pyjama trousers and a T-shirt, though someone had slung a coat over her shoulders. He couldn't tear his gaze from the scene, unbearable though it was to witness.

He'd put his hand in his coat pocket and fished out a packet of pills, allowing himself two tablets to cope with the stress. Now he regretted the fact, as he only had the one pack with him, and after what had happened there was no chance of his going home to fetch more. It hadn't achieved the desired effect either, since the numbness hadn't spread through him until after the police operation was over. He'd had to watch, stone-cold sober, as a member of the SWAT team opened the rear door of a police car, put a hand on Aldís's head and guided her inside. Then the door had slammed and Aldís had vanished from view. The car had reversed out of the parking space and driven away.

Rögnvaldur refused to let himself think about where Aldís might be now. He couldn't allow his mind to go there. He had to stay alert. He had already taken various measures to cover his tracks. The moment he judged it safe, he had returned to his car, driven to a cashpoint and taken out as much money as the machine would let him. Then he had driven to the Skeifan retail park, where he'd bought a cheap new outfit of coat, trousers and jumper. After that he had ditched the car at the Laugar sports complex, then walked back to Skeifan, carrying Bríet's laptop in a cloth bag, and finished buying what he thought he would need.

there would be no sense of satisfaction when he achieved it? He consoled himself that it wasn't a question of feeling good; that condition no longer existed for him. The pleasure centres in his brain had died along with Íris. No, this was a question of justice.

He opened the register and saw that it contained the information he was looking for. It took him almost no time to collect the names of the children who hadn't been vaccinated against measles. Having done this, he listed them according to address, creating a special file of those who lived in the Reykjavík area. However, this didn't narrow the field that much since there were apparently a greater number of idiots living in the capital than in the countryside. He also removed all the children who'd had the first, but not the follow-up jab that was necessary for complete protection against the virus. That reduced the number considerably.

Rögnvaldur clasped his hands behind his neck, leant back in his chair and surveyed the results. He was aware of a faint sense of achievement.

Bending down to the screen again, he began to read about each child. The sheer number of them didn't surprise him. He knew that around five to ten per cent of children had not received the complete vaccination against measles. But it didn't matter. He was in no hurry. He had a gut feeling that the name he was looking for was in here somewhere and he had the whole night ahead of him.

As it turned out, Rögnvaldur didn't need the whole night.

In search of motivation before starting on the long list of names, he minimised the register and went online, logging in to the Cloud where he and Aldís stored their photos. He wanted to see a picture of Íris. However painful it was, he had to remind himself why he was doing this and what he had lost. To heighten the effect, he plugged the laptop into the projector. Seeing Íris's image blown up to more than life-size on screen would be bound to fill him with fighting spirit, lending him the strength of Hercules.

Although photos were the quickest and easiest way to preserve memories, they were also pitiless. There were no photos in the Cloud of Íris on her deathbed. Neither he nor Aldís would have dreamt of taking one, not even when their daughter was first admitted to hospital with measles and there was still a chance. And definitely not towards the end, when their fear was growing and there was no longer any doubt about what was going to happen.

This meant that Rögnvaldur could open the most recent photo without any risk of being distressed by the content. The directory was organised according to date: this picture had been taken ten days before Íris first developed a fever, on one of the most likely days for her to have been infected. He double-checked the day. When compiling his table, he had gone through all the pictures taken in this period, on both his and Aldís's phones, to find out what they had been doing on those days. There hadn't been a single photo from this date. Photos taken on all the other days during the infection window had been on their phones, yet to be uploaded to the Cloud. In fact, both the more recent and the older pictures were still on their phones, so it appeared that only the photos from this day had been uploaded.

That was odd.

He opened the file and looked up at the wall. A huge photo of Íris appeared and he felt a stabbing pain in his heart that even the sedative couldn't dull. But Íris wasn't alone in the picture; she was posing with two other girls her age and a boy who looked a little younger. He scrolled through the rest of the photos, pausing on the final one. Rögnvaldur stared at it for a while, the tears running unchecked down his cheeks. Then he closed his eyes, unable to bear it any longer. His body was shaken by sobs. Only now did he understand why Aldís had lost her will to live as quickly as she had.

Rögnvaldur opened his eyes again, giving free rein to his feelings.

He felt angry. Then hurt. Then sad – sadder than he had ever been before. After a while, all the other feelings retreated before an overpowering sense of rage.

The children's proud, happy faces beamed down at him from the wall. Although he had no proof, he was convinced that one of them had been the carrier. It was obvious. And that child's name would be in the register. That was obvious too.

Rögnvaldur glanced at the clock in the bottom corner of the screen. It was too late for him to ring up and ask for the names of the children in the picture. That would have to wait until morning. The delay didn't cause him any particular disappointment or impatience. He was only two steps away from his goal. One phone call, then all he had to do was look up the names in the register. After that, he would know who the infection carrier had been. He could feel it in his bones.

Again, the expected feelings failed to materialise. His lack of pleasure probably wasn't only due to the sedative. Getting hold of the register had taken its toll. He pushed away the thought of Bríet's fate. Like the satisfaction, any feelings of regret or penitence would also have to wait.

Rögnvaldur stood up, switched off the computer and put it back in the cloth bag. Then he left the meeting room and took the stairs down to the basement. There he could lose himself in dreams of a fitting revenge until the alarm clock woke him at seven tomorrow morning. Because although the sedative had a deadening effect on his emotions, it was no match for the rage that had taken up residence in his soul. No drugs, no therapy, no words could lessen its force. Rage and thoughts of revenge were the fuel that kept him going. Without them, he would have shrivelled up and died long ago.

Chapter 21

The montage of pictures and information on the meeting-room wall had just got a lot more crowded. In addition to all the material on Bríet's murder, they now had documents relating to the disappearance eleven years previously of a baby called Mía Stefánsdóttir. Of all the horror that confronted the onlooker, the photo of the empty pram was the starkest. Huldar was sitting beside Erla, contemplating the wall display. He wasn't focusing on anything in particular, just trying to grasp the bigger picture. He guessed that Erla was doing the same.

She looked exhausted as she sat there slumped in her chair, repeatedly massaging her temples. They should both have gone home as it was unclear what they were achieving by working so late. For the last hour, Huldar had been finding it hard to concentrate for more than a few minutes at a time. He kept opening files, only to close them again almost immediately; drinking mugs of coffee, nipping out for a smoke. When he'd come back in from his last cigarette break he had spotted Erla in the meeting room and decided to join her.

'How could it happen?' Erla sounded as shattered as she looked. 'How could a ghost pop out of the woodwork like that, just as we were finally getting somewhere?'

Huldar puffed out his cheeks, then slowly released the air. 'It's pretty fucked up. But there has to be an explanation. It can't be a coincidence that this old case has become mixed up in the inquiry.'

This did nothing to cheer Erla up. 'I'm not so sure. Couldn't it be some fucking accident that we'll never be able to untangle? The girl who vanished would be eleven now. I'm not even going to try to imagine where she's been all these years, but she could simply have been passing, looked in the boot and thrown up when she saw what was inside, then continued on her way. It's not impossible.'

'No. No chance. That would be one hell of a coincidence.' Huldar was still staring at the wall but now he was searching for something to support his assertion. He couldn't see anything, though. They were two separate incidents that had happened eleven years apart. There was no link between the main protagonists, or at least none that the police had yet found. 'But if it is, we'll work it out. Somehow. That's for sure. Let's start by finding Rögnvaldur, then the rest will fall into place. He has to have some connection to the missing baby. We just have to discover what it is.'

'It won't change anything. If the DNA results aren't some kind of mistake, I'm in deep shit. Even if the two cases do get solved.'

'How do you work that out? I'd have thought you'd be the hero of the hour if you manage to find a little girl who was written off as dead.' Huldar turned from the wall to study Erla's profile. Her jaw was clenched, the muscle prominent even through the puffiness of fatigue that had blurred her features ever since the forensic technician had left her office that afternoon. Unless it had nothing to do with this latest setback and was merely due to the salt content of all the chips she'd eaten earlier.

'A hero? Oh come on, I wasn't born yesterday. Who do you think will get the blame if the old inquiry turns out to have been a complete cock-up? Certainly not the bloke who was in charge at the time – he's left the police for some cushy position in a government ministry. He'll never have to answer for his mistakes. You know how it works. I'll be the fall guy. I'll have to reopen the old inquiry, and that'll make it mine. I'll be left literally holding the baby. And because I'll be on maternity leave, I won't be able to defend myself. Believe me, I'll end up taking the blame. And if we don't solve this case, I'll be blamed for that as well. So I'm buggered whatever happens.'

Huldar turned back to the wall. He didn't want to lie but nor did he want to agree with her and make her feel even worse. Instead, he shared with her the only solution he could think of. 'Then you'll just have to crack both cases before you go on leave. That way you'll be here to defend yourself if the media starts putting the boot in. You can just point the finger at the guy who was in charge of investigating the missing-baby case back in the day and you'll be off the hook. Seeing as you're . . . you know . . . pregnant . . . the reporters will immediately turn their guns on him. No one's going to start giving grief to a woman who's about to give birth.'

Erla laughed drily. 'Then we'll have to move fast.'

Here it was. Finally Huldar would get to know Erla's due date. 'How fast?'

'Fast.' Checkmate.

Huldar smiled, conceding defeat. 'How about calling it a day? Turn up fresh as a daisy tomorrow morning with a good night's sleep behind us and our heads in gear?'

'Nope. I'm hanging around until the guys who are out looking for Rögnvaldur get back. I feel I should be here to meet them. They've been scouring the streets since three this afternoon. It'd be a bit crap for them to come back to an empty department, especially when none of their efforts have produced any results. And judging by the way the search has gone so far, the last half-hour isn't going to turn anything up either.'

'I'll wait for them. You go home. Everybody happy.'

Erla turned to him and for a moment he thought she was going to accept his offer, but she just shook her head.

'Are we chasing the wrong guy, Huldar? Supposing I've put out a wanted notice for a man who hasn't killed anyone? And arrested his wife too? Locked her up in a mental ward? This is a couple who've just lost their child. I mean, Jesus.'

'Firstly, Aldís was admitted to hospital, she hasn't been locked up. And no one could claim that was unnecessary. Anyway, I heard from a nurse at the psych ward that she's expecting Aldís to be discharged soon. She wants to go home and they can't persuade her to stay indefinitely. She's not been sectioned, so she's free to go. Which is a pity as Freyja thinks she knows something. But according to the nurse, she refuses to talk about her husband. She recommends we give her time. Pressuring her now won't work. Unfortunately.' Huldar gestured at the wall, jabbing his finger towards a CCTV capture of Rögnvaldur's car entering Bríet's neighbourhood. 'Secondly, it's unthinkable that Rögnvaldur's not our man. His fingerprints were in her flat, remember? He had blood on his shoes. His car was caught on a recording at a time that exactly fits her time of death. He was after data stored in her laptop, which has been stolen. He bombarded her with text messages and threats. He's on the run. It's him. Definitely.'

'There's nothing definite about this, Huldar. We can't see his face in the recording. It could be someone else driving the car.'

'Who? You mean someone stole his car, then returned it? His wife? Extremely unlikely. Judging by the height, it looks to me like a man.'

Huldar stood up and went over to the latest additions to the wall, drawn by the photo of the empty pram. He stopped in front of it and bent a little to take a closer look. In the photo, the cover that usually lay over the pram was dangling from its fastening. Inside, it was shockingly empty. A small white quilt lay crumpled at the foot. Apart from that, there was nothing: no sheet, blanket, dummy or bottle. On the tiled terrace lay the broken baby monitor that Númi, one of the fathers, had dropped when he realised Mía was missing.

Huldar's gaze shifted to the next photo, which showed the remains of a woman. This was Droplaug, baby Mía's biological mother. Huldar instantly averted his eyes. The body was a mess after being in the sea for ten days, and, as if that wasn't bad enough, it appeared to have tangled with the propeller of a boat with an outboard motor. Since the boat owner hadn't come forward, it was assumed that he simply hadn't noticed what had happened.

The woman had drowned, her lungs had filled with seawater and her body had sunk. Then the decomposition process had begun, with bacteria forming gases which had collected in her abdomen and chest cavity. When enough gas had formed, the body had floated up to the surface where it had been trapped under an expanse of seaweed. In the end, it had been washed up on the beach at Ægisída on Reykjavík's southern shore, tangled in weed, battered and badly decomposed after almost two weeks in the sea.

Her post-mortem report had not been stuck up on the wall but Huldar had skimmed it earlier and reckoned he'd grasped the gist. The time of death was necessarily vague, given how many days had passed before she was found. But the disappearance of Mía fitted within the time frame. The corpse had been badly hacked about by the propeller, and seabirds had pecked the back of the woman's head to the bone while she was floating face down in the mess of seaweed. It was believed that she had received all these injuries after her death, though it was hard to be sure, given the state of the body. Nevertheless, it seemed fairly certain that she had died from drowning, rather than from her injuries. This was shown by the histological analysis and the acute alteration of her alveoli and bronchi. All the documents relating to the post-mortem had been sent to the pathology department at the National Hospital for review, in case there had been a mistake, but Huldar wasn't expecting anything new to emerge.

Beside the gruesome photo of the body was another of a matted, ragged woollen blanket lying on a steel table in the lab. It had also been found on the shore a week after Droplaug's body turned up; not on Ægisída but in a small cove by the Hvassahraun lava field on the Reykjanes Peninsula, some fifteen kilometres south of Seltjarnarnes as the crow flies. A vigilant walker had spotted it and made the connection with the media's description of Mía, who it was thought might have been wrapped in the blanket that had vanished from her pram.

Although it had been in the sea for such a long time, analysis of the blanket had discovered biological traces from the baby girl and her biological mother, Droplaug. The traces were not enough to provide intact DNA profiles but they were sufficient to confirm their identities.

As baby Mía's body had never been found, she was presumed dead. The conclusion of the inquiry was that her birth mother, Droplaug, must have snatched the child and thrown herself into the sea with her. After the baby drowned, her tiny body had been consumed by sea creatures while the blanket had been washed south by the currents and ended up on the coast at Hvassahraun. In time, the search of the beaches was called off, Mía's name was added to the list of missing persons, and the case was closed.

The investigation concluded that Droplaug had been driven to this desperate act by the fight over custody of her daughter. She lived on Unnarbraut in the suburb of Seltjarnarnes, where it was only a few steps down to the beach and the marina. During the day there was rarely anyone around, so there would have been little risk of her being seen and stopped. And, sure enough, it transpired that no one had seen her.

Mía's parents were a gay couple called Númi and Stefán. Droplaug had carried the child, who was fathered by Stefán, in an attempt to get around Iceland's anti-surrogacy law.

The two men had adopted Mía as parent and step-parent, which was easier than primary adoption, in which there is no connection between the child and the prospective parents. Stefán was Mía's biological father and Droplaug wasn't married or in a civil partnership. This was important as the little girl would otherwise have been legally registered as the child of Droplaug's husband or civil partner, and Stefán would have had to bring a paternity suit to prove that he was the father. But as she had been single, none of this had been necessary. She had simply registered Stefán as the father on the birth certificate and relinquished custody to him. Stefán's husband, Númi, had then been able to adopt the newborn baby who had, up to that point, been his stepdaughter. Once this was done, Droplaug had effectively surrendered all claim to the child, and the two men had become Mía's parents in the eyes of the law.

To begin with, everything had gone smoothly and Droplaug had even confirmed the adoption three months after signing the preliminary papers.

Copies of both documents were pinned to the wall. Perhaps it was fanciful, but Huldar thought he could detect a difference between Droplaug's signature on the first and on the second set of papers. Both were unmistakably signed by the same hand, but the writing appeared a little shakier on the second document. Perhaps she'd had regrets. She must have hesitated, if only because signing the second set of papers would make the arrangement irrevocable.

The moment she put the pen down, there was no turning back. Whether by accident or design, shortly afterwards she found herself shut out: Droplaug was no longer allowed to enter the two men's house, though up until then she had been coming round regularly to breastfeed Mía.

According to her sister, it had come as a bad shock to Droplaug when the fathers refused to let her see her baby, and she'd tried to persuade them to grant her access rights. Droplaug had bonded with Mía during pregnancy and breastfeeding, and hadn't fully understood the role intended for her. It now became clear that the plan had never been for her to be involved in Mía's upbringing. There had been a terrible misunderstanding.

Droplaug soon realised her situation was hopeless. The adoption had gone through and been confirmed: she had given away her child and had no right to any contact with Mía. If the new parents didn't want her to be part of the child's life, their decision was final. This situation was believed to have pushed the poor woman over the edge. She had apparently decided that if she couldn't have access to her daughter, then no one could. Her decision was tragic, especially for the innocent child who had paid with her life. Or so everyone had believed until now.

The final report of the inquiry included a harshly worded paragraph about how Stefán, Númi and Droplaug had conspired to break the law on surrogacy. It was recommended that the case be investigated, particularly in light of the disastrous consequences of their actions. As a rule, surrogacy cases were hard to prove without a confession. If everyone involved stuck to the story that the child had been conceived as the result of adultery, and that the adoption had been a subsequent arrangement, there was little the police could do about it. In the Mía case, one of the fathers had blurted out the whole story during interview, whereas the other, who had legal training, had refused to answer any questions about Mía's conception and adoption. Apparently it was Númi who had opened up about it and Stefán who had been more circumspect. This fact was only mentioned in the closing words of the report, and so far Huldar had failed to track down Númi's confession in any of the numerous statements that had been taken from him.

As far as Huldar had been able to ascertain, the police had lost their enthusiasm for investigating the surrogacy question after the couple hired a crack lawyer, who argued that Númi hadn't been in his right mind when he'd given his statement. There had been no denying this; indeed, Huldar had seen various references to Númi's mental state in the investigation notes. He also discovered why he hadn't been able to find Númi's admission about the agreement with Droplaug in the original case files. It turned out that the couple's lawyer had arranged for his testimony to be destroyed. Even the digital version had been deleted. As a result, the case against the couple had been incomplete and the police had decided there was no point trying to pursue it any further. The two men had already received a devastating punishment for their actions and there was no call to kick them when they were down.

Huldar could find nothing in the files to suggest that the conclusion of the inquiry had been ill-judged. The alleged sequence of events was supported by numerous witness statements and also fitted with the couple's own stories. According to Stefán and Númi, their immediate assumption was that Mía had been snatched by her mother, who wasn't answering her phone. After receiving a call from a hysterical Númi, Stefán had gone storming round to Droplaug's house, but she hadn't answered the bell. He had hammered on the door until his knuckles ached, then put his ear to it but heard nothing. When the police were summoned to the address, they got the same response. Given the gravity of the situation, they had forced entry to the flat, but it was empty; neither Droplaug nor Mía were there.

After that, all efforts were concentrated on trying to find Droplaug. The police had questioned her parents, her sister and closest friends but none of them knew anything. They were all aware of the situation with Mía, however, and

Droplaug's sister had harsh words for Stefán and Númi. She had also become extremely agitated when asked if she thought Droplaug could have harmed the baby. She couldn't rule out the possibility that her sister might have snatched her daughter in despair as a result of being denied access to her, but she vehemently denied that Mía could be in any danger. It was totally out of the question. Droplaug's other family members agreed, if not as fiercely.

There was evidence that Droplaug had been in the area that morning, at around the time the baby had vanished. For example, tracking data on the mobile phone, left behind in her flat when she vanished, showed that she had been over to Skerjafjördur where the two men lived. Her car turned out to be in the garage, but the on-board computer confirmed her movements. The timing fitted: she had driven to Skerjafjördur while Mía was asleep outside in her pram.

Everything pointed to the same conclusion. Stefán and Númi's neighbour reported having seen Droplaug's car outside that morning, and the builders, who had come by to pick up their tools, said they'd encountered her car leaving the street. They insisted that Droplaug had been behind the wheel, since they were familiar with both her and her car. The woman had been a frequent visitor while they were working on the house, initially going inside but later being turned away at the door.

In addition, the builders had witnessed a number of scenes, including several blazing rows between Númi and Droplaug when she had turned up unannounced, wanting to see her baby. Their shouting had been so loud at times that it had drowned out the noise of the builders' tools, and occasionally Stefán had got involved too, when Númi had rung and asked him to come home. Once, Droplaug had arrived with back-up in the form of her sister. That was when things had really got nasty. The builders all agreed that Droplaug seemed to have completely lost the plot by then, but they'd added that it wasn't exactly surprising. They'd heard enough to grasp what was going on, and said it had been a relief to finish the job and get out of there.

The neighbours had told the same story, as most of the screaming matches had taken place at the front door. They'd also seen the woman sitting crying in her car outside the house on more than one occasion; something the builders had witnessed as well.

All the evidence suggested that the woman had been on the brink of despair, and this was apparently confirmed when her body washed up on the beach at Ægisída. After the subsequent discovery of the child's blanket, the sequence of events seemed clear. The baby's mother had stolen her from the pram. So great was her desperation that she had walked into the sea with her daughter in her arms. Case closed. No one could have dreamt that, eleven years later, Mía would turn up again, alive.

Huldar looked at the photo of Íris, Rögnvaldur and Aldís's daughter, then at the picture of the hairless baby Mía, smiling her happy, toothless smile.

The photo of Íris had been confiscated from the couple's flat while it was being searched, together with other material that had been part of Rögnvaldur's collage on the sitting-room wall. The photo of Mía, on the other hand, had been given to the police by her adoptive parents, to be circulated to the media at the time of her disappearance. It had never been returned to them, perhaps because a member of the investigation team had scrawled the dates of Mía's birth and disappearance on it in marker pen.

Huldar peered at the clumsy handwriting, then turned his head to Erla. 'I didn't know they were born in the same year.'

Erla looked up, her face a mask of exhaustion. 'Who?'

'Mía and Íris. Weird.'

'So?'

'Oh, nothing. I just can't work out if it's a coincidence or significant in some way. Though I don't know how it could be.'

'Yes. Right.' Erla appeared to be falling asleep, which, in these rock-hard chairs, took some doing.

'And I can see another connection between the cases too.'

Erla yawned as she answered, drawing out the word: 'What?'

'They both involve longed-for children.' Huldar tried to come up with some further links but his mind was fogged by tiredness. 'Joy, loss and grief.'

'God, don't start getting all sentimental on me.' Erla tipped her head back, contemplating the ceiling for a moment, then stretched her arms and yawned again. 'There's no place for that in an inquiry like this.' She gripped the edge of the conference table and levered herself to her feet. 'But while you're feeling inspired, try and picture where Mía's been hiding all these years. Who knows, maybe you could dash off a poem about it?'

Huldar ignored her jibe. 'Abroad. It's the only explanation. You can't hide a child in Iceland that easily, let alone get away with suddenly pretending you've given birth to a baby that you've stolen.'

Erla waddled over to the door. 'Maybe not. But don't forget that no one was looking for her. She was believed dead.

That would have made it easier to conceal her identity.' She turned, and the weariness seemed to recede for a moment. 'I'll have to give Númi and Stefán a call to let them know their long-lost daughter may be alive, and arrange a meeting with them ASAP. Finally, a job that won't be hard to do.'

Huldar couldn't imagine what it would feel like to be on the receiving end of a phone call like that. A mixture of madness, joy, confusion, incomprehension and tears, shot through with anticipation. The police had better bloody find the girl or the men would have to endure her loss all over again. 'They'll be overjoyed. But don't forget to warn them that we don't have anything concrete.'

'I'm not a complete fucking idiot.' Erla turned and suddenly she looked almost prostrate with tiredness. 'How the hell are we supposed to find the time and manpower to handle both inquiries? I know they're linked and ought to be seen as part of the same investigation, but in practice that's not how it'll pan out. Until we know how the girl's connected to Bríet's murder, it's going to double our workload, or worse. The search for Mía, the search for Rögnvaldur, the investigation of both crimes. I just can't see how the hell we're supposed to manage it.'

'It'll get done somehow.' Huldar spoke against his own conviction. The next few days would be crazy, and those were exactly the kind of conditions that gave rise to mistakes or oversights. 'Tell you what, you take tomorrow to deal with Mía and placate the top brass. I'll concentrate on the murder inquiry and the search for Rögnvaldur. Remember, I've been in charge of this team before and I'm perfectly capable of delegating tasks and keeping people occupied. Just accept my help.'

Erla nodded dully. It was unlike her to accept help with anything to do with managing the department, and she didn't comment on Huldar's offer now, just started itemising the tasks that lay ahead. He would have to take her faint nod as acquiescence. 'The most urgent job, of course, is finding the fucker. You can send all the main media outlets the CCTV capture of Rögnvaldur at the Laugar sports complex. Permission's come through. The picture should revive the public's interest in finding him. Let's just hope he's still wearing the same clothes. It's a pain that there wasn't anything else useful on the footage.' Rögnvaldur had been caught on camera parking his car, getting out and walking away in a southerly direction. He had not got into any other vehicle that they could see.

Erla paused to catch her breath, then continued: 'You'll have to finish ringing round the people we want to interview, prioritising anyone who talked to Bríet on the day she died or in the days beforehand. Particularly Andrea, her dissertation partner, and her two old friends, since their names turn up repeatedly in Bríet's phone log.'

'Sure, will do.' Huldar knew which two friends she meant; the few remaining names on the list included the women in question. He had tried without success to call and email Andrea. The same applied to the two old friends, though he had made do with trying to phone them. Neither had answered. One was a photographer, the other a teacher.

'And you'd better make sure you get hold of them tomorrow. It's vital we get a statement from this Andrea, seeing as she had a brush with Rögnvaldur as well.' Erla grimaced. 'Though it's quite possible that the unidentified blood in Bríet's flat was hers. If so, we can assume she was there when Bríet was attacked.'

Huldar tried to visualise the scene. 'Isn't that a bit far-fetched? Andrea's supposed to be abroad. Surely no one would jet off on a foreign holiday like nothing had happened if they'd just been present at a murder? Especially not on a yoga retreat.'

Erla shrugged. 'If she's implicated in the murder, a trip abroad would be ideal. Don't forget that.'

He smiled. 'Are you suggesting she and Rögnvaldur were in cahoots?'

'Who the fuck knows? Nothing would surprise me about this case.'

'No. Sorry, I don't buy it. But don't worry – I'll take care of it. We've got the whole weekend ahead and we'll make good use of it.' He gave her what he hoped was an encouraging smile. 'I'm sure the team will be up for working right through. Pulling late shifts.' He didn't remind her of all the witnesses they might have to question in relation to the reopened Mía case. Anyway, that could wait. After eleven years, people's memories were bound to be hazy. But there was no doubt it would be a long list: Númi and Stefán's neighbours, Droplaug's friends and relations, a whole army of builders, the pathologist and the police officers who had worked on the original inquiry . . . 'It'll all sort itself out.'

'Yeah, right.' Again, Erla sounded highly sceptical. 'Oh, and one other thing: maybe you could arrange for Bríet's parents to see the body. We've been given the go-ahead. The sooner the better, because the pathologist's waiting to start the post-mortem on the head. You just need to follow through; most of the preparation's already in place.'

Huldar glanced inadvertently at the photos of Bríet's body parts. No one had got round to adding a picture of the head yet and he certainly wasn't going to remind them. 'Are you sure that's a good idea?'

'No, I'm not. Far from it. But it's out of my hands. The guy from the Identification Commission put it to the committee and they agreed unanimously. I'm too tired to do anything but obey. Let's hope to God the mortuary can piece her together well enough to minimise the shock to the parents. I gather the head is the only part that will be visible and they'll spread a sheet over the rest. But get Freyja to talk to them beforehand. She offered to prepare them.'

Erla didn't seem able to remember anything else. She put a hand to the small of her back and shuffled out. She may not have been born yesterday, as she had said earlier, but judging by her gait it might have been better if she'd given birth yesterday.

Chapter 22

Huldar sat down and ran through the checklist he'd prepared as soon as he got into the office that morning. He crossed off two jobs that had been done. While Erla was attending a meeting with senior management and the police PR representative about the Mía case, he had handed out the assignments, making sure that everyone had enough to keep them busy. He allocated to himself the job of contacting the people who had spoken to Bríet on the phone shortly before she died. There were only two names left on the list: the photographer, Ólína Traustadóttir, and Bríet's dissertation partner, Andrea Logadóttir. The third friend, a teacher, had answered her phone and explained that she and Bríet had been discussing plans for an imminent girls' trip to a summer house that they were supposed to be organising. The friend had heard what happened from Bríet's mother and, although Bríet's name hadn't yet been made public, she hadn't kept the information to herself. Apparently their circle of friends were devastated by the news. They were even thinking of cancelling their trip. This was followed by a pause, as if she hoped Huldar would encourage them to stick to their plans and go anyway. He said a curt goodbye and hung up.

The net was closing around the two women left on the list. It was more urgent to get hold of Andrea than Ólína, since she had also had dealings with Rögnvaldur. But her mobile phone was still off and there had been no response to the emails or messages Huldar had sent her. He had resorted to tracking down her mother, from whom he learnt that Andrea was in Thailand and wasn't due back until tomorrow. Andrea had flown out at the crack of dawn on Saturday morning and there would be no way of contacting her until she got back. She was on a combined yoga and meditation retreat, where no phones or computers were allowed. Her mother had the idea it might be a silent retreat too. She gave Huldar the name of the place where it was being held but all his attempts to get through on the phone went unanswered.

This was incredibly frustrating, as Bríet and Andrea had been in regular contact. Not only was it vital to get Andrea's testimony about Rögnvaldur, but the two women had attended lectures, studied and worked on the dissertation together. It went without saying that they must have talked about more than just their studies, which meant that Andrea was almost certainly in possession of information that no one else knew. According to Bríet's mother, they had been planning to put in a session on the dissertation together on the Friday. It was even possible that Andrea had been at Bríet's flat when Rögnvaldur forced his way in, and that the unidentified blood found at the scene was hers. On the other hand, there had only been one plate on the kitchen table and nothing to suggest that two people had been sharing the pizza.

Huldar had studied a sketch of the flat with the locations of all the biological traces marked in, but this did nothing to help explain the unidentified blood-stains. According to the plan, Bríet's blood had been found in the kitchen, the other blood-stains in the hall. As they were from a different woman, this suggested that Bríet had not been alone in the flat. Perhaps Andrea had been with her but hadn't felt like any pizza.

He reminded himself that the unknown blood could be that of the killer. Bríet's attacker could conceivably have been a woman. But he had no intention of airing this view at the moment, since Erla already had quite enough on her plate. Besides, Rögnvaldur's behaviour strongly implied that he was guilty.

Huldar abandoned his speculation temporarily and returned his attention to the job at hand. He was getting seriously pissed off with this Andrea and her yoga retreat. If it were being held in Iceland, he could have barged in and dragged the woman out with her mouth open in a silent scream. But since this wasn't an option, he resorted instead to asking the International Department to submit a request to the Thai police to contact her. He wasn't expecting a response until this afternoon at the earliest.

Ólína, the other elusive friend, wasn't abroad, but whenever they tried her phone, all they got was an automated message in English: *I'm in a meeting, I'll call back later.* Since they had tried her both in the evening and during the day, either the woman was keener on meetings than a procedure committee or her phone was set to give this message whenever she didn't pick up.

Although talking to Ólína wasn't top of their list, they still needed to get hold of her at some point as she was one of the people Bríet had spoken to on the phone in the days leading up to her murder. Earlier this morning, Huldar had called Bríet's mother to arrange a time for the couple to visit the mortuary. He had grabbed the opportunity to ask her about Ólína and learnt that she wasn't one of Bríet's closest friends. Which was odd, considering the high volume of phone calls between the two women recently.

Bríet's mother had been surprised to hear this and said they had been close at school but had drifted apart as they'd got older. They hadn't quarrelled or fallen out, it was just that their lives had led them in different directions. Bríet had studied biomedical science, Ólína photography. It was possible they had revived their friendship but, if so, the mother was surprised Bríet hadn't mentioned it to her. Then she backpedalled, saying it must have been because Bríet had been so busy. At which point she broke down in tears.

All the police needed to know was what Ólína and Bríet had been talking about on Friday and in the preceding days. Nothing else. But Huldar was itching to cross the task off his list and move on to the next. It was good for the morale to be able to mark jobs as done, however minor they were. So he got in touch with the IT department and asked them to track Ólína's phone. He wanted to cross off as much as he could before Erla got back, to cheer her up. Once her meetings were over, she was due to go and see Mía's parents, which meant he still had a bit of time. Everything else on the to-do list had been assigned. Gudlaugur had gone with Freyja to prepare Bríet's parents for the viewing of their daughter's body, and the rest of the team were busy with other tasks, including the hunt for Rögnvaldur.

The phone rang. It was the man from IT with the coordinates for Ólína's phone.

Huldar watched as Lína deliberately adopted a commanding stance. She drew herself up, raised her chin and arranged her features in a stern expression. He wasn't too impressed with her much-vaunted police science degree course if this is how they taught students to pose. The small, hard pellets of snow falling from the sky seemed to agree. They collected on Lína's red hair, pale eyelashes and shoulders, sparkling in the streetlights as if she had poured glitter over herself, and undermining her attempt to look professional.

School children in colourful anoraks were trickling out of the building. Apart from their coats, most of them weren't dressed for the snow that was now coming down heavily. The day had started out clear and dry but the weather gods had subsequently changed their minds. Only a handful of kids, whose parents had had the foresight to check the forecast, were equipped with hats, gloves and moonboots.

'What's a photographer doing at a school?' Lína stared over the playground at the grey two-storey building without much enthusiasm.

Huldar shrugged. 'Taking class pictures? Unless she's working here. Maybe they offer photography courses. It wouldn't be the stupidest thing they teach.'

Lína gave him a glance and from her pursed lips it was clear that she didn't agree. 'Shall we go in?'

'No reason to hang about.'

They set off against the tide of children. Huldar had to dodge a snowball but it hadn't been aimed at them. They were wearing their police coats and it was clear that the girl who'd thrown it was terrified when she realised she'd almost hit a cop. She raised her snow-caked mittens to her face with a look of horror and melted into the crowd. The warmly dressed kids were noticeably keener to take part in the snowball fight, while those in unsuitable clothes made the most enticing targets, as is so often the case.

Huldar and Lína went inside and the door swung to behind them, muffling the shouts and screams in the playground. Once they had found the office, Huldar knocked on the door and opened it. A woman who was squatting down, putting magazines in a box, glanced up in surprise. 'Hello. Can I help you? Are you here about the fire alarm?'

Huldar said no, they were from the police.

The woman stood up. 'Sorry about the misunderstanding. Our fire alarm's developed a fault and it keeps going off. It's impossible to get any work done, so we've had to send the children home.'

Lína looked up at the ceiling, then around her, clearly doubting the truth of this, given the silence, and the woman hurriedly added: 'It's not constant. It keeps stopping and starting.'

'No problem. Actually, we're here about another matter.'

'Why, has something happened?'

'No. We're just looking for Ólína Traustadóttir.'

'Is she a pupil?' The woman's worried frown deepened.

'No. She's an adult. Possibly a member of staff.' The moment Huldar had said this, he realised how unlikely it was. The school wasn't that big a workplace and the woman would have recognised the name immediately if Ólína had been employed there.

'Erm, no. There's no Ólína working here. I'm not the secretary, though. I work in the library. I just popped into the office.'

'She's a photographer. Is it possible she could be here to take class pictures?'

The woman shook her head. 'No. Those were done last month. I don't know if this Ólína took them – the photographer was a woman, but she hasn't been back, as far as I know. I can't see why she would need to, either. The pictures arrived ages ago and the children have all got theirs.' The woman brightened up. 'Could she be one of the cleaners? I don't know all their names.' Then she looked embarrassed. 'The turnover's so high.'

'It's possible. Are the cleaners here yet?'

'No. I'm afraid not. They don't start till four. So not for a while yet.'

It was just past eleven.

Lína weighed in. 'Could she be a parent?'

'Maybe. I don't know all their names. But I'm not aware of any parents in the building. The children have just gone home, as I said. If she's a mother, she could be outside. We emailed all the parents earlier when we had to call it a day because of the noise.' The woman's eyes narrowed suddenly. 'Why do you think the woman's here?'

Huldar didn't answer, merely thanked her and exited the office, with Lína in tow. She stopped before they reached the front door. 'Try calling her number.'

It was a good idea. Huldar pulled out his phone, selected the number, then, once he'd heard that it was ringing, pressed it to his thigh, to prevent the sound from interfering with any faint ringtone from Ólína's phone, should it be in the vicinity.

They stood without moving, straining their ears.

Nothing.

Lína gave up first. 'Couldn't she be one of the parents, like the woman said? If so, she's probably left by now.'

Huldar sighed. 'Maybe. But IT said they'd tracked the coordinates twice, half an hour apart, to see if the owner of the phone was on the move, and the location was here both times. The second time was just before we left the station.' He put his phone back in his pocket.

Once they were outside in the playground, he decided to try again. Maybe Lína was right and the woman was still there, waiting for her child.

He selected the number. Over the voices of the remaining kids, they heard the faint sound of ringing. It was such a common ringtone that lots of the kids instinctively reached into their pockets or backpacks before realising it wasn't theirs. Meanwhile, Huldar and Lína were trying to work out where the sound was coming from, hampered by the hubbub of shrill voices around them. Then, with a deafening screech, the fire alarm went off, drowning out both phone and kids.

Just before the alarm finally fell silent, Huldar felt a tug at his coat. Looking down, he saw a little boy gazing up at him admiringly. 'Have you got a gun?'

Huldar answered hastily, before Lína could jump in and start citing the rules on the handling and use of weapons and force by the police: 'No.'

'Are you going to arrest us?' The little boy didn't seem particularly daunted by the prospect.

'No. Don't worry.' Eager to get rid of the child so he could try the phone again, Huldar wished he'd let Lína drone on about rules. That would have been guaranteed to drive the boy away. 'But now we need a bit of peace to do our job. You go back to your game.'

But the boy wasn't going to be fobbed off so easily. 'What are you doing?' Children and questions: they went together like blueberries and *skyr*.

Huldar asked Lína to deal with the kid while he tried the phone again. This time it was even harder to locate the ringing over the sound of Lína lecturing the boy on the importance of the police's job and how vital it was that members of the public didn't get in the way while they were trying to perform their duty. He glanced round at the children who were now all staring at him and Lína. The freshly fallen snow seemed to have lost its appeal. Cops in the playground wasn't something they got to see every day – luckily.

The ringing fell silent before he could locate it. The children had started wandering away from the playground in dribs and drabs, the interruption to their snowball fight having apparently killed the mood. Since Huldar towered over them, it wasn't hard for him to reassure himself that Ólína wasn't among them. As they were streaming past, he tried the phone again. This time the shrieking had moved away and the ringtone was clearer but, instead of coming from the departing children, it originated from the spot where they had all been gathered earlier.

With the kids gone, it was easy to track down the phone, lying abandoned in the snow.

Huldar slammed the car door harder than he intended. He put the key in the ignition and started the engine. 'I don't know who had the phone but there's no way it's been lying there all morning. There was hardly any snow on the screen, for one thing, and if it was there before the children arrived, one of them would surely have spotted it and picked it up, or trodden on it by mistake. But no, it was lying there, untouched.' Huldar broke off while he checked to see if it was safe to reverse out of the parking space. 'One of the kids dumped it there. Perhaps because they guessed we were looking for it.'

Lína fastened her seat-belt. She was holding the phone in a plastic evidence bag. 'Is it possible that Ólína could have lent her kid the phone, and he or she dropped it during the snowball fight? It could be that simple.' She was silent briefly, while checking something on her own phone, then added: 'No. She doesn't have any kids. According to the National Registry, she's single and childless.'

Huldar eased his way out into the traffic. 'She could have lent her phone to a friend's kid, or a niece or nephew or something. Maybe she's a yoga freak like Andrea and likes to go on silent retreats.'

'I'd never lend my phone to a child.' Lína assumed her pompous tone again. 'Not under any circumstances.'

She was right. Huldar would certainly never trust any of his nephews with his. He'd be guaranteed to get it back all sticky, with a crack in the screen, cluttered up with stupid games. He threw a quick glance at Lína. 'What do you say to a coffee? A good one, at a café?'

Lína's face took on the expression of Little Red Riding Hood contemplating her grandmother's dodgy appearance. 'Shouldn't we just head back to the office? I don't want to get into any trouble.'

'Lína, in our job trouble means breaking a witness's arm, accidentally arresting a government minister or dropping a piece of evidence down a drain. Grabbing a coffee does not even make it onto the list.'

She didn't look convinced but Huldar wasn't going to be deterred. They had a long day ahead and after that a long weekend at work. The traffic was still reasonably light and a quarter of an hour at a café wouldn't change that. 'Well, I need a coffee, so that's settled.'

Chapter 23

Friday

Bríet's parents were sitting side by side in the waiting room. They had pushed their chairs together and were holding hands, in silent solidarity. No doubt the same thoughts were passing through their minds, the same grief. They had dressed up for the occasion: she was wearing a dress, tights and modest heels; he was in a suit and tie, and his best shoes. Neither Freyja nor Gudlaugur had commented on the fact when they'd gone round to collect the couple from their home.

They were sitting a little apart from the parents now, Gudlaugur staring blankly at the wall, Freyja snatching regular glances at them. It didn't occur to either of them to get their phones out to help pass the time.

It wasn't really a waiting room so much as a corridor where a few chairs had been placed against the wall here and there. All the doors in the corridor were closed and few members of staff passed by. Those who did kept their eyes straight ahead and walked briskly. There was no telling if they'd got wind of the purpose of this visit or were simply very busy.

The clock on the wall clicked every time the minute hand moved, sounding absurdly loud in the silent corridor. Nobody needed such a regular reminder of the inexorable passage of time, especially not those who were waiting.

Freyja caught the movement as Bríet's mother raised her
free hand to one eye and wiped it. Then she gave a polite little
sniff, so polite that in different circumstances it would have
been inaudible. Her husband tightened his hold on her other
hand.

'Is everything all right?' Freyja leant over in an attempt
to make eye contact. She had sat with them for half an hour
before they set out for the mortuary, giving them plenty of time
to ask questions and get everything they needed to off their
chests. Before meeting them, she had turned off her phone
in case Saga's nursery phoned to tell her they were closing
early for some reason and she would have to collect her niece.
This was unlikely, but still. She mustn't mess this up. These
people needed consideration and the sort of gentle touch that
no one on the investigation team seemed to possess. She had
concluded the conversation by saying a few words on loss and
grief, but the couple would not be drawn on the subject of
their decision to view Bríet's body. At least they had already
been notified that the head had been found, so that wouldn't
come as a surprise. 'You know you can change your mind at
any point,' she reminded them now.

The couple had been slumping in their chairs but now drew
themselves upright. It was the husband who answered. 'We're
not changing our minds. But it would be good if we didn't
have to wait much longer.'

Freyja agreed. They had turned up at the appointed time
and had now been kept waiting twelve minutes, according to
the noisy clock. 'They know we're here. They'll open the door
soon.' She hoped the couple wouldn't take it into their heads
to get up and open it themselves. It would be a disaster if they
got a look inside the room before all the preparations had

been completed. 'Perhaps they're waiting for the chaplain. He was invited at rather short notice.'

At the last minute, Bríet's parents had asked if the hospital chaplain could come along and say a few prayers. Freyja had thought this was an excellent idea and immediately got on the phone to relay the request. It would provide them with some sort of formal closure, otherwise they would simply go in, take a look, cry and leave again. She hoped they would accept the chaplain's help afterwards as well. Few people had as much experience of providing bereaved family members with pastoral care, independent of their faith, than a hospital chaplain. It was clear that they needed help but it seemed unlikely they would turn to her. Sometimes therapists failed to develop the necessary rapport with their clients to invite confidences, and in those cases it was important to find an alternative solution. Perhaps Bríet's parents thought she was too young, the wrong sex, irritating or not sincere enough. She hoped the chaplain would suit them better.

Freyja didn't have to wait long to find out. A woman – young, blonde, looking not unlike her – appeared at the top of the stairs and came over. Instead of wearing the black attire and ruff of a Lutheran vicar, she had on a white coat over conventional, neat clothes. But as she came closer, Freyja noticed that she was wearing a shirt with a priest's white collar.

The couple appeared rather put out, so presumably their resistance to Freyja had been to do with her age and possibly her sex as well. She didn't take offence: everyone was different.

The chaplain introduced herself and apologised for keeping them waiting. She said nothing about the short notice, just focused her attention on Bríet's parents, ignoring Freyja and Gudlaugur. As it should be.

Once she had spoken quietly to the couple and established that they had no questions, she announced that everything was ready. Freyja was familiar with most of the things the chaplain had said to prepare them. They were similar to what she herself had pointed out to them this morning, though couched in rather more religious language. Freyja consoled herself with the thought that the couple had at least been prepared as well as they could be for the sight of their daughter's body.

Bríet's parents rose to their feet. The mother wobbled as if her knees were giving way and her husband gently took her arm. He didn't release his hold, even though she recovered her balance almost at once. Their eyes met, then they followed the chaplain to the door.

The chaplain knocked lightly, then opened it a crack to peer in. After this she turned to the couple and asked if they were ready. Both nodded without speaking.

Freyja and Gudlaugur stayed behind in the corridor and heard a man, presumably the pathologist, receiving the couple as had been agreed. Freyja had been fully briefed about what would happen, so that she could explain the procedure to the parents. Nothing must come as a surprise at a time like this. The loss of their daughter was difficult enough, and viewing her body would play a central role in the grieving process. Everything had to go as smoothly as possible.

Through the crack in the door, Freyja heard the pathologist expressing his condolences. He told them he would remove the sheet from Bríet's face when they were ready and reminded them that her eyes would be closed, as if she were asleep. They mustn't touch her, however much they wanted to. Freyja knew why: the head and body parts that had been assembled under the sheet had just been brought out of the freezer. Apparently it would come as a horrible shock to the parents if they touched her icy flesh, even though they had been forewarned. She knew, too, that small plastic moulds had been inserted under the eyelids to prevent them from appearing sunken. She could have done without this particular piece of knowledge.

The pathologist told them to take their time and just let him know when they were ready.

'I'm ready.' The mother's voice sounded as hoarse as if she had just inhaled a lungful of volcanic ash. The father sounded no better when he chimed in.

The silence which followed lasted longer than Freyja had been expecting. She was impressed by the composure the parents were showing, as she couldn't hear so much as a sniff. She sighed, filled with pity for the poor couple. She'd been expecting weeping and perhaps that they would say something. But what was there to say at a time like this? What had she thought they'd say?

Certainly not what the father now blurted out:

'That's not Bríet.'

The body was lying on a steel trolley that had been wheeled into one of the labs following the fiasco. The sheet was pulled back from the head, the plastic moulds still in place under the eyelids. Freyja would have given anything not to have to see it, but she had no choice. As if the face of a dead person wasn't bad enough, how much worse to know that the body under the sheet was in pieces. Freyja couldn't help wondering if the poor woman would be stitched together like Frankenstein's monster for the funeral. She shivered.

Huldar looked devastated. He seemed as upset by the sight as Freyja since he kept turning away, although he did remark that the head looked better than when he had last seen it down at the beach. She'd heard that it had been cleaned up, once samples had been taken for analysis, to facilitate identification. The cleaning didn't seem to have achieved much, though. There was a conspicuous wound on the lower part of the neck and another on the right side of the forehead, which had been turned away from Bríet's parents.

Gudlaugur was sitting with his hands in his lap on an adjustable metal stool, the only seat in there. Normally, he was the epitome of good manners, so the fact he had collapsed onto the stool without offering it to anyone else first was a fair illustration of the state he was in. When the commotion had broken out, he had at least had the presence of mind to call Huldar, after failing to get through to Erla. Apparently she was still in a meeting; in other words, still in a world where their investigation was on the right track. A little shaky, perhaps, but still holding up. Freyja had stopped Gudlaugur from sending her a text about the latest twist. This wasn't news that anyone, let alone a heavily pregnant woman, would want to receive via SMS in the middle of a meeting with senior management.

Afterwards, Freyja had talked to the parents, who were taking the whole thing with extraordinary composure. At first, the colour had flooded into their cheeks and it was clear that they interpreted the mistake as meaning that their daughter might still be alive. It was painful to have to snuff out this spark of hope but Freyja didn't want them to embrace this joy, only to have to go through the grieving process all over again. They couldn't assume that Bríet was alive, in spite of the debacle. Freyja had spent most of the time with them apologising for the blunder.

The hospital chaplain had been there too but lacked the appropriate words for the situation, having never experienced anything like it. But then, short of a natural catastrophe or being bombed in a war, nothing could excuse a cock-up like this. Freyja didn't even try to play it down or deny responsibility. Since she had no previous experience to rely on either, she had to fall back on sincerity. As a result, the couple's attitude to her seemed to have softened, which made the conversation more bearable. Most people find it easier to sympathise with someone who's found themselves in the wrong.

'I'm not taking responsibility for this.' The head pathologist was suffering from a combination of fury and stress. 'This is the first time I've been anywhere near the head. I was supposed to perform a post-mortem on it, that was all. This fiasco is entirely the police's fault. I didn't even supervise the taking of samples or cleaning. And I would like to point out that I was completely opposed to this viewing.' He took a pen from the pocket of his white coat, pointed it at Huldar and repeated his words: 'Completely opposed to it. As I'm sure I said in one of my emails. I can prove it.'

Freyja admired the way Huldar kept his cool, especially as he wasn't known for his ability to control his temper. Perhaps it was the shock. The news had reached him just as he was sitting down to enjoy a double espresso at his favourite café. Lína had tagged along to the mortuary, as she had been with him at the time, though she was at pains to point out that she hadn't ordered anything herself. She had whispered in an aside to Freyja that she didn't think it was appropriate to take a break in town like that in the middle of an investigation. From the way she said it, she appeared to regard the café visit as even more scandalous than the mix-up with the head.

Huldar waited until the pathologist lowered his pen. 'Have we not got the right head?'

'The right head? What do you mean? Is it Bríet's head? No. Is it the head that fits the body? Yes.'

'Good.' Huldar ran his hands through his hair, glanced at the trolley, then quickly averted his eyes. 'Do you have any idea who it could be?'

The head pathologist flushed dark red. 'Me? How should I know? I don't want to see you lot back here until you've worked it out. And I want X-rays of the teeth before I write a death certificate.' The wind suddenly seemed to go out of his sails, but it turned out to be from relief rather than a sense of defeat. 'Phew. At least I had the sense to add a disclaimer to the post-mortem report on the question of identity. And I haven't issued the death certificate yet.'

No doubt this was a great comfort to him, but the others were not so lucky: Erla and her team had gone full steam ahead in the certain knowledge that the body was Bríet's.

A phone bleeped in the man's pocket and he took it out, read something on the screen, then looked at Huldar. 'What bad luck. I sent a request to Bríet's dentist when we took delivery of the head yesterday, asking for X-rays of her teeth for comparison. They've only just been sent over.' The pathologist picked up a scalpel from the worktop beside him.

'I'm sorry but I can't watch you open up the head,' Freyja exclaimed in horror as the man walked over to the body. She couldn't take any more. 'I've got to leave the room.'

He paused and regarded her in surprise. 'I wasn't intending to open it up. I just want to check something.' He turned the knife and used the handle to raise the upper lip. Then he gestured to Huldar. 'Look.'

Freyja turned away. She had no desire to see inside the mouth of a severed head. Huldar seemed equally unenthusiastic, but he swallowed and stepped over to join the pathologist, wearing a resigned expression.

When Freyja felt it was safe, she turned back, just in time to see the pathologist remove the knife handle, causing the lip to fall back into place. 'As you can see, this is a completely different set of teeth. Bríet's had obviously been straightened.' He handed Huldar his phone and Freyja assumed that he was showing him a dental X-ray.

'I can't see any difference.' Huldar handed it back.

This didn't surprise Freyja at all. She had seen Huldar checking Tinder and he had seemed oblivious to everything about the women's pictures apart from the filters, which he was unusually adept at spotting. He'd also had an eye for designer labels. If the picture featured a filter or label, he'd swiped left, dismissing the woman. He'd also had his own elimination method when it came to the women's profiles. This rather slapdash approach, which could hardly be described as forensic, left him almost exclusively with women in a certain age bracket, who he swiped right on. Freyja was inclined to scoff at first, but had to admit that it was efficient. Yet, for some unexplained reason, the more women had fallen into this category, the more uneasy she had felt.

'You must be able to see the difference.' The pathologist shoved the phone back at Huldar, who shook his head again.

All this talk about teeth was making Freyja increasingly agitated. She was desperate to get outside into the fresh air. What on earth were they achieving here? Surely they should be heading back to the office, preparing themselves to get down on their knees and bleat out an apology, prepare a statement.

But the truth was, she didn't want to do that either. On reflection, it was actually better to be here.

It seemed she wasn't alone in thinking this. No one appeared to be in a hurry to leave. But the dental examination was only delaying the moment of doom. With any luck, it would help their case that it was the Identification Commission that had recommended the parents be allowed to view the body, but this was by no means certain. Faceless committees were much better at evading responsibility than named individuals. And this time, she and the CID team were those individuals.

Even Lína no longer seemed eager to get back to the office. If anyone had invited her to a café now, she would have jumped at the offer. She was standing to one side, watching impassively and taking no part in the proceedings.

Something dawned on Freyja. She'd seen a photo of Andrea on the wall at the police station, and it struck her now that the two women weren't unalike. They were a similar height and weight; both had light-brown hair. She wouldn't trust herself to identify Andrea from the head, based on that picture alone, but Huldar or the pathologist would be in a better position to do it. 'Huldar. Could you call up the photo of Andrea and compare it to the head? It has to be her, doesn't it? No one's been able to get hold of her for nearly a week and Rögnvaldur threatened her too, didn't he?'

It was an excellent idea but Huldar didn't seem particularly grateful to Freyja for suggesting it. 'Sure. I can do that.' Reluctantly, he took out his phone. If it got anywhere near the head, he'd probably insist on stopping to buy a new one on his way back to the station.

The pathologist intervened. 'I want to see the woman on a proper-sized screen, not a phone.' He moved over to the computer and Huldar followed, looking slightly happier.

Freyja watched over their shoulders. She had a hunch that she was right.

She turned to smile at Lína and Gudlaugur, the latter still rigid with horror, his head buried in his hands. But Lína had her back to her. She was standing over by the head, having seized the opportunity to take a closer look while Huldar and the pathologist were otherwise occupied. Freyja was amazed by the girl's lack of squeamishness. Then she turned back to the screen where all she could see over the men's shoulders was a woman's forehead and hair. 'Is it her?'

Before they could answer, they heard the click of a phone unlocking behind them. Freyja spun round, outraged, ready to reprimand Lína for taking a photo of the head, but it transpired that this wasn't what she had been doing.

Lína had turned and was staring at Freyja, her eyes wide. 'I know who it is.' She held up a phone in her gloved hand. The screen was lit up and activated. 'It's Ólína, the photographer.'

Chapter 24

Friday

Gudlaugur, Erla and Freyja were sitting outside the house in an unmarked police car. Gudlaugur, who was driving, had parked by the kerb and switched off the engine, but none of them could bring themselves to open the doors and get out. Instead, they sat there without speaking, gazing at the rough sea where it could be glimpsed between the houses. Although the sun was up, it was making little impression on the dark snow-clouds obscuring the sky. The sea was a matching black, apart from the white crests of the waves that vanished almost as soon as they appeared.

No one had said a word on the way there from the police station. Shortly after Huldar, Gudlaugur, Freyja and Lína had got back from the mortuary, Erla had appeared, looking reasonably satisfied after her meeting with the top brass. Her satisfaction was short-lived. Huldar took it upon himself to inform her what had happened and when he emerged from her office shortly afterwards, he told Freyja and Gudlaugur to put their coats back on. They were to go with Erla to see Mía's parents. The visit had already been arranged and couldn't be postponed. According to Huldar, Erla had refused to discuss the latest bombshell until after the visit was over. She simply couldn't cope with anything else at the moment. Huldar had warned Freyja not to discuss it on the way. He must have mentioned it to Gudlaugur too because there couldn't be any other explanation for the awkward silence. They were all pre-occupied with the mistaken identification of the head and body, and its fallout. But since the subject was off limits, it made sense to keep one's mouth shut.

In the end, it was Freyja who broke the silence with a general observation. 'How much does something like that cost?' She was studying the swanky modern house that stood on one of Reykjavík's desirable oceanfront plots. The properties on either side, which dated from several decades earlier, testified to the changing trends in architecture. One had columns flanking the front door that would have looked more at home on the Acropolis hill than in Skerjafjördur. But despite their stylistic variety, the houses had all clearly been built by people with deep pockets, and were so oversized for their plots that, ironically, there was hardly any space between them.

Neither of the others replied to Freyja's comment, but then the amounts involved must be way beyond anything their pay packets would stretch to, even if they were all combined. Gud-laugur gripped the steering wheel and shook it slightly. 'Right, guys. Shall we get this over with?'

Erla still looked like a thundercloud but at least she made the effort to answer: 'Yup. It's time.'

They got out just as a plane took off from the domestic airport, which cut right through the middle of Skerjafjördur's residential streets. By the time they reached the men's front door, the plane had vanished into the dark mass of cloud. They formed an unusually large delegation but there was a reason for that. As a rule, two officers were sent out in cases where it was considered unnecessary or inappropriate to ask people to come to the station. But Erla's phone conversation with the men late yesterday evening had revealed that communication with them was likely to prove a minefield. The old files on Mía's disappearance had been strangely unforthcoming on the problems that had dogged the police's relations with the little girl's parents, which had apparently begun badly and gone downhill from there.

This time, as the top brass had stressed to Erla, the fathers were to be given the full kid-glove treatment. Freyja gathered that they were hoping Erla would manage to butter them up sufficiently to prevent their anger about the original investigation from spilling over into the press. As it was, media outlets would be fighting for interviews with them the moment the results of the DNA analysis leaked out. Even the international press and TV stations were likely to take an interest in the miraculous reappearance of a child who was believed to have died more than a decade ago.

Erla also had private reasons for wanting to get on the men's good side. Normally she would have delegated someone else to talk to them, in light of the latest setback, but she was in charge of the inquiry and if Mía's fathers went to the papers, she would bear the brunt of the negative coverage. To increase the chances that these tactics would work, the senior management had ordered her to take the others along; Freyja, presumably to pacify the men, armed with her psychological expertise; Gudlaugur, perhaps because he was gay, although this had not been stated in as many words. Freyja couldn't see what they thought this would achieve.

The front door opened to reveal a man in his thirties. He had dark hair, glasses, was of average height and looked in good shape – from running or cycling, Freyja guessed. His

face, which would no doubt have been friendly in normal circumstances, now appeared anxious, but the crease between
his brows disappeared and his eyes opened wide when he saw
how many of them there were. 'Are you all from the police?'

Erla said they were and introduced them. When the man
showed no signs of inviting them inside, she prompted him by
asking if they could come in for a minute.

They could see into a hall with a floor and walls of large,
shiny black tiles, which looked as if they had been polished
that morning. The man called out: 'Stebbi, the police are
here!' Then he retreated into the gloomy hall as they stepped
in through the absurdly high, wide entrance. The massive
door must have weighed at least fifty kilos.

Beyond the hall was an open space, from which some steps
led down into a breathtakingly grand living room. The ceiling
was so high one could almost have fitted in an extra storey,
but it was well worth sacrificing a room or two for the floor-
to-ceiling glass wall. The dramatic view of the choppy, dark
ocean completely stole the show, putting the designer furniture in the shade. The men could just as well have chucked a
few pallets in there, plonked some cushions on them and hung
IKEA posters on the walls, as few visitors would have eyes for
anything but the view.

The man who'd let them in – Númi, presumably – showed
them down into the living room and invited them to take a
seat on the stylish, brown leather sofa. As they sank into the
huge cushions that must have been stuffed with goose down,
Freyja wondered if she would have to haul Erla to her feet
at the end of the meeting. Númi sat down facing them in a
large, black leather chair, which was as stylish as the sofa
but didn't look anywhere near as comfortable. Perhaps that

was why he appeared so ill at ease. He didn't meet their eyes or say a word while they waited for his husband, Stefán, to join them.

'What a stunning house,' Freyja said to break the awkward silence. She received no reply. Númi had turned away from them to stare out of the window. Freyja found herself thinking about what it must have been like for the fathers living in that house for all those years after their daughter Mía was believed to have drowned in the sea. The view must have lost its charm for them, especially while there was still a risk their baby might one day be washed ashore. The thought made her shudder and she wondered why they hadn't sold up and moved somewhere inland.

Stefán appeared on the landing from another part of the house. He stormed down the steps, his face livid, and took a chair matching Númi's, but in contrast to his husband he made no attempt to avoid eye contact. He was taller and darker than Númi, with thicker eyebrows, but looked in similarly good shape. He was dressed in a smart shirt and suit trousers, which were a bit on the short side, in Freyja's opinion. Above the expensive leather shoes, there was a flash of colourful socks. His shirtsleeves were rolled up, giving him the look of a banker who was spoiling for a fight on his way to work. He wasn't a banker, though – according to Erla, Stefán was a lawyer, partner in one of the bigger legal practices in the city. He immediately struck Freyja as the kind of arrogant prick who'd be a nightmare to work for. Númi came across as a much gentler character: he worked for an investment fund, dealing in securities.

Erla explained that she was the person they'd spoken to on the phone yesterday evening and again this morning. She went on to introduce Freyja and Gudlaugur, but had barely finished speaking when Stefán jumped in. 'Is this some kind of joke? They send along a pregnant woman, a psychologist and – what? – a gay man? Is this supposed to win us over and make us forgive the way the police treated us in the past?'

Erla quashed this immediately, though Stefán wasn't actually that wrong. 'No. We aren't clairvoyant enough to have planned the interview nine months in advance. The reason there are three of us is so we can answer all your questions and provide assistance, should you require it. The news is bound to be hard to take in.'

Stefán's knuckles whitened as he gripped the shiny steel arms of his chair. 'I'm speaking for both of us when I say we want absolutely no assistance from the likes of you. You're the very last people we'd turn to if we needed help. We're not interested in fake sympathy from you or anyone else in the police. Why don't you just get on with your job and stop wasting our time?'

The meeting was already going off the rails but Erla reacted stoically. No doubt she had recovered from her initial shock at the misidentification and had progressed to the numb stage. 'Regardless of what happened between you and our colleagues eleven years ago, we're not faking anything. We urgently need to find out how your daughter's DNA has suddenly turned up like this. But before we go any further I must repeat what I said yesterday: although all the indications are that she is alive, nothing's guaranteed.'

'What's the matter with you people?' Númi had turned back to face them when Stefán joined them. His voice was shaking, but whether from rage or overwhelming emotion, it wasn't immediately obvious. 'How dare you break the news to us like this? Mía's alive – except maybe she isn't. You can't do this to us. Why don't you go out and search for her instead of trying to prove she's not alive after all, just to cover up your mistakes? I bet that's what you're up to. Why else are you here? Do you think we're hiding her down in the cellar or something? Seriously?'

Erla seized her chance to dive in at this point. 'No. Of course not. Nor are we trying to excuse the people responsible for the original investigation. Our priority is to find Mía.' Before Númi or Stefán could interrupt, she continued: 'We've been through the case notes from the time of her disappearance, searching for anything that could shed light on this latest development. But I can't say there's much to go on. The conclusion of the investigation was reasonable, given the information available at the time.'

'Oh, it was, was it?' Stefán shot back. 'That's quite a surprise, considering that the officer in charge was totally incompetent. And a homophobe too. Does it mention in the case files that they suspected us for a long time?' This last sentence emerged almost in a growl.

'Yes, I saw that.' Erla was struggling to sit upright, which meant perching on the edge of the squashy sofa as if it were a park bench. 'It's standard practice for suspicion to fall on family members in serious crimes like this. In your case, the assumption was wrong. In the majority of cases of this type, it proves correct.'

Númi was rubbing his hands together in his agitation. 'I couldn't care less about the old inquiry. Don't waste any more time on that now. We can come back to it later. The only thing I'm interested in knowing is what's happening about the search for Mía. When do you think you'll find her, so she can come home?'

Erla had sunk back into the sofa but struggled upright again before answering. 'The investigation is at a very early stage, so I'm afraid we can't realistically give an estimate of when we'll track her down. So much is still unclear. As I told you yesterday, all we know is that we have a DNA profile that matches the one taken from her umbilical cord during the original inquiry.'

Freyja had heard about this from Huldar, who had read it in the old case files. After Mía was presumed dead, a sample of her DNA had been required for the Trace Database, in case her remains were ever washed up by the sea or turned up in some other context. The biological material had been extracted from the dried-up stump of her umbilical cord that her fathers had kept in a bag at the bottom of the freezer. They'd been planning to have it preserved in a plastic mould to commemorate her birth but had never got round to it. Huldar had never heard of such a bizarre idea. He had added that, as far as he was aware, none of his five sisters in Egilsstadir had ever dreamt of doing such a thing. When their sons shed their umbilical cords, the stumps had been tossed straight in the bin. He assumed it must be some weird city custom and Freyja didn't contradict him.

'Where did her DNA turn up?' Stefán kept his eyes fixed on Erla's. 'You wouldn't tell us yesterday but I insist you do us the courtesy of informing us now. Mía's our daughter and she's still a minor. I can't see how it would compromise the interests of the police or the investigation to give her parents this information. It's our right. I'm warning you now that if you don't respect our wishes, we'll take the matter as far as we have to – to the Children's Commissioner, the courts . . . We'll go to the papers, if necessary. Perhaps I should take your full names now in case I need to mention you in an interview.'

Erla hesitated, evidently conducting a quick risk assessment in her head. When she spoke, she had obviously concluded that sharing the information was less risky than dragging the police through the kind of unpleasantness Stefán was threatening. 'We found her DNA at a crime scene.'

Erla could hardly have expected to get away with leaving it at that, though she'd thought it was worth trying.

'A crime? What crime?' Númi raised a hand to his heart. Naturally, he was imagining the worst.

'A murder.'

Númi's stunned expression showed that this hadn't even occurred to him. 'Murder? Murder? I don't understand. Is she dead? What the hell's wrong with you people? First you say she's alive, then that she's been murdered. What the hell?' He started to rise to his feet but Stefán reached out and grabbed his arm, forcing him down again.

Stefán rounded on Erla, looking as if he'd like to see her boiled in oil. 'Are you referring to the murder in the news? Or is this some other case that the media don't yet know about?'

'The one in the news.' Erla braced herself.

Númi clasped a hand over his mouth, his eyes huge above it. Then he dropped his hand and said, his voice trembling: 'The woman found in the boot of the car? Has the murderer got Mía? Why aren't you out there looking for her?'

'Unbelievable,' Stefán broke in. 'She's been alive for eleven years and you lot haven't been able to find her. Eleven years. And you turn up here now. Couldn't you have come six months ago?' He glared at them all contemptuously. Freyja felt like a defendant in the dock. 'This must be some sort of world record in incompetence. Not to be able to find a missing child in a country as small as Iceland.'

Númi had turned his head away to stare out to sea again. When he finally spoke, he sounded exhausted. 'No one was looking. Everyone was satisfied with the theory that she'd vanished in the sea. Everyone except me. But no one would listen to me.'

There was no answer to that. Erla returned to the point of the visit. 'Do either of you know a woman called Ólína Traustadóttir? Or Bríet Hannesdóttir?'

Both men shook their heads and Stefán asked: 'What do they do?'

'Ólína's a freelance photographer and Bríet's a lab technician at the National Hospital,' Erla replied. 'She's also studying public health at the University of Iceland. More specifically, researching childhood immunisation. Are you by any chance opposed to vaccinations?'

'No, of course not.' It was Númi who answered. 'And I don't know any lab technicians.'

Stefán nodded in agreement.

'What about Rögnvaldur Tryggvason? Do you know him? Or Aldís Ellertsdóttir? They're married; he works for an insurance company, she's an accountant, though she hasn't worked much in the last few years. Their daughter had leukaemia. Her name was Íris and she was ten when she died – Íris Rögnvaldsdóttir.'

'I don't know any of these people.' It was Stefán who replied. 'I've seen the photo of Rögnvaldur in the papers and I'm quite sure I don't know him. The wife and daughter's names don't ring any bells either.' He glanced at Númi, who shook his head. 'Did he murder the woman? Is that why you put out a wanted notice for him? Has he got our daughter?'

As Erla showed no signs of answering these questions, Freyja came to the rescue by changing the subject. 'It goes without saying that it must be extremely difficult for you to take in this news, especially as it's bound to reopen old wounds.' She had taken her card out of her coat pocket and now placed it on the coffee table. 'I urge you to get in touch with me when it's convenient. I may be able to help you work through your feelings. I can also refer you to another psychologist, if you'd prefer. Whichever you choose, I strongly recommend that you accept the offer of help.' Freyja paused to allow Númi or Stefán to speak but, when neither said a word, she continued: 'When . . . if . . . Mía is found, it's going to be a real emotional rollercoaster for the three of you, and how you handle the situation will make all the difference. As yet, we have no idea where she's been all these years but you need to be prepared for the possibility that the person who abducted her hasn't looked after her properly. Let's hope it's no more serious than that. I'm a specialist in child psychology and will be there to ensure that Mía's interests are protected at every stage of the inquiry. Everything will be done to make the process as painless as possible, whatever your previous experience of the police. But I won't pretend that it's going to be easy.'

Stefán and Númi were each looking in different directions, Númi at the name card on the table, Stefán at Freyja. He might not be directing quite the same hate-filled glare at her as he had at Erla, but it wasn't far off. 'We don't need *your* help.'

Freyja didn't let this disconcert her. 'Nevertheless, the offer's there if you change your mind.'

She was alarmed by Stefán's rage, which seemed to be intensifying rather than subsiding, but neither Erla nor

Gudlaugur appeared remotely intimidated. Erla's voice was perfectly level when she spoke again. 'If we could get back to the point. Can you think of anyone who could have abducted Mía, now that all the evidence suggests it wasn't her birth mother? Seeing as Droplaug quickly became the focus of the original inquiry, perhaps you never seriously considered any other possibilities?'

'No. Of course not,' Stefán snapped. 'If we'd suspected anyone else, we'd have noticed if that person had suddenly acquired a child – especially a child who looked like Mía.'

Númi didn't say anything, just nodded his agreement.

'Children change a great deal during their first year.' Gudlaugur now entered the conversation for the first time since they'd sat down. 'It would probably only have been necessary to hide her for the first few months to a year. After that, it's not certain that you would have recognised her. It says in the files that she didn't have any distinguishing features that would have made her stand out.'

'We'd have recognised her after a year. We'd recognise her today, for that matter.' Númi folded his arms across his chest, as if waiting for someone to contradict him. None of them shared his conviction, but they all remained silent.

'There is one person who springs to mind.' It was Stefán who spoke. Númi's lips parted in surprise. 'Droplaug's sister,' Stefán went on. 'Ellý. She's as crazy as her sister was.'

Erla noted this down. 'We'll look into it.'

She didn't get any further because at that moment the front door opened and there was a commotion in the hall. A cheerful child's voice called out: 'Hi, Dad! Hi, Dad! I'm home. We got the day off school, so we went round to Rósa's, but now we're going to play here.'

All heads turned towards the hall where three little girls appeared in their socks. One came down the steps into the living room, examining the assembled company with interest. She was small and skinny, her hair in two thin plaits, wearing dungarees and a roll-neck jumper that had ridden up on one side. Her glasses, which had slid down her nose, were noticeably smeary. 'Why are you home? Who are these people?'

'We got the day off too. And these are just visitors.' Stefán waved a hand at the girl. 'Take Selma and Rósa to your room. You can play there. We need a bit of peace.'

'Are you getting a divorce?' The girl didn't seem particularly bothered by the prospect.

'No, we're not getting a divorce. They're just visitors.'

The other two girls came closer to get a better look at the guests. Neither seemed particularly impressed. The smaller one elbowed the daughter of the house. 'Come on. They're probably just debt collectors.'

The third girl watched over the shoulders of the others, which was easy as she was considerably taller. 'Or social workers. They sometimes come round to my house.'

'Go and play, girls.' Stefán made as if to stand up and they scuttled off in the direction of the bedrooms.

'So you have a daughter?' Erla voiced what they were all thinking. Freyja assumed the others were as taken aback as she was herself. From what she had read so far in the old case files, she'd assumed the two men wouldn't try engaging the services of a surrogate mother again until it was legalised. No magistrate would agree to another step-adoption after their arrangement with Mía's mother had been exposed, especially since the magistrate who'd approved Mía's adoption had come in for harsh criticism. But it seemed that some people's sins were soon forgotten. 'How old is she? Who's her mother?'

Stefán lost his temper again. 'She's eleven and it's none of your business who her mother is. But before you start getting your knickers in a twist, let me assure you it's all perfectly legal.' He stood up, pulling down his sleeves. 'Right, I need to get back to work. Númi will see you out. If you ask me, your time would be better spent searching for Mía.' Instead of observing the usual social niceties in parting, he simply barked an order: 'Find her!'

Stefán vanished in the direction of the bedrooms, presumably to go and don a tie and jacket. Númi, meanwhile, sprang to his feet, saying he'd see them to the door. He seemed nervous and kept rubbing his hands together. Freyja, sensing he had something on his mind, asked him straight out. She was right.

'She will be allowed to come home to us, won't she?' Númi asked in a rush.

Freyja answered, full of sympathy: 'She'll almost certainly be in the care of children's services to start off with. The situation will be incredibly hard for her because she won't know you. But I promise you her interests will be prioritised at every stage and she'll be allowed to come home eventually. We – and you, of course – want that homecoming to be as happy as possible, but it's going to require some preparation.'

Númi nodded slowly. 'But you promise me she'll come back to us in the end?'

Freyja drew a deep breath. 'Yes, I don't see why she shouldn't. She's your daughter.' She gestured to her card on the table. 'Do, please, consider my offer. I wasn't aware that you had another daughter. It'll be an equally big adjustment for her when Mía's found. I don't know if you've told her she has a sister but, if not, it's terribly important that you do and that you prepare the ground carefully. I urge you to get in touch so I can either help you myself or recommend another psychologist.'

Númi didn't answer, just stared blankly at her card. Then he escorted them back to the dark entrance hall, which looked a little less gloomy now that it was decorated with three pairs of children's shoes, which had been kicked off and left where they fell on the tiled floor. One expensive pair of moonboots, some grubby trainers and a battered pair of wellies that must belong to the tallest girl. The moment Erla, Gudlaugur and Freyja were outside, Númi shut the door on them, his manner still oddly jittery.

When she was sitting in the car again, Freyja noticed the girls at the window, their elbows propped on the sill, their faces pressed against the glass. The three little faces watched intently as she and the others drove away.

As he turned out of the street, Gudlaugur started speaking. Finally, they had something else to discuss apart from the cock-up over the body. 'Was it just me or was that a weird reaction to the news? Shouldn't they have been over the moon?'

Freyja got in before Erla: 'There's no standard, natural reaction to the kind of news they received yesterday. But didn't it strike you as odd when Stefán asked why we couldn't have come six months ago? What did he mean by that?'

Erla was staring moodily out of the passenger window. 'Who knows? The main thing on my mind right now is how downright weird it was to adopt another kid – not just a girl like Mía but the same age as her as well. That's pretty fucked up, surely.' She twisted round to Freyja. 'What does your psychologist's brain have to say about that?'

Freyja couldn't answer. But she agreed with Erla in a way: under the circumstances, the existence of another daughter the same age was singularly unfortunate.

Chapter 25

Friday

Huldar didn't bother trying to lighten the atmosphere in the meeting room. Any attempt would only raise the threat level from red to the danger zone. Erla was ready to tear her hair out, Gudlaugur and Freyja were mute. He himself was pacing around the room, in spite of repeated requests to stop. His agitation was getting on Erla's nerves, and she was wound up enough already. Poor Lína was leaning sheepishly against the wall as if the whole thing were her fault, absurd though that was.

Erla had ushered the four of them into the meeting room after returning from the visit to Mía's parents, and made it clear that this was in order to hush up the mistaken identification for as long as possible. Huldar guessed it was also because no one could see into the room. If she'd taken them into her goldfish bowl of an office, everything they did would have been on display to the rest of the team. She had managed to hang on to her composure when Huldar originally informed her about the mix-up, only asking if the discussion could wait until she got back from the meeting about Mía.

'It must be a mistake. It shouldn't be possible. Surely the eyes have to be open for the phone to unlock with Face ID?' Erla was still clinging to the faint hope that this latest setback was all a terrible misunderstanding.

'No. Not if the user's got it on the default settings.' Lína's voice was barely more than a whisper. She was clearly reluctant to explain, in case this tipped Erla over the edge. 'But the lock mode hadn't been selected.'

Freyja glanced at the smartphone at the centre of the furore. It wasn't the phone's fault that the body had been wrongly identified. If anything, they should be thanking Lína for her quick-wittedness. They would be in a far worse position if they'd had to start the identification process from scratch. She also deserved praise for having unlocked the device via facial recognition, then having the presence of mind to change the settings to keep it open.

Erla raised her eyes to the ceiling with a groan. 'I am so fucked.'

No one contradicted her. Huldar reckoned he was pretty well acquainted with the senior management and that Erla had no grounds for optimism. For understandable reasons, it was essential to maintain public trust in the police. Anything that eroded that trust was frowned on, and these days it was no longer possible simply to wait for a crisis to blow over.

To make matters worse, it looked as if Freyja might be in hot water too. Only this morning Huldar had overheard someone saying that she had accessed the Police Information System for private purposes. He had spun round and nipped that rumour in the bud. He didn't for a minute believe that she would be tempted to do anything of the sort, but the station gossips weren't too fussed about the truth. And the story could prove serious for her, since management frowned on such breaches.

Huldar paused in his pacing to bend down and peer at the phone on the conference table. What he thought he would achieve by this, he didn't know. Raising his head, he caught Freyja's eye. She didn't immediately drop her gaze. What was the point of carrying on with this stupid pantomime that any idiot could see through? It didn't matter now if their relationship was on everyone's lips. In fact, their attempt at secrecy had always been pointless.

Especially now that she might be about to lose her job.

Freyja drew a deep breath and appeared to be steeling herself. She wasn't the type to whinge when things went wrong, a quality Huldar greatly appreciated. She could be angry, moody and silent, but at least she was no cry-baby.

She stood up. 'Is there anything I can do?'

Erla turned a weary face to her. 'Yes. You can make bloody sure you don't say a word to anyone. I need time to think before the news spreads in-house.'

'I won't,' Freyja said tersely. She didn't bother with any long speeches about how reliable she was. If Erla didn't trust her, no amount of words would help.

'Maybe you should concentrate on working out how best to tackle Bríet's parents. We'll need to talk to them again, without giving them any reason to believe she could be alive and well.' Erla rubbed her eyes. 'Jesus Christ.'

Huldar caught Freyja's eye again. 'I'll go with you, when the time comes.'

'No one's going to talk to any members of the public – not at this stage.' Erla sounded as if she was pulling herself together. Or perhaps she had become resigned to what had happened. She looked at Freyja. 'Not until I've worked out a new action plan.'

Huldar straightened up. 'How about doing it now? Is there any reason to wait? There's no way we're going to experience any more upsets on that scale – we must have hit rock bottom, surely? The situation can't get any worse. I mean, what else could happen?'

'Well . . .' Typical Lína; she couldn't leave well alone, however subdued she was. 'Bríet hasn't been found. Her head could turn up on the doorstep of a TV station. Or—'

'Stop. Please.' Erla leant forwards so she could rub the small of her back. She seemed ready to throw in the towel.

Lína opened her mouth to continue but the look Huldar sent her made her snap it shut again. He jerked his chin towards Ólína's smartphone. 'Why don't you go through the contents of the phone, Lína? It's bound to reveal some communications that might help us get a handle on this. Check the photos Ólína's been taking recently. The emails she's sent. It would be a good idea to get a list of all her Facebook friends too, and her email and phone contacts. We might find something that ties her to Stefán, Númi, Rögnvaldur or Aldís. They're all linked. We just need to find out how. Once we know that, we'll have solved the case.'

Erla emitted a bark of sarcastic laughter. 'Yeah, right. You forgot that we still have to find Rögnvaldur, the place where the body was cut up, the kid Mía, and Bríet's dead body. Or Bríet alive. I'm not sure how any contacts will help us with that sodding nightmare.'

Huldar didn't answer. He just nodded at Lína to take the phone and get to work. She didn't wait to be told twice but pulled on her rubber gloves, picked it up and exited the room. As she closed the door, there was no hiding the relief on her face.

'Four with all the trimmings, please. And two Cokes.' Huldar held out his card. The sales assistant fished the hot dogs out of the deep-fat fryer and placed them in the buns. Then he passed them to Huldar, one at a time, and Huldar demonstrated considerable deftness in conveying both hot dogs and Cokes to the round table at the front of the shop, where he placed them in the plastic holder, managing not to drop anything. 'There you go.'

Erla gaped at the food, then at Huldar. 'Are you joking? You don't seriously think I can put away four hot dogs?'

'Sure, you can. It'll do you good.' He'd got up to go for a smoke after making a string of phone calls to people they needed to talk to, but one look at Erla had been enough to tell him that she was in urgent need of fresh air.

She had protested, but mostly for show. When he discovered that she hadn't eaten since the chips in the canteen yesterday, he had insisted on taking her out to get something down her. He chose the petrol station for its lack of seats, since he was afraid she'd crash out if she sat down. He'd extracted an admission from her that she'd worked until half past two in the morning and come back in at half past six. 'This is to make up for the meals you missed yesterday and this morning. It'll do you good,' he said now.

Erla took a bite without much enthusiasm. While she was chewing, she checked her phone. Huldar thought she was looking at her inbox.

'I don't think the inquiry's going to collapse if you ignore it for a few minutes, Erla.'

'It can hardly be more buggered than it is already. I expected Gudlaugur to keep me updated. He has to find CCTV footage of the car soon. It's not like we live in Los Angeles.'

'Sure, but what could possibly emerge from that that can't wait? You'll hear the news as soon as we get back to the office.'

Erla took another mouthful, with a little more appetite this time – enough for the hot dog to leave behind smears of ketchup and mustard at the corners of her mouth. 'I won't be able to relax until we've caught the bastard who did this, and found Mía and Bríet. Where in God's name are they?' Her bump twitched and Erla fell momentarily silent. But when she started talking again, it was not about her pregnancy or the baby. 'I want to solve this case before I go on maternity leave. If I don't, you know as well as I do that the person who stands in for me will deflect any criticism of the inquiry onto me. Regardless of whether I was there at the time.'

Huldar handed her a napkin. 'Depends who stands in for you.' He reviewed a mental list of the candidates. On reflection, few of them were likely to shoulder the responsibility for their own failures, but he didn't say as much to Erla. 'You needn't worry.'

Erla snorted but when she replied she sounded more conciliatory than usual. 'I don't want to come back to work after my maternity leave to find I've lost my job, Huldar.'

'Forget it. There's absolutely no chance of that happening.' Sometimes it was better to lie. He'd been eight years old, his sister ten, when they were out playing and she'd fallen and torn a hole in the backside of her jeans. He had lied and said no one could see the tear. If she'd been on her way out of the house, he'd have told the truth, but there was no reason to upset her when they still had to walk home. The truth wouldn't have changed anything – her knickers would still have been on show. When you're ten, that's a big deal. But she hadn't exactly been grateful for his tact when they'd got home and she'd caught sight of herself in the mirror.

Huldar repeated his words: 'Absolutely no chance.'

Erla went on eating, looking a little less despondent.

Huldar reckoned this was a good moment to go over a few points in the investigation. It was so easy to lose sight of the bigger picture when it felt as if they were dealing with two separate cases. He'd noted down some things he wanted to put to Erla, suspecting he wouldn't get another chance once they were back at the office. Since there were no other customers and the sales assistant didn't speak Icelandic, they were safe to talk freely. 'One thing, Erla.'

She nodded with her mouth full.

'That business of Ólína's phone. I'm convinced one of the kids in the playground had it. You say Númi and Stefán's daughter had been given the day off. Well, the kids were given the day off at the school Lína and I visited. It has to be the same one. It's in their area, after all.'

Erla glanced up and said something indistinct that sounded like: 'So what?' The words were accompanied by a blast of mustard.

'It can't be yet another coincidence. I reckon Stefán and Númi's daughter had the phone.'

Erla swallowed. 'OK. Then where did she get it from?'

'Well, that's the thing. Maybe Ólína knew her dads.'

'No. At least, they claimed they didn't know her.' Erla took a swig of Coke. 'Though they could've been lying, of course. Are you suggesting they killed Ólína – one or both of them?'

'Not necessarily. My money's still on Rögnvaldur. But it's a strange coincidence, don't you think?'

Erla answered wearily: 'Yes, Huldar. It is.'

He was silent while he watched Erla take her first mouthful of hot dog number two. As soon as she'd swallowed, he raised the next point. 'I've been thinking about Bríet – about where she could be.' When Erla didn't answer, he continued: 'Droplaug's body and Ólína's head were both found in or near the sea in the west of town. Isn't it likely, then, that Bríet's body's there too? Assuming she's dead. Perhaps Rögnvaldur thinks it's the best, or at least the most convenient, dumping ground.'

'Droplaug killed herself, Huldar. That had nothing to do with Rögnvaldur.' Erla paused and frowned thoughtfully. 'Or not as far as we know. It might be worth asking his wife, I suppose. Aldís is still in hospital. She's still refusing to answer our questions, though.' Erla picked up the hot dog and seemed in a hurry to finish what she was saying so she could take another bite. 'Why did he drive Ólína's body to the housing estate, in that case? And why didn't he get rid of both of them? Assuming Bríet *is* dead.'

Huldar couldn't answer that. 'I don't know.' He glanced at his notes. 'What about insurance? Rögnvaldur sold health insurance and we haven't examined that angle. Could there be a connection?'

Erla swallowed as she shook her head. 'How? You mean the vaccination register could provide him with some kind of inside information? Like not insuring people who aren't vaccinated? I don't think we need to bother pursuing that angle. He's after the person who infected his daughter – we already know that.'

Huldar was distracted, remembering his phone call with the man from the insurance company's IT department, who had looked Rögnvaldur up in the access log. Jóhannes, he thought the man's name was. There had been an odd note in his voice, though Huldar couldn't quite put his finger on what was wrong. Had the guy been nervous? Or upset that his colleague was wanted by the police? Or did he just have a slightly strange voice?

Huldar spared Erla these thoughts and moved on to his next point. 'Andrea's meant to be getting back to the country tomorrow. You know – the yoga freak. It shouldn't be difficult to get her to come in for interview. She won't be able to stop talking after spending a whole week in a silent retreat. I'm just hoping she'll be able to tell us something useful.' Huldar pushed the second Coke towards Erla. 'How about trying to put a positive spin on this whole mess and working on the basis that Ólína's the lynchpin – the person connecting Bríet, Rögnvaldur, his wife, Mía and her dads? We know virtually nothing about her, only that she's a freelance photographer who spends a lot of time taking pictures in the Faroes. I found that out from her homepage.'

Erla yanked a napkin out of the steel holder and wiped a blob of remoulade off her chin. 'Did you notice that she takes class pictures for schools too? You're not the only one with an internet connection, Huldar.'

Huldar decided not to mention that he'd already clocked that. Erla needed to be able to contribute something.

She carried on: 'I got hold of the head teacher and she was able to look it up from home. Ólína took some class photos for them about a month ago. She probably lost her phone then and some kid picked it up and put it in their pocket.'

'You think her phone was lost for a whole month?' Huldar shook his head. 'I don't buy it. She'd have searched for it. Or had it blocked. Of course it would be easy enough to charge it, so it doesn't necessarily mean anything that the battery still had juice, but it's still highly unlikely.'

'Maybe she went to the school to deliver the pictures and dropped her phone then. The head teacher didn't know how the class photos had been delivered to the pupils. But she did say something else that I found interesting. I asked if she knew Bríet. She remembered that a woman had come to the school to talk to some children in connection with a study on immunisation and that her name had been Bríet. She's going to check on Monday but she thought she still had a copy of the letter the woman showed her, which gave her permission to speak to the kids.'

'Who granted her permission?'

'The head didn't remember but thought the letter had been issued by the Directorate of Health. This was about three weeks ago, she reckoned.' Erla took a sip of Coke before continuing. 'She didn't know which children Bríet spoke to but thought she'd visited two classes.'

Huldar frowned. 'That doesn't square with what Bríet's supervisor said. She told me that there had been no plan to contact any of the children who hadn't been vaccinated. Is it possible that the head teacher was mixing up studies? And names?'

Erla shrugged. 'Maybe. It's also possible that Bríet wasn't there to talk to children who hadn't been vaccinated. Could she have been talking to a control group? To compare them with the results for kids who hadn't been vaccinated, for example?'

'It's possible. I don't know much about their study. But I do know that it's easy enough to forge a letter of permission. Could Bríet have been there to look for Mía?'

'Why the hell would Bríet have been looking for Mía? I'd have thought she already had enough on her plate with work, studies and childcare. No, I reckon there must be some perfectly natural explanation. Though I have to admit it's a weird coincidence that she turned up at the school Stefán and Númi's daughter attends. Still, who knows? Maybe she went to all the schools in the Reykjavík area.'

'Maybe.' Huldar glanced down at his notes. He had one point left. 'Then there's Rögnvaldur. I was wondering if we should try to find out who infected his daughter. He's almost certainly got hold of the register of vaccinations. Tomorrow, Bríet's dissertation partner will be back and she might be able to give us some likely names. It must be possible to get around data protection when it's a case of saving someone from Rögnvaldur's planned revenge. He's shown that he's capable of anything. If we find the infection carrier, chances are we'll find Rögnvaldur.'

'You're optimistic. In my experience, the privacy laws trump everything else. Which is ironic considering that most of the population broadcast the most intimate details of their private lives every day on social media. But who knows? It's not the stupidest idea you've ever come up with.' Erla eyed the third hot dog.

Huldar passed it to her. 'Go on. It'll do you good. You've got a long afternoon of phone calls and meetings ahead of you. You don't want your stomach rumbling loud enough to drown out the people you're speaking to.'

This was enough to make Erla take a large bite out of the third hot dog. 'Huldar, do you realise you're the first person to invite me out for a meal in months? And you've brought me here – to a petrol station.' She took another swig of Coke, then picked up the tray with the final hot dog and pushed it towards him. 'You'll have to eat this one. I'm stuffed.'

Huldar winked at her. 'I promise to do better next time. I'll take you and the baby for a burger. Believe it or not, kids love me.'

Erla rolled her eyes. 'Right.'

Despite the miserable failure of his previous attempts to get Erla to confide in him about the baby's father, Huldar reckoned this might be a good moment to have another go. Erla seemed as mellow as her nature would ever allow, the subject of the baby had been broached and he was, after all, the first person to take her out for months. That should count for something, even if the location left a bit to be desired. 'I know you don't want to talk about it, Erla, but what about the dad? Is he going to be in the picture at all? To help out and stuff?'

Erla raised her eyebrows and Huldar braced himself for an earful about sticking his nose in where it wasn't wanted. But the forbidding look softened and when Erla spoke again her tone was mild. 'He says he will, and he's been OK during the pregnancy. But let's just say that my hopes aren't all that high. The baby wasn't planned and neither of us expected to be permanently linked like this.' Her eyebrows lowered again. 'You do realise that you don't have a monopoly on one-night stands, Huldar?'

He ignored the swipe, not wanting to go there. 'So, the two of you aren't in a relationship?'

Erla shrugged. 'Not really. Or maybe. I don't know what to call it. Time will tell. We're both on the fence – me more than him, actually. I'm not sure we're compatible or likely to make a good couple. We're so different.'

'Sometimes that's a positive, Erla.' Huldar didn't add that he couldn't imagine how two people as prickly as Erla could ever live together. She would be better off with a super-cheery, easy-going type. Feeling that he was on a roll, Huldar decided to ask the question he had been longing to ever since he'd found out she was pregnant. 'So, is it someone from the office? A cop?'

His only answer was a smirk that implied Erla was amused. What it meant, he couldn't begin to guess. But it seemed the conversation was over. Erla scrunched up the mess of napkins and packaging on the table and chucked it at an open bin two metres away. The ball of paper landed on the floor. 'Let's go.'

Huldar shoved the rest of the hot dog in his mouth and hastily retrieved the rubbish and put it in the bin before Erla could attempt to bend down herself. She might get stuck down there or, horror of horrors, her waters might break. He didn't want to regret having invited her to his favourite petrol station. She'd eaten quite a lot too – supposing she puked up on the floor? Then he'd be *persona non grata* and would be forced to find himself a new source of hot dogs.

Chapter 26

Friday

Erla and Huldar had gone out, to take care of important business, no doubt. Freyja scanned the open-plan office in search of a friendly face, but everyone was immersed in their screens or had their phones clamped to their ears, their expressions grave. Lína was sitting bolt upright at her desk, wearing a frown of intense concentration. She gave the impression that she was solving not just the case, but the mystery of life itself. Gudlaugur, on the other hand, didn't appear quite so focused as he sat watching recordings from the town's CCTV and private security cameras, but then it was hard to imagine a more mind-numbing task. Freyja decided against asking him if he could suggest a job for her. She didn't want to end up sitting beside him, staring at traffic.

Freyja's main reason for coming upstairs had been to tell Erla about her phone conversation with Bríet's parents. She'd thought of calling her, but her fingers had stalled as she was on the point of selecting Erla's number. She was bound to get a bollocking for disturbing her. There was no point ringing Huldar either, since he was with Erla. It would only rile Erla further and land Huldar in her bad books too. The fact that Freyja had good news to impart would be irrelevant.

There had been no hint during their conversation that Bríet's parents were planning to take their story to the papers or make a formal complaint. Of course, Freyja hadn't been able to ask them straight out, but she had read between the lines. If she'd pressed them about it, it would have given the impression that the police were mainly concerned with their image. Which was absurd. Their main concern was the investigation.

Freyja had also had a call from her brother, Baldur, to say he'd be getting back to town on Sunday and asking if everything was OK. She said it was, since there was never any point moaning to Baldur when she had problems. He was too laid-back and happy-go-lucky to listen to a litany of complaints and would only tune out halfway through, as Freyja had discovered on the rare occasions she had tried it. So she let him yak on, telling story after story about dissatisfied elderly foreigners with more money than sense. The dark was too dark. The waterfalls were too wet. The snow was too cold and the Icelanders were too Icelandic for their taste. In parting, Freyja had consoled him by pointing out that neither of them was destined to moulder away under a pile of money in their old age. He sent his love to Saga but, at that moment, was interrupted by some disgruntled old git. Freyja heard him insisting that Baldur do something to prevent the sun from shining in his eyes so he could enjoy the view in more comfort. Baldur hung up before she could say goodbye.

There was something unsettling about conversations that were broken off before they had officially ended. Silly though it was, she was left with the feeling that something remained unsaid between them. If the past was anything to go by, it was probably bad news that he would blurt out at the last minute. She could only hope and pray it had nothing to do with another stint in jail. She also acknowledged the possibility that her unease might not have anything to do with Baldur. Maybe it was just her own bad conscience niggling at her. She hadn't exactly been forthcoming with her brother about her precarious fling with Huldar.

Freyja hovered awkwardly on the sidelines, looking around the maze of desks, but no one made eye contact or gave any sign of having noticed her. It was embarrassingly clear that she wouldn't be given anything to do unless she tackled every member of CID individually.

Her gaze wandered back to Gudlaugur. She was itching to ask if he could access the files relating to Mía's disappearance for her but didn't dare to in light of their previous exchange about the Police Information System. She didn't want to put him in an awkward position. It would be better to apply to her manager for authorisation and discuss with him the rules governing access to the database. Perhaps she wouldn't be allowed to view old cases unless she put in a special request. She'd soon find out. The worst part was not knowing her status with any of these things, since that increased the risk of doing something wrong.

Her manager's cryptic reference to abusing the system had been bugging her, especially since Gudlaugur had sounded so serious when describing access limitations. Did her boss suspect her of breaking into the system? Surely not. Still, it might be a smart move to go and see him to set the matter straight.

Freyja glanced around. She might as well be invisible, so there was nothing for it but to wait until Erla got back. Until then, she would just have to occupy herself with the paperwork generated by all the committees she was involved in. Or speak to her manager.

But before she could make a decision, her phone rang. Several people looked up, only to go straight back to work when they saw whose it was. Freyja didn't recognise the number but answered anyway as she was heading for the exit. It could be anyone: the bank, Saga's nursery, the residents' association complaining about Molly's barking. One of Baldur's countless girlfriends trying to get hold of him. The intuition she'd had that he wanted to tell her something might relate to his latest relationship fiasco. It wouldn't be the first time he'd messed up in that area and needed to vent. Nor would it be the first time he hesitated before doing so. He knew her opinion of his love life.

But it wasn't a betrayed girlfriend on the line. It was Númi. Sounding stressed and hesitant, he asked if they could meet, only to backpedal as soon as he'd said it – before subsequently repeating his request. She didn't have to think twice before answering yes, she'd be there, then saying a hasty goodbye before he could change his mind.

Half an hour later she was back in the dark entrance hall of the swanky house. The little shoes were still there, but now they had been neatly lined up, side by side, the wellies looking conspicuously bigger and clumsier than the others. Númi had opened the door to her, seeming as flustered as he had on the phone. He was dressed more casually than he had been that morning, in jeans and a jumper, but that was the only relaxed thing about him.

Instead of extending a hand in greeting, he ushered her inside as if he feared a storm was brewing or that she might

have been followed by someone who would force their way in
behind her if he didn't close the door at once.

His fear wasn't that far-fetched. Before leaving the station, Freyja had rung Erla, guessing that she would not be
pleased if Freyja went off without telling anyone. Better to
risk being castigated for the interruption than to find a tor-
nado waiting for her when she got back to the office. Erla
had tried to insist that a police officer should accompany
Freyja, but in the end Freyja had managed to dissuade her.
Númi had appealed to her as a psychologist, not as an inves-
tigator. If she turned up with a police escort, he was unlikely
to let her in.

He invited her to take a seat on the same sofa as last time
and took the same chair himself. She half expected the cushion still to be warm but of course it wasn't. In fact, the soft
leather felt chilly to the touch.

'I'm afraid calling you was a mistake.' Númi fiddled with
the seams of his seat cushion. 'Stebbi's so angry with the police
that he wouldn't hear of talking to any of you, not even for
counselling. He doesn't know about this and I'd rather keep
it that way.'

Freyja assured him she wouldn't tell his husband about her
visit. But this wasn't enough to allay his doubts.

'It's a mistake, I know it. But I didn't know where to turn.
I'm afraid I'll go out of my mind if I have to struggle with these
thoughts all weekend. And it's impossible to get a same-day
appointment with a therapist.' His gaze flickered to Freyja's
and away again. 'I can't discuss this with anyone close to me.
Not any more. Everyone's lost patience with me.' He shook
his head, rubbing his hands nervously. 'But I still shouldn't
have invited you here.'

'Wouldn't it make sense to grab the chance now that I *am* here?' Freyja folded her hands in her lap to prevent them from moving in sympathy with Númi's. 'If you have no one else to talk to, you could hardly hope to find a better listener. This is my job, in case you've forgotten.' Strictly speaking, this wasn't quite true since she'd left the Children's House and consultancy, but all her therapist skills were intact nonetheless. 'As I said this morning, the news is bound to have stirred up some powerful emotions. It'll take more than a few hours or days to process them. I imagine it must rake up a lot of difficult memories for you, about all the trauma you went through eleven years ago. It's never easy when old wounds are reopened.' Freyja left a gap for Númi to say something, but he didn't bite. He appeared to be holding his breath, his chest perfectly still under his jumper.

Freyja resumed where she had left off. Sometimes it was necessary to talk for a while before people could be persuaded to open up, even when they'd had far less of a shock than Númi. 'I imagine you and your husband had accepted that you'd lost Mía. It may sound counterintuitive, but it's not going to be easy to handle the feelings stirring inside you now that it seems the loss may not have been permanent after all. On top of that, there's the uncertainty about if and when Mía will be found and about what sort of care she's received all these years.'

Númi was still plucking at the seam of the chair, but less frantically now. 'I've been waiting in suspense for eleven years. I always knew she didn't end up in the sea.' He raised his eyes to Freyja's. 'You think I'm just saying that, now that it's obvious, but you're wrong. I never believed it. No one would listen to me, though. Even Stebbi gave up on me.' The nervous plucking grew more frantic again. 'Sooner than I'd have expected. He just gave up.'

'People cope with trauma differently,' Freyja said. 'Sometimes couples experience relationship difficulties when something terrible happens and one person displays more emotion than the other. The less forthcoming partner in the relationship feels obliged to provide constant comfort and support to the partner who's more open. As a result, they don't have a chance to process their own pain. It's not uncommon. In the end, they can't take any more, because they're suffering too.'

Númi nodded. 'He suffered all right. God, we both did. We were complete wrecks. Maybe that's why I can't bring myself to talk to him about it now. Or to my friends and family. They all believe I had a breakdown at the time and lost my mind. But I was right: I wasn't seeing things.'

'What do you mean? I don't quite follow. Did you see Mía after she was presumed dead?' Freyja managed to keep her voice steady, concealing her eagerness. She wondered why he hadn't reported it at the time. 'When was this?'

Númi's chest heaved. 'I didn't see her.' He met Freyja's eye again, his head tilted on one side, looking puzzled. 'Haven't you read up on the background?'

Freyja hadn't seen the files. She was relying on the rather scrappy account of the events that she'd gleaned from Erla and other members of the team, together with what she remembered from the news at the time. 'No, I haven't read the reports. But then I'm not part of the investigation, I'm only a consultant, so I'm sorry but I don't know what you're referring to.'

Númi was silent. From another part of the house there was a thud, followed by a burst of shrill children's laughter. Freyja longed to ask if their daughter knew about Mía. She hadn't noticed any photos of Mía in the house but neither had she seen any of their other daughter. Perhaps there were framed pictures of one or both in another part of the house. Or perhaps not. Framed photos were mostly a thing of the past. These days people tended to store their pictures in electronic folders.

A gust of wind blew in off the sea and the big picture window rattled. Freyja turned instinctively and looked out. The waves were rougher than they had been that morning and the house was so close to the shore that the glass kept being spattered with spray. The water trickled down the window, leaving a film of salt behind, turning the glass matt. 'It's an incredible view. Never the same.'

'I hate that window.' Númi had found his voice again. 'For a while I thought about having it covered up. For a long time after Mía died, I couldn't bear to look out of it. Now I often do, but it's lost all its charm.'

Freyja turned back to him. 'Even though you were always sure that Mía hadn't disappeared in the sea?'

Númi shrugged. 'I was and I wasn't. I had no proof except what I'd witnessed with my own eyes, and I often had doubts. About my own sanity, even. For a while I believed what everyone said – that the shock had made me hallucinate.'

He needed to hear the truth. 'It can happen,' Freyja said. 'Hallucinations aren't unheard of following a major shock. But what was it you thought you saw and when was this?'

Númi's face hardened. 'I thought you were different. You seemed nice. But you're just like all the others. You won't believe me; you'll gang up on me with all the rest of them who think I was just seeing things.'

'Try me. If I do, one more won't make much difference. You've got nothing to lose.'

Númi smiled dully. 'That's true, I suppose.' He closed his eyes for a moment and drew a deep breath, his nostrils flaring. 'When I got to the pram there was another baby in it.' He locked eyes with Freyja, closely observing her reactions. 'A dead baby.'

She kept her face carefully blank. 'A dead baby? I haven't heard any mention of that. Whose was it?'

Númi began picking at the seams again. 'I don't know.' He dropped his eyes to his knees. 'It disappeared. I freaked out and left it in the pram while I went to ring Stebbi, then waited for him inside the house. I couldn't go back out, couldn't even look in the direction of the door to the terrace. But by the time Stebbi got home and ran out to the pram, the baby had vanished.'

More shrieks of laughter from the daughter's room. They lasted longer this time and Númi seemed poised to go and tell the kids to pipe down. Freyja hoped he wouldn't. It was a relief to hear that someone in this house was happy. She started speaking to distract him. 'I can't judge if that was a hallucination or reality. But it sounds a bit implausible. Why didn't you ring the police?'

'Because I was sure Droplaug – Mía's mother – was to blame. We'd been involved in a nightmarish dispute with her and she wasn't in a good way. I was sure she'd snatched Mía and all I wanted was to get her back. You see, our arrangement with Droplaug was a bit hazy and I was desperate to keep the police out of it as long as possible. It didn't occur to me that she would harm Mía in any way. I just thought she'd stolen her, so I phoned Stebbi at work. I didn't have my glasses on when I went outside, and while I was waiting for him I tried to convince myself that it had just been a horrible doll or something. That Droplaug had painted it to look as if it was dead – as a kind of symbolic revenge or something. But really I knew better. It wasn't a doll. It was a dead baby. And someone took it away. Just like they did with Mía.'

Freyja nodded while she was turning the man's story over in her mind. First somebody came and swapped Mía for a dead baby. Then the person in question came back and took away the dead baby too. It sounded so far-fetched that she wasn't surprised they'd dismissed Númi's account as the sign of a nervous breakdown. 'Well, all I can say to you is that it won't be long now before you get an explanation. When Mía's found, we'll finally learn from the person who took her what happened. I simply can't begin to guess what could explain it. There's always a possibility that you *were* hallucinating, though. It would be dishonest of me if I didn't point that out.'

Númi didn't react badly this time. 'There's more.'

'Oh? Like what?'

'The blanket found on the beach wasn't the one from her pram. Mía was wrapped in a different blanket.'

'That's the first I've heard about this, too,' Freyja said, then added in a level voice: 'But like I say, I haven't read the files.'

'If it's even in there. No one would listen to me when I finally got to see the blanket. They'd closed the case and written me off as some neurotic gay who was talking a load of nonsense.' Númi ran his hands down his thighs as if smoothing creases from his already smooth trouser legs.

'Am I right that they found Mía's DNA on the blanket? And Droplaug's too? Or is that a misunderstanding?'

Númi ran his hands down his trousers again. 'No. It was her blanket, all right. But it wasn't the one from her pram. She'd thrown up on it a couple of days earlier and we'd been meaning to take it to the dry cleaner's. Stebbi and I turned the whole house upside down after I realised, but it wasn't there.'

Freyja was becoming increasingly convinced that Númi couldn't have been in his right mind. 'Then who do you think took the blanket from your house?' she asked. 'It washed up on a beach.'

Númi's hands stiffened halfway down his thighs. 'I don't know. But they wouldn't have had to come into the house to get hold of it. The blanket was outside the front door in a plastic bag – because of the smell. It had been sitting there for a while because we kept forgetting to take it with us when we went out. Our cars are kept in the garage, which has a connecting door to the house, so we rarely use the front door.'

'I see.' But Freyja could make no sense of it at all. 'In other words, anyone could have taken it. Do you have any idea who it could have been?'

'Yes. I think the person who took the dead baby wrapped it in the blanket, then threw it in the sea.'

Freyja nodded and was silent for a minute or two while she was trying in vain to picture the series of events. The only sensible explanation she could come up with was that the bin men had mistaken the plastic bag for rubbish and taken it with them. How the blanket had subsequently ended up in the sea was hard to explain, though – assuming it was the same blanket. The man could simply have been muddled. 'You do realise, Númi, that it's quite a complicated and confusing explanation for what happened.'

'Yes, I do.'

Freyja didn't want to end their conversation on a negative note. Númi was visibly distressed and desperately in need of support. 'Well, you can be sure of one thing – the case will be reopened now. All the evidence will be re-evaluated. After all, it appears the original inquiry came to the wrong conclusion, perhaps because no one listened to you.' Freyja watched the man facing her undergo a transformation. His spine straightened, he took his hands off his thighs and his eyes were shiny with unshed tears.

'Thanks. I've been waiting a long time to hear someone say that.' He gave her a pale smile. 'Ever since Mía vanished.'

There was a muffled sneeze from the landing above them and they both jerked round. Númi and Stefán's daughter was standing there with her two friends. The taller girl had her hand over her mouth; it was she who had just sneezed. The scruffy daughter of the house was giving her father a puzzled look.

'Daddy, who's Mía?'

Chapter 27

Friday

The wind whipped Lína's red hair over her face. She tried in vain to push it behind her ears but in the end gave up, took an elastic band from her pocket and gathered her hair into a high pony-tail. This had the effect of making her look far too young to be on official business. The height difference between her and Huldar did nothing to help. Anyone who saw them would think he'd brought along a school kid on work experience, despite Lína's efforts to draw herself to her full height and adopt a stern expression.

'Where is it?' She put her hands on her hips and peered down the street as if she expected the answer to come driving along it. Huldar pointed to the ministry building that was their destination. Since Lína was from the northern town of Akureyri, she didn't know Reykjavík that well. In fact, Huldar doubted many young people had a clue where the top echelons of the executive were housed. Even he had been forced to look up the address.

They entered an unexpectedly cramped lobby and encountered a stream of people coming out as it was Friday and the weekend was beginning. Everyone appeared eager to leave the office, so eager that few had bothered to do up their coats before hurrying outside to freedom.

In contrast, the woman on reception looked thoroughly pissed off. She graced Huldar and Lína with an expression of barely concealed contempt. He guessed she had been asked to stay on late because of them and was now picturing the Friday queue at the state off-licence growing longer with every minute that passed. She didn't bother to greet them when they came to stand in front of her desk, pretending instead that something urgent had just caught her attention on her computer screen.

Huldar ignored the unfriendly reception. He rapped hard on the desk, forcing the woman to look up, told her the name of the man they had come to see and said he was expecting them. She gestured towards the lift, with a brusque: 'Second floor.'

'What's wrong with her?' Lína asked as the lift doors closed behind them.

'You can't expect everyone to be sunny, Lína.' Huldar watched the number above the door change from 'G' to '1', then from '1' to '2'. 'I mean, would you want to work here? I'd be as sour-faced as her within a week.'

The door opened and Lína shrugged. 'I suppose.'

The civil servant they had come to meet was waiting for them outside the lift. He was about sixty, with greying hair and a pair of reading glasses in the pocket of his jacket. The slightly too-tight shirt did little for his physique, straining over an impressive belly that recalled Erla's as it had been about two months ago. Smiling broadly in welcome, he extended a hand and introduced himself to them each in turn. Huldar reflected that he preferred the receptionist's honest unfriendliness to this insincere geniality.

On second thoughts, he could be reading the guy wrong. Perhaps the man really was that amiable and he himself was just prejudiced by his encounters over the years with so many high-ranking gits in the police. Petty tyrants who had forgotten the purpose of their job and thought only of wielding the limited powers their positions gave them. But then this phenomenon was hardly unique to the police.

The civil servant, whose name was Valgeir, showed them down an empty corridor to his office. 'Do come in. Take a pew. I'm afraid I don't have anything to offer you but, if you like, there's a coffee machine outside.'

They declined the offer and sat down, and Valgeir followed their example. He leant back with his hands clasped behind his head. Judging by how bare and uncluttered his desk was, he must do a lot of this. 'So, what news of the old Police Commissioner's Office? Same as ever?'

Huldar pretended he hadn't heard the question. Valgeir knew why they were there and his small talk was only an attempt to put off the inevitable. Huldar and Lína did not have time to waste. He'd almost had to drag her away from the contents of Ólína's phone with the promise that they wouldn't be more than half an hour, tops, and he intended to keep his word. Lína was chafing to get back to her desk because she still hadn't managed to open the app that she believed Ólína had used most to talk to friends, including Bríet. So far, the only account Lína had managed to access was the woman's Facebook page, as Ólína was one of the few people who bothered to lock their social media accounts on their phone. Any minute now, the device would be taken away from her and handed over to the IT department.

'As I explained on the phone, we'd like to discuss the inquiry into the disappearance of baby Mía. I know it was years ago, but you had the best overview at the time and I'm hoping you won't have forgotten anything major.'

Valgeir loosened his hands and lost his smile. 'Yes, of course. Absolutely. Fire away. I've been thinking it over since you rang, but I can't say there's anything that stands out. Anything abnormal, I mean. Apart from the fact that the crime itself was abnormal, of course.'

Huldar nodded. 'Let's start with three names. We've been looking for them in the old case files but can't find any mention of them. I realise it's unlikely, but I wanted to check if you remember them cropping up in the course of the investigation, even though they didn't make it into the reports.'

'Try me.' Valgeir smiled. 'But bear in mind that it was eleven years ago.'

'Firstly, there are two women, Ólína Traustadóttir and Bríet Hannesdóttir.' Lína did the talking. Huldar had suggested she take this opportunity for interview practice. Although Valgeir had changed career, he was still tied to the police through his former job, which made him the ideal guinea pig. Huldar wasn't worried that she would commit any blunders. On the rare occasions that she'd spoken up during other interviews she'd attended with him, her contributions had always been carefully considered. Well, almost always.

Lína placed some photos on the table. 'These are the women, in case it helps.'

Valgeir picked them up, unhurriedly reaching for the glasses in his jacket pocket. He studied the pictures, his expression thoughtful, then replaced them on the desk, shaking his head. 'No. Sorry. Neither of them are at all familiar. If the files have been properly archived, all the reports, witness statements and other information should be there. We didn't cut any corners, if that's what you're implying.'

'There's no suggestion of that.' Huldar picked up the photos and handed them back to Lína. 'One of the women is a technician in a biomedical lab, the one called Bríet. Ólína's a photographer. Does that jog your memory at all?'

Again, Valgeir shook his head. 'No. I can't say it does. But we spoke to a huge number of people, as it was such a serious incident. No photographers, though. But I do remember talking to a nurse or midwife at some point. The baby's GP, too. We needed confirmation that the two men were—'

'The child's parents,' Lína corrected him. She didn't seem to have done so inadvertently since she neither blushed nor looked at all awkward.

Valgeir regarded her in surprise over his reading glasses. Recovering quickly, he corrected himself: 'Yes, of course, the parents. We needed confirmation that they'd been caring for the child properly. Since suspicion fell on them at first, it was a necessary part of our investigation. It just occurred to me, as you mentioned a lab technician. It's possible that in our conversations with health workers, we did speak to a lab technician – I can't recall. I didn't conduct all the interviews myself, though naturally I read all the reports.'

'Were these health workers from the National Hospital?' Huldar tried to remember how long Bríet had worked there. But if he'd ever heard, he hadn't taken it in. If Bríet had been working there eleven years ago, she must have only just started, since she would have been quite young.

'Yes. I think so. The midwife was, anyway. But I have a feeling there was someone from the local surgery, too. A woman, if I remember right – their GP. She wasn't a lab technician, at any rate.'

Lína glanced at Huldar, who gave her a sign to continue. She brought out another photo. 'What about this man? Rögnvaldur Tryggvason. He sells insurance.'

Valgeir took the picture and examined it. 'Hang on, isn't this the guy who's wanted by the police? You think he snatched Mía?'

Lína handled this well. Rather than answering, she persisted in her line of questioning. 'Do you remember him from the original inquiry?'

'No. Definitely not. Neither the name or the face. There was no insurance angle either, or at least not as far as we were concerned. It's possible Mía's mother had life insurance but, like I said, that wasn't passed on to us if she did. And I very much doubt the two men . . . the *parents* . . . had insured the baby's life. But what do I know?'

Huldar took over again. 'What about the conclusion of the investigation, given what we now know? What do you make of this new information?'

Valgeir laid his hands flat on his bare desk and leant forwards a little, as if to reduce the distance between himself and his visitors. 'Honestly, I don't know what to say. Naturally, I was delighted when you told me that all the evidence suggests the girl's alive. But I was astonished too. Flabbergasted, actually. There was nothing in the results of the inquiry that gave me pause or nagged at me afterwards. Not a single detail. The events, as we reconstructed them, were based on witness statements and evidence. We didn't leave a stone unturned. I simply can't see where we could have made a mistake.' He removed his hands from the desk and settled back again. 'If it *was* a mistake. I don't know what to call it. We worked round the clock and conducted a scrupulous investigation. I stand by that. But of course I've left the police, as you know, so it's your job, not mine, to find out what went wrong. An inquiry is much more than one man. The whole force has to shoulder the responsibility, not just me.'

Huldar remained impassive. Valgeir was in an unenviable position, but then so was Erla. 'I'm not actually interested in that side of things,' he said. 'Our concern is with finding Mía.'

'Yes. Of course. I just wanted to make the point.'

Huldar didn't waste any more time on the blame game; right now it was a side issue. 'Can you think of anything, in retrospect, that could help us find Mía? Anyone who strikes you as a possible suspect? You say her parents were under suspicion, but were there other names too – even if they were only of vague interest at the time?'

Valgeir took off his glasses, pulled a cloth from his pocket and began to polish them, though as far as Huldar could see they were already spotless. Still, if it helped him remember the case . . . Valgeir finally looked up. 'I can assure you that there were no other suspects apart from Droplaug and the fathers; we didn't have a single other person in our sights. If we had, you can be sure we'd have carried out a thorough investigation of them. Anyway, it would have been an incredible coincidence for someone else to have been involved. The child was snatched at exactly the same time as the mother gave up the fight and killed herself. It simply doesn't make sense for it to have been anybody else. We had countless witnesses who confirmed that the woman had been in the vicinity at the time the child was abducted. I just can't see what else could have happened.'

Huldar wasn't surprised by this answer. After going through the files, he found it difficult to imagine any other explanation himself. 'There are a large number of formal and informal witness statements connected to the case. We may need to re-interview some of the people concerned. Is there anyone in particular you'd advise us to talk to? Anyone who, in your opinion, is more likely to have lied or accidentally provided inaccurate information? Those are the ones we'll probably concentrate on. We're not going to review the inquiry only to come to the same, wrong conclusion.'

'Hm. You're not asking much.' Valgeir clasped his fingers and raised them to his lips, apparently thinking it over. 'Look, at the time I believed people were telling the truth. I don't remember suspecting anyone of lying.' He reflected again, then continued, 'No, I can't think of anyone. But of course we relied mostly on the statements of those who saw the mother at the scene when the child disappeared. They included one of the neighbours in Skerjafjördur, an old woman who's probably dead by now. She was adamant about the time of the row next door because it disturbed her while she was listening to a particular radio programme. She recognised the voices too, as there had been rows outside the house almost every day. Then there were the workmen who met the mother's car as they were leaving the house. Their story was crucial because there were several of them and they were all in agreement. But I doubt you'll be able to get hold of them all, as they were mostly foreigners who are bound to have gone back home by now. Though there was an Icelandic electrician, and a carpenter, I think, as well as the contractor himself. Come to think of it, he wasn't quite as confident as the others. He claimed he hadn't seen the mother's car and thought it was more likely the fathers had done something to the child themselves.'

'Oh?' Huldar didn't remember that. He vaguely recalled the accounts of the foreign and local workmen, who had been travelling together in two vehicles. The contractor's statement had mostly been concerned with the scenes he'd witnessed between the fathers and Droplaug while his men were working on the house. He hadn't been certain that he'd passed Droplaug's car on his way there but he'd met the two vehicles containing his crew, who were leaving just as he arrived, so perhaps he'd been too preoccupied with looking at them to notice the other traffic. 'I don't remember reading that he suspected the fathers.'

'No. He implied it but when it came to the crunch he didn't want to be quoted. He said he didn't have any proof beyond the fact that he'd liked the mother and felt sorry for her. He felt she'd been badly treated and he didn't have a good word to say about the two men. Though bear in mind that he was involved in a dispute with them about surcharges at the time, so he wouldn't have been completely neutral. I reckon he was a reliable witness, though. In fact, his statement was unfortunate for Númi, the one who discovered the empty pram, because the contractor claimed he hadn't heard any shouts or cries when the baby was supposedly found to be missing. Then again, he arrived at the house at around the same time, so it's possible he missed the commotion. And Númi wasn't sure if he'd called out or not. One minute he was certain he had – the next he couldn't remember.'

A silence descended and lasted until Lína broke it. 'Was there anything odd about the case that wouldn't be clear from the witness statements and reports?'

'Odd? Isn't what I've just been describing odd enough?' Valgeir smiled at Lína but when she didn't reciprocate, he addressed Huldar instead: 'We were investigating a case involving two individuals with mental health problems. The mother, Droplaug, was believed to have been suffering from post-natal depression, while Númi completely lost the plot when the baby vanished. He came out with the most unbelievable rubbish, which didn't make our job any easier.'

Huldar replied to this, since he wasn't sure whether Lína had been given access to all the files, as he had. 'I read somewhere that he'd been in a bad way, but it wasn't specified what form this took. His statement was quite short and there was nothing odd there. Was the rubbish, as you call it, included in the report that was destroyed?'

'Yes, it was. It was in the statement taken at the station the day it happened, when Númi was beside himself about his daughter's disappearance. He let slip the business of the surrogate mother and some other stuff that didn't make sense. When his husband realised, he acted fast. Their lawyer immediately pounced on two points: one, that we'd failed to inform Númi of his right not to make a statement, given that he and his husband were suspects, and, two, that Númi had suffered a breakdown and should have been seen by a doctor. We hadn't treated him with the due consideration required by the police code of conduct. Whatever the truth of it, the lawyer kicked up such a stink that the decision was taken to destroy the offending statement. Not that this changed much because Númi came in again later and gave a more detailed and plausible description of the events. He was very lucid on that occasion, not hysterical and gabbling like he had been when he gave his first statement, or when the police originally arrived at the scene.'

Like Huldar, Lína had been listening attentively. She'd sat stony-faced during Valgeir's speech, except when he mentioned the bit about violating the code of conduct, at which her expression had grown indignant. Now she slipped in a question: 'What exactly did Númi say that was dismissed as rubbish?'

Valgeir told them and Huldar couldn't help nodding during the description of the dead baby in the pram that had subsequently vanished without trace. Crazy nonsense. But then he noticed out of the corner of his eye that Lína was frowning sceptically. That was all it took to make him think again. Lína was sharp. Maybe there had been something in Númi's original story after all.

Chapter 28

Friday evening

Síðumúli wasn't yet empty of people. Rögnvaldur had the hood of his cheap anorak up and kept his head down as he walked. The cold wind and flurries of snow meant he wasn't the only one, and no one paid him any attention. It would have been far more suspicious to walk tall, with a bare head. In this respect at least, the weather was on his side; on the other hand, the intense cold had forced him to leave the caravan earlier than intended. It was either get into the warmth or die of hypothermia. And he wasn't ready to freeze to death – not yet.

Rögnvaldur raised his head. He had no choice if he were to cross the road without being run over. He waited while two cars went past, then waded quickly through the slush to the other side. His feet were so frozen that he barely even noticed when the icy water leaked through the seams of his shoes. His first few steps after leaving the caravan had been as jerky as those of a scarecrow, his extremities numb, his joints too stiff to work. Walking had loosened them up a little but he still felt stiff. Even worse was the way his body was screaming out for warmth. The pain was so bad that he couldn't stop grimacing. Still, this would help with his disguise, along with his three-day growth of stubble. The photo

accompanying his wanted notice was of a completely different man from this scowling, bearded scarecrow; a man who
worked in an office on Síðumúli and was eager to visit people
and talk to them about health insurance, whether they were
interested or not.

He darted a sideways glance at the insurance company
offices as he walked past. All the lights were off except in the
lobby, where the advertisements stuck to the glass wall looked
suddenly so forlorn. When they'd first been put up, he'd
thought they were great, and believed that this advertising
campaign and the new logo would have a big impact on sales.
When this failed to materialise, he was as surprised as anyone.
The talk around the coffee machine had put the blame on the
colour combination: it was too yellow – that had to be it. Now
he found it incredible that he should ever have cared enough
to have an opinion.

At the corner he turned abruptly and slipped round the
back of the building, having decided, since the lights were off,
to take a chance on the fact that everyone had gone home. He
couldn't stay out in the cold a minute longer. With shaking
hands, he drew his staff card from his pocket and held it up to
the sensor by the door. His numb fingers had so much trouble
hitting the right buttons on the little keypad that he had to
enter the code three times. It worked at last and he stepped
into the blessed warmth.

The first item on the agenda was to eat something. There
was nothing on offer in the cafeteria but biscuits, since fruit
and other perishable foods that would spoil over the weekend had been locked away in the kitchen larder. He opened
the small fridge where the employees kept their private sup-
plies and saw that there was plenty of *skyr* and yoghurt. He

scooped up all the pots, though they were clearly marked with the owners' names. He had to eat.

There was enough light entering the cafeteria through the windows for Rögnvaldur to be able to eat in comfort. He sat at a table by a radiator, feeling the heat flowing towards him as he devoured the dairy products. The warmer he got, the more agonising the pain in his fingers and toes became, but in the end the aching faded. By the time he stood up again, he felt almost back to normal. His guts had stopped rumbling and his joints were working again.

Leaving the cafeteria, he headed to reception where he grabbed a car key, having first turned off the lights so he wouldn't be on display to passers-by like a goldfish in a bowl. He turned them on again when he left, doubting that anyone who had seen the lights go off and on would give it a moment's thought. No one would care.

Inside the dark office all was quiet. Rögnvaldur decided to see if his work computer was still connected, rather than relying on Bríet's rather inadequate laptop. He groped his way to the lift and pressed the button. When the doors opened, he flinched back from the glare for a moment, before stepping in and being forced to confront his own reflection in the large mirror. He wasn't too taken with this new version of himself. In addition to his shabby appearance, he had an odd glint in his eyes. The shadows around the sockets made it look as if they had sunk into his head and his expression was a little unhinged too, as if the mechanism behind his eyes had been wound up a notch too tight.

The steel doors closed behind Rögnvaldur before he could tear his eyes from this vision, but the clang broke the hypnotic effect and he hurriedly selected the right floor. He'd got careless. Last time, he had taken the stairs to avoid the risk of someone spotting the light from the lift. He would just have to hope that no passers-by would give a damn about what happened in an office building on a Friday evening. They'd be too interested in getting home to give it any thought.

His workstation was a depressing sight. His belongings had been thrown into two cardboard boxes. One would have been enough if it had been carefully packed. But no, it looked as if someone had simply swept everything off his desk and shelves. He stared at the framed photo of Íris sticking out at an angle. It felt as if a burning-hot spike had been rammed down his spine. Would it have killed the person who cleared his desk to lay the photo respectfully in the box?

Rögnvaldur picked it up and traced a crack in the glass with his finger. It ran from corner to corner, cutting right across his daughter's beautiful face. Only one eye had escaped, and half her mouth. He licked his dry, split lips, holding the photo to his chest. He stood like that for a few moments, trying to control his breathing, until all thoughts of setting fire to the building had passed.

Before sitting down, he propped the picture up in its old place on his desk. While he focused on Íris's one visible eye, he reminded himself that the sloppiness had a positive side. Whoever they had got to do the job hadn't bothered to finish it properly: his computer was still connected and his access card hadn't been deactivated. A more conscientious employee would have made sure to deal with those things.

The computer bleeped and started up with a familiar whirring from the clapped-out fan. He'd been meaning to ask for a new one but had never got round to it. Pity. It would have given him pleasure to think of the company wasting money on him. But it was too late. The cardboard boxes indicated that he'd been sacked. It seemed that being wanted by the police was bad for your career. But the access card and computer suggested that the process hadn't been completed. He'd been half sacked – from half a job. A quarter employee.

Once the computer was ready, Rögnvaldur got down to work. He needed information and although it wouldn't take long, there was no reason to tempt fate by dawdling. Plus there was a danger he'd fall asleep in his chair now that he was finally warm.

He fished a pen out of one of the boxes and tore a crumpled page from a notepad that had been dumped in there. The pad reminded him inescapably of Bríet's exercise book, which had been lying on the floor of her flat, battered by its fall. Determinedly pushing this image to the back of his mind, he started hunting for the information he needed.

As Rögnvaldur was scribbling down the last detail on the already full page, he was distracted by a noise. He stiffened, his head jerking up, recognising the creak of the door to the department. Someone had opened it. To see who it was, he would have to peer over the partition round his workstation. But there was no way he could risk sticking his head above it. All he could think of was to dive under the desk. He wriggled as close to the partition as he could, hoping that whoever it was didn't have any business with him or with any of the neighbouring workstations.

Rögnvaldur groaned inwardly when he realised that his illuminated screen was reflected in the window. Since there was nothing he could do about it, he just held his breath and squinted along the floor of the office.

The lights came on. Two feet in dirty snow boots appeared and started walking towards him, coming to a halt by his desk.

'I know you're under there.'

Rögnvaldur considered staying where he was, waiting until the man who was talking had to bend down to him. Then he decided to see who it was. The voice was familiar and although the man didn't sound exactly happy, he wasn't outraged either. Rögnvaldur wriggled out from under the desk and got to his feet, to find himself face to face with Jói from IT. 'Hello.'

'Hello? Hello? Are you out of your mind? What are you doing here?' Jói's face turned red with indignation. Or anger. Or both.

'I needed to use a computer.' In awkward situations it was generally best to stick to the truth.

'Use a computer? Use a computer?'

'There's no need to repeat everything.' Rögnvaldur pulled over the sheet of paper he'd been writing on and shoved it in his coat pocket, for fear that Jói would grab it and tear it to pieces.

'You've got to get out of here. Do you know why you've still got access?'

'No. I thought maybe I'd only been semi sacked.'

Jói didn't understand what he meant. 'No. You've been sacked, all right. Sacked sacked.' He put his hands on his hips. 'You've still got access because I didn't cancel it. I needed to talk to you and this was the only place I had a chance of catching you. I've got a connection at home and I can keep an eye on the access log. When your name popped up, I came straight over.'

'I see.' Rögnvaldur didn't see at all.

'I lied for you. Lied to the police. Don't ask me why. I said something really stupid: that you couldn't possibly have been seen in the building since there was no record of your having accessed it. Then I deleted the records of your entry when you brought in the laptop and picked it up.'

It wasn't hard to guess why Jói had lied: he didn't want to have to explain why he had helped Rögnvaldur with the laptop. 'You didn't do anything wrong,' Rögnvaldur said reassuringly. 'They hadn't put out the wanted notice yet when I was here.'

'I realise that. That's why I said I'd been stupid. I panicked. But you have to leave right now.'

'Did you come here just to tell me to leave?' Rögnvaldur scratched his cheek. His beard was beginning to itch in the heat. 'Or did you come to ask why the police are after me?'

'No. I don't want to know. I'd feel better if I could believe it was for something trivial. I came here to ask you not to tell them about the business with the laptop – when you're caught. Because you will be caught. That's all.'

Rögnvaldur could see the man's agitation. He knew Jói enjoyed his job and didn't want to get fired like him. Rögnvaldur found himself feeling sorry for him. 'No problem. I won't say a word. Why would I?'

Jói was so relieved he let out a sigh that echoed around the empty office. Then he tensed up again. 'What do you want from me in return?'

'Nothing. Not a thing. You've done quite enough for me. Thank you. We're more than quits.'

'OK then. But I'm going to take you off the system now. You won't be able to get in again. And I'll delete all your visits. You won't mention them to anyone, will you?'

'No. You needn't worry.' Rögnvaldur hesitated. 'Should I go then?'

Jói nodded. 'Yes. That would be best.'

Rögnvaldur couldn't actually go anywhere, though, since Jói was blocking his way. Realising this, Jói stepped awkwardly aside. Neither said goodbye; social niceties seemed out of place in the circumstances.

Rögnvaldur went downstairs and exited the building.

Then he lurked nearby, waiting for Jói to appear and drive away. Once he was sure Jói wasn't coming back, he went over to the staff entrance and tried his access card. It didn't work.

Rögnvaldur hurried to the spaces where the company cars were parked. He searched for the number plate matching the key he had taken, found the vehicle and got in. His former colleagues would have a major headache on Monday morning, trying to work out what had become of the missing car. Suspicion wouldn't fall on him, though, as he hadn't been there, according to the system. He'd been fired and didn't have access to the building. Which was fine. He didn't want to get Jói into trouble. The IT guy had no need to worry that he'd grass on him.

He had no intention of talking to the police. He had no intention of being caught. Not alive, anyway.

Chapter 29

Friday evening

Saga and Erla were eyeing each other balefully: it was hard to tell which of them was less impressed. Huldar could see that Freyja had noticed, because she was trying to distract the little girl's attention, as if she were afraid of an explosion. It was probably just as well, since Erla was near the end of her tether. She was still recovering from the shock of learning that the body wasn't Bríet Hannesdóttir but Ólína Traustadóttir. Huldar couldn't remember ever having seen her this pale and silent. Her usual reaction to setbacks was to blow her top, generally with those who deserved it least. Her team had learnt to live with this. New recruits were easy to recognise by their mortified expressions when she bawled them out. The old hands merely shrugged it off and got on with their work.

Mind you, there had been a glimpse of the old-school Erla in the car on the way there, as she fumed about Freyja's 'endless bloody babysitting'. This rant had given way to a barrage of questions about Saga, which Huldar hadn't been able to answer. Why couldn't the child's mother take her? The kid was a bit weird, wasn't she? Was she born like that? Was it hereditary? What about the father? Was the whole family a bunch of losers? Was Freyja going to have to babysit for much longer? To all of which he replied: 'I don't know.' By the end, he had begun to suspect that the reason for Erla's irritation wasn't that Saga was getting in the way of Freyja's work but that Erla was picturing herself in the same predicament before long. This wasn't about Freyja, Saga or the girl's useless parents, but about Erla's own future.

She had become subdued again when he changed the subject to ask about her conversation with Ólína's family. It turned out she'd spoken to the woman's father on the phone. He was a widower, who lived somewhere in the west of Iceland, and the news had hit him hard. He said he'd had a good relationship with Ólína but when he didn't hear from her, he'd just assumed she was taking photographs up in Svalbard. He must have misremembered the date of her planned trip to the Arctic. The phone call hadn't lasted much longer as he had been too choked up to talk any more.

Erla and Huldar were now sitting with the other four at a restaurant by the hot-water beach in Nauthólsvík Cove. They were the only customers as lunchtime was long over but it was still a bit early for supper. Huldar had dragged Erla over there after Freyja had rung, following her visit to Númi, explaining that she'd sat with him far longer than she'd intended and now had to dash to pick up Saga.

When she called, Huldar had only just got back to the office after interviewing Valgeir, the ex-detective at the ministry who had headed the original inquiry into Mía's disappearance. Less had emerged from that conversation than Huldar had hoped.

In contrast, it sounded as if Freyja's visit to Númi had thrown up something new that she wanted to discuss with him and Erla. The problem was she didn't have a babysitter. She offered to bring Saga into the office but he suggested she meet them at the restaurant instead. Erla needed to eat again – it was as if the three hot dogs earlier had awoken her appetite and she was now ravenously hungry, her body trying to make up for all the meals she had recently missed. Besides, employees bringing their children into the police station was frowned on. And none of them needed any more criticism in-house right now. He was desperate to get out of the office too. When things were going badly like this, he couldn't stand being cooped up inside. His depressing thoughts seemed to bounce off the walls, growing ever more insurmountable until he thought they'd drive him nuts.

Gudlaugur and Lína, spotting Erla and Huldar leaving together, had quickly pulled on their coats and insisted on coming with them. Gudlaugur was so cross-eyed from staring at the footage of traffic that he would have seized the chance for a break even if they'd been heading down the city's sewers.

Huldar didn't know why Lína was so keen to join them. When they'd got back from their visit to the ministry, she had headed straight to her desk to get on with work. Perhaps she just wanted to stay in the loop. Apart from Huldar, few of the detectives bothered with her. They hardly spoke to her and next to no one shared important information with her when it came in.

It was possible, too, that neither Lína nor Gudlaugur wanted to be left alone with the rest of the team, who still hadn't got wind of the mix-up with the body. Huldar could understand that: he could think of few things more uncomfortable than the weight of a secret that he couldn't share.

Erla hadn't kept it entirely quiet, though. She had broken the news to her boss and he had taken it as expected – badly.

At his request, Erla had delayed telling the rest of CID. But she had told her team to dig up everything they could on Ólína Traustadóttir, Bríet's childhood friend, promising more information by the end of the day. No one reminded Erla that the long working day was already almost over.

The waiter came to their table and asked if they'd like coffee. They all accepted, including Saga, who nodded vigorously, though she had no idea what she was agreeing to. Freyja ordered a glass of apple juice for her. Nobody spoke while their empty plates were being cleared. They had chosen to sit in a corner of the glass building, as far from the counter as possible, in order to have a bit of privacy. None of what they had to discuss was for public consumption.

While the waiter was wiping the table, Huldar stared out of the window at the largely uneventful scene outside. A jogger ran along the illuminated path past the sailing club, continuing on round the foot of Öskjuhlíd hill, before vanishing from sight. Three people, each carrying a bag, walked down to the heated beach for a swim in the sea. With a shiver of sympathy, Huldar turned away from the chilly, dark winter evening, back to the warmth.

He watched Lína put a cross by something on the page in front of her. She had brought a sheaf of papers with her and had hardly looked up from them since they'd sat down. When their food arrived, she had simply moved the papers next to her plate so she could carry on working while she was eating her salad. Such was her preoccupation that she had scarcely said a word, and it didn't look as if she was going to venture any opinions for the rest of the meal either.

Up to now, they had been talking about the dead baby Númi claimed to have seen in the pram. The fact that

Huldar had already heard about it and had told Erla rather took the wind out of Freyja's sails, but she was quick to recover. She had a trump up her sleeve, since Huldar wasn't aware of the blanket – presumably because the head of the original investigation hadn't heard about it. According to Freyja, the detail had only emerged after the inquiry had been closed, so it was conceivable that Númi's statement had been overlooked – or dismissed as nonsense. It wouldn't be the first time such a thing had happened at the police station.

'I haven't seen anything in the files to say it wasn't the blanket from Mía's pram.' Erla screwed up her face as she tried to remember the details. 'But maybe that's not surprising since the first I heard about the dead baby was when Huldar told me earlier. In all other respects, Númi's account fits with what the head of the original inquiry had to say.' Erla shrugged.

Freyja put down the paper napkin she had been using to wipe Saga's mouth. 'Why wasn't it looked into? Both the business of the blanket and the dead baby?'

'Because Númi omitted to tell you why his version isn't recorded anywhere,' Huldar answered. 'He and his husband had the statement destroyed. That's how they avoided being prosecuted for illegally using a surrogate mother. And that wasn't the only thing that went in the shredder. When Númi gave his later statement, they had clearly planned what he would say and rehearsed it carefully, no doubt to prevent him from accidentally blurting out any details of their arrangement with Droplaug again.'

Freyja didn't seem satisfied. 'Still. He did say it. I'd have thought it was standard practice to look into his story, at the very least.'

She was right. Huldar had made the same point during his conversation at the ministry. 'It was looked into. Everything was looked into, according to the guy who was in charge. But they found nothing. No dead baby turned up afterwards and there was no sign that it had ever existed. And, given that there was zero evidence, I can understand why people didn't take it seriously. All Númi's bizarre story achieved was to cast suspicion on him.'

'Why?' Freyja handed Saga the teaspoon the little girl had been vainly trying to reach. Saga didn't seem to realise that her arms were at least half a metre too short. 'It's not like it was the first time the police had interviewed someone who was in shock. You must be used to dealing with all kinds of reactions.'

Erla was looking more like herself. Clearly, she was less than amused by Freyja's criticisms of the police's performance, even though she herself hadn't been involved. Huldar hastily dived in to answer Freyja first. 'You have to bear in mind that Númi was hysterical when the police arrived and it must have seemed as though he'd murdered his own daughter in a fit of madness. At first, our guys guessed he'd dumped her body in the sea before ringing his husband and coming to his senses. Their house is right on the shore, so he wouldn't have had far to go. Then, later, the series of events got muddled in his head when the madness wore off and he was hit by the terrible truth. He convinced himself the body he'd been holding had been some unknown baby.'

'He said he'd never been arrested or anything.' Freyja slipped a napkin under the spoon that Saga was banging noisily on the table. The little girl's perma-scowl deepened as the napkin muffled her blows. 'If he was a serious suspect, why wasn't he arrested?'

Huldar pre-empted Erla again, nervous that she was about to go off the deep end. 'No one wants to arrest the father of a missing baby. And anyway, the focus soon shifted to the child's mother. They couldn't arrest her either.'

Lína looked up. 'You do realise that if there really was a dead baby in the pram, that solves the problem of where Mía's been all these years. It would explain the whole thing if she was swapped for a baby who'd died. That would be much easier than concealing a child who had never existed. I believe there was a dead baby in the pram. It's the only rational explanation.'

No one contradicted this, though Erla couldn't resist sniping at her. 'Since you've got the whole thing worked out, Lína, what happened to the dead baby?'

Lína's pale cheeks flushed slightly. 'I don't know. Maybe it was thrown in the sea or buried somewhere.'

Erla hadn't finished. 'And who would do a thing like that? Kill their child and steal another to replace it?'

'I don't know.' Lína looked to Freyja for help.

'No one knows how the baby died – if it ever existed,' Freyja said. 'It could have been the result of SIDS – you know, cot death – or something. An illness. There's no reason why it should have been killed, is there?' She paused to give Erla a chance to respond, then continued: 'There are people who steal babies. Both women and men. But it's not a large group and your average person wouldn't do it.'

Erla folded her arms on top of her bump. As she couldn't scowl at both Freyja and Lína simultaneously, she directed her glare at Saga instead. The little girl responded by sticking her tongue out at her. This did nothing to soften Erla's expression. 'What kind of person would be most likely to do it?'

Lína looked relieved when Freyja answered this. 'Someone with a child the same sort of age. I assume it's more likely to have been a single parent, because I can't see how it would be possible to hide the switch from a partner. Unless the partner lived abroad, or simply wasn't in the picture. It would be difficult but not impossible to conceal it from the wider family. This was in the middle of winter, so the child would have been well wrapped up whenever it left the house. It wouldn't have had any teeth yet and not much hair either. Young babies tend to look quite similar, much more so than when they get older. If you kept friends and relatives at a distance for a while, I imagine it would be possible. Babies develop and change so fast.'

'How many children would have been born in that year?' Huldar chipped in. 'Or rather, how many girls?'

It didn't take Lína long to find the answer. She took out her phone, tapped at the screen, then raised her eyes. 'About two thousand three hundred. Fewer if we rule out the children born several months before Mía. The babies must have been around the same age.'

Huldar turned to Erla. 'In a case as serious as this, we have the authority to take biological samples from more than just the accused. We could blow our budget on DNA tests for the lot – if we didn't spend any money for the rest of the year.' When Erla didn't smile, he added: 'Of course, we'd have to get extra funding.'

Erla shook her head. 'No chance. It would take far too long and I can't see the kids' parents agreeing. Still, if we can't solve the case now, we can dream.' She inhaled so deeply it sounded like a reverse sigh.

'Rögnvaldur's daughter, Íris, was the same age as Mía. They were born only two months apart.' Lína dropped her eyes to her papers the moment she'd spoken. She'd obviously been itching to say it.

'Right.' Gudlaugur seized on this. 'Rögnvaldur's connected to Bríet's disappearance and Ólína's murder. That would link the two cases. Very neatly.'

It was all a bit too much of a coincidence for Huldar's liking, but he didn't say so. It would be oddly fortuitous if Droplaug, Mía's mother, had just happened to drown herself the very day the child was snatched. But Gudlaugur so rarely spoke up when there were other people present that Huldar didn't like to be dismissive. He tried to picture it. Rögnvaldur steals Mía. Droplaug throws herself in the sea. Mía – or Íris – dies after being infected with measles. Rögnvaldur kills Ólína for some reason that must relate to his mission to exact revenge for the death of the daughter he snatched from her pram all those years ago. And he probably kills Bríet as well. No, it just didn't add up.

At that point, Freyja's comment at her first meeting with the inquiry team came back to Huldar. The person who dismembered the body had almost certainly done something terrible before. Huldar had been picturing mutilation or some such scenario, but switching one's own dead baby with someone else's child would have involved crossing a pretty major line, morally speaking. There might be something in what Gudlaugur and Lína had said. 'We need to check any possible links between Rögnvaldur and Ólína, that's clear. And any connection between him and Númi and Stefán. The person who snatched Mía must have known she was sleeping outside in her pram.'

Erla looked at him. 'They claim they don't know him. But I suppose he could have been knocking on doors, selling insurance, and noticed the pram. Maybe he was invited in and happened to see her outside but they've forgotten the incident. After all, this was eleven years ago. You're forgetting something, though. Rögnvaldur's daughter, Íris, was dead and buried by the time Ólína was murdered. So how could she have vomited in the boot of the car?'

They were all silent while the waiter served their coffee and apple juice – all except Saga, who was dissatisfied about getting her drink last. When the glass was finally put in front of her, she dragged it clumsily towards her, spilling juice on the table. Lína, who'd only just managed to rescue her papers from the puddle, looked highly disapproving – as did Erla, who narrowed her eyes as she watched Saga's behaviour and Freyja's attempts to mop up the worst of the juice before it started dripping on the floor. Huldar was sure Erla was picturing her own future: nappy changing, nose blowing, sleepless nights, spillages and stickiness. He wanted to nudge her and remind her that the good times would probably outnumber the bad. But he held back. He wasn't exactly experienced when it came to having kids, so if he knew this, the odds were that she was already aware of it herself. And no one likes having the blindingly obvious pointed out to them.

'Does she have an unusually big head or are all babies like that?' Erla was still staring at Saga, although her question was directed at Freyja, who could guess what might have motivated it.

'No, don't worry. It runs in the family. My brother was born with a huge head as well, but thankfully the rest of the body seems to catch up with time. I'm sure your baby will be much easier to pop out than this one was. She was referred to as pumpkin head on the maternity ward.'

Erla did not seem reassured. Her frown only deepened.

'What else did Númi have to say?' Gudlaugur, having got his coffee before the others, had had time to sip it, put down his cup and resume the previous conversation. The subject of babies' head sizes was thankfully closed.

Freyja put down the soaking paper napkin. 'He said a number of things I can't share with you, which have nothing to do with the case and more to do with his worries about the future: how their other daughter will react, how Mía's going to adjust, the effect on his marriage, and so on. He's not blowing anything out of proportion – these are all pretty big challenges to have to face.'

Huldar saw Erla open her mouth and, afraid she was going to put pressure on Freyja to betray her professional confidentiality, he hastily changed the subject. 'Where did their other daughter come from? Could she be Mía?'

Freyja answered this flatly: 'No. She's not Mía. It's no secret how she came to them. She's adopted, but not in the same way as Mía. It wasn't a step-adoption. They went through the conventional process, since she's not related to them. They got her when she was three, which was around three years after Mía vanished. According to Númi, it wasn't easy for them to be recognised as fit parents after what had happened, so when they were offered Gudbjörg, they leapt at the chance. And I believe they've been very good parents to her.'

'What about the biological parents?' Huldar was eager to spin out the conversation, to distract Erla from demanding more details from Freyja's confidential chat with Númi.

'The father died of an overdose and the mother was judged unfit as she was an addict. There has to be a hell of a lot wrong before the authorities will take a child away from its

332

parents these days and I gather the little girl carries the scars of her early life. She's got galloping ADHD and she's behind at school. Her eyesight's badly affected too because she was very premature as a result of her mother's lifestyle. Still, at least she's lucky to have found a good home.'

Lína glanced up. 'So Mía's bad luck was her good luck. That's sad.' She immersed herself in her papers again without waiting for a response.

Freyja raised her eyebrows at this comment, then continued. 'I suppose so. I also asked him why his daughter had been let out of school early. Apparently it was due to a malfunctioning fire alarm. So, in other words, Gudbjörg is a pupil at the school where Ólína's phone turned up.'

Erla's expression didn't change. She'd asked Freyja to check this, and no one was surprised as the school was the local one for the Skerjafjördur catchment area where Númi and Stefán lived. 'I thought so.' She raised a hand to her forehead as if checking whether she had a temperature. 'How the hell does it all hang together?'

'Shouldn't we just ask to talk to the girl?' Huldar winked at Saga, who had been staring fixedly at him ever since she'd spilt her drink. Perhaps she was fascinated by the fact that he was the only adult who hadn't reacted with disapproval. As far as he was concerned, it wasn't a big deal. Drinks got spilt and ice-creams fell out of their cones. Such was life.

'We can try. But we won't get permission. Not as matters stand. Stefán's a lawyer, remember, and he's not exactly well disposed towards us.' Erla shook her head in defeat. 'He'll dig his heels in and the only argument we've got is that she's at the school where the phone turned up. Along with five hundred other kids.'

Freyja agreed. 'They won't let us talk to her, if only because she doesn't know about Mía.'

'What?' Huldar couldn't hide his amazement. 'Why not?'

'Because they've had to break a lot of very difficult news to her over the years, so they decided it could wait. They didn't want her to feel second best.' Freyja handed the teaspoon back to Saga, who immediately began banging it on the table again. As the soaking napkin no longer muffled the noise, Freyja put her hand underneath and got hit for her pains. It didn't really hurt but she flinched and withdrew her hand anyway. 'I don't blame them at all. It's their decision and they know Gudbjörg better than anyone. She overheard us mention Mía and asked who we were talking about. Númi just said no one she knew and sent her back to her room. Clearly, though, if Mía's found, it won't be possible to put off telling her any longer.'

'Not *if* – *when* she's found—' Erla broke off and put a hand to her belly. It looked to Huldar as if she was pushing a foot back into place. There had definitely been a movement in there. 'Who the hell can have taken the baby?'

'Bríet?' Gudlaugur suggested. 'Isn't her daughter eleven?'

'No, ten. And she's only recently had a birthday. She's big for her age but that doesn't mean anything.' Freyja opened her mouth as if to say more, then changed her mind.

'Droplaug's sister? What's her name – Ellý?' Although Huldar thought it unlikely, it was the only name he could come up with.

Erla seemed to agree it was unlikely, judging by her lack of enthusiasm. But Lína raised her head from her papers, her eyes wide. 'Ellý? What's her patronymic?'

'Er . . . Droplaug's was Thórdardóttir, if I remember right. As far as I know, they had the same father.'

Lína bent over her papers again and started leafing through them. When she found what she was looking for, she held out a page. 'Ellý. Ellý Thórdardóttir. She's friends with Ólína on Facebook. They must have known each other.'

Erla immediately perked up. At last they had a link of sorts between the murder case and Mía. Ólína, who had been sawn into pieces, and Ellý, Mía's aunt, had known each other. It was tenuous – but it was a link, nonetheless.

Chapter 30

Friday evening

The girls were giggling as if at something forbidden or something they weren't old enough to understand. Sædís remembered that kind of whispering from her childhood, but then it wasn't that long since she'd been eleven years old herself. Even though, strictly speaking, it was half a lifetime ago, as she was now twenty-two.

'What are you lot whispering about?' Sædís shot a glance over her shoulder at the three friends.

'Nothing.' More giggles.

Sædís felt suddenly overcome with anxiety. She bent down and caught sight of herself in the wing mirror. Her smile had gone and her brow was knotted with worry. If she went on like this, she'd end up with deep furrows between her eyes – long before she reached the age when the salesmen of eternal youth would start swooping down on her in the cosmetics aisles.

But her foolish fear of wrinkles did nothing to distract her from her other worries, and after a moment her thoughts returned to her young passengers and the secrets they might be keeping.

She was most concerned about Rósa. Sædís suspected that her home circumstances left a lot to be desired. She didn't know much about the family except that Rósa's father was an electrician and her mother was unemployed. On the rare occasions that Sædís had met the couple, the woman had reeked of booze and the man had been surly, bad-tempered and hard-faced. The poor kid was often shabbily dressed, her appearance screaming neglect. As she was taller than the rest of her year at school, she was very conspicuous and couldn't hide her unkempt hair or ancient bobble hat, just like Sædís at her age. Sædís hadn't been properly looked after either, but for different, more forgivable reasons. It wasn't her mother's fault that she was ill or her father's that he couldn't cope. He'd done his best. It was just unlucky for the family that it hadn't been enough.

Gudda was the complete opposite of Rósa: small and slight, always smartly dressed, with brushed teeth and combed hair. But it was as if her clothes and her body operated on different networks. Her garments were always askew, as if they were trying to come off. And it was the same with anything in her hair: her plaits unravelled, her clips got dislodged and her hair ties slid off, fell on the floor and were lost. Her glasses, too, were always crooked, smudged and forever being mislaid. But there was one thing Gudda never lost and that was her happy temperament and the smile she wore at every opportunity.

Selma, Sædís's sister, was in the middle, in height, appearance and behaviour. They made quite a threesome.

Sædís stopped at a red light and stole another glance over her shoulder. Sure enough, Selma was sitting in the middle, between big Rósa and scruffy Gudda. All properly strapped in, preoccupied with each other and living in the moment. Untroubled by past or future. They could have given lessons in mindfulness, despite never having heard of the phenomenon.

She smiled at them.

Then fear reared its head again. Would they manage to stay friends into adulthood? Or would some conflict arise and ruin it? She prayed it wouldn't. None of them found it easy to make new friends, and the three of them fitted so well together. Like a three-legged stool, they were strong and solid together, but if one leg was removed, it would fall over.

Sædís hoped her decision wouldn't spoil everything. Would the child she was carrying upset the balance? She hadn't given it any thought when she'd embarked on this journey. Naively, she had just assumed that it would strengthen the bond between the girls. At least between Selma and Gudda, who would be forever tied through the child. But the reality would be different. Sædís had forgotten that her own relationship to the baby would be terminated as neatly as an umbilical cord being cut, and with it the ties between her little sister Selma, and Gudda. If she herself became *persona non grata* at Gudda's house, the same would presumably apply to Selma. And Sædís would not be welcome – that was part of the deal. It hadn't been stated openly but it was there between the lines.

She wasn't to approach the child, either in person or on social media, by email or phone. For the first six months she was to express her breast milk, put it in the freezer and hand it over daily or every other day. They would pick it up from her. If she saw them with the child in public, she was to steer clear and stay out of sight. She had no right to news, photos or anything else. And so it went on. Her only possible role in the child's future would be if it ever needed a kidney or bone marrow. Then they might turn to her, but she gathered that she was allowed to refuse. This point had been a bit hazy, though. The contract was long and often unintelligible, with tortuous sentences and a drily authoritative tone. She had found it so difficult to follow that in the end she had given up the struggle to understand some parts.

Hopefully that wouldn't matter. She trusted them and understood what lay behind their overcautiousness. It wasn't as if they'd made a secret of it. Once bitten, twice shy. They were decent people, or at least Númi was.

But even decent people sometimes do bad things. They become blind to everything but their goal and forget those they trample underfoot to reach it.

She reminded herself that it had been her idea. She had volunteered. They had even been reluctant to accept her offer.

Because the girls generally preferred to play at Gudda's house, Sædís had often dropped by to pick up Selma – and Rósa too, as her parents never offered to do any of the lifts. Just under a year ago Sædís had gone round on a Saturday, only to find that the girls hadn't got back from swimming yet. Númi had taken pity on her and invited her in. It was the first time since Selma and Gudda had become friends that she had been further inside than the hall. She'd found it hard not to stare, dazzled by the stylish affluence of the interior. Númi had invited her into the living room where there was a huge glass of white wine on the coffee table and a half-full bottle with a cork, rather than a screw-top, and a French label.

At first she had felt like the country mouse in the story she used to read to Selma. She hadn't expected to be invited in, which involved taking her shoes off, and there was a hole in one of her socks.

But Númi didn't seem to notice it. Or her ugly T-shirt. He had even hung her worn anorak in the hall cupboard, as if she'd turned up in a fur coat. Once she had sunk into the big leather sofa, he'd offered her a glass of wine but she had declined as she was driving. The moment she said it, she turned bright red. He must have known she was driving since she was there to collect her sister. At least she'd had the sense not to add that she didn't drink; it might have made him feel awkward, as if she were judging him.

The girls had kept them waiting and she had ended up sitting with Númi for over an hour. To begin with, he had asked innocent questions about her and the girls, in an attempt to make conversation, but she was so flustered she simply answered in monosyllables. She blamed this on being shy and stressed. He was quite a bit older than her and somehow so smart and self-assured. But gradually she found herself relaxing, perhaps because Númi gave up trying to get her to talk and started telling her things instead, regularly refilling his glass until the bottle was empty and his eyes were glittering.

Towards the end of the hour he confided in her about how much he and Stefán longed for a child. A baby. He told her about the ordeal they had gone through when their daughter Mía was abducted and all the problems they'd had before that. Then he added quickly that she mustn't misunderstand him – they adored Gudda and regarded her as their own daughter, just like Mía had been. Sædís had nodded, trying to hide how uncomfortable she was finding the conversation. She suspected that later he'd regret having shared all these confidences with her. When he began talking about how much the name Mía meant to them and how awful he found the nickname Gudda, she was no longer in any doubt: he would regret opening up like this.

What followed was a rather incoherent account of their failed attempts to change their adopted daughter's name. Gudbjörg was supposed to be rechristened Ísold, which would have ensured that she was no longer referred to as Gudda. But the Child Protection Agency had got wind of their plan and kicked up a fuss. Apparently you're not allowed to change a three-year-old child's name for what the agency described as trivial reasons. Númi rolled his eyes at the memory and took a big slug of wine.

It was then that Sædís spoke up unprompted, for the first time since she had arrived. Without even stopping to think, she offered to carry a child for them. She'd be up for it, she said.

Númi was momentarily silenced. Then he laughed off the idea, yet she could tell from the gleam in his eyes that he wanted to leap up, throw his arms around her and accept her offer. Next time she'd come round to collect Selma, he had dropped hints about the subject, and then again every time she turned up after that. Eventually, he invited her out to dinner with him and Stefán, which was the first time they had seriously discussed the possibility. The men had talked so much, and asked her so often if she was absolutely sure, that they didn't even notice that she hadn't touched the weird fish on her plate. Shortly after that, they had produced the contract, which she had read and duly signed.

Her offer had been impulsive, not thought through at all, and she wasn't even sure why she had done it. She had just been gripped by the desire to restore joy and harmony to their elegant home. She was the child of an alcoholic and had settled into the role of co-dependent. She longed to make the two men happy again. In her mind the universe had shifted things around to make this happen. It was meant to be.

Even if it left her in a mess.

Her eyes grew hot and she felt tears pricking at them. But giving in to the urge to cry was out of the question with the girls in the car. She'd promised to take them to the cinema and it would spoil the mood if she started blubbing. They'd been looking forward to it so much. She opened the car window in the hope that a blast of cold, fresh air would revive her. Sure enough, it did.

Right up until an image from her scan appeared in her mind's eye. A tiny creature with a head out of all proportion to its body, like an alien in a film. Her pregnancy wasn't even half over but it looked to her as if most of what a child should have was already in place: fingers, stomach, nose and umbilical cord. Thank God. She'd been worried that there might be something seriously wrong with it. What would have happened in that case? Would she have been left holding the baby, forced to bring it up without any help from the fathers or support at home? What kind of life would that be for the poor little thing? And for her? There must have been something about that eventuality in the contract but she couldn't face reading it again to find out.

Bloody scan. She hadn't meant to look but the woman doing the ultrasound had prompted her, telling her she just had to see. Númi had encouraged her too, presumably to avoid suspicion. They had to come across like a couple who were expecting a baby together. Sædís had had no choice but to obey and raise her eyes to the screen. It hadn't done her any good, only made her emotional. The child growing inside her had acquired an image. And a gender. It was a little girl.

There was no way of erasing, on demand, what you had seen. Or heard.

From the back seat Rósa piped up: 'Can we go to a horror film?'

'No.' Sædís glanced in the rear-view mirror and caught Selma's eye. 'You're not old enough and it's out of the question.' She realised her voice had been overly shrill but the girls didn't seem bothered.

'But we know it's all make-believe.' Rósa wasn't about to give up. 'Pleeease?'

'No. I'm not even discussing it.' Sædís turned into the cinema car park. 'We're going to a film that's age appropriate, and that's final.' She glanced in the rear-view mirror again and could have sworn Selma was looking relieved. Hopefully this would be the end of the discussion.

There were plenty of spaces by the cinema but she chose to park at the furthest end from the entrance because of the street lamp. All the other lights in the area were switched off. She'd caught sight of a van in the mirror which seemed to be following them; a thought which had filled her with trepidation. She'd first noticed it just after Rósa had got into the car, but the man could have been following them before that. If he was. Perhaps it was just a coincidence. After all, he hadn't turned into the car park after her.

Sædís had no sooner stopped than the girls tumbled out. They charged off, keeping pace with one another, almost as if they were joined at the hip, all talking at once and gesticulating excitedly.

Sædís locked the car and set off after them more slowly. They were waiting impatiently by the entrance now, beckoning to her to hurry. They were anxious to sit together and didn't seem to have noticed how empty the car park was. They'd be able to bag three seats in any row they wanted, by the aisle, in the middle or anywhere in between.

Just as well the cinema wasn't busy. One of the things Sædís had failed to take into account was that once she started to show, she would have to forgo her usual company.

Her friends were sure to ask about her bump and she wouldn't be able to tell them the truth. Firstly, they'd never understand how she could have agreed to do it: other people's problems with having children, or the subject of children at all, were so far outside their area of interest. And secondly, she was afraid they'd accuse her of being cold and unfeeling. What kind of person would offer to give their child away? So there was no alternative; she would have to stop seeing her few good friends. She could only get away with meeting them for another month – and then only in settings where she could keep her coat on.

Then there were the people she couldn't hide from. Although she lived with her parents, she still hadn't told them. Of course it would be better to do it before they worked it out for themselves, but she was reluctant. She had turned down the offer of being put up in a summer house for the last few months of her pregnancy, but the offer still stood; it was in the contract. If she accepted, no one need ever know. She wouldn't lack for anything – she'd seen pictures. But that wasn't the problem.

The problem was that Sædís didn't want to be parted from Selma for months. That would actually be worse than moving into her own flat and leaving Selma at home. At least in that case she would be able to see her regularly and wouldn't have to pretend to be working abroad – doing what? – as she would if she accepted the men's offer of accommodation.

She'd forgotten to zip up her coat and hurriedly did so as she was walking, shivering from the cold. It felt noticeably tighter. Naturally the girls didn't know about the baby. So far she'd got away with hiding her bump under baggy jumpers and cardigans. But their questions would be the most difficult and embarrassing of all. She was assuming that Númi and Stefán still hadn't told Gudda, since the little girl hadn't shown the slightest interest in Sædís's expanding waistline. And hopefully she wouldn't any time soon.

All these dreary thoughts made Sædís conscious of the empty car park behind her. She had a sudden powerful instinct that there was somebody out there. It wasn't impossible, as there was more than one entrance. Perhaps the van that had been following them was lurking in the darkness behind her. She told herself not to be silly. Of course it wasn't. It had just been an ordinary little van, marked with some company logo, she thought. There was nothing inherently mysterious about that. But the driver had been alone in the van and the sun visor had been down, in spite of the dark winter evening, which was undeniably odd.

Sædís tried to reason with herself. As if anyone would start following her. What for? The man could hardly be planning to rob her. He would have to be blind or at least have failed to take a good look at her old junk heap of a car. It was glaringly obvious that she wouldn't have anything worth stealing. Unless the sun visor had blocked his view.

The other possibility was that it was someone who wanted to hurt them. She picked up her pace as much as she dared but the tarmac was slippery with frost, so she couldn't go any faster. Instinctively she put her hands over her belly to protect the little creature inside. She was responsible for seeing that the baby came to no harm. There had been no need to mention that specifically in the contract – and yet there had been a clause to that effect.

Only a few steps left until she reached the pavement and the girls. Pretending nothing was wrong, she followed them in through the double glass doors, then paused and turned to scan the car park. She couldn't see anything out of the ordinary, just the odd car here and there in the darkness and her old banger, illuminated by the street lamp, all alone. Her precarious situation must have made her imagination run riot. She needed to calm down.

She was relieved when the door automatically closed behind her. Turning to follow the girls, she didn't see a small van marked with the logo of an insurance company drive into the car park and come to a halt in the darkest corner.

Chapter 31

Saturday

Huldar pushed the small milk jug towards Droplaug's sister, Ellý. She hadn't poured herself any coffee yet and it occurred to him that she might want some milk. But she shook her head, lips tightening. He got the same response when he offered her a biscuit, so he didn't bother pestering her with the water jug. The woman clearly didn't want anything. It was possible that she simply wasn't thirsty or hungry, but he suspected that wasn't the reason. After all, she'd made no secret of her animosity towards the police.

Huldar had been given the job of interviewing Ellý with Erla. He'd called her yesterday evening to ask her to come to the station but she'd refused, saying she wasn't going anywhere. It was only when he pointed out politely that if she didn't come in voluntarily, she'd be slapped with a court order that she gave in. She'd be there at eight.

Sure enough, Ellý arrived in reception at five to and was on the right floor on the dot of eight. Huldar had gone down to fetch her and found the ride up in the lift excruciating. Ellý had stared fixedly at the number indicator above the doors all the way up, her arms folded uncompromisingly across her chest, her coat buttoned up to the neck. She wore the strap of her handbag across her body, instead of over one shoulder, as if afraid Huldar would try to wrestle it away from her and run off with it.

Even here in the meeting room, she hadn't unbuttoned her coat or put down her bag. Instead, she sat facing Huldar and Erla, straight-backed, waiting defiantly for what was to come. Her harsh expression made it difficult to see if she resembled Droplaug. She had the same blonde hair as her sister, according to the photos, but it was longer and she didn't have a fringe.

Erla kicked off with: 'Do you know a woman by the name of Ólína Traustadóttir?'

The question seemed to take Ellý by surprise. Her uncompromising expression softened, her eyes widened slightly and her lips parted. Although the resemblance to her sister wasn't striking, it was there. 'Er, yes.'

'How do you know each other?'

'We're cousins. Our mothers were sisters.' Ellý undid the top button of her coat. 'What's this about? Has something happened to her? Is she suspected of something? I'm not testifying against my cousin, if that's what you think.' The frown had returned, accompanied by an eye-roll. 'Of course that's what you think. Obviously, nothing's changed around here.'

Erla and Huldar let her talk. When she paused for breath, Erla resumed, saying in a level voice: 'Ólína's dead. She was murdered.'

It was as if the stormy expression had melted off Ellý's face. Huldar wouldn't have been surprised if a black puddle had formed on the table in front of her. 'What are you talking about?'

'You don't find it odd that you haven't heard from her in over a week?' Huldar was careful to keep his voice gentle.

Ellý didn't immediately answer. Understandably, she seemed to be having trouble taking in the news. She gave a sudden sniff and wiped a tear from the corner of her eye with a clumsy movement. 'We don't talk every day, just from time to time. As it happens, I did try to get hold of her last week but she wasn't answering her phone. I just assumed she was away on an assignment. She often goes . . . used to go . . . abroad to take landscape photos and didn't pick up or answer messages. She said it disturbed her concentration.'

'I see.' Huldar glanced at Erla, but she seemed happy for him to continue. 'I'm afraid that's not why she didn't respond this time.'

'Then what was the reason? Who killed her? You said she'd been murdered, didn't you?'

Erla took over. 'That's right. Ólína was murdered a week ago on Friday. That's why you're here. We can see from her phone that you spoke to each other the day before. Can you tell us what you talked about?'

Ellý picked up the mug and held it under the thermos spout with a trembling hand. She pumped coffee into it, then put it back on the table. But she didn't take a sip, just seemed to have been buying herself time. 'I don't exactly know. She said she had a surprise for me – hopefully.' Ellý's voice shook but she didn't break down.

'Hopefully?' Huldar asked, puzzled. 'Was she hoping to surprise you? What did she mean?'

'I don't know. She said she had news that would make me incredibly happy. Maybe. Things would become clear very soon. When I didn't hear from her, I assumed the hopefully-maybe hadn't gone as planned. That's why I rang her during the week. I was curious to hear more.'

'She wasn't more specific about what kind of news it was?' Erla picked up her pen, ready to write the answer down. But she needn't have bothered.

'No. Not a word. I kept asking her but she refused to say any more. All I could think of was that it might be about a prize. That she'd won some photography prize. Or one of her pictures had been chosen for some posh magazine.'

'Wouldn't she have phrased it differently if it had been about her success as a photographer?' Huldar repeated Ellý's own words back to her. 'Why should it have made you "incredibly happy"? I can understand that you'd be pleased for her, but it sounds a bit over the top to say you'd be incredibly happy.'

'She was my cousin. Of course I'd be happy if she did well.'

Erla put her pen down. 'Would you excuse us a minute?'

She made it sound as if Ellý had a choice in the matter but of course she didn't. Instead of answering, the woman just waved a hand at them as if batting away a cloud of midges.

Huldar followed Erla out and closed the door. Although the interview room was thoroughly sound-proofed, he lowered his voice to a murmur. 'Are you thinking what I'm thinking?'

Erla snapped back irritably: 'How should I know?' She leant against the wall. 'But I have a suspicion that the incredibly good news was about Mía. It must have been that, surely? It can hardly have had anything to do with Bríet's measles study?'

Huldar shook his head. 'No, you're right. Maybe Ólína had found out that Mía was alive. It would be strange to sit on the news, though. Unless she'd been intending to get hold of the girl – steal her back and take her round to her aunt's, for example.'

'No way. The girl wouldn't have gone with her, even if she'd told her the story. As far as Mía knows, she's someone completely different. And how could Ólína have found out? I'm assuming the people who snatched Mía would never reveal their secret, so I doubt the girl would have marched up to Ólína when she was taking class photos and told her who she was. The kid can't be aware herself.'

Huldar racked his brains to think what could have alerted Ólína. 'Bríet, then? Could she have spotted something in the medical records that gave away the girl's true identity? She worked at the hospital and had access to the vaccination register. If so, surely she'd have got in touch with her childhood friend Ólína, who she must have known was related to Mía?'

Erla shrugged. 'Christ knows. And how the hell did Rögnvaldur get mixed up in the whole thing? Could he have blundered into it by total coincidence?'

'Search me.'

Having spent a minute or two deciding on their line of questioning, they went back into the room. Ellý didn't turn or look up at them once they were sitting down again.

Erla launched into her next question. 'Do you know Bríet Hannesdóttir?'

'Bríet? Yes, but not well. She's an old friend of Ólína's. I met her a few times back when we were younger but I haven't seen or heard from her for at least ten years. They both went to different sixth-form colleges, which is when people often go their separate ways.' Ellý paused, then added: 'What's she got to do with it?'

Instead of answering, Erla continued: 'We believe the unexpected news Ólína was planning to tell you had nothing to do with photography. We believe she was referring to something quite different.'

'Like what?' Ellý's face radiated genuine curiosity.

Erla and Huldar exchanged glances before Erla replied. 'When her body was found, we discovered the presence of DNA from an unidentified person. It was sent off for analysis and the person was identified on that basis.' Erla paused, swallowed, then went ahead. 'The DNA turned out to belong to your niece, Mía.'

Ellý frowned. She lifted her hand to the collar of her coat and gripped it. 'Has her body been found?'

Huldar fixed and held her gaze. 'No. The DNA came from a living person.'

Ellý's fingers tightened on her collar. Her knuckles whitened and Huldar feared for a moment that she would tear it right off. But the seams held. Her voice thickening, she asked: 'Is Mía alive? Where is she?'

'Do you have children yourself?' Huldar asked.

'Yes. Two.' Ellý's voice broke. She sounded suddenly as hoarse as a worker in an asbestos factory.

'Age and sex?' Erla picked up her pen again. They were putting on an act to fool Ellý into thinking they didn't already know about her children. In fact, they'd done a background check on her yesterday and discovered that she had a ten-year-old son and a twelve-year-old daughter. They were simply asking in order to observe her reaction. From that, they were hoping to work out whether there was any reason to suppose her daughter might be Mía.

Ellý cottoned on immediately. 'Hang on. You think I've got Mía? That one of my kids is Mía? That I stole her? Are you out of your minds?'

Erla's pen was still hovering over her notepad. 'Age and sex, please.'

Ellý was visibly seething. By the time she walked out of there the roller coaster of emotions this conversation must be provoking would leave her feeling as battered as a fillet of dried cod. She snapped: 'Oh, just google it. You're the fucking police. You must have access to the National Registry. But neither of my kids is Mía, you stupid bastards.'

Both Huldar and Erla were inured to such insults. Huldar's next question was designed to placate the woman. 'Do you have any ideas about where Mía could be? Or who could have taken her?'

It had the desired effect. Ellý calmed down a little. 'Funny. Back when I was trying to tell you that my sister would never do anything to harm Mía, I was almost kicked out of here. Now that it turns out I'm right, you have the nerve to come to me for help.'

Huldar continued: 'We're not asking you to go out and look. We just want to know if you can think of anyone. Anyone who knew about Mía's existence and could have taken her. That's all.'

Ellý didn't take any time to reflect. 'No. I can't think of a single person who'd steal someone else's baby.' Then she added sarcastically: 'Oh. Apart from Númi and Stefán, of course. They stole Mía from Droplaug when she was born. Who knows, perhaps they did it again? Don't ask me why. I don't understand those men. But I advise you to check up on them as well while you're looking at the National Registry. After all, they've got a daughter the same age as Mía.' Ellý leant back in her chair with an air of triumph.

'Their daughter isn't Mía. She's adopted.' Huldar took a deep breath. 'So you have no idea who it could have been?'

Ellý sat up again. She was red in the face, but then she must be boiling in that coat. Without raising her eyes from the table top, she spoke, but not to answer Huldar's question. 'They're not nice guys. Did you know that Droplaug and Númi used to be best friends? Childhood friends? That's why she did it for him. She wanted to help her best mate. And what did Númi do? He turned his back on her as soon as he and Stefán didn't need her any more. He locked her out. Literally. Droplaug didn't get a penny from them, if that's what you think. She was doing her friend the biggest favour anyone could ask for, but he wouldn't lift a finger to help her in return. She wasn't even allowed to see Mía once a month. She'd have accepted that.' Ellý's gaze alighted on Erla's bump. 'You of all people should understand. How crazy it is. To have a baby, then give it away.'

Erla's face remained blank. 'Surrogate motherhood is illegal in Iceland. There's a reason for that.'

Ellý didn't let this wrong-foot her. 'Surrogate motherhood! They should call it something else. You're not asking the woman to be a mother. Quite the opposite. A woman's not a mother during pregnancy. She becomes a mother when the child is born, which is when the role of a surrogate mother ends.' Rage was dripping off every word. 'It should be called rent-a-womb – or get one for free, in Droplaug's case.'

Huldar felt the interview was going nowhere. Instinct told him they wouldn't get much more sense out of Ellý now. He'd seen countless people sit in the chair she was now warming and he could generally identify those who had something to hide or were lying through their teeth. Ellý wasn't hiding anything. He didn't believe she had anything on her conscience. She was Droplaug's sister and had stood on the sidelines back in the day, watching and trying to help. That was all. There was no reason to keep her any longer.

Erla had obviously reached the same conclusion. 'If anything occurs to you, I urge you to get in touch. I don't think there's anything else for the moment.'

But the woman who had initially refused to come in, now didn't want to leave. 'What about Droplaug's death? Are you going to look into that again? Since you fucked up the investigation of Mía's disappearance, chances are you probably came to the wrong conclusion in Droplaug's case as well. My sister wasn't the type to kill herself. Surely you're going to reopen her case?'

Huldar answered that. 'They're reviewing the results of her post-mortem and other aspects touching on her death. But I doubt it'll change anything.' He gripped the edge of the table, conveying the message that he was about to stand up.

It had no effect on Ellý. 'Who'll get Mía when she turns up?'

The question caught them both unprepared. As was often best in circumstances like these, Erla answered with the truth: 'That's out of our hands. But I assume she'll go to Stefán and Númi. They are her parents, whatever you may think of them.'

Ellý was silent. She untwisted the strap of her bag. 'I'm going to insist she comes to me. They've already got another daughter, and, anyway, they're up to their old tricks again with the whole fucking surrogacy thing.'

'What?' Huldar's fingers loosened from the table. 'What do you mean?'

Ellý's face brightened. She had finally managed to disconcert them. 'I've got a friend who works at the National Hospital. She saw Númi with a pregnant girl, waiting for an ultrasound. A very young girl – hardly more than a kid. He doesn't have any younger sisters. I know that. And I think it's safe to assume that he doesn't have a girlfriend on the side. So what do you think is going on there?'

Neither Erla nor Huldar replied. There was no need.

Erla hauled herself to her feet. 'Right. Thanks for coming in. We'll be in touch.'

Finally recognising that there was no point sitting there any longer, Ellý got up too and Huldar escorted her down in the lift. She was as uncommunicative as she had been when she arrived. Only, out of the corner of his eye, he saw that tears were running down her cheeks. He pretended not to notice. When the lift doors opened, she marched out without a backward glance or a word. He watched her stomping off down the unploughed pavement, before crossing the road and vanishing from view into the dark morning.

Chapter 32

Saturday

There were two suitcases parked by the wall outside the interview room, one a carry-on item, the other a large case that looked as if it was bursting at the seams. Both belonged, Freyja knew, to Andrea Logadóttir, who had arrived back in the country early that morning. She'd been picked up from Keflavík Airport in a police car and brought straight to the station. She was later than expected as her flight had been delayed and, after she'd landed, Customs had gone through her luggage with a fine-tooth comb. It wasn't surprising as the reek of patchouli, mingled with some other hippy scent that Freyja associated with joss sticks, could be smelt a mile off.

Thanks to the delay, Freyja had managed to catch a glimpse of Andrea when she arrived. She was wearing a long, bulky coat over clothes that looked totally inappropriate for the Icelandic winter. Wide, patterned trousers of thin cotton flapped around her calves and she was wearing socks and sandals – never a good combo, as out of place in the hot country Andrea had just come from as it was in Iceland. A bit like her; on the one hand, so summery and beautifully tanned, on the other, bundled up in a knee-length winter coat.

She also showed all the signs of someone who has been travelling too long. Her clothes were creased, her fine features weary, and her shoulder-length hair so full of static electricity that it floated around her head like a halo. She looked as stale and dishevelled as anyone would after a long-haul flight. And it couldn't have helped that she'd received the news of Bríet's disappearance the moment she walked through the arrivals gate at the airport. The wellbeing and energy she had been seeking through her yoga retreat must have evaporated in an instant. What she had to say in her interview would probably also go a long way towards undoing all the good of her vow of silence. She'd have done better to stay at home and spare herself the expense and fatigue of travelling.

Freyja stared at the closed door of the interview room, fighting the temptation to go and press her ear to it. She had yet to learn how the team had got on after she'd parted from them yesterday evening. If it hadn't been for Saga, she'd have turned up early, eager not to miss anything. Instead, she'd had to wait until it was late enough to ring her friends and ask if any of them could babysit, knowing that the chances of a positive reception were greatly enhanced if she didn't drag them out of bed. This tactic had paid off, as it had taken no more than two phone calls to sort out her little niece. Saga had put up no resistance since the friend in question had two cats that were too fat to run away. The little girl wouldn't hurt them; all she wanted was to stroke them and pick them up – an almost impossible feat for a small child given their great weight. But at least the challenge stopped Saga from getting bored. And Baldur was due back in town after lunch, hopefully before the cats got fed up with having their fur stroked both the right and the wrong way, or with being hoisted up until only their hind paws remained on the ground.

Staring at a closed door never achieved anything. It remained firmly shut. Huldar had promised to let Freyja know as soon as he and Erla had finished questioning Andrea, but in her impatience she was afraid he might have forgotten. She would just have to resign herself to waiting – which was easier said than done.

A woman she recognised from the IT department came in. She'd helped sort out an ID for Freyja when she'd first joined the police. The woman strode over to Erla's office, only to turn away, looking tight-lipped, when she saw that Erla wasn't there. Freyja hurried to try and intercept her before she left again. She tapped the woman on the shoulder and smiled when she turned round, but instead of returning her smile, the woman looked oddly shifty, as if it was the end of the month, Freyja was her landlady and she herself was a tenant behind with her rent.

'Hi, I won't keep you,' Freyja said brightly. 'I just wanted to ask you about a small misunderstanding that needs sorting out.'

'Oh?' The woman still seemed reluctant to engage.

'I'm told I'm suspected of having logged on to the Information System for private purposes – out of curiosity or something.' As she said this, Freyja noticed the woman shuffling her feet and avoiding eye contact. 'I've never done anything of the sort, so I just wanted confirmation from you that it's all a big mistake. I hear that kind of thing's taken very seriously, so I wanted to clear up the misunderstanding before it goes any further.'

The woman stared past Freyja as if there was someone standing behind her. 'I'm afraid I can't help you.'

This was annoying. 'Then who can?' Freyja asked. 'Doesn't IT manage the access log?'

'Yes, we do. The problem is that according to our records, you logged on to the Information System to carry out a search unrelated to a case. I saw it with my own eyes. So there's no mis-understanding to correct.' The woman was directing her words over Freyja's shoulder. 'It's all logged. You accessed the system to look up your brother. That's against the rules and you'll just have to take the consequences. The IT department isn't involved in that side of things; we just monitor how the system's used.'

'Hang on a minute. My brother? Am I supposed to have looked Baldur up? Why on earth would I do that?' Freyja was stunned. She had been expecting to be able to sort out the mis-understanding then and there, and mentally cross the matter off her to-do list. But now she was completely thrown. 'I don't even have a log-in,' she protested. 'I've never once accessed the system. Your records are wrong.'

'Our records are not wrong. And you did get access. I organised your log-in myself.' The woman took hold of the door handle. 'I don't know what to say. You'll just have to take responsibility for your own mess. Maybe someone forgot to tell you the rules. What do I know? But the records don't lie. You logged in.'

'But I didn't.' Freyja considered blocking the door with her foot to prevent the woman from leaving, but this would only lead to more awkwardness. 'I don't doubt you created a log-in in my name but the fact is I never received it. Either on paper or by email.'

'Talk to your manager. I sent him the details.' The woman opened the door. But rather than hurrying out, she took pity on Freyja, leant over to her and whispered: 'If someone's log-ging on with your ID, it wouldn't be the first time.' The instant she'd finished speaking, she was gone.

Huldar turned to Freyja before pressing the doorbell. 'Are you sure there's nothing wrong?'

Freyja forced a smile. 'Yes. There's nothing wrong with me.' She'd decided to keep quiet about her conversation with the woman from IT. At least until after the weekend. Her colleagues had enough on their minds; Huldar too. But she had a bone to pick with her manager, who'd received her log-in details. She'd scoured her inbox in vain for any notification, then sent him an email, asking what was going on. The message would be waiting for him on Monday morning. Until then, she would just have to push the problem to the back of her mind.

On the way there she had asked Huldar about Andrea. According to him, nothing in her statement had changed the substance of what they already knew. Andrea had had an encounter with Rögnvaldur and was able to confirm that he was trying to access the vaccination register. She believed him capable of anything and said she was grateful to have emerged unscathed from their meeting at the café. He had reacted so badly when she refused his request that she didn't like to think what might have happened if they hadn't been in a public place.

Andrea had last spoken to Bríet on the Friday before she herself had left the country. They had put in a session on the dissertation at Bríet's flat, finishing at about five in the afternoon. To begin with, Andrea claimed that Bríet had been her normal self that day, but later in the interview she had taken this back and said that actually Bríet had been strangely hyper. She had been expecting her friend Ólína, who Andrea knew only by name, to drop round that evening. Andrea also confirmed that Bríet and Ólína had been in close contact in the weeks before Bríet's disappearance, but said she hadn't heard her mention Ólína before then.

The only surprise to come out of the interview had been in connection with Andrea and Bríet's vaccination study. She'd explained there was no way the register could be used to track down the contact who had infected Rögnvaldur and Aldís's daughter, even assuming that the individual in question was a child and in the database. There were far too many children who hadn't received the measles vaccination, most of them for valid reasons but some through parental neglect or due to the ludicrous idea that it would be a risk to their health. Andrea assured them, moreover, that she and Bríet had never spoken to any of the children or made any attempt to approach them. She added that the head teacher, who claimed that Bríet had gone to her school to meet a pupil in connection with the study, must have been mistaken. Nothing like that had ever been part of their project or indeed been possible – and this applied equally to the children who hadn't been vaccinated and those in the control group.

Huldar added that although Andrea had been baffled by their question, she had told them there was nothing in the register that could reveal the heredity of a child or its relationship to anyone else. She'd never heard Bríet mention Mía either, though she remembered hearing about the baby's disappearance at the time.

As far as Huldar could remember, nothing else of interest had emerged from the conversation with Andrea.

'Are you ready?' His finger was on the doorbell. 'You're in charge of this interview. I'm just the bodyguard.' He ran his eyes appreciatively up and down her body before winking at her. 'May I remind you that I also provide out-of-hours body-guard services. Of the happy-ending type. On the house.'

'Jesus, Huldar. This is hardly the place.' Freyja wouldn't actually have minded the ridiculous come-on if they'd been anywhere else. But they were standing in the lobby of the building where Rögnvaldur and Aldís lived. Erla had sent them to talk to Aldís, who had been discharged from the psychiatric ward yesterday evening, at her own request. Erla was hoping they would manage to extract something from the woman now that she should be in a better mental state. Freyja had nodded, while privately doubting that Aldís would be any more forthcoming. Nevertheless, she was prepared to give it a go. No one involved in the investigation could fail to realise how vital it was that they find Rögnvaldur, dead or alive. And at least Aldís hadn't refused to see them when Erla had called her earlier. 'Go on, then,' she said. 'Ring the bell . . . body-guard.'

Huldar went ahead, thankfully skipping the opportunity to offer to ring her bell, too.

They were waiting for Aldís to answer the entryphone when there was a buzz from the lock and only Huldar's quick reactions saved them from having to ring the doorbell again. Aldís probably didn't care whether they got in or not.

But she opened the door promptly enough after Huldar knocked, and regarded them silently through the gap, without saying hello. She was looking a little better than the last time Freyja had seen her, but not much. Her eyes were still sunken and her shoulders bowed but at least her hair was clean and she was properly dressed.

Still without saying a word, Aldís turned and walked away from the door, apparently taking it for granted that they would follow. It was gloomy inside, the lights were off and the curtains drawn. Nothing seemed to have changed since the police had entered the flat on Wednesday. They went through to the sitting room, which was still a shambles, with paintings and pieces of shattered vase on the floor, and papers and pens strewn everywhere. The main difference was that the wall that had been papered over with Rögnvaldur's chart was now bare. The odd bit of Sellotape or Blu Tack were the only traces of his efforts.

Before sitting down, Freyja removed a pair of scissors from the sofa. Huldar joined her after clearing away some papers. Aldís took a chair facing them, without bothering to remove the piece of paper that was on it.

There was no reason to hang around. 'How are you doing, Aldís?' Freyja asked.

The woman looked Freyja straight in the eye. 'Absolutely brilliant. Never been better.'

Freyja smiled faintly at her. The fact she was capable of sarcasm was a good sign, suggesting that her stay in the psychiatric ward had had a beneficial effect. She wasn't as passive as the last time Freyja had seen her, and if she was on medication it was an improvement on whatever she had been taking before. Or at least she was taking the right dose. Previously the woman had been so drugged up that any sort of conversation had been almost out of the question. Maybe she would finally open up now that she was in a better state. 'I doubt that. As you know, we're still looking for Rögnvaldur. There's been no sign of him since Wednesday and it would be best for both of you if he turned up as soon as possible. There's a storm forecast for later and if he's out in the elements, he could be in danger.'

Aldís dropped her gaze. 'I haven't a clue where he is. I keep telling you. If I knew, I wouldn't hide it from you.'

'You know him better than anyone, Aldís. Maybe you don't know exactly where he is but you might have an idea where he'd go looking.'

The woman was silent. Her gaze strayed to the blank wall behind Freyja and Huldar, and she gnawed her lower lip meditatively. 'I don't suppose it's any secret that he's looking for the person who infected Íris.'

Freyja glanced at Huldar who nodded almost imperceptibly to indicate that she was on the right track. She turned back to the picture of misery sitting before them. 'You saw him working on his wall chart, so I'm guessing you must have got an idea of his main suspect. Or at least of where he thought the infection might have taken place. Can you remember that for us?' Freyja took out her phone and opened the photo of the wall chart that she had taken during the search of the flat. 'If it'll help jog your memory, I've got a picture here of the wall as he left it.'

Aldís examined the photo briefly, then looked away, resting her gaze on the curtains. 'I don't think there was anything there that would help him find the person who infected her.'

Huldar intervened. 'Why not?'

Aldís handed Freyja back her phone, behaving as if she hadn't heard the question. In fact, she behaved as if Huldar wasn't there, never looking at him, her attention constantly returning to Freyja. 'Just . . . that chart won't help you find Rögnvaldur.'

Freyja took back her phone and examined the picture. She had printed it out when she'd got back to the office and tried to work out what it meant. It hadn't been difficult to guess, and a brief search online about how and when measles infections take place had filled in the blanks. 'Do you mean there's nothing there to explain the infection?'

'Yes. Something like that.'

Freyja was still concentrating on the photo. 'If I understand this right, all the boxes for the days when it's most likely Íris was infected have been filled in. From what I can see, she was mainly at home on those days. Either with you or with both you and Rögnvaldur. If she wasn't infected during the very few trips out of the house that are listed here, how do you think it could have happened?'

The silence hung heavy in the sitting room, unbroken until Aldís sniffed. It was too dim for Freyja to be sure but she thought there was a tear trickling down the woman's cheek.

Aldís sat up straighter. 'I lied to him.'

Freyja hesitated before asking her to explain, afraid the woman would retreat into her shell again. Employing the gentlest tone she was capable of and being very careful not to reveal her own excitement, she said: 'We all tell lies from time to time, Aldís. Sometimes to keep the peace. Sometimes so as not to hurt another person. I don't know what you lied about but if it's been weighing on you, you'll feel better if you share it with us. I imagine it'll have to come out sooner or later anyway.'

Aldís met her eye and now the shadows couldn't hide the tears pouring down her cheeks. 'Íris took part in a children's poetry competition held by the City Library. She was so happy when she got the notification in the post that she'd won. It was the first time she'd had a letter in the post and the first time she'd ever won a prize. When we told her she couldn't go and collect it in person, it was the end of the world for her. She cried and cried, and her dad constantly going on about how the ceremony would be nothing special didn't help. It was lucky he didn't ruin the prize for her altogether with his insensitive comments. To Íris, it was as important as the Nobel Prize for Literature. By saying the ceremony didn't matter, he was belittling her achievement. He backed down in the end and said he'd been wrong, but he wouldn't change his mind about her having to stay at home, however nicely she asked him, or pestered him, or cried.'

Aldís paused briefly to wipe the tears from her face. Then, having recovered her composure a little, she went on: 'And what did I do? I gave in. She wanted it so much and I thought it would be OK.' Aldís broke off to heave in a breath. She closed her eyes but that did nothing to halt the flow of tears. 'Rögnvaldur was working half-days at the office, which made it easier for him to be strict. But I was with Íris round the clock. So, going against everything we'd agreed, I let her go and pick up her prize. The ceremony was in the afternoon, while he was at work, so all we had to do was agree to tell him that the prize certificate had come in the post. Íris promised not to let on to her dad. It was supposed to be our little adventure that we could tell him about later, once it was clear that no harm had come of it. But that's not what happened. It ended in disaster.'

'I see.' Freyja took in the implications of Aldís's words. No wonder she was in a terrible state. This was the secret that had been torturing her. 'You couldn't know what would happen, Aldís.'

Aldís gave a brief, dry laugh, devoid of any amusement. 'Oh, yes, I could. Sadly I can't comfort myself that I didn't know any better. I knew as well as Rögnvaldur that Íris had to avoid crowds after her bone-marrow transplant until she could have her booster shots. But I just thought it would be

OK. I desperately wanted to make her happy because she'd already missed out on so much. And it was so easy. It wasn't supposed to take any time: we were just going to pop in for the prize-giving itself. But Íris was so happy and started talking to the other kids who'd won. She'd been so isolated and loved company so much that I couldn't bear to rush her home straight away as we'd agreed. In the end we stayed longer than intended and I let her enjoy a little time with the other kids. I don't know what I was thinking.'

Freyja studied the woman in front of her, full of pity. 'So when Rögnvaldur was working on his chart, you didn't tell him about it?'

'No. I couldn't. I felt bad enough already, knowing that Íris's illness and death were almost certainly my fault. So I lied. To him, to the doctors and to the representative from the epidemiologist's office. After that there was no going back. I should have told Rögnvaldur the moment she fell ill. But that day passed, then the next and the next, and then it was too late.'

'When was the prize-giving, Aldís? Are you absolutely sure the infection can be traced back to that?' Freyja felt compelled to try to ease the woman's desperate sense of guilt.

'It was on a Thursday. During the week when it's almost certain she was infected. On one of the three days the epidemiologist regarded as the most likely. We didn't leave the flat on the other two days. So, yes, I'm pretty sure it happened then.'

Huldar asked the next question: 'Did you take pictures of the ceremony, Aldís?'

Aldís nodded. 'Yes. I deleted them from my phone and uploaded them to the Cloud, so Rögnvaldur wouldn't come across them. He hardly ever goes in there. The idea was to show them to him later, when everything was over and Íris had recovered. But then she fell ill. After that, I had other things on my mind. And I'm not sure I'd have deleted them anyway. They're the last pictures I have of her where she's enjoying life like a normal child. As she would have done later, if only I'd been stricter with her.'

'Could we see the pictures?' Huldar did a good job of hiding his excitement, but Freyja knew him too well. The tense muscles, the light in his eyes and the pulse in his neck all gave him away. Although the circumstances were completely different, it was exactly the same expression he wore when he was inside her, about to reach the finishing line.

Aldís shifted in her chair to reach her back pocket and pulled out her phone. She tapped the screen a few times, then handed it to them. 'It's connected to the Cloud folder. Just scroll through if you want to see them all.'

Freyja let Huldar take the phone, suppressing the urge to snatch it out of the woman's hands. She leant close to him to see the screen.

Three girls and a boy appeared, posing for their picture. They were beaming from ear to ear, holding rather sad bunches of flowers and certificates with florid writing. Behind them was a glimpse of more kids and some bookshelves.

Freyja pointed to one of the girls. 'I know who that is, Huldar. She's a friend of Stefán and Númi's daughter. I have a feeling she's called Rós or Rósa.'

He nodded and moved on to the next picture, which turned out to be of Íris and the Rós, or Rósa, in question. They were leaning their heads together and smiling. Rósa's forefingers and thumbs formed a heart that she was holding up over Íris's nose and mouth.

The infection carrier had been found.

Chapter 33

Saturday

Huldar saw Freyja check her phone for the third time since the meeting with Erla had begun. He knew a friend of hers was babysitting Saga and guessed this meant she would have to pick her up soon. Erla didn't appear to notice, although there weren't many other people in the meeting room.

Despite the ongoing inquiry, the department wasn't fully staffed today. The team had to be allowed some time off at the weekend, especially those who had been working late every day since Monday, when Ólína's remains had been discovered in the boot of the car. Of course, this applied to Huldar as well, but he had come in anyway. He couldn't possibly hang about at home, watching the English footie, while his heavily pregnant boss was in the office, working her guts out, her nerves jangling with stress. He wasn't that kind of guy. There would be another weekend after this one and it wasn't like it was the last football match that would ever be played in the history of the world. Another lot of teams with equally over-paid players would take each other on next week.

'And you're sure Rögnvaldur has seen these photos?' Erla's question was directed at the IT expert who'd been given the job of examining Rögnvaldur and Aldís's Cloud data, to work out if Rögnvaldur could have known about the pictures and therefore about the prize-giving.

'Yes. Pretty sure. The Cloud was accessed using his log-in on Thursday evening. These pictures were opened and presumably viewed. Of course, I can't prove who it was, but by far the most likely answer is that it was him. When I spoke to his wife to get the details of their Cloud, she said the couple were the only users and that no one else knew of its existence.'

Erla digested this news before carrying on. 'So we can assume that Rögnvaldur believes he's found the carrier. None of the kids can be ruled out but, from the photos, it looks as if this Rósa got closest to Íris. And it can't be a coincidence that she's linked to Stefán and Númi through their daughter. I refuse to believe it, however small Iceland is.'

'Hasn't she been vaccinated?' The young policeman who asked was unaware of Erla's efforts to access this information via the Directorate of Health's vaccination register. Andrea had cited the personal privacy laws and refused to reveal a thing to Erla, saying she had no authority to hand over information from the database. The same had applied to the man Erla had managed to get hold of at the Directorate of Health. Data protection matters would not be dealt with over the phone at the weekend. End of story.

Erla didn't try to hide her exasperation when she snapped: 'We don't fucking know. Maybe after the sodding weekend.'

The young policeman retired in confusion.

Huldar was staring at one of the pictures projected onto the wall. It showed Íris and Rósa hugging, the thin, frail Íris being almost crushed in the arms of the bigger girl. They were still holding their bouquets, but Rósa's was looking rather battered. The prize certificates were nowhere to be seen, suggesting that the adults accompanying the girls must have rescued them. 'Can you scroll through the photos a minute, Erla?'

She did so without comment and everyone present watched the succession of images changing on the screen. There weren't many, but in some it was possible to glimpse people in the background who might be of interest. When Huldar and Freyja had seen the pictures on Aldís's phone, it had been difficult to see the details clearly on the small screen. 'Are there any familiar faces? Apart from Rósa?'

Gudlaugur and Freyja both pointed almost simultaneously to Stefán and Númi's daughter, who was just visible in one of the shots. Beside her stood a young woman who appeared to be straightening the coat on the girl's shoulders. She was holding a piece of paper that was probably Rósa's prize certificate. No one present recognised her.

Erla had little interest in the young woman's identity. 'It's probably Rósa's sister,' she said dismissively. 'It can hardly be her mother. She's far too young.'

'Rósa's an only child.' Lína had done her homework – of course. It was she who had tracked down the girl's patronymic after a bit of online detective work, since there had been nothing about the prize-giving ceremony on the City Library website. A phone call to the library had drawn a blank as it was closed for the weekend. The person who'd answered had asked Erla to call back on Monday, but he was able to tell her that their news page had fallen victim to a foreign cyber-attack in which a lot of older posts had been lost. He assured Erla that the report on the prize-giving had definitely been posted at the time. This did nothing to cheer her up.

'She hasn't got any sisters,' Lína added.

Erla shot her a murderous glare before continuing: 'OK, let's concentrate on the essentials. For example, is there any chance Rögnvaldur could have dug up the girl's name? Will he track her down and, if so, what'll happen when he finds her? Those are the questions we should be asking ourselves, not who was with Rósa at the ceremony. Also, how the hell did he access the internet?'

The IT specialist jumped in. 'The IP number is registered at Sídumúli, at the insurance company where he worked. But that doesn't necessarily mean he went inside. He could have accessed their wi-fi from outside the building. He must know their password or maybe he managed to get hold of a guest log-in. We don't know what computer he was using, though. That's harder to establish.'

'My bet would be Bríet's laptop,' Huldar said. 'He's almost certainly got it. I'm guessing that Rögnvaldur has found out the girl's name, too. As it sounds as if he made the discovery on Thursday evening, he could have rung the library yesterday and acquired the information that way. Don't forget that if he's got Bríet's computer, he's also got access to the vaccination database. If the girl hasn't been vaccinated, he'll know about it.' Huldar watched Freyja shifting anxiously in her chair. 'What about the next steps, Erla? Shouldn't we go round to Rósa's and talk to her parents? Put a guard outside?'

Erla didn't answer immediately. She leant forwards a little, clutching at her lower back, her face grey with pain. Everyone around the table watched helplessly. Everyone except Lína, who was observing her closely, poised to spring into action if she went into labour. Not to make a run for it, but to assist. It proved unnecessary, however, as Erla straightened up, took a deep breath, then started speaking again as if nothing had happened. 'Yes. I'm going to call them now and see how the land lies. But we can put a guard outside straight away.' She pointed at Lína and Gudlaugur. 'You two take the first shift. Use an unmarked car and park somewhere with a clear view.'

Huldar saw Freyja raise her hand. 'I'm afraid I've got to run. Is there anything I can do? It's no problem for me to come back.'

Erla hit the roof. 'What? You're choosing to fuck off now, just when we need to interview a minor?'

'I'm not fucking off. There's something I urgently need to do but I can come straight back.'

'Fine, off you go, then.' Erla pouted like a sulky child. 'The rest of you know what to do. Unless any of *you* have urgent hairdresser's appointments to go to?'

Freyja opened her mouth to protest, but luckily thought better of it. Huldar leapt up and followed her out as the meeting room began to empty. She was almost as incensed as Erla. Apparently anger could spread without losing any of its force. But perhaps there was some other reason for her temper – she'd been in an odd mood even before the meeting began.

'You don't have to show me out. I know the way.'

'I'm going outside anyway.' Huldar brandished the cigarette packet in her face. 'Can I offer you one? They're very good for calming the nerves.'

She declined. Not politely either. Huldar guessed that now wasn't the time to offer to swing by this evening to feed the snake. Armed with a bottle of red wine. That could wait until she came back and had cooled down a bit. He didn't doubt that by the end of the day the general mood would be buoyant. Even Erla would be happy. The case was close to being solved.

He said goodbye and watched Freyja stomp over to her car as he leant against the wall, savouring his cigarette.

Erla hadn't raised any objections when Huldar said he was driving. This was just as well, since judging by the way she kept writhing in her seat, she would have driven them straight into a wall. When he asked if everything was all right, she had bitten his head off, which was reassuring, indicating that she wasn't about to conk out. Delivering a baby in a car wasn't top of his wish list. Or delivering a baby full stop.

He parked in front of a three-storey building on Dunhagi, which looked as if it had once had shops on the ground floor. Now, curtains were drawn over the large display windows, suggesting that the demand for living space in the area outweighed the demand for retail.

Gudlaugur and Lína were sitting in an unmarked car in a nearby parking space. Gudlaugur had his head bent over his phone; Lína was staring unblinkingly at the block of flats. Huldar honked the horn at them, causing Gudlaugur to jump guiltily, whereas Lína didn't remove her gaze from the house, even for a second. She was the right woman for the job: if Rögnvaldur so much as put a toe on the pavement in front of the house, Lína would be on him, brandishing a pair of handcuffs.

As Huldar and Erla got out of the car and headed towards the building, he noticed that she was walking oddly, as if she had aged several decades on the way there. She was clutching her back with one hand, and every step she took seemed to hurt. Despite knowing what to expect, he felt compelled to ask again: 'Are you sure you're all right, Erla?'

Instead of snapping at him, she emitted a loud groan: 'This pregnancy lark is one big fucking pain in the arse. Who the hell came up with the idea?'

Huldar was silent, waiting for her to answer herself, blaming it on the patriarchy. He had no intention of being dragged into that debate. But she didn't say anything, just let out another groan, so violent it was almost a scream, then straightened her back, shook herself and appeared to have recovered. The curative powers of a good bellow shouldn't be underestimated.

'Let's get it over with.' Erla shot Huldar a glare, as if he had been the one creating the delay.

They found the doorbells, which were outside the house, as there was no lobby. A rasping voice said hello, and Erla introduced herself and asked the man to open the door. The answer was drowned out by crackling. Huldar took hold of the handle to be ready when the lock buzzed, but nothing happened. Instead, after a short wait, the door was opened from inside.

The man standing there, scowling at them, was unshaven, with dirty hair and bits of food in the corners of his mouth. 'What?'

'I rang earlier and spoke to your wife. We're here about your daughter, Rósa. Could we come in and have a quick chat with you both?'

'No.' The answer was blunt, and Huldar saw the man block the door with his foot, as if he thought they were going to throw themselves against it.

'It's urgent. If you'd rather, we can talk to you down at the station.' Erla took out her phone. 'If you refuse, we'll have you brought in. Just say the word.'

The man puffed out his chest. Huldar had seen his share of these guys over the years; men whose default response was to be bolshie, who seemed to thrive on aggression and conflict. 'What's this bullshit? The wife told me you were claiming Rósa might be in danger. Maybe us too. You must have got the wrong family, mate. There's no one after us. Anyway, I can look after myself and my family without the cops getting involved—'

Huldar cut him off. 'Did Rósa get ill about six months ago? Did she have a rash on her face?'

This brought the man up short. 'Rósa? Nah. She's as strong as an ox.' Nothing about the man's manner suggested he was lying. 'A rash on her face? No. Definitely not.'

'It was around the time she got the prize. For her poem.' Huldar hoped this milestone might refresh the father's memory.

'Prize? For a poem?' The man shook his head. 'Rósa's never won any prizes. She's not that good at anything. And she doesn't write poems. We're not fucking commies. You're barking up the wrong tree, mate.'

'We've got a picture of her receiving the prize.' Erla searched for the photo on her phone and showed it to him. 'Isn't that Rósa?'

The man took her phone. His hands were coarse, his fingers grazed and swollen. 'Yeah, that's Rósa. But that's not her prize. She picked it up for a friend who was ill and couldn't go along herself. I remember because they let Rósa keep the flowers. It wasn't much of a bloody bouquet. The flowers were all dead by the next day.' He handed the phone back to Erla. 'I told you you'd got the wrong family.'

Erla kept her cool. 'What's the friend called?'

'Selma. Selma something.'

'Where's Rósa now?' Erla asked.

'Round at their other mate's – at Gudda's place. They're always hanging out there. It's in Skerjafjördur, somewhere. The poor kid's got two dads – no mum. Not exactly healthy, if you ask me.'

Huldar smiled coldly. 'I wouldn't worry about it. People who adopt go through a very strict vetting process. Personally, I'm more concerned about parents who have their own kids. Some of them could do with vetting, if you ask me.'

In Skerjafjördur, Númi answered the door to them. Huldar, who hadn't met him before, introduced himself, but Númi merely nodded. He made no move to let them in, just asked what they wanted. Perhaps he suspected that they'd uncovered his and Stefán's attempt to have a second child with the help of a surrogate mother. But now wasn't the time or place to go into that. Erla had been very firm when she'd informed the investigation team that the inquiry was already messy enough. There was no reason to complicate it further, based on nothing more than a rumour.

'We're looking for your daughter's friend – friends, actually: Selma and Rósa.' Erla was brusque, to match their reception. 'We understand they're here.'

'What do you want with them?' A chill blast of wind hit them and Númi hugged himself. He was wearing only a thin shirt, unlike Huldar and Erla who were well bundled up.

Neither of them answered his question. Erla just said: 'Are they here or not?'

Númi's jaw tensed with anger but he answered anyway: 'They were here but they left with Selma's sister about a quarter of an hour ago. She has a cleaning job on Seltjar-narnes on Saturdays and they were going to play on the beach while she's working. She often lets them go with her. They usually end up going for an ice-cream on Grandi afterwards. They're not doing anything illegal, if that's what you think.'

'Where does Selma's sister clean?' Erla asked.

'At a workshop, apparently. At the far end of the industrial area out by Grótta. I think her dad has a business there – or a workshop. Something like that.'

Huldar knew the place: a small industrial estate, the relic of early zoning mistakes by the city planners, situated between the Grótta nature reserve and the suburb of Seltjarnarnes. Various mechanics, repair shops and garages had set up shop there, and recent attempts to relocate them had failed. No wonder, as it would be hard to replicate the view and proxim-ity to the ocean if they were to move.

Erla asked her second question: 'Have you noticed any unusual activity outside your house today? Have you seen any-one who could be following the girls, for example?'

Númi frowned. 'No, not right outside. But when I came home from the gym earlier there was a van parked at the end of the road. The man behind the wheel sank down in his seat when I drove by. It struck me as a bit odd but I didn't give it much thought. There are plenty of strange types around, especially at weekends.'

'Did you see the man's face?' Huldar thought it was unlikely to have been Rögnvaldur as he didn't have the use of a car, but anything was possible. It wasn't that difficult to steal one.

'No. He had his hood up. But it was a man. Or else a tall woman.' Númi paused, apparently searching his memory. 'It was a small van. A white Toyota. Marked with a company logo.'

'Which company?' It was Erla's turn to frown.

'Oh, it was one of those new brands. There was no company name, just the logo.'

Erla got out her phone, tapped at the screen, then turned it to face Númi. 'Was that the logo?'

Númi nodded. 'Yes, I have a feeling it was.'

Huldar intercepted the phone as Númi handed it back. On the screen was the new logo of the insurance company where Rögnvaldur worked. 'Can you show us where the van was parked?'

Númi did as they asked, but the space was empty.

It didn't take them long to find the Toyota. It was parked out near the point at Grótta, in one of the spaces at the end of the road. It was only two days since they had last been there, to pick up the head. It felt like years ago.

Huldar drew up beside the small van. 'Should we wait for the others?' On the way there, Erla had called for back-up, in case Rögnvaldur tried to resist arrest. She herself would be of little use in her current condition, and although Huldar felt confident in his ability to take care of Rögnvaldur on his own, this was not in accordance with procedure. Which was a pity, because he could do with letting off a bit of steam. Erla had also called Freyja and asked her to come straight over. Or rather, she hadn't *asked* Freyja, she'd *ordered* her. Huldar heard Freyja protesting that she was waiting for her brother to pick up Saga, but Erla had snapped that her useless bloody brother could just fetch his brat from Grótta. Surely he could manage that? She hung up.

Before Erla had a chance to answer Huldar's question, they became aware of distant shouting and screaming. Although the sounds were faint, there was no mistaking their urgency. Huldar didn't wait for Erla's reply but flung open the door; the calls were clearer now and he was sure they were children's voices. Hearing the desperation, he set off at a run in the direction of the beach. Behind him, he heard Erla slamming the passenger door. But he didn't slow down, just sprinted as fast as he could, up onto the shore ridge, from where he could get an overview.

The sight that met him was an ugly one. The tide was in, unlike the last time he'd been there, and although it didn't reach all the way to the sea defences, only a narrow strip of sand remained above water. There, he saw two terrified little girls trying to clamber onto the slippery rocks, hampered by the ice and their panic. It didn't help that they were both soaked to the skin.

Looking further out to sea, he saw a man wading towards the shore. The water reached up to his waist but judging by his wet clothes, he'd been even further out.

Behind him, a small figure was floating face down in the unusually calm sea. Huldar started leaping and scrambling over the rocks, not caring if he fell. The two girls finally noticed him and screamed something he couldn't hear. They also changed direction, tripping over each other in their frantic haste to reach him. He was a grown-up and therefore represented help. But Huldar had no time to spare for them. They would have to wait, and anyway Erla would appear any minute. He plunged into the freezing sea, hardly noticing the cold in his furious haste. Pulling the small truncheon from his belt, he gripped it tight in his hand.

There would be no time to arrest Rögnvaldur. The truncheon would have to do. All that mattered now was to get the girl to shore.

Chapter 34

Saturday

Freyja sat down to catch her breath. She'd poured too much coffee into her mug and spilt it as she was carrying it with trembling hands to the empty meeting room. She felt close to collapse but consoled herself that at least she had managed to stay calm while in the midst of the action. There simply hadn't been time to give way to the feelings that had broken over her like waves.

Now she put her mug down on the conference table and concentrated on getting her breathing under control, grateful for the quiet. It wasn't completely silent, though; outside the closed door there was a hum of activity. Freyja breathed slowly in and out, her eyes on the wall display with its photos and documents relating to the investigation. As yet the three girls from the beach had not been added, but there was Rögnvaldur, staring back at her. She dropped her gaze.

It had taken her only a few short minutes to reach the scene after Erla's phone call, since she had been in the car park outside her building on Seltjarnarnes, about to drive Saga over to Baldur's place. She'd considered dropping the little girl off first but Erla's tone of command had been uncompromising: Freyja was to drop everything and come that instant.

She had been meaning to tackle Erla about this business of her log-in for the Police Information System. Although it was the weekend, her manager had replied to her email straight away, explaining that he'd sent the information to Erla, asking her to pass it on to Freyja and explain the rules of access. Astonished to hear this, Freyja had been determined to find out what Erla was playing at, but the matter had faded into insignificance as soon as she had registered what was happening at the beach.

She had a vivid flashback to the scene she had been met with when she'd hurried out of the car to join Erla on the shore ridge. Luckily, she had left Saga behind, strapped into her child-seat, on the grounds that it would be less damaging for her to be left alone in the car than to witness God only knew what kind of appalling sight on the beach. Maybe she was too young to have processed it anyway, but Freyja was still glad she'd taken that decision.

Two soaking-wet girls had been trying to haul themselves up the heap of boulders that formed the sea wall between the beach and the land. One had lost a snow boot; it was floating, conspicuously pink, at the water's edge. Erla was squatting on the ridge, unbalanced by her bump, reaching out a hand to them and shouting words of encouragement. She was in no state to climb down to help them. The girls were out of their minds with terror, their screaming and crying incongruous in the otherwise tranquil surroundings. Equally incongruous was the scene out in the mirror-like sea, beyond the strip of sand.

Huldar was wading towards the third girl, who was floating face down, some way further out. And a man was heading towards Huldar, on his way back to shore. When they met, Huldar raised his arm without hesitation or warning and struck the man a violent blow on the head with some implement he had in his hand. The man toppled into the water and a streak of dark blood stained the surface by his head. Huldar didn't so much as pause to check if he was alive, just ploughed on through the waist-deep sea until he reached the girl's prone figure.

He turned her over and took her in his arms, where she hung, an inert weight. Her arms and legs were limp, her head hung backwards as if staring away towards the golf course. Seawater poured from her hair, limbs and coat. She had lost both her boots: they must have sunk since they were nowhere to be seen. At the time, Freyja had been distracted by wondering what had happened to them. Where were her boots? It was a simple, manageable question, unlike the other, more urgent ones raised by what she had witnessed.

Huldar's shout brought her back down to earth. He was calling her, apparently telling her to get down to the beach. She quickly searched for the least dangerous route and set off, ignoring the ice and slimy seaweed on the rocks. Next minute she had lost her footing and fallen, landing on her backside, though that hurt less than her hands, which she'd flung out to save herself. There was nothing for it but to get up and carry on.

When she made it down to the sand, Huldar was close enough for her to hear what he was shouting. He was ordering her to wade in and rescue Rögnvaldur. She had balked, but when he repeated the order, she had braced herself and floundered into the waves. The deeper she went, the higher up her body the icy pain moved. By the time the water was up to her waist, she felt as if she had been beaten with a club. But, by then, Rögnvaldur was only a short distance away and the water didn't get any deeper. Freyja had to tread carefully, though, as the seabed was uneven and slippery, and she couldn't see her feet in the murky water.

Finally, she had reached him. Grabbing hold of the man's anorak, she'd started towing him behind her towards the shore. The closer she got to the beach, the heavier he became until he was no longer floating and she couldn't shift him any further. His head was still bleeding. She tried to grasp him under the arms and haul him up onto the sand but his clothes kept snagging on the rocks and stones until eventually she was forced to give up. She looked down at the man who had caused so much grief and pain in his failed attempts to find relief for his own suffering. As he lay there bleeding on the weed and gravel, tugged to and fro by the ankle-deep sea, he cut a pathetic figure.

Freyja turned and saw Huldar kneeling over the girl who he had laid on the sand, alternately pounding on her chest and trying to blow life into her lungs. Freyja felt her heart shrink when she saw that it wasn't having any effect. In between breaths, he called out to her, asking if Rögnvaldur was bleeding. When she said yes, he replied that this meant he was still alive, so she'd better get back to Erla as quickly as possible.

Freyja managed to clamber back up over the line of boulders without falling and hurting herself this time.

Erla was waiting at the top with the two girls, who she'd told to sit on a bench by the path. The bench was intended for walkers who wanted to enjoy the view, but neither child was looking towards the sea. Instead, they were huddled together, sobbing. Not until Freyja reached them did she notice how cold she was. She'd completely forgotten that her bottom half was drenched from the icy sea.

Freyja bent down to the girls and saw that one was Stefán and Númi's daughter, Gudda; the other was her friend. She assumed the third friend, Rósa, was the girl lying on the sand with Huldar.

Like Freyja, they were soaked to the skin, but too traumatised to realise that they were freezing. They asked about the bad man and Freyja assured them that he wouldn't come up here. Then Gudda started crying even harder, sobbing to Freyja that she had lost her glasses. Just as Freyja had fixated on the lost boots of the girl in the water, it was probably easier for Gudda to fret over this minor matter than over the bad man who had attacked her friend, dragged her into the sea and tried to drown her.

Freyja's memory of what had happened next was confused. Police cars had arrived with sirens wailing and soon the small parking area was full. They had been followed by an ambulance that had parked behind them. It had hardly stopped moving before the paramedics and a doctor leapt out. Erla directed them down to the beach and they raced off with a piece of equipment that Freyja didn't recognise. She didn't watch to see how they got down over the rocks.

Not long after that, a young woman without a coat on came running across the snow-covered grass between the beach and the collection of low-rise buildings that made up the industrial estate. When she reached the fish-drying frames, she paused to catch her breath and Freyja noticed that she was holding her stomach. Then she came over and asked breathlessly what was going on. Gudda's friend flung her arms round her neck and told her in between bouts of weeping that a man had attacked Rósa.

Afterwards, things became so chaotic that Freyja had difficulty remembering in what order they had happened. There had been countless police officers and paramedics running

back and forth between the beach and the ambulance. A
stretcher had been carried down and returned with Rósa,
who was then loaded into the ambulance. Another stretcher
was brought out and the paramedics scrambled down to the
shore with it to fetch Rögnvaldur. While this was happening,
the ambulance sped away, taking Rósa to hospital. Rögnvaldur
was left behind with one of the stretcher bearers and a crowd
of police officers standing around him.

While all this was going on, Saga had been staring,
huge-eyed, out of the car window. She didn't seem to have
suffered any harm from being left there, and once Freyja's
work at the scene was done, she had been able to drop her
round to Baldur's as planned. Baldur's eyebrows had shot
up when he saw the state of his sister, but she had still been
in too much shock to explain. He asked her to come in as
there was something he wanted to tell her – more anecdotes
about annoying rich tourists, no doubt – but that would
have to wait. The two girls had been driven to the police
station and Freyja needed to be present while their statements were taken.

That had now been done, and both had told exactly the
same story: the three of them had been playing on the beach
when the man appeared. They didn't recognise him and had
no idea what was happening when he charged towards them,
grabbed hold of Rósa and dragged her into the sea. The other
two kept trying to stop him but he had shoved them away and
they had repeatedly fallen into the water while Rósa screamed
and struggled to break free. Once the man had got quite a
long way out, he had put his hands round Rósa's neck and
held her head under water. The others had stumbled back to
shore, terrified out of their wits, sure they would be next. It

was shortly after this that Erla and Huldar had appeared on the shore ridge, and they had been saved.

The interviews had been exhausting for the girls, who had shed a lot of tears. Almost every time they answered a question, they asked how Rósa was. But there was no information yet. The doctors had managed to revive her but she was being kept in an induced coma, and it was touch and go whether she would escape brain damage.

A doctor had been called to examine the other two girls as well and confirm that it was safe to send them home. The moment the examination was finished, they would be released. Their family members were sitting out front, waiting for them. Terrible though they must be feeling, it was nothing compared to what Rósa's parents were going through by their daughter's bedside in hospital. Freyja hadn't spoken to any of them, only seen them in passing: Stefán and Númi, Selma's sister and her father Einar, who Freyja thought looked vaguely familiar. She got the impression the two families didn't get on particularly well, judging by the way they were sitting in silence, staring into space. She didn't like to look at them too obviously, though, in case one of them called her over. She needed time to recover herself before she could see to anyone else's needs.

Freyja took a mouthful of coffee, then leant back and closed her eyes. She meant to enjoy this brief respite as there was still a long day ahead. And she would have to spend it in a pair of police-issue trousers. There had been no time to go home and change after dropping Saga off, but when she got back to the station she realised she would have to get out of her soaking, salt-stained trousers. Gudlaugur had come to the rescue, finding her a pair of police ones, which were so loose on her that she had to keep hitching them up.

Still, things could be worse. Rögnvaldur had recovered consciousness on the stretcher while still out at Grótta. When the second ambulance arrived, he had been taken on board, where they had put stitches in the gash in his forehead and measured his vital signs, after which he'd been transferred to a police car. They had brought him directly to the station for questioning. He wasn't offered a change of clothes. All he got was an aspirin for the headache he kept complaining about.

The door of the meeting room opened and Huldar stuck out his head. 'There you are. Want to come outside with me while I have a smoke? We're taking a short break from interviewing Rögnvaldur.'

It was a welcome offer. Freyja felt in dire need of some oxygen. She rose to her feet, hitched up her trousers and followed him out to the yard where they huddled under a canopy, sheltering from the huge snowflakes that had started falling. On the short dash across the yard, Freyja's hair had got covered in snow and she shook it off before it could melt. At this, her trousers fell down again and she only just managed to grab the waistband before they dropped to her ankles.

Huldar grinned. 'Cool trousers. I can lend you a duty belt, if you like.'

She declined. 'How's it going? Is it all becoming clear?'

'Yes and no. He's admitted to attacking Rósa, but got a bit of a shock when he discovered that her name's not Selma. It turns out he thought he was drowning her friend. He'd got Selma's name when he rang the library to ask about the winners of the poetry competition. Apparently he pretended he was writing an article for some paper that was going to publish the poems. The library even told him where the kids lived. Unbelievable. Selma's name was on the register of children who haven't been vaccinated, so he reckoned he'd finally found the infection carrier. What he didn't know was that Rósa had picked up the prize on Selma's behalf. Hence the confusion.'

'How did he call without his phone? Was someone hiding him?'

'He used Bríet's laptop. Connected to the wi-fi outside his office building and used a program she had for making phone calls. No one was sheltering him. He claims he broke into a caravan parked in one of the streets close to where he lives and hid in there. Forensics are examining it now, so we'll soon know if his story checks out. He denies having entered his office and says he just used the wi-fi outside, and happened to have the key to one of the company vans in his pocket. He'd forgotten to return it. That fits with the information from the company's access log. The bastard's in a bad way. Suffering from cold and hunger after his stay in the unheated caravan. I'm guessing that was what finally tipped him over the edge. He hadn't originally been intending to hurt a child. The parents, maybe, but not a kid. He wasn't in any physical shape to take on an adult, though, so maybe that's why he attacked the poor girl. He couldn't have won a fight with Rósa's dad, that's for sure.'

Freyja made a face. 'Jesus. Then what? How did he track them down to the beach?'

'He'd been lying in wait outside Selma's house. Apparently he followed them to the cinema yesterday but said he had no chance to get to Rósa because the girls weren't alone. Then, earlier today, he followed Selma and Rósa when they left Selma's house to go and see Gudda in Skerjafjördur. He said there was too much traffic around for him to be able to drag Selma – Rósa, that is – into the van, so he lurked a little way off, waiting for her to come out again. When Selma's sister came to pick them up, he followed them. Then he saw the girls walk out to Grótta and knew he'd finally got his chance.'

'What about the sister? She arrived at the scene on foot, not in a car. Where had she come from? The girls were a bit vague about that. They told me she was at work but they couldn't explain in any more detail. They mentioned a workshop but didn't want to talk about it. I suppose they thought the sister's job was unimportant compared to what they'd just been through.'

Huldar lit a cigarette, took a long drag, then blew the smoke out from under the canopy to disperse among the snowflakes. 'Einar, the father of Selma and her sister, has a workshop there. He's one of those medium-sized contractors who manages to survive somehow. The sister cleans the workshop on Saturdays and often takes the girls along.'

Freyja nodded, preoccupied. Now she stopped to think about it, the girls' reaction to the question about the workshop had been odd. They'd become shifty and started crying even harder when the conversation touched on it. Although this hadn't struck her as suspicious at the time, it had been frustrating. She pushed the thought away as Huldar carried on with what he was saying.

'Rögnvaldur flatly denies killing Ólína. He claims he had nothing to do with Bríet's disappearance either. But he says she's dead.'

'Seriously?' Freyja couldn't fathom why the man would admit to having tried to drown a child while denying the murder of a woman – two women.

'Yes. He admits that he drove round to Bríet's flat at suppertime on Friday, but then he had no choice but to admit it because his car was caught on CCTV. He slipped into the building with one of the other residents, but says Bríet wouldn't let him in when he knocked on her door. He'd assumed that would happen, since his attempts to talk to her on the phone had been unsuccessful – which is why he'd sneaked into the building in the first place. According to him, they had an argument while he was standing in the corridor, then she slammed the door on him and refused to open it again. Which is consistent with what her neighbour overheard. Rögnvaldur blames Andrea for spoiling things. As far as he was concerned, what he was asking wasn't unreasonable – he just wanted access to the register of vaccinations. He doesn't seem to understand that they weren't authorised to pass the records on to him.'

'How did he get hold of her computer then? If his visit was unsuccessful.'

'He says he sat in his car, wondering what to do, and decided to sneak inside again when the next resident came home. But he was too slow to react when the pizza delivery guy arrived, and again when a woman appeared – Ólína, presumably. So he moved the car closer and managed to enter behind a man who arrived after that. He said the man walked straight in because the door to the lobby turned out to be unlocked, a possibility that hadn't even occurred to him. According to him, the man headed straight to Bríet's flat, so Rögnvaldur had to pretend he was going somewhere else and went upstairs to wait on the floor above. From there, he claims he heard screams and crashing noises coming from below. When he heard the sound of slamming, he crept downstairs, put his ear to Bríet's door and says he heard a faint groaning and mumbling. In other words, he's claiming he heard the women being murdered, though at the time he was under the impression it was only Bríet.'

Realising that she'd been holding her breath, Freyja filled her lungs with the cold, clean winter air. 'Do you believe him? I mean, weren't his fingerprints found in the flat? How does he explain that?'

'He says he went round the back of the building to see if he could peer through the windows and saw the man coming out of a garden that he guessed belonged to Bríet's flat. He hid and waited until he believed the coast was clear. The garden door turned out to be open, as there was no way of locking it from outside. So he went in.'

Freyja waited while Huldar had another puff on his cigarette. He was looking good. He'd changed into a fresh pair of trousers and shirt, and seemed to have had a shower too. If they hadn't been in the police station yard, she'd have been tempted to pull him aside and let her police trousers fall down. A quickie right now would be just the thing to relax her, but this wasn't the time or place.

Luckily Huldar didn't pick up on what she was thinking. He tapped the ash from his cigarette and carried on with his tale. 'He says he was met by dead silence inside the flat and crept across the sitting room without hearing anyone. When he glanced into the kitchen, he saw two women lying dead on the floor, one of them Bríet, the other nobody he recognised. In other words, his story is that the stranger had killed them before he entered the flat himself.'

'And it didn't occur to him to ring the police or an ambulance?'

'No. He saw a laptop on the kitchen table and thought it was a better idea to grab it and get out of there. He says he didn't check the women for signs of life because he was sure they were both dead. Or pretty sure, anyway.' Huldar took another puff. 'Unbelievable.'

'Can his story be true?' Freyja watched a huge snowflake float lazily to the ground and melt on the black tarmac.

'I doubt it. It does fit with the movements of his car, but on the other hand we know he came back later to fetch the bodies and take them away in Bríet's car. So what's missing from his statement is the fact that he returned that evening either on foot or by bus to clean up after himself. He's still sticking to his story about the stranger he pretends he saw. But he'll tell us the truth in the end. He just doesn't know it yet.'

'What about the DNA profile? From Mía? How on earth did that get there? Has he said anything about that?'

'Only that he knows absolutely nothing about it.' Huldar stubbed out his cigarette and disposed of the butt in the ashtray that was fixed to the wall. 'He seems to be mainly interested in whether he can get a divorce while he's in prison. I told him not to worry his head about that. His wife's bound to divorce him first.'

They went back inside and the moment they entered the office, Freyja felt oppressed at the sight of Stefán, Númi, and Selma's father and sister waiting there. She knew she was unlikely to be able to avoid talking to them. None of the detectives would be prepared to speak to them alone, except maybe Erla, and she was currently busy with Rögnvaldur. Freyja didn't want to have to explain what had happened; she got a bad taste in her mouth just thinking about it. She'd give anything to be able to wipe away the memory of Rósa's body lying face down in the sea. Every time she was forced to relive the events, she knew they would become more indelibly imprinted on her memory.

But she was saved at the last minute. They'd no sooner entered the CID office than the woman from the IT department came bustling over and drew Huldar aside. Freyja followed because she couldn't face having to brave the girls' families alone. If she waited for Huldar, she could make it look as if they were in the middle of an important conversation when she walked past the waiting relatives.

'We've had a look at the laptop found in the suspect's car. It's Bríet's, no question. And we've come across a folder that appears to be key.' The woman addressed Huldar, ignoring Freyja, though her eyes wandered to the trousers that she was holding up with one hand. Her expression suggested this outfit had done nothing to raise her opinion of Freyja following the Information System debacle. Still looking down her nose, the woman turned back to Huldar. 'The folder's called "Mía".'

Huldar peered over the heads of the IT woman and Freyja, as if scanning the room for someone. 'Where's Erla? She needs to hear this.'

'I can't find her anywhere. Presumably you'll be able to fill her in later. I need to get back to examining the computer, but I assumed this couldn't wait.'

Huldar turned back to the woman. 'Sorry. Go on.'

'The folder contains a number of things you should have a look at. It appears Bríet believed she knew what had happened to Mía – that she was sure of Mía's identity. In fact, she seems to have sent some DNA for analysis, to prove it. At least, the folder contains the results of a mitochondrial DNA test for a sample labelled Mía Stefánsdóttir. Judging by the date, it was sent recently. In other words, it's not old.'

Huldar frowned. 'Mito what?'

'Mitochondrial.' The woman looked impatient. 'The mitochondria contain DNA that is inherited exclusively from the mother. Forensics are comparing the profile to Mía's. The results should be available very shortly.' She was silent for a moment. 'One other thing. The name of the girl she believed was Mía is there too.' She went on to tell them what it was. Huldar and Freyja both glanced simultaneously at the families of the two little girls who were still sitting in the corridor, pointedly ignoring each other.

Chapter 35

Sunday

The man in the interview room looked exhausted. When he'd first sat down he had been stiff and silent but that had now changed. His name was Einar Brjánsson and he was an unusual character, in spite of his very ordinary name. There wasn't a hint of arrogance or insolence in his manner, let alone aggression, which was pretty astonishing in light of the crimes he was suspected of. He had sat down, folded his heavy arms across his chest and declined the offer of a lawyer. Repeatedly. Then he had begun to answer their questions, with a simple yes or no where he could get away with it. He didn't fidget or shift in his chair and didn't want anything to drink. It was like interrogating an automaton that was suspected of murder. Apart from his appearance, that is. No self-respecting designer would have dreamt of creating such a dour, taciturn robot.

Huldar recalled blokes like him from his days working with builders. They were generally the most experienced men on the site, and on the rare occasions they expressed an opinion on the job in hand, they were usually right. They had little truck with innovations and were reluctant to deviate from the set way of doing things. They were men who drank from large mugs in their coffee breaks and grumbled if pasta was on the lunch tray instead of meat and potatoes. Apart from that, they spoke little, unless the talk turned to one of two professions – politicians or engineers. That was guaranteed to make them tut and shake their heads. As a rule they were slow to anger but could lose their tempers if seriously provoked.

So far, Huldar and Erla had been treated to Einar's forbearing side and now they were getting a glimpse of his weariness. But there hadn't yet been the slightest hint of his violent temper. No one was in any doubt that the man had a temper, though, as they had ample evidence of the fact. All available manpower had been set to working until late last night and performed a Herculean task in gathering the necessary proof. Huldar and Erla had enough in hand to demolish any attempt on his part to claim innocence. There was no way out for him now. Sooner or later, Einar would be forced to face up to how much they knew.

He had conceded early on that his daughter Selma had not received her childhood vaccinations. And not long after that he admitted that she had been ill – possibly with measles. The family hadn't been aware of the risks associated with it as his elder daughter had gone on an online chat forum where she had been told that the virus was no more dangerous than flu. So they had made do with keeping Selma at home until her fever had gone.

Einar believed he knew how his daughter had been infected. One of his foreign workers had contacted the Directorate of Labour from abroad to inform them that he had been ill with measles. The man had proved incapable of doing any useful work, so he had been sent home after only a few days but, in spite of that, Einar's daughter Selma had come into contact with him. She'd accompanied her elder sister, Sædís, when she brought food to the workshop for the crew, and the man had still been there at the time. A couple of weeks later, Selma had come down with something. She'd coughed repeatedly over her friend Rósa, who had dropped by to see her before going with Sædís to pick up Selma's poetry prize on her behalf. And Rósa had passed on the virus to Íris. He was prepared to admit all this. But he obstinately refused to admit that the reason his daughter hadn't received her childhood vaccinations was that he and his wife hadn't dared to take Selma to the doctor when she was small. They had been terrified it would somehow be discovered that she wasn't their child.

Einar went on stubbornly insisting that Selma was his daughter. Huldar had the feeling that his denials became all the more vehement when they told him that they also suspected him of murdering Droplaug. The pathology department's review of her post-mortem results had revealed that not enough attention had been paid to the speed at which she appeared to have drowned. There had been less seawater in Droplaug's stomach than would have been expected had she been fully conscious at the time, regardless of whether she had intended to kill herself or not. The conclusion wasn't indisputable, but those who had reviewed the evidence believed it was more likely than not that Droplaug had been either unconscious or close to losing consciousness when she entered the sea. It had also emerged that Droplaug's DNA, which had been found on the baby blanket washed up on the shore at Hvassahraun, was unlikely to have got there because she had handled it. It was far more plausible that it came from the vomit stain left on it by Mía, who had been fed a bottle containing her mother's expressed breast milk from the freezer, just before she developed an upset stomach. A mother's breast milk contains her DNA.

Einar also flat out denied any responsibility for Bríet's disappearance or Ólína's murder, saying he didn't know either of them. But Huldar noticed that his denial wasn't as vehement as when they'd implied that he'd killed Droplaug.

On the table between them lay some of the evidence they had shown him to convince him to come clean: CCTV captures, data from Bríet's laptop, a phone log, incomprehensible information about DNA profiles, the results of the fingerprint analysis, various reports and countless photos. Two of these stood out. One was a class photo taken by Ólína; the other was of a massive machine used for cutting through concrete pipes. The latter had been taken by Forensics during a search of the man's workshop in the industrial estate by Grótta.

Huldar pushed the class photo across the table. The children in it were grinning broadly at the photographer. 'Judging by the data from Bríet's computer and the messages she and Ólína exchanged, it's fairly clear that this is the picture that sparked off the whole business.' Huldar pointed to one little girl. 'That's your daughter Selma, isn't it?'

Einar glanced at the photo and nodded. Then, remembering that Huldar and Erla had repeatedly reminded him to speak aloud for the recording – that movements of the head wouldn't do – he said: 'Yes. That's her.'

Huldar pushed another picture over to him. This one was of Mía's mother, Droplaug, at the same age as Selma was now. Ólína had added it as an attachment in one of her first emails to Bríet. 'Alike, aren't they?'

The man obliged by taking a quick look at the picture. 'I can't see it myself.'

'Funny. We think they're almost identical. The resemblance is striking. Enough for the photographer, Ólína, to have noticed it. She was Droplaug's cousin and remembered her well as a girl. Like most of the family, she never believed Droplaug would have done anything to harm Mía. This photo comes from her family album, by the way. It was bad luck for you that Selma has the exact same hairstyle.'

'Lots of kids look alike. That doesn't mean anything.'

'That's just what Ólína thought. So she appealed to her friend, Bríet, who was doing a study of childhood immunisations, and persuaded her to help. She showed her the pictures and convinced her that there was something strange going on. We know all this from the messages they exchanged. Bríet went to the school and took a DNA swab from your daughter. They sent it off with a sample from Ólína for comparison, and what do you know? Bingo! They turned out to be related.' Huldar took the two pictures back. No need for Einar to know that Bríet had falsified the letter authorising her to approach his daughter. In the circumstances, that was unimportant. 'But you know all this, don't you?'

Einar was mute.

'Don't you?' No reaction. 'Look, you do realise we don't actually need your confirmation? We have evidence that after Ólína and Bríet received the results of the DNA test, they got in touch with your wife. Ólína rang her on the Friday morning and the call lasted for nearly ten minutes. We're not quite sure what Ólína and Bríet were after but we suspect they were worried that the results weren't conclusive enough. They had acquired Selma's DNA without your permission and were afraid of getting into trouble if they went to the police, only for it to turn out that they were wrong. After all, the DNA test only showed that Selma was probably the child of Ólína's cousin. The average amount of DNA shared between first cousins once removed is only about six per cent. They wanted to be absolutely sure that there wasn't an innocent explanation for the relationship. Their messages contain some speculation about whether you or your wife could have been adopted and related to Ólína without her knowing it. They'd have done better to use a DNA sample from Droplaug's sister, Ellý, but they didn't want to get her hopes up. It was a mistake for them to get in touch with your wife, though, because we all know how that ended.'

Huldar paused to give Einar a chance to speak but the man remained silent. So Huldar persevered. 'We take it that your wife told you and you decided to shut the women up. You traced Ólína's address from her phone number and lay in wait for her, then followed her to Bríet's flat, where you forced your way inside. Have we guessed right? You attacked them, probably knocking Ólína out with the door when she answered it instead of Bríet – perhaps because she thought you were another man Bríet didn't want to talk to. You strangled her, then dealt with Bríet when she came to see what was going on. Did you chase her into the kitchen and kill her there? Let me remind you that we have a witness who saw you enter the flat. The same witness saw you leave by the back door. And rest assured that we'll soon have security-camera footage from the bus or we'll track down the person who gave you a lift back to the flat just before midnight to remove the bodies. So why don't you save us all a lot of time and confess now? It's totally pointless to go on denying it.'

When the man still made no move to answer, Erla intervened: 'As we speak, your wife is sitting in a prison cell, waiting for her turn. I saw her brought in and I'm pretty sure she's not a hard case like you. I'm confident that she'll tell us exactly what happened—'

Erla broke off, her features twisting in a grimace. Huldar was becoming increasingly concerned about the twitches of pain that kept contorting her face. He took over again in the hope that she would recover and that it wasn't her contractions starting. 'Yes, and then there's your daughter – your real daughter, Sædís. She's not as tough as you either. She'll spill the beans. Right now, she's sitting in the cell next door to her mother, waiting to talk to us.' He saw the man's shoulders suddenly sag. 'I just don't understand why you're digging your heels in like this, Einar. We've got a witness who saw you enter Bríet's flat the evening she vanished and Ólína was killed. We've got the saw you used to cut up Ólína's body. Bríet's too, no doubt. We've been over your workshop with luminol, which allows us to see bloodstains that are invisible to the naked eye. The place lit up like a Christmas tree, in spite of your efforts to clean it. So did the saw.' Huldar smiled mockingly at the man. 'You shouldn't have used such environmentally friendly products to clean up after yourself. But never mind. I could go on: your company's replacing the water mains in the road next to where Bríet's car was abandoned. And your old firm was working on Númi and Stefán's house, just before you went bankrupt. That must have taken its toll. You couldn't have predicted then that you'd set up as a contractor again one day. Could you?'

No response.

'It's useless, mate. If you want to protect your nearest and dearest, I recommend you come clean. Selma and her friend are over at the Children's House now, being interviewed, and I'm telling you that Selma's testimony is the kiss of death for you. Because you may not be aware of this but she saw Ólína's mutilated body parts in the boot of Bríet's car. She's just admitted the fact. That's what was in the text messages we were looking at earlier. I'm assuming this was when she went with her sister to clean the workshop. Or with your wife, perhaps, if she had some errand to do there.'

Erla had recovered sufficiently to take over, though her face was shiny with sweat. 'Right, well. I think we'll call it a day and talk to your wife and elder daughter instead. We know it was one of them that drove Bríet's car from Grótta to the housing estate. You couldn't have done it yourself because you were sleeping it off in a police cell at the time, remember? Did you think we wouldn't notice? Not a chance. Since you didn't move the car, it must have been your wife or Sædís. That means one or both of them are your accomplices. Which is a pity for them. And for you. What happened? Did you go on a bender after your little butchery job with the saw? Or were you already pissed when you forced your way into Bríet's flat? We know you're a recovering alcoholic.' Erla put air quotes round the word 'recovering'.

Einar was showing signs of being about to cave. He kept running his big hands through his hair, he had slumped in his chair and beads of sweat had formed on his upper lip. Huldar added: 'We believe your wife or daughter – or possibly both – may have been with you when you murdered Ólína. And presumably Bríet too. You do realise that sharing the blame with a couple of other people won't do anything to reduce your sentence? You'll all suffer equally heavy penalties.' In fact, this was nonsense: the police had no evidence to suggest that his wife or daughter had been present during the murders.

Einar lowered his gaze and Huldar decided to tighten the thumbscrews. 'Do you know how poor the care is in prison for mentally ill people like your wife? Have you thought about what it will be like for Sædís if she goes down for murder at her age? Do you think she'll ever escape its shadow? Do you really want to find out the answers to these questions?'

Erla suddenly doubled up, her face a rictus of pain, and Huldar fell silent, wondering if he should suspend the interview and tell her to go home. Or to hospital. Of course it was a disastrous moment to break off, just as the exhausted man was on the verge of crumbling. But Erla toughed it out. Sitting up again, she stared coldly at Einar and said: 'Prisoners are not permitted to have their children with them for any length of time. Are you aware that your daughter's pregnant?'

Judging by Einar's stunned expression, the answer to that was no.

Freyja was looking good, much brighter than she had yesterday when her nausea had almost got the better of her. It helped that she was wearing her own clothes again and wasn't constantly having to hitch them up. She'd made an effort with her appearance, too, though not quite as much as the time she'd turned up in the skirt and hoop earrings. Huldar guessed this was because she had been to the Children's House for the girls' interview. Revisiting your old workplace was a bit like meeting your ex. You wanted to look your best. It wouldn't do for your ex, or your ex-colleagues, to leave the reunion thinking, 'Phew – lucky escape!'

Huldar went over to her, feeling his spirits lifting with every step. By the time he reached her he had shrugged off the tiredness that had weighed him down after Einar's interview. The solution of a case was never as rewarding as he expected. When the crime was as irrevocable as murder, it was too late to change anything. The victims were as dead afterwards as they had been before, and too many people's lives would never be the same again.

'How did it go?'

Freyja sighed despondently, evidently experiencing the same sense of anticlimax as him. 'Well – whatever that means, under the circumstances. When I sent you the message, Gudda had told us what happened, and Selma then confirmed her story. Of course Rósa won't be able to give us her version any time soon, but they say she was there as well. They both told exactly the same story and there's no reason to doubt what they say. According to them, all three of them accompanied Sædís when she went to clean on Saturday last week. They found a phone on the ground beside a car in the parking spaces outside the workshop and Rósa decided to keep it, though they couldn't unlock it. She was the only girl in her class who didn't have a phone and she wanted to show off. After that they discovered the car was unlocked and had a look inside, including in the boot where they saw some bags, took one out and opened it.' Freyja broke off and shuddered. 'There was a head inside.'

'So all three of them saw Ólína's severed head?' Huldar had a hard time picturing it. Children and amputated body parts just didn't go together, especially not heads.

Freyja nodded. 'Selma threw up and Gudda took the bag and flung it away from the car. After that, they decided to look inside the other bags and Selma puked up again, splashing them. At that point Sædís came running out, having heard their screams. They say she looked inside one of the bags in the boot, was silent for a while, then turned back to them and said they were props for a horror film. They mustn't tell anyone because it would spoil the film, she said. They believed her – almost. Anyway, they kept quiet. According to them, Sædís then said that she didn't need to clean after all, so they could go and buy ice-creams. After they got home, Selma says Sædís went out again and didn't come back until after she'd gone to sleep.'

So, as Huldar had suspected, Einar's daughter had taken it upon herself to clean up after her father. How the head had ended up caught in the rocks above the beach was a mystery, however. Perhaps the bag had accidentally got left behind when Sædís moved the car and either she or her father had thrown it in the sea near the workshop when they realised. The incoming tide must have washed the bag and its grisly contents ashore again, where it had been trapped between the rocks. All would become clear in due course.

Freyja glanced around distractedly. 'Where's Erla?'

'She went to the ladies' to splash some water on her face. She wasn't looking too good.' Huldar smiled at Freyja. 'She'll be back. I've got great news, by the way. Einar has confessed to the murder of Ólína. And Bríet. He blames it on the fact he was drunk and temporarily lost his mind.

When he discovered that Bríet and Ólína had found out who Selma was, he fell off the wagon after being dry for a decade.'

'So he's admitted that too? That he stole Mía?'

'Yes. He didn't have any choice – we'd got him backed into a corner by then.'

For a psychologist, Freyja was showing remarkably little interest in Einar's mental state. 'And? How on earth did it happen?'

'He says he and his wife had a daughter called Selma. She died – of SIDS, he thinks. When he found his wife with the dead baby in her arms he decided to swap her for Stefán and Númi's child. He was drinking at the time and his anger with the men had clouded his judgement. His firm was on the brink of bankruptcy and they were dragging their feet about paying for some extra work his crew had done. On top of that, he believed it was wrong for two men to bring up a child. And he thought the way they treated the mother was a disgrace.'

'Then what happened to the baby who died? Who took her from the pram after Númi saw her?'

'Einar did. It dawned on him as he was driving away that it would be possible for the police to find out whose daughter she was. So he took Mía home to his wife, then came back to fetch his baby's body. He could hear Númi screaming inside the house, but he slipped round the back and grabbed the body. Apparently she's buried in their garden. Originally behind their old flat but he moved her when they sold up and bought a new house. He was afraid someone might discover the bones. And he wanted to have her near the family. We've disinterred her remains and it might be possible to find out what caused her death, although there's only a tiny chance the post-mortem will be able to draw any conclusions after such a long time. We need to send a diver out to Grótta too. Einar took Bríet's body there in several bags, weighed them down with rocks and sealed them up with duct tape, then threw them in the sea. It shelves down quite steeply beyond the lighthouse. After that he went back to the workshop, cut up Ólína's body with the saw and packed it into the boot of Bríet's car. It was early in the morning by then and the tide had come in, flooding the causeway out to the lighthouse. He lay down at the workshop, intending to wait for the next low tide, but he didn't wake up until his daughter arrived to clean. He says he told her to go home and not to worry: there had been an accident and that's why there was blood everywhere. Then he asked her to drive the car over to the housing estate and leave it there. He swears she didn't know anything. He was intending to hide Ólína's remains in the ditch that his company was digging, and to cover it up that night. But he started drinking and ended up in the cells.'

'According to the girls, Sædís knew about it, Huldar.'

He smiled. 'I don't doubt it. He's trying to protect her. Of course it won't work. Any more than his insistence that his wife didn't realise he'd switched their daughter for Mía. That's obviously total rubbish. But it'll all become clear when we interview the women.'

'Does that mean you've got everything out of him that you need?' Freyja reached for her phone, which had just bleeped in her pocket.

'Yes and no. I get the feeling he knows more than he's letting on. But that wasn't his last interview. Not by any means.' Huldar paused. Freyja's attention was fixed on her screen.

When she looked up, she sighed. 'Am I the unluckiest person in the world?'

'What now?'

'Baldur's asking me to take Saga.'

'Can't you just say no?' Freyja seemed to have a very different relationship with her brother from the one Huldar had with his sisters. He said no to them more often than he said yes. And vice versa.

'He says it's a total emergency. Jesus.'

Huldar tried to cheer her up. He was hoping to drop by and see her after work, since he hadn't managed to yesterday evening. 'I don't think you'll miss anything. You're free for now. Just go. I was thinking of swinging by later. If you've still got Saga, I could grab some junk food on my way over.' Saga had the same taste in food as him, which was very convenient. Anything round would do: pizzas, burgers, tortillas, biscuits, pancakes, doughnuts . . . Though pizza wouldn't be on the menu any time soon, a fact for which he had Einar to thank.

Freyja didn't reply. She was looking agitated, her eyes on the door to the ladies'. 'It wasn't only the girls' statements I wanted to talk to Erla about. I also need a word with her about the Police Information System. Apparently my log-in details were sent to her but she never passed them on to me. I wanted to know if she maybe forwarded them to someone else by mistake. I don't want this bloody business hanging over me for the rest of my time here.'

Huldar raised his eyebrows. 'Can't Baldur just bring Saga here, then? The top brass aren't in today and we don't mind if she's here. That'll buy you a bit of time and Erla's bound to come out soon.'

Freyja duly sent her brother a message. The phone bleeped again almost immediately and she checked it before returning it to her pocket. 'He says that would suit him perfectly. He'll be here in five.' She hesitated, her eyes still on the door to the ladies'. 'What do you think? Should I just put my head round the door and ask about the log-in mix-up?'

'No. No way. That's the worst idea I've heard in a long time.' Huldar could just picture the explosion if Freyja marched in and tackled Erla through the cubicle wall.

Before Freyja could reply, they heard a muffled cry from the ladies'. They exchanged glances, then set off at a run. They weren't the only ones to react – but they were the first to get there. Huldar told Freyja to open the door and look in. It would be more tactful for her to do it, in case something was happening in there that Erla would rather the whole office didn't get an eyeful of. While Freyja had her head round the door, Huldar waved everyone else away except for Lína. Since she had googled *delivering a baby*, she might actually come in useful. Lína rolled up her sleeves, her face purposeful.

Freyja now disappeared inside, closing the door behind her. Huldar and Lína could hear the sound of a conversation. Then another muffled cry. After a short interval, Freyja came out again. 'Right, people. It looks to me like Erla's gone into labour.'

Huldar took a step backwards, Lína a step forwards. But she was halted by a glare from Freyja. 'For goodness' sake, she's not about to give birth in the loo. What's wrong with you? But she's having strong contractions and needs to get to hospital *now*.'

Every face in the open-plan office was turned their way, all ears were pricked. Someone called across the room: 'Does she need a lift?'

Freyja rolled her eyes and for a moment Huldar thought she was going to say that it would do Erla good to walk, but her answer was free from mockery. 'No. She's got a lift.'

'Should I take her?' The instant he'd said it, Huldar remembered all the stories he'd heard about women giving birth in the car on their way to hospital.

Freyja shook her head. 'No, I told you, she says she's got a lift. I'm going to take her downstairs. If you want to help, it would be good if someone could fetch her coat.'

Huldar didn't wait to be told twice. He dashed into Erla's office, grabbed her coat off the peg and was back just as Freyja helped Erla out of the ladies'. The moment she appeared, all heads in the office ducked back to their computer screens. Her face was a mask of pain, covered in a sheen of sweat, and she was clutching her lower back with both hands. She was in such a bad way that she couldn't even put her arms into her sleeves, so Huldar hung the coat over her shoulders.

'I can get downstairs on my own. For Christ's sake, let go of me.' Erla tried to shake Freyja off. Normally, this would have been easy for her as she was much stronger and knew all kinds of wrestling moves that Freyja had never even heard of. But in the circumstances she was in no fit state to put up a fight, and Freyja did not let go of her arm.

'Don't be like that. I'm going with you. I'm not leaving you until you're safely in the car. No arguments.'

Erla grimaced but Huldar couldn't tell if it was resentment at Freyja's high-handedness or a new contraction beginning.

Erla clenched her jaw and turned to Huldar. 'Don't get too comfy in my chair, Huldar,' she said, her voice strained. 'I forgot to tell you earlier but they want you to be my maternity cover. As long as you do it like you did last time, I can be sure of getting my job back.' She tried to smile but couldn't. Instead she closed her eyes, clamped her lips shut and bit back a groan. After that, she allowed Freyja to help her out of the department and into the lift without further protest.

Huldar was left standing there with Lína. She gave him a jab with her elbow, but the height difference between them was so great that it hit him on the hip. 'Wow. Congratulations.'

Huldar groaned like Erla. But inwardly. The last thing he wanted was this position. But he'd take it on. For Erla's sake. The powers that be would far rather have her back than keep him in the job, whereas all the other potential candidates would do their utmost to brown-nose senior management in the hope of being kept on full time. He looked down at Lína, smiling faintly. 'Yes. Thanks. Yippee.'

Lína obviously couldn't understand why he wasn't celebrating the news. But he couldn't do it, not even to please an ambitious intern. Puzzled and disappointed, she went back to her desk.

Erla's announcement hadn't passed the other members of CID by. He could feel their eyes on him. No doubt some were thinking vengeful thoughts, but it wasn't Huldar's fault he'd been chosen. He could look forward to long months of form-filling, meetings and human-resources issues, so he might as well make the most of his last day as an ordinary detective.

Freyja came back into the department. She was carrying Saga, who immediately started straining towards Huldar. Baldur must have arrived while she was downstairs. He noticed that Freyja was looking oddly pale and distracted.

'Hi Saga!' Huldar took the little girl in his arms. 'Is everything OK?'

'Yes. Yes, sure,' Freyja replied, though evidently it wasn't.

'Everything's OK with Erla, isn't it?'

Freyja nodded. 'Yes. She's fine. She was yelling something about an epidural when I said goodbye. It'll help with the pain – if it's not too late.'

It was blindingly obvious that she was holding something back. 'You didn't tackle her about that log-in business?' he asked. It was all he could think of. It had been Freyja's last chance to get things straight as Erla would be away from work for months now.

Freyja shook her head. 'No, I didn't. I didn't need to. Not when I saw who her lift was.'

'Oh?'

'It was Baldur. My brother Baldur. He's the father of Erla's baby.' Freyja closed her eyes and put a hand to her forehead. 'Baldur's the father of Erla's baby.'

That explained everything. Erla had used Freyja's log-in to run a background check on Baldur. She couldn't have been too happy about what she read, but that was her problem.

If he knew Freyja, she would never bring the subject up again. She'd rather take the blame for having used the database herself. He just hoped Erla would appreciate her sacrifice. Hoped – but he couldn't be sure. Still, now that he was taking over Erla's position, he'd do his best to resolve the issue without it impacting too badly on Freyja.

He had difficulty replying as Saga had his neck in a stranglehold. When she loosened her arms, all he could think of was to repeat his suggestion that he pay them a visit that evening. To his surprise, Freyja positively welcomed the idea. He'd been expecting her to be too shocked and preoccupied to hear what he said, let alone answer with enthusiasm.

'Oh, yes. Do come round. Absolutely. And bring wine, please. Lots of it.'

He wanted to say that everything would be all right. He wanted her to tell him the same thing. But neither of them said anything.

They didn't need to. They'd get by. Whether apart or together. Together or apart.

This evening, clearly, together. One day at a time.

Huldar smiled. With any luck, he'd get the chance to play off-duty bodyguard. They both deserved a happy ending.

Five months later

Chapter 36

Saturday

Sædís was gripped by an overwhelming urge to push; nothing else could get through to her brain. She couldn't even tell if she was bellowing or just grimacing. She threw her head back and concentrated on trying to force the child out. While she was straining, she was less aware of the pains that ripped through her at regular intervals, making it feel as if her pelvis was being torn apart, her kidneys were bursting, her abdomen was on fire. She had refused the epidural, although she had known exactly what she was in for. Her sufferings were cathartic.

From the moment she had rung the bell in the maternity ward, bent over and panting with the pain, there had been few surprises. She had been preparing for this moment for months. Much of what she'd read hadn't been directly relevant to her situation, assuming as it did that the woman wouldn't be going through this alone but would have someone there to lean on. One sentence in particular that she had read in a booklet on childbirth from the GP's clinic had stayed in her mind: *The prospective father provides support with his presence, love, encouragement and care.*

Admittedly, Númi was sitting in the chair beside the delivery bed but his entire demeanour couldn't be more of

a contrast to the rose-tinted images in the childbirth literature. He was deliberately avoiding her eye and they hadn't
exchanged a single word since he'd arrived. She'd noticed that
he glanced at her from time to time, but his expression did
nothing to encourage her to turn to him for support. He hated
and despised her and saw no reason to hide the fact.

The midwife made up for it with her kindness and warmth.
Holding Sædís's hand, smiling and praising her. Various other
people kept wandering in and out of the delivery room: doctors, nurses, assistants and a woman who appeared from time
to time, asking if she was hungry or thirsty. Having never
given birth before, Sædís had no idea if this endless coming
and going was normal or whether she was the reason. The latter seemed more likely. After all, she was notorious, so it was
only natural if people wanted to see the young woman who
was linked to Mía's disappearance; the daughter of a baby-
snatcher and murderer, who was now alone and penniless,
and carrying the child of one of Mía's fathers. The papers had
given her a rough ride since the story had hit the news.

'Nearly there, Sædís. It doesn't look as if you'll have to
do too many more pushes.' The midwife was smiling at her
from between her splayed legs. 'You're doing really well, dear.
Quite the opposite of some women I've helped. We had one in
here a few months ago who swore like a trooper throughout
the birth. Still, when her little boy popped out, I could understand why. He had the biggest head I've ever seen on a baby.
Almost like a pumpkin. Healthy and normal, though. It ran
in the family, according to the father. But your little one's head
seems perfectly sized.'

Sædís was too busy catching her breath to reply. The midwife turned to Númi and invited him to come and see the

head. When he declined sulkily, the woman snapped: 'Why are you here, then? Why don't you just wait outside?'

'No.' Númi was affronted. 'It's my baby. I've got a right to be here.'

The midwife wasn't having any of it. 'No one has a right to be here except the mother.' She turned to Sædís. 'Do you want him to go outside, dear? Don't hesitate to say if you do.'

Sædís gasped down some air and managed to answer just before another wave of pain snatched her breath away. 'He can stay. I don't care.'

And it was true. She didn't care. She had learnt a lot over the last few months, including the fact that it was possible to go on living your life even when people hated you. She had come to this realisation after a particularly horrible phone call from a woman named Ellý who had introduced herself as the sister of Droplaug, Mía's mother. Her contempt for Sædís had been palpable during the mostly one-sided conversation. She had repeatedly asked how Sædís could live with herself after withholding the truth all these years and letting everyone think Droplaug had killed her own baby. The woman had also said she didn't believe for a minute that Sædís hadn't known about the baby swap. She had called her all the worst names imaginable, adding further insults in English when the supply of Icelandic ones ran out. But, oddly enough, the excessive hate Ellý had unleashed on her turned out to have a healing effect. Nothing Sædís said or did would ever earn forgiveness from this woman or any of the other people who held her in contempt. This would simply be her reality from now on, and accepting it had helped.

Her desperation to please everyone, to keep the peace, had gone. It was like tilting at windmills. All that really mattered was to live in peace with those you loved and who loved you in return. That group had been greatly reduced, which made it pretty simple. The only people left were her friends. Everyone else had turned their backs on her. Her friends didn't understand her but stood by her anyway. At first, they had asked her warily about the case and all the stuff that was going on, but when she was reluctant to answer, they had backed off. As good friends should. Her parents had vanished behind bars, where they were awaiting trial. Although they were no longer in solitary confinement, she was forbidden to visit them as she was a party to the crimes. Sædís could count herself lucky that she wasn't also in prison. But the fact she had escaped custody so far didn't mean she wouldn't eventually be charged. She had picked a lawyer at random from a list she'd been shown, and he had explained various things about which she had been ignorant. Firstly, that she had been questioned as a suspect rather than as a witness. That was a bad sign, according to him. He hadn't liked to predict whether she would be charged or what sort of sentence she was likely to get if she was convicted. But he had gone on to say that the fact she had been cooperative might work in her favour. It would also help that she hadn't been directly involved in the most serious crimes, that is, in the murders or the abduction of Mía.

Since Sædís had been a child when Mía was stolen and therefore below the age of responsibility, her lawyer said she needn't worry too much about that. Though, that said, she might conceivably be held accountable for the years after she had reached the age of responsibility, but only if it could be proved beyond a doubt that she had known Selma was Mía, which he considered highly unlikely. He thought it more probable that the prosecution would accept that she had been unaware that the babies had been swapped. All the witnesses agreed that her little sister had spent most of her short life in the darkened bedroom with her sick mother. In addition, both Sædís's parents were adamant that she hadn't known anything. According to the reports the lawyer had read, her mother was pleading diminished responsibility as she hardly had any memories from that time. It was possible, then, that her mother would be deemed not to have been responsible for her actions, in which case she would most likely be sent not to prison but to a prison unit at the psychiatric hospital. Sædís didn't know whether this was good or bad, nor did she ask. The lawyer probably wasn't the best in town, but then she had only chosen him because he had a nice name.

The murders were another matter. There Sædís would almost certainly be facing criminal charges and a sentence. The lawyer had explained at length how it appeared to the prosecution, but she had understood little of what he said. He'd talked about concealment, assistance, complicity and the ill treatment of a body, or a combination of these. But he had informed her with apparent satisfaction that at least collusion was out of the question. Sædís had smiled and pretended to be pleased as well, rather than asking why that was a good thing.

He must have seen the fear and incomprehension in her eyes because he had quickly turned to the positives. She had been consistent in her statement, which also matched her father's account of events. But then, she reflected, it was easy to be consistent when you were telling the truth.

She had gone to the workshop to do the cleaning, as she did every Saturday. The girls had come with her but, thank God – since the place had looked like a slaughterhouse – they had stayed outside. There was a large, heavy-duty band saw in the middle of the room and the whole place was awash with blood. She'd found her father crashed out on the sofa in the coffee room, half drunk, half hung-over. On the floor lay a set of blue overalls, the legs dark with stains, and an inside-out waterproof. But the crumpled clothes he was wearing were mostly clean. She had shaken him and asked what on earth had happened. It had taken him a long time to sit up and open his mouth. When he could finally speak, he said there had been an accident. 'Who got hurt?' she had asked, and he had mumbled that it was no one she knew and she shouldn't worry.

At that moment she'd seen no reason to doubt this. Before she could question him any further, she heard the girls screaming outside and discovered just how serious this supposed accident had really been. When she looked inside one of the bags in the boot of the car, her heart had stopped. Then she had got a grip on herself and hurriedly slammed the boot shut. All she could think of was to get the girls away from there and prevent them from telling anyone. She needed time to think.

After buying them ice-creams and driving them home, she had returned. Her father had vanished but the workshop was still covered in blood and the car was still parked outside. Unsure what to do, she started cleaning. It wasn't a conscious decision, she'd just automatically started following the same routine as she did every Saturday, as if instinct had kicked in, compelling her to purge the workshop of the grisly evidence of what had happened there. The cleaner it became, the better she felt. Once she had finished, she had driven home and tried to pretend to her mother and sister that nothing had happened. When her father didn't come back that evening, she'd become increasingly worried. She'd been hoping he would know what to do. She couldn't ring the police without talking to him first, in case there was a reasonable explanation for what had happened. Perhaps the man in the car boot had been dangerous and deserved to die.

She'd simply assumed it was a man – it hadn't even crossed her mind that it could be a woman, since it's hard to guess someone's gender from the amputated stump of a limb. When they said on the news that a woman's body had been found, it had come as a terrible shock but by then it had been too late. There was no going back. If she were honest, she wasn't sure she'd have reported her dad to the police even if she had realised straight away. Perhaps she would have convinced herself that it had been some evil woman who had deserved it and wouldn't be missed.

According to the lawyer, her father had said that he went into town after Sædís left the workshop. He'd headed to a bar, started drinking and ended up in a police cell. He'd returned to the workshop on the Sunday, seen that the car had gone and decided to carry on drinking. All his plans of disposing of Ólína's dismembered remains in the sea, as he had Bríet's, had been thwarted, though he had spotted the bag containing her head in the car park and thrown it in the sea by the causeway out to Grótta before hitting town again to drink himself into oblivion.

Sædís had removed Bríet's car the night before. Too anxious to sleep, she'd got dressed and driven over to the workshop to check if the car was still there. Again, she had acted on an irrational impulse, obeying an urgent need to get rid of it. She had become increasingly worried that Gudda or Rósa would tell their parents about what they had seen in the boot and the

parents would contact the police. If there was no car containing body parts outside the workshop when the police turned
up, they would probably dismiss it as kids' nonsense. Discov-
ering the keys in the ignition, she had got behind the wheel
and set off. The only question had been, where to? All she had
been able to think of was one of her father's sites, reasoning
that he would be able to take over from there once he came
back. She had left the car in the neighbouring street to some
roadworks his men were engaged in and had headed over to
the Portakabin. As she had duplicates of all her father's work
keys on her key ring, she had opened the door, gone inside
and sat there, wondering what to do, unable to think of any
solution. In the end, she had decided to walk home. Before
leaving, she had wiped all the places outside and inside the car
that she or her dad might have touched. Just in case he didn't
come back. Then she had embarked on the long trek back to
the west of town, abandoning the car as it was. She'd been in
such a hurry to get out that she hadn't had the presence of
mind to park it properly or to lock it and remove the keys.

Her dad hadn't come home that night either, so it wasn't
until Monday that she had finally encountered him. Then it
had been the same old silence between them; he said nothing
and she said nothing, both waiting for the right time that never
transpired. Her chance to tell him about the car expired the
day after he returned, when the news about the discovery of a
body hit the news. After that, the days had passed, one after
another, and still she didn't tell anyone. This was where she
had been guilty of the 'ill treatment of a body' that her lawyer
kept going on about; the fact she'd moved it across town, from
Seltjarnarnes to the housing estate. It seemed extraordinary to
her that this constituted 'ill treatment', and made her wonder

what language they used to describe what her father had done to the women's bodies.

'Aha!' The midwife was beaming at Sædís again. 'I think we're there. Now we just need you to push as if your life depended on it during the next set of contractions, and after that we should be home and dry.'

Sædís tried to focus her mind as she waited. She felt a drop of sweat trickling down her forehead and remembered the descriptions of childbirth she had read online. In those, the father or another helper would be on hand with a wet flannel to cool the woman's brow and wipe away her sweat. Whereas Númi just sat there staring at the bed.

When Sædís arrived in hospital, the midwife had been astonished to hear that she had walked all the way from her home in the west end. There had been such genuine concern in her eyes that Sædís had struggled not to burst into tears. She had given the midwife a feeble explanation about worrying that she might get a parking ticket if she was kept in. The truth was, she had to watch every penny and taking a taxi was like burning money. She had lost her job. When the shit hit the fan, the company's clients had terminated all ongoing projects and called on the performance bonds. After that, the bank had taken over the running of the company and their first action had been to sack her. The only bright spot had been that the one-armed payroll clerk and the other employees had kept their jobs. She tried to be grateful for the fact that her parents had been allowed to hold on to their house, which meant she had somewhere to live. When the company was doing well, her father hadn't only splashed out on the jeep, he had also paid off all his debts. There had been nothing else to do with the money.

Sædís gathered herself for the final push, inhaling deeply and blowing out. She left it as long as she could, then pushed with all her might just as the contractions reached their peak. She clenched her jaw, feeling as if the blood vessels in her forehead would burst, but the effort paid off. The midwife told her the head was out and all it needed now was one last little shove. Sædís pushed again and the baby slithered out. With that, the pressure was gone and she felt so relieved and happy that she began to cry.

The midwife lifted up the child for Sædís to see. Númi was on his feet, but Sædís paid no attention to him. All she was aware of was the sticky head, the blood-flecked body, the swollen eyelids, clenched toes and splayed fingers on the slender arms. She had never seen anything more beautiful or heard anything lovelier than that shrill wailing.

'A fine baby girl.' The midwife smiled at Sædís and laid her newborn daughter on her chest. The umbilical cord had yet to be cut. 'Keep a good hold of her while you're passing the afterbirth. Don't worry. It's a whole lot easier than bringing a child into the world.'

Sædís became aware of mild contractions and started pushing in time to them. While she was doing so, she gazed into the little face and touched a finger to the skin that was so soft it almost felt as though it wasn't there. She was still weeping, unable to stem the flow of tears.

Númi had come to stand beside her. The contempt was gone and instead his face radiated wonder over this tiny new person. Sædís instinctively tightened her hold. When he reached out to touch the baby, she had to discipline herself not to turn away. He was the child's father, in spite of everything.

The midwife announced that the afterbirth was out and invited them to see. Neither knew what to expect or had the presence of mind to refuse. The woman produced a disgusting, bloody lump, put her hand inside it and lifted it up to show them the caul. 'Some people believe it helps with breastfeeding if you eat it. There's a recipe for placenta lasagne on the internet, if you're interested.' Númi gagged. As he did so, he drew back his hand from his daughter, much to Sædís's relief. She couldn't shake off the feeling that he was about to snatch her baby away and rush off home with her.

But all he did was return to his chair. The midwife took the little girl, snipped the umbilical cord, then wrapped her loosely in a blanket before replacing her on Sædís's chest. 'I'm just going to pop out for a minute to let you two have a chat. Then I'll come back and sew you up. I'll give you the local anaesthetic now, so it will have time to take effect.'

Sædís felt a brief sting between her legs that felt no worse than a flick of a finger after all she'd gone through since entering this room. The midwife closed the door behind her. After she had gone, the oppressive silence was unbearable. This was the most incredible, emotional moment of Sædís's life and Númi's presence did nothing but cast a shadow over it. She couldn't understand what she had been thinking of to let him know that she was in the labour ward.

Better get what she had to say off her chest. The sooner Númi left, the better. 'How's Selma – Mía, I mean?'

'Don't even ask. She's nothing to do with you any more. And she doesn't want to be called Mía. She insists on being Selma.' Númi's face softened slightly. 'Don't take it badly. The whole thing's terribly complicated and it's better if you don't get involved. She's angry with you too, you know. She's convinced you knew but never said anything.'

Sædís swallowed a lump in her throat. 'I see.' She gazed down at the tiny face of the child in her arms. The little girl opened her pitch-black eyes as if she were looking back at her. 'I have to tell you something, Númi. You're not having her.' Sædís didn't even look at him, just kept on gazing, entranced, into her daughter's eyes.

Númi was silent for a few moments. Searching for the right words, perhaps, or waiting for his anger to subside. 'We made a deal, Sædís. You knew what you were doing.'

'No. I didn't know.' Sædís stroked the sticky black hair, flinching when her finger ran lightly over the soft spot where the skull had yet to close. 'I didn't know. As you were fully aware.' She stopped speaking for a moment as she turned to him. She had to look him in the face when she said the next bit. 'And there's another thing I know now that I didn't then. Something very important.'

Númi looked baffled. 'What? That it was difficult to have a child? Everyone knows that, Sædís.'

'No. I was well aware of that. But I wasn't aware that Stefán had killed Mía's mother, Droplaug. He's not having my baby.'

Númi's mouth fell open. He looked like the goldfish Sædís had once owned. 'What kind of bullshit is that? Did they give you some drug before I arrived?'

'It's not bullshit.' Sædís proceeded to share with him the contents of the letter she had received from her father. The letter hadn't reached her by the conventional route but had been passed on to her by her father's lawyer with the words that she wasn't to tell anyone how she'd got hold of it. He was doing her father a favour by smuggling it out of prison and he didn't want to get into trouble for it.

The letter had consisted of four densely written sides. It contained more words than had passed between her and her dad for months, if not years. Most of the letter had been about regret, penitence and a plea for forgiveness. She should always remember that the whole thing was his fault. His helplessness in the face of her mother's illness and the fact he was incapable of talking about things. He'd always clammed up at critical moments instead of discussing things and confronting and sharing problems. As a result he had slid further and further into the abyss, constantly lowering the bar of what he was prepared to do to sweep complications under the rug. To keep their secret and their family safe. To keep her safe. If he had only addressed the original mistake, things would never have turned out like this. He would have been forced to face the inevitable outcome: that their house of cards would come tumbling down.

But there was more. He said he couldn't understand why she had agreed to carry a child for Stefán and Númi. They would only treat her badly, just like they had Mía's mother. He went on to confide in her that he had been intending to give little Mía back to her mother because he had thought it was the right thing to do in the circumstances. But Stefán's car had been parked outside her house when he got there, so he had stopped a little way off and waited for him to leave. He'd had no reason to think Stefán would stay there long, not after the scenes he had witnessed between them. But then he had seen Stefán carry Droplaug out, wrapped in a blanket; seen him manhandle her limp, unresisting body into his car before driving away. He had followed, hanging back a little, and so witnessed the moment when Stefán had thrown Droplaug into the sea by the marina below the road where she lived. That was the moment when he had decided to take Mía home with him. He had felt it was important Sædís should know this, so that she could decide what to do with the information. He wasn't going to expose Stefán unless he was forced to, because he cared too much about Selma, who had now gone back to live with him and Númi.

Sædís could tell that Númi was hearing this for the first time. 'Ask Stefán,' she said. 'If it helps at all, Dad said he'd also seen Stefán take the bag containing the dirty blanket with him that morning. He must have been intending to take it to be cleaned. But instead he used it to get rid of Droplaug. That's why it was found washed up on the beach. You told me you'd insisted it was the wrong blanket. Well, there's your explanation.'

'You're lying.' Númi was staring at her as if she had grown a pair of horns. 'You're lying.'

'No.' Sædís shook her head. 'I'm afraid not. But surely you must understand that things look very different now. I have nobody left in the world. Nobody at all. You two knew that. But all I've had is two text messages from you in the last few months. Nothing else. You weren't there for me. I didn't kill anyone, remember? I wished you well. I still do. But there are limits.'

Númi didn't speak, just slowly shook his head. Then, after a moment or two, he asked: 'What are you saying?'

Sædís savoured the warmth from the child on her breast. It was a struggle to keep her eyes open but she had to stay awake a little while longer. She could sleep afterwards. Forcing herself to concentrate, she said: 'I think we need to make a new contract. I'm not unreasonable, Númi. You're the father and you must have access to your daughter. But there's no way Stefán's going to adopt her. I'll never back down over that. In return, I'll make sure Dad's story doesn't go any further. I can't promise the police won't take action – they've been asking questions about Droplaug's death – but I have no control over that. Still, my lawyer says they don't have any evidence apart from a different interpretation of the post-mortem results, so they'll probably drop the inquiry in the end. One interpretation's not obviously any more correct than the other. He told me this because the police think my dad killed Droplaug.'

Númi had risen to his feet. He had that goldfish look again, his mouth hanging open, his eyes wide. But the fact he wasn't protesting Stefán's innocence told Sædís that he had his doubts. When he finally spoke, it was to ask about her, not Stefán. 'Why did you offer to carry a child for us, Sædís? Did you never have any intention of keeping your end of the bargain?'

She managed with an effort to stop her heavy eyelids from closing. 'I wanted to be kind. I wanted to do something for you. That's all.'

He shook his head and sighed heavily. 'Yeah, right.'

Sædís didn't let this get to her. All of a sudden she felt a flash of pity for Númi. He wasn't a bad person, any more than she was. 'Would you like to try holding her?' she asked.

Númi's eyes lit up as he gazed at the tiny creature, and he came closer. Sædís sat up a little, taking a gentle but firm hold of her daughter's blanket-wrapped form, and passed her over. Númi took her in his arms. Heedless of his smart clothes, he began to rock her and dropped a kiss on her forehead. Then he whispered something in her ear that Sædís couldn't hear, though she knew it must have been an endearment.

Nothing further was said. He handed back his daughter, with a reluctant parting gaze at the little head, then left the room without saying goodbye. But he didn't slam the door.

Everything would be OK. They would never be friends but that had never been on the cards anyway. According to their original contract, Sædís was supposed to disappear from her daughter's life shortly after the birth. But now some contact would be inevitable and she might even get to see Selma again. She desperately hoped so. Just as she hoped that in time Selma would forgive her. In spite of everything, they were sisters. And sisters didn't have to be related by blood.

It was also vital that Númi should stay in touch with his daughter. Have her to stay every other weekend, once she was a bit older. If Sædís went to prison, the child would stay with him. But now she had ensured that she would get her back again. That was one reason she had told him about Stefán. There had been no need to do so in order to break their contract: her lawyer had told her that. It was impossible to force people to honour an illegal contract. And surrogacy was exactly that: illegal.

Sædís was also banking on another thing that would make co-parenting easier. Númi would leave Stefán. Maybe not today or tomorrow but at some point in the near future. He was not the sort of person who would be able to forgive the murder of an innocent woman. Sædís and her baby daughter wouldn't be forced to have anything to do with Stefán, as he wasn't her daughter's father. But he was Selma's father, as Númi was, in the eyes of the law. Sædís hoped Númi would use the information she had just given him to compel Stefán to grant him primary custody of Selma and Gudda. After all, Sædís knew she would never be allowed to see Selma if she remained with Stefán, and she couldn't bear the thought of her sister being brought up by him.

Her tiny daughter mumbled and opened her eyes but the hospital lights were too bright and she immediately closed them again. Sædís felt tears welling up but didn't try to stop them this time. She wept with happiness over her baby; wept with sorrow over her situation and the wretchedness of fate. How could it be fair that innocent people had had to pay with their lives for the mistake she'd made as a child? Was it her fault or were childhood transgressions forgotten in time?

One day. It had only been one day. All the other days of her childhood she had been a little angel and never put a foot wrong. Or not that she could remember, anyway. But that one day she had done a terrible thing.

She had just turned eleven. She had come home from school to a dark house, but then that was nothing out of the ordinary. As usual, she began by looking in on her mother and letting her know she was home. Her mother was lying there in the darkened bedroom, as ever, but that day she had Sædís's tiny sister, Selma, in her arms. She was rocking to and fro, wailing as if she were possessed. Sædís had gone to her, overcoming her alarm, to find out what was wrong.

It was the worst that could have happened. Worse than when her mother cut both her wrists with the glass from her watch; worse than when she took too many pills; worse than when she thought there was cancer in the walls.

Her sweet little baby sister looked odd somehow. In the light from the doorway she appeared to be a strange colour and was sleeping in her mother's arms with her eyes and mouth open. It took Sædís a moment or two to understand the gravity of the situation. It didn't help that there was no sign of any injuries on Selma; she just looked as if she had decided not to live any more. Even now, after the police had done a post-mortem on her bones, they couldn't tell how she had died. Sædís had watched from the sitting-room window as the police dug her up in the back garden, where she had been resting, unbeknownst to Sædís, because the family had never talked about it. Or about Selma and what Sædís had done in an attempt to make everything right again.

In those days, her father hadn't been silent but talkative. Whenever her mother felt up to joining them for supper, he used to tell them about the men he was working for. He would go on about how weird it was that two men should be allowed to bring up a baby the same age as Selma and that in his opinion it wasn't right. Children should have a mother and a father. Sædís had long ago realised how prejudiced this view was. What children needed were parents who loved them and cared for them. Their gender was irrelevant. But she had been a child herself at the time and everything her father said had sounded like the truth. He had also gone on about how badly the men were treating the woman who'd had the baby for them.

Sædís knew where they lived because once, when her father was giving her a lift to the dentist's, he'd had to stop off at the men's house on the way. Acting fast, she had prised Selma's cold, peculiar-looking body from her mother's arms, wrapped her in a blanket, put her in her bicycle basket and cycled over to the men's house. It wasn't far from her home in the west end to Skerjafjördur and the ride only took her ten minutes.

When she got there, she wasn't quite sure how to swap the babies. She crept round the back of the house in the hope of finding an unlocked door. But luck was with her. Their baby daughter was asleep in a pram behind the house. In her ignorance, Sædís had thought that if she put their daughter's hat on Selma, the men would believe that their daughter had just decided to give up and die, like her little sister. So she had put Mía's hat on Selma's poor little lifeless head, then switched the babies, all without Mía waking up, beyond a brief murmur of complaint.

Sædís had had practice at this. When her father was at work, she had often fetched Selma from her parents' bedroom and laid her down somewhere to gaze at her pretty baby mobile or given her a wooden spoon to hold. All of this had to be achieved without a sound, so as not to disturb her mother. A gentle hushing usually did the trick.

Sædís put the sleeping baby in her bicycle basket and cycled home. When she got there, she took the baby upstairs and laid her in her mother's arms. Although her mother looked dazed, she didn't say anything. The baby girl cried a little but quietened down as soon as she was put on the breast and started sucking eagerly.

Not long afterwards, her dad had come home and seen instantly that it wasn't their child. But her mother had started howling hysterically when he tried to take the baby away and Sædís had been forced to intervene and tell him what had happened. He had been struck dumb. Now that she came to think about it, that was the moment he had stopped talking, more or less for good. He had rushed out and when he returned an hour later, he had gone into the back garden with a spade. Catching sight of Sædís watching from the window, he had waved her away and she had obeyed. After a while he had come back inside, without saying a word, gone straight to the drinks cabinet and poured himself a shot. Then another and another, on and on.

Next day, nothing was said. Or the next day, or at any time after that. If news of baby Mía appeared on TV, he would switch it off and drain his glass. He began every morning by disposing of the newspapers that were put through the letter box. They saw less and less of him at home as his company was in freefall. Once it had gone bust, he had picked himself up, gone into rehab and returned as a workaholic. He had set up a new company and spent as much time at work as possible without actually sleeping there at night. During this time, the new Selma grew up, filling the void that the original Selma would have left in their lives had it not been for Sædís's intervention. It wasn't long before it felt as if nothing had happened. They carried on with their lives. Admittedly, her father was a changed man, but her mother remained the same invalid and Sædís became obsessed with the need to do everything right.

Ever since Selma and Gudda had become friends, Sædís had known who Gudda's parents were. But she had generally been able to avoid them as their dealings had mostly been limited to occasionally bumping into one another on the doorstep. Although this was extremely uncomfortable, Sædís had pushed away all thoughts of their grief and loss. She had convinced herself that Gudda had taken Mía's place and that everything was fine. There was no need for compensation.

Until, eleven years after that terrible day, she had sat listening to Númi describing the suffering they had gone through following Mía's disappearance. Tormented by guilt, she had unthinkingly offered him the use of her womb. If she could give them a new baby, she had reasoned to herself, they would be quits.

But it's pointless putting a plaster on a malignant tumour. In the end, it will force the plaster off, by which time it will be incurable.

Her foolish, ill-thought-out attempts to compensate two parents for their loss had led to three women losing their lives: Droplaug, Bríet and Ólína. It had been her fault that a contemporary of Selma's had died of measles and that Rósa had come close to dying or being crippled for life. That was the only good thing in all of this – that Rósa had made a good recovery.

About a month ago, Sædís had been missing Selma so much that she had waited outside Rósa's home to get news of her sister. She had wanted to ask for a message to be passed on to her. But Rósa had been so frightened when she saw her that Sædís had stumbled away without being able to do more than stammer out a few words. After sitting, crying in her car for a while, Sædís had decided to focus on the positive. At least Rósa had seemed like her old self.

She hadn't looked up any of the other victims of the situation to apologise on her father's behalf. She knew it would be a disaster. Most of all she was afraid of Bríet's family, who would have to be content with only getting to bury part of her body. Divers had retrieved a few body parts from the seabed but in the end they had been forced to abandon the search. Missing from her coffin had been one leg and both arms. Sædís just hoped Bríet's daughter didn't know.

Sædís had cried until she had no more tears left. After that, she had decided there was no point dwelling on the past. She was standing at a crossroads and from now on everything would be about the future – not the past. She kissed the soft little head and told her daughter how beautiful she was and how much she loved her.

The midwife appeared and smiled at them both. 'So. Ready?'

Sædís nodded and went on talking to her baby.

The midwife took up position between her spread legs. 'Now that's what I like to see. It's good for children to be talked to. If you two are left alone together, make sure you keep it up. Don't bring her up in silence. That can never end well.'

Sædís felt her tears spilling over again. Because no one knew that better than she did.

Comparative Government and Politics

Visit the companion website for this
text at:
http://www.palgrave.com/politics/hague

COMPARATIVE GOVERNMENT AND POLITICS
Founding Series Editor: The late **Vincent Wright**

Published

Rudy Andeweg and Galen A. Irwin
Government and Politics of the Netherlands

Nigel Bowles
Government and Politics of the United States (2nd edition)

Paul Brooker
Non-Democratic Regimes: Theory, Government and Politics

Robert Elgie
Political Leadership in Liberal Democracies

Rod Hague and Martin Harrop
Comparative Government and Politics (6th edition)

Paul Heywood
The Government and Politics of Spain

B. Guy Peters
Comparative Politics: Theories and Methods
[Rights: World excluding North America]

Tony Saich
Governance and Politics of China (2nd edition)

Anne Stevens
The Government and Politics of France (3rd edition)

Ramesh Thakur
The Government and Politics of India

Forthcoming

Judy Batt
Government and Politics in Eastern Europe

Robert Leonardi
Government and Politics in Italy

Comparative Government and Politics
Series Standing Order
ISBN 0–333–71693–0 hardcover
ISBN 0–333–69335–3 paperback
(*outside North America only*)

You can receive future titles in this series as they are published by
placing a standing order. Please contact your bookseller or, in the
case of difficulty, write to us at the address below with your name
and address, the title of the series and an ISBN quoted above.

Customer Services Department, Macmillan Distribution Ltd
Houndmills, Basingstoke, Hampshire RG21 6XS, England
